continued . . .

Just the Sexiest Man Alive

"Fantastic, frolicking fun . . . Read *Just the Sexiest Man Alive*, and you will be adding Julie James to your automatic-buy list!"
—Janet Chapman, *New York Times* bestselling author

"Witty banter and an amazing chemistry . . . bring this delightful story to life."
—*Chicago Sun-Times*

"Remind[s] me of Katharine Hepburn and Spencer Tracy movies: they have that funny edge."
—Eloisa James, *New York Times* bestselling author

"Witty and romantic."
—*Publishers Weekly*

"James['s] familiarity with both the law and the film industry lends credibility to this fast-moving contemporary romantic comedy."
—Booklist

"A wonderful debut novel . . . James had me laughing out loud . . . Fabulous."
—*Romance Novel TV*

"Great dialogue . . . A quick and breezy read that generate[d] a lot of smiles."
—*Dear Author*

"Ms. James tackles what happens . . . with wit [and] humor. The one-liners will keep you laughing all the way through this book."
—*Night Owl Reviews*

"Laugh-out-loud funny."
—*Fallen Angel Reviews*

"The sparks fly . . . Engaging . . . James has done an excellent job."
—*The Romance Studio*

"A spectacular beginning of what I hope is a stellar career . . . [An] awesome novel that rightly deserves my Perfect Ten award."
—*Romance Reviews Today*

"Smartly written."
—*All About Romance*

"Witty, competent, and thoroughly charming escapist fantasy . . . Romantic comedy at its best."
—*The Romance Reader*

JUST THE SEXIEST MAN ALIVE
PRACTICE MAKES PERFECT
SOMETHING ABOUT YOU
A LOT LIKE LOVE

A Lot Like Love

JULIE JAMES

BERKLEY SENSATION, NEW YORK

THE BERKLEY PUBLISHING GROUP
Published by the Penguin Group
Penguin Group (USA) Inc.
375 Hudson Street, New York, New York 10014, USA
Penguin Group (Canada), 90 Eglinton Avenue East, Suite 700, Toronto, Ontario M4P 2Y3, Canada
(a division of Pearson Penguin Canada Inc.)
Penguin Books Ltd., 80 Strand, London WC2R 0RL, England
Penguin Group Ireland, 25 St. Stephen's Green, Dublin 2, Ireland (a division of Penguin Books Ltd.)
Penguin Group (Australia), 250 Camberwell Road, Camberwell, Victoria 3124, Australia
(a division of Pearson Australia Group Pty. Ltd.)
Penguin Books India Pvt. Ltd., 11 Community Centre, Panchsheel Park, New Delhi—110 017, India
Penguin Group (NZ), 67 Apollo Drive, Rosedale, North Shore 0632, New Zealand
(a division of Pearson New Zealand Ltd.)
Penguin Books (South Africa) (Pty.) Ltd., 24 Sturdee Avenue, Rosebank, Johannesburg 2196,
South Africa

Penguin Books Ltd., Registered Offices: 80 Strand, London WC2R 0RL, England

This is a work of fiction. Names, characters, places, and incidents either are the product of the author's imagination or are used fictitiously, and any resemblance to actual persons, living or dead, business establishments, events, or locales is entirely coincidental. The publisher does not have any control over and does not assume any responsibility for author or third-party websites or their content.

A LOT LIKE LOVE

A Berkley Sensation Book / published by arrangement with the author

PRINTING HISTORY
Berkley Sensation mass-market edition / March 2011

ISBN: 978-1-61129-329-6

BERKLEY® SENSATION
Berkley Sensation Books are published by The Berkley Publishing Group,
a division of Penguin Group (USA) Inc.,
375 Hudson Street, New York, New York 10014.
BERKLEY® SENSATION and the "B" design are trademarks of Penguin Group (USA) Inc.

*To my sister,
for the Western Barbie story
and many other timeless classics.*

Acknowledgments

To my fabulous editor, Wendy McCurdy, for her insight, suggestions, and support, and to my wonderful agent, Susan Crawford, for her dedication and tremendous enthusiasm. Thanks as well to the entire team at Berkley, all of whom do such an incredible job and whose contributions are extremely appreciated.

A special thanks to Denise and Martin Cody, for showing me the ins and outs of running a wine store, and for being so gracious in answering all my pesky questions. Thanks as well to wine educator and sommelier John Laloganes for his fantastic wine appreciation course.

To Maria and Brian Guarraci, Matt and Melissa Boresi, Jen Adamo, and most especially to Pete Montenaro, my New York consigliere, for their insight and wonderful stories about Italian families. I only wish I could've used every story they shared with me—particularly the one about the tomato plant.

Thanks as well to my father-in-law, for his investigative expertise and that of his mysterious "sources," for helping me develop the setup of this story in its early stages.

To my incredible beta readers, Elyssa Papa and Kati Dancy, for all their helpful suggestions, and an extra-special thanks to Elyssa for the title of this book.

Thank you to my family and friends, for all their love and support, and particularly for putting up with me when I'm on a deadline. And finally, to my husband, for always listening, helping, advising, and being all-around amazing.

One

FROM THE MOMENT Nick McCall walked into his boss's office, he knew something was up.

Being a special agent for the FBI, he was an expert at both observing body language and reading between the lines, often gleaning all he needed to know from a carelessly chosen word or the subtlest of gestures. A skill that frequently came in handy.

Upon entering the room, he watched as Mike Davis, the special agent in charge of the Chicago field office, toyed with the sleeve of his venti Starbucks coffee cup (even he refused to drink the crap they had in the office)—a gesture many of the senior agents in the office had noted long ago. It was Davis's tell, and Nick knew exactly what it meant.

Trouble.

Another long undercover job, he guessed. Not that working undercover bothered him—in fact, for the past few years, that was almost exclusively the type of investigation he'd handled. But having just finished a particularly grueling assignment, even he was ready for a break.

He took a seat in one of the chairs in front of Davis's desk, watching as his boss now twisted the sleeve around the base of the Starbucks cup. Shit, he was screwed. Everyone knew that twisting of the sleeve was even worse than sliding.

Nick saw no point in beating around the bush. "All right. Just lay it on me."

Davis greeted him with a grin. "Good morning to you, too, sunshine. And welcome back. How I missed our pleasant chats while you were working on Fivestar."

"Sorry. I'll start over. It's good to be back, sir. Thank you."

"I assume you were able to find your office without too much trouble?" Davis asked dryly.

Nick got comfortable in his chair, letting the sarcasm bounce off him. True, while working on Operation Fivestar over the last six months, he hadn't been in the office much. And it felt good to be back. Surprisingly, he realized that he *had* missed his chats with Davis. Sure, his boss could be prickly at times, but with all the crap he had to deal with as special agent in charge, this was to be expected.

"I wandered around the floor until I found a door with my name on it. Nobody's kicked me out yet, so I figure I must be in the right place." He looked Davis over. "You're looking a little grayer around the temples there, boss."

Davis grunted. "Spent the last six months of my life worrying that you'd screw up your investigation."

Nick stretched out his legs in front of him. He didn't screw up investigations. "Have I ever given you any reason to doubt me?"

"Probably. You're just better at covering it up than most."

"That's true. So you want to go ahead and give me the bad news?"

"You're so convinced I've got something to tell you." Davis feigned innocence as he gestured to his Starbucks cup. "Can't a guy simply catch up over coffee with the top agent in his office?"

"Oh, so I'm your top agent now."

"You've always been my top agent."

Nick raised an eyebrow. "Don't let Pallas hear you say that," he said, referring to another agent in their office who'd recently been on a run with some very high-profile arrests.

"You and Pallas are *both* my top agents," Davis said, as diplomatically as a mother who'd just been asked to name her favorite child.

"Nice save."

"Actually, I wasn't kidding about the catching up part. I heard the arrests last week got a little rough."

Nick brushed this off. "That can happen with arrests. Funny enough, it's typically not an experience that catches people at their best."

Davis studied him through sharp gray eyes. "Coming off an undercover job is never easy, especially a rough one like Fivestar. Twenty-seven Chicago police officers charged with corruption is quite a coup. You did a great job, Nick. The director called me earlier this morning and told me to extend his personal congratulations to you."

"I'm glad both you and the director are pleased."

"I can't help but think that the arrests might've struck a nerve, given your background."

Nick wouldn't necessarily say the case struck a nerve, although it was true: busting police officers wasn't high on his list of fun things to do. Cop blood ran through his veins, after all—he was a former police officer himself, having worked vice for the NYPD for six years before applying to the FBI. His father had served on the New York Police Department for thirty years before retiring, and one of Nick's brothers was a cop. But the twenty-seven police officers he had arrested last Friday had crossed the line. In his opinion, the fact that the bad guys happened to wear badges only made them less worthy of sympathy.

"They were dirty cops, Mike. I didn't have any problem taking them down," Nick said.

Davis seemed satisfied. "Good. Glad we got that out of the way. And I saw that you put in for some time off."

"I'm heading back to New York for a few days to surprise my mother. She's turning sixty this Sunday and my family's having a big party."

"When are you leaving?"

Nick sensed that this question was less casual than Davis's tone would suggest. "Tonight. Why?" he asked suspiciously.

"What would you say if I asked you to consider postponing your trip a few days?"

"I'd say you obviously don't know my mother. If I don't get back home for this party, you'll need a bulldozer to dig me out of the layers of guilt she'll pile on me."

Davis laughed at that. "You don't need to miss her party, you can still be in New York in plenty of time. Say . . . Saturday night. Sunday morning at the latest."

"You're joking, obviously. Seeing how I've asked for all of about two days off in the last six years, I'm thinking I'm kind of due for this vacation."

Davis turned more serious. "I know you are, Nick. Believe me, I wouldn't ask if it wasn't important."

Nick held back what would normally be his sarcastic reply. He respected Davis. They'd been working together for six years, and he found Davis to be a fair boss and a straight shooter. And the entire time Nick had worked in the Chicago field office, he'd never heard of Davis asking anyone for a favor. Which made it virtually impossible to say no.

He sighed. "I'm not saying yes. But out of curiosity, what's the assignment?"

Davis sensed the beginnings of his capitulation and leaned forward in his chair. "I'd call it a consulting job, of sorts. There's been an unexpected development in an investigation being run jointly by the financial crimes and organized crimes divisions and I need to bring on someone with your level of undercover experience. Things might get a little tricky."

"What kind of case is it?" Nick asked.

"Money laundering."

"Who's in charge of the investigation?"

"Seth Huxley."

Nick had seen Huxley around the office, but probably had exchanged less than ten words with him. His first—and only—impression had been that Huxley seemed very . . . organized. If Nick remembered correctly, Huxley had come to the Bureau by way of the law program and had gone to some Ivy League school before joining the financial crimes division. "What do you need me to do?"

"I'll let Huxley fill you in on the details of the case. We're meeting him in a minute," Davis said. "I've assured him that you're not being brought on board to take over— he's been working on this case for a couple months now."

Nick realized that his agreement had been somewhat of a formality the entire time. "So why do you need me?"

"To make sure Huxley isn't in over his head. It's his first undercover assignment. I don't like holding back an agent, and Huxley hasn't given me any reason to do that here. Everyone has to have his or her first undercover assignment sometime. But the U.S. attorney has her eye on this case, and that means there's no room for error."

"Is there ever room for error in any of your cases?"

Davis acknowledged that with a grin. "No. But this time, there's particularly no room for error. It's the way I classify things: basically no room for error, no room for error, and *particularly* no room for error. It's very technical."

Nick thought about something Davis had just said. "You mentioned that the U.S. attorney is watching the case. Is it part of the Martino investigation?"

Davis nodded. "Now you understand why there can't be any mistakes."

He didn't need to say anything further. Three months ago, a new U.S. attorney, Cameron Lynde, had been appointed after a scandal that resulted in the arrest and resignation of her predecessor. Ever since Lynde had been appointed, she'd made the Martino investigation her top priority. As such, it was the top priority of the FBI's Chicago field office as well.

For years, Roberto Martino had run the largest crime syndicate in Chicago—his organization was responsible for nearly one-third of all drug trafficking in the city, and his people extorted, bribed, threatened, and killed anyone who stood in their way. Over the course of the last few months, however, the FBI had arrested over thirty members of Martino's gang, including Roberto Martino himself. Both the attorney general and the director of the FBI had declared the arrests to be a major victory in the war on crime.

Since he'd been working undercover on Operation Fivestar for the last six months, Nick hadn't been involved in any of the Martino arrests. Some of the other agents had received all the glory on that front, a fact that somewhat rankled his competitive ego.

"Want to find out more?" Davis asked, a knowing gleam in his eyes.

Hell, it was less than a week, Nick figured. Over the next few days, he could lend his much-learned undercover expertise to a junior agent, score brownie points with his boss, kick some gangster ass, and still be in New York by Sunday to sing "Happy Birthday" to his mother. From where he stood, it was a win-win situation all around.

"All right," Nick nodded. "Let's go meet Huxley."

AGENT HUXLEY WAS already waiting for them in the conference room. Nick did a quick assessment of his new partner: carefully groomed blond hair, wire-rimmed glasses, and an expensive three-piece suit. His eyes held on the article of clothing Huxley wore underneath his suit jacket.

A vest.

And not the bulletproof kind. A *sweater*-vest. As in, Huxley wasn't wearing just a suit; he had this whole ensemble going: dark brown pants and jacket, crisp pinstriped shirt, V-neck vest, and tan silk tie.

Nick, on the other hand, was dressed in his standard-issue, no-frills gray suit, white shirt, and navy tie. Because men who grew up in Brooklyn didn't *do* ensembles. And they certainly didn't do sweater-vests. True, it was early February in Chicago and about ten degrees outside, so he supposed the vest served some sort of functional purpose in keeping Huxley warm, but still. In Nick's opinion, the only accessories an FBI agent should pair with a suit were a shoulder harness and gun. Maybe handcuffs, depending on the formality of the occasion.

Nick nodded at Huxley and said a quick greeting as he took the seat opposite him at the marble conference table. Davis sat at the head of the table and got things started. "So

I told Nick how you've been working on the Eckhart investigation for the past couple of months."

At least he had a name now, and one he was familiar with—a name many people in Chicago were familiar with. "Xander Eckhart? The restaurant guy?"

"Nightclubs and restaurants, actually," Huxley corrected him. He adjusted his glasses, sitting straight in his chair. "Eckhart owns three restaurants and four bars in the Chicago area, all expensive, upscale establishments. The crown jewel is a French restaurant, Bordeaux, located just west of the Loop. It sits on the river and has an exclusive VIP-only wine bar that caters to a wealthy clientele."

"I've already filled Nick in on the fact that the investigation is connected to the Martino cases. Why don't you pick up from there?" Davis suggested.

Huxley had his laptop out, prepared to do just that. He picked up a remote control, and with the push of a button, a screen dropped down from the ceiling in the front of the room. The lights in the conference room dimmed, and Huxley began his presentation. "Subsequent to the arrests of Roberto Martino and other members of his criminal organization, we've begun to realize that the scope of Martino's illegal activity is far wider than we'd suspected. Like his connections to this man here."

On the screen before him, Nick found himself looking at a photograph of a man in his midthirties who had medium-length brown hair stylishly swept back from his forehead. He wore a suit that appeared even more expensive than Huxley's and had a tall, willowy brunette in her early twenties on his arm.

"That's Xander Eckhart," Huxley said. "The girl's inconsequential, the flavor of the month. Based on evidence we've acquired over the last few months, we believe that Eckhart has been laundering large sums of drug money for Roberto Martino. Martino combines his money with the profits of Eckhart's restaurants and bars—the nightclubs in particular deal heavily in cash, providing the perfect cover. Eckhart then reports the dirty money as part of his revenue, and voilà, it's clean. We've been working with the IRS to find proof in the tax records that Eckhart has filed for his businesses over the last couple years, but in the meantime the U.S. attorney has asked us to come up with additional evidence."

"Something a jury would actually pay attention to," Davis explained to Nick.

Nick understood the U.S. attorney's thinking behind this. He'd worked with enough prosecutors to know that they disliked cases where the evidence was primarily document-driven. Putting a boring IRS investigator on the witness stand to walk through pages and pages of indecipherable tax filings was the surest way to put a jury to sleep—and lose a conviction.

"So what other evidence do we have?" he asked.

"I've been watching Eckhart for the last few weeks and observed him meeting with this man." Huxley pulled up another image, a photograph of a man with jet black hair who appeared to be in his mid to late forties. He wore a dark overcoat with the collar turned up as he hurried into a building Nick didn't recognize.

"That's Carlo Trilani, being photographed outside Bordeaux," Huxley said. "He's been there on several occasions to meet with Eckhart, always when the restaurant is closed. We suspect that Trilani is one of Martino's men, although we don't have enough evidence yet to make an arrest. Hopefully, we'll nail both him and Eckhart as part of this investigation."

Nick was quickly catching on. "I'm guessing the tangible evidence we want lies in those meetings."

Huxley nodded. "What we need is a way to listen in on Eckhart and Trilani's conversations."

Nick saw where Huxley was going with this: electronic surveillance. More commonly used by the FBI than he suspected the average person realized, it was an investigative technique that often provided them the hard evidence they needed. The trick, however, was setting up the recording devices without tipping off the suspects. But the FBI had its ways.

"You said they meet at Bordeaux?" Nick asked.

"I should have been more clear. They don't actually

meet in the restaurant. Eckhart, or more likely Trilani, is smarter than that." Huxley pulled up computer-generated blueprints of a building with two levels. "This is the layout of the building where Bordeaux is located." A progression of images flashed across the screen, with different areas on the blueprints highlighted in yellow as Huxley continued. "There's a restaurant on the main level, with an outdoor terrace overlooking the river. The VIP wine bar is located next to that, in this space right here. Below the restaurant and the wine bar is this lower level, where Eckhart keeps a private office. That's where he and Trilani meet."

"Can you get into the lower level through the bar?" Nick asked.

"Yes and no." Huxley zoomed in on the blueprints for the main level. "There's an interior door in the wine bar that leads to a staircase to the lower level. There's also this separate exterior entrance here, right next to the back door for the main bar. The problem is that both doors to the lower level—as well as all the windows—are protected by an alarm system."

"Eckhart has a separate security system for his office?" Nick asked.

"I think he's more concerned with this space here." Huxley brought up the blueprints for the lower level and highlighted a large space located down the hall from Eckhart's office. "This is the wine cellar for the VIP bar and the restaurant. That's the reason for the security system—Eckhart's got over six thousand bottles of wine down there. Really top stuff. I did some research; apparently Eckhart's a huge collector. Last year, *Wine Spectator* did a whole cover story on him and the cellar at Bordeaux. And a few weeks ago, he made a big splash in the wine community by paying two hundred and fifty-eight thousand dollars for a case of rare wine."

"A quarter of a million dollars for *wine*?" Nick shook his head in disbelief. The things rich people did with their money.

"And that's just one case out of six thousand bottles," Huxley continued. "By all accounts, between wine and champagne, Eckhart's got over three million dollars in drinkable, easily transportable goods sitting underneath his restaurant."

Davis whistled. "Explains the security system."

Nick scoffed at this, not so easily impressed. Sure, maybe Eckhart's collection was worth a ton of money, but it was still just *wine*. Call him unrefined, but he wasn't about to get all hot and bothered over a bunch of fermented grape juice. A man's drink should be strong, and burn a little on the way down. Like bourbon. "Who has access to the password for the security system?"

"Only Eckhart and his two general managers, one of whom is required to be at Bordeaux whenever it's open. And according to our reports, they change the password every week."

"What reports?" Nick asked.

"We've got a female agent working undercover as a bartender—we set her up in the position a few weeks ago," Huxley said. "We'd planned to use her to get into the lower level of the restaurant, but Eckhart's security has proven to be more of a challenge than we'd expected."

Nick shrugged. "I don't see why we even need her—our next step seems simple enough. We get a court order forcing the alarm company to turn over the password to Eckhart's security system, then go in and bug the place in the middle of the night."

"Unfortunately, that's not an option in this case," Huxley said. "Eckhart uses a company called RLK Security. I checked them out—they do security for private homes and businesses. Including, notably, Roberto Martino's home."

Nick was impressed by Huxley's thoroughness. "I doubt that's a coincidence. I'm guessing Martino hooked Eckhart up with his security team once they went into business together."

"Even with a gag order, it's too risky to let RLK Security in on the plan. Anyone Martino trusts is not a friend of the FBI," Huxley said.

No disagreement there. "So where does that leave us?" Nick asked.

Huxley looked over at Davis. Nick sensed that this next part was the reason he'd been brought in for consulting.

"It means we do this in plain sight," Huxley said. "Every Valentine's Day, Eckhart hosts an exclusive charity event at Bordeaux. One hundred people on the list, five thousand dollars per head. As part of the event, Eckhart offers tastings from some of the rare wines he owns. He keeps a security guard stationed in a private tasting room near the cellar as a precautionary measure, but guests have general access to the lower level. Which means that an agent posing as a guest could slip away from the others during the party, break into Eckhart's office, and set the microphones in place." He cleared his throat. "That will be me."

Nick was missing something here. "Why not just have this agent we've already got on the inside plant the recording devices? Why else do we have her pretending to be a bartender?"

Huxley conceded this with a nod. "Originally, that was the plan. But Agent Simms has learned that employees don't have access to the lower level during the party—Eckhart has hired a private sommelier to pour the most expensive wines from his cellar for the guests. That was an unexpected development, but not a total loss—Simms can serve as backup upstairs while I plant the bugs in Eckhart's office."

"And how, exactly, do you plan to get into the party?" Nick asked. "I'm guessing the FBI isn't on Eckhart's invite list."

"True. So instead, I'm going to pose as the date of one of the guests."

Nick paused and eased back in his chair, taking that in. "That means getting a civilian involved." Generally, he didn't like using civilians in undercover operations. They were unpredictable and, frankly, a liability. Sometimes, however, circumstances made it necessary.

Huxley was quick to continue. "It's a one-shot deal, and the risk of harm to the civilian is minimal: she doesn't have to do anything except get me into the party. Once inside, I can take it from there."

Davis spoke for the first time since Huxley had begun outlining the parameters of the assignment. "What do you think, Nick?"

Nick studied the blueprints on the screen before him. Without the ability to bypass the alarm system, he didn't see any other way. "I'm not saying it can't work. But clearly this isn't the most typical way to plant recording devices."

"Good. The boys in Rockford can handle the typical stuff," Davis said.

Nick smiled at that. "True enough. But the trick will be to find Huxley here a date to this party. One who will be willing to play ball with us."

Huxley turned back to his computer, efficient as always. "Actually, I've already gone through the guest list. I've got the perfect candidate in mind."

"Just out of curiosity, how much longer is this presentation of yours?" Nick asked.

"Only eighteen more slides to go."

"We're going to need more coffee," Nick muttered to Davis. Then he looked over and saw the photograph on the screen before him of the woman Huxley apparently wanted to bring into the Eckhart operation.

Oh, *hell*.

Nick recognized the woman instantly. Not because he knew her personally, but because everyone in Chicago—and probably half the country in light of certain recent events—would recognize her. "Jordan Rhodes?" he asked incredulously. "She's the richest woman in Chicago."

Huxley brushed this aside with a wave. "Not quite. There's Oprah, of course. Nobody tops Oprah."

Davis pointed, throwing in his two cents from the head of the table. "And don't forget the Pritzkers."

"Good call. I think I'd put Jordan Rhodes more around fourth richest," Huxley mused.

Nick leveled them both with a stare. "Fine, let's just say top five, whatever."

"And technically it's her father's money, not hers," Huxley noted. "The *Forbes* list of the four hundred richest

Americans puts Grey Rhodes's net worth at one point two billion dollars."

One point two *billion*. "And we want to drag this man's daughter into an undercover op?" Nick asked. "*This* is our best option?"

"The list of people attending Eckhart's party is extremely exclusive," Huxley said. "And we don't exactly have the luxury of interviewing candidates. We need someone that we can be certain will agree to help us. Someone who has a great deal of incentive to agree."

Nick took in the photograph of Jordan Rhodes on the screen. Reluctantly, he had to admit that Huxley raised a good point—fourth richest woman in Chicago or not, they did have leverage over her. Significant leverage.

"What's the matter, McCall? Afraid she's out of your league?" Davis asked with a sly grin. "Professionally speaking."

Nick had to fight back a laugh. Over the last six months, he'd posed undercover as everything from a drug dealer to a thief to a con artist, he'd spent nearly thirty nights in jail, and he'd taken down twenty-seven corrupt Chicago cops. He could certainly handle one billionaire heiress.

Xander Eckhart was his target now, at least for the next five days, and Jordan Rhodes appeared to be their best shot at making the investigation a successful one. Which meant that it was no longer a question of whether she cooperated with them, but when.

He nodded at Davis, all business. "Consider it done, boss."

Two

THE CHIME RANG on the front door of the wine store. Jordan Rhodes came out of the back room, where she'd been sneaking a quick bite for lunch. She smiled at her customer. "You again."

It was the guy from last week, the one who'd looked skeptical when she'd recommended a cabernet from South Africa that—gasp—had a screw top.

"So? How'd you like the Excelsior?" she asked.

"Good memory," he said, impressed. "You were right. It's good. Particularly at that price point."

"It's good at any price point," Jordan said. "The fact that it sells for less than ten dollars makes it a steal."

The man's blue eyes lit up as he grinned. He was dressed in a navy car coat and jeans, and wore expensive leather Italian loafers—probably too expensive for the six to eight inches of snow they were expected to get that evening. His light brown hair was mussed from the wind outside. "You've convinced me. Put me down for a case. I'm having a dinner party in a few weeks and the Excelsior will be perfect." He pulled off his leather gloves and set them on the long ebony wood counter that doubled as a bar. "I'm thinking I'll pair it with leg of lamb, maybe seasoned with black pepper and mustard seed. Rosemary potatoes."

Jordan raised an eyebrow. The man knew his food. "Sounds delicious." The Excelsior would certainly complement the menu, although she personally subscribed to the more relaxed "drink what you want" philosophy of wine rather than putting the emphasis on finding the perfect food pairing—a fact that constantly scandalized her assistant store manager, Martin. He was a certified level III sommelier, and thus had a certain view on things, while she, on the other hand, was the owner of the store and thus believed in making wine as approachable as possible to the customer. Sure, she loved the romance of wine—that was one of the main reasons she had opened her store, DeVine Cellars. But for her, it was also a business.

"I take it you cook," she said to the man with the great smile. Great hair, too, she noted approvingly. Nicely styled, on the longer side. He wore a gray scarf wrapped loosely around his neck that gave him an air of casual sophistication. Not too fussy, but a man who appreciated the finer things in life.

He shrugged. "I know my way around food. It comes with the job."

"Let me guess—you're a chef," Jordan said.

"Food critic. With the *Tribune*."

Jordan cocked her head, suddenly realizing. "You're Cal Kittredge."

He seemed pleased by her recognition. "You read my reviews."

Yes, she did, along with many others in Chicago. "Religiously. With so many restaurants in this city to choose from, it's nice to have an expert's opinion."

Cal relaxed against the counter. "An expert, huh . . . I'm flattered, Jordan."

So. He knew her name.

Unfortunately, a lot of people knew her name. Between her father's wealth and her brother's recent infamy, rare was the person, at least in Chicago, who wasn't familiar with the Rhodes family.

Letting this sit for a moment, Jordan moved behind the counter and opened the laptop she kept there. "A case of the Excelsior it is." She pulled up her distributor's delivery schedule. "I can have it in the store next week."

"That's plenty of time. Do I pay for it now or when I pick it up?" Cal asked.

"Either one. I figure you're good for it. And now I know where to find you if you try to skip out."

Yes, she may have been flirting a little. Maybe more than a little. For the last few months, her family had been living under an intense spotlight because of the mess with her brother, and, frankly, dating had been the last thing on her mind. But things were finally starting to settle down— as much as things could ever settle down when one's twin brother was locked up in prison—and it felt good to be flirting. And if the object of said flirtation just so happened to have polished, refined good looks and was a first-class connoisseur of cuisine, well, all the better.

"Maybe I *should* skip out, just to make you come look for me," Cal teased.

And maybe she wasn't the only one flirting a little.

He stood opposite her with the counter between them. "Since you read my reviews, I take it you trust my opinions on restaurants?"

Jordan shot Cal a look over the top of her computer as she finished entering his wine order. "As much as I'd trust a complete stranger about anything, I suppose."

"Good. Because there's this Thai restaurant that just opened on Clark that's fantastic."

"Glad to hear it. I'll have to check it out sometime."

For the first time since entering her wine shop, Cal looked uncertain. "Oh. I meant that I thought you might want to go there with *me*."

Jordan smiled. Yes, she'd caught that. But a little warning alarm had gone off in her head as she wondered how many other women Cal Kittredge had used his "Do you trust my opinions on restaurants?" line on. There was no doubt he was charming and smooth. The question was whether he was *too* smooth.

She straightened up from her computer and leaned one hip against the bar. "Let's say this—when you come back to pick up the Excelsior, you can tell me more about this new restaurant then."

Cal seemed surprised by her nonacceptance, but not necessarily put off. "Okay. It's a date."

"I'd call it more . . . a continuation."

"Are you always this tough on your customers?" he asked.

"Only the ones who want to take me to new Thai restaurants."

"Next time, then, I'll suggest Italian." With a wink, Cal grabbed his gloves off the counter and left the store.

Jordan watched as he walked past the front windows and noticed that snow had begun to fall outside. Not for the first time, she was glad she lived only a five-minute walk from the shop. And that she had a good pair of snow boots.

"My God, I thought he'd never leave," said a voice from behind her.

Jordan turned and saw her assistant, Martin, standing a few feet away, near the back hallway. He walked over, carrying a case of zinfandel that he'd brought up from the cellar. He set the box on the counter and brushed away a few unruly reddish brown curls that had fallen into his eyes. "Whew. I've been standing back there holding that thing forever. Figured I'd give you two some privacy. I thought he was checking you out when he came in last week. Guess I was right."

"How much did you hear?" Jordan asked as she began to help him unpack the bottles.

"I heard that he's Cal Kittredge."

Of course Martin had focused on that. He was twenty-seven years old, more well read than anyone she knew, and made no attempt to hide the fact that he was a major food and wine snob. But he knew everything about wine, and he'd grown on her. Jordan couldn't imagine running the shop without him.

"He asked me to go to some new Thai restaurant on Clark," she said.

Martin was instantly impressed. "I've been trying to get

reservations there for two weeks." He lined the remaining
bottles on the bar and tossed the empty box onto the floor.
"Lucky you. If you start dating Cal Kittredge, you'll be
able to get into all the best restaurants. For free."

Jordan modestly remained silent as she grabbed two bottles of the zin and carried them to a bin near the front of the
store.

"Oh, right," Martin said. "I always forget that you have a
billion dollars. I'm guessing you don't need any help getting into restaurants."

She threw him an eye as she grabbed two more bottles.
"*I* don't have a billion dollars." It was the same routine virtually every time the subject of money came up. Because
she liked Martin, she put up with it. But with the exception
of him and a small circle of her closest friends, she generally avoided discussing finances with others.

It wasn't exactly a secret, however: her father was rich.
Okay, extremely rich. She hadn't grown up with money; it
was something her family had stumbled into. Her father,
basically a computer geek like her brother, was one of those
success stories *Forbes* and *Newsweek* loved to put on their
covers: after graduating from the University of Illinois with
a master's degree in computer science, Grey Rhodes went
on to Northwestern University's Kellogg business school.
He then started his own company in Chicago where he developed an antiviral protection program that exploded worldwide. Within two years of its release to the public, Rhodes
antivirus protected one in every three computers in America
(a statistic her father made sure to include in every interview). And then came the money. A lot of it.

One might have certain impressions about her lifestyle,
Jordan knew, given her father's financial success. Some of
these impressions would be accurate, others would not. Her
father had set up guidelines from the moment he'd made his
first million, the most fundamental being that Jordan and
her brother, Kyle, earn their own way—just as he had. As
adults, they were wholly financially independent from their
father, and Jordan and Kyle wouldn't have it any other way.
On the other hand, their father was known to be extravagant

with gifts, particularly after their mother died nine years ago. Take, for example, the Maserati Quattroporte Jordan had sitting in her garage. Probably not the typical present one received for graduating business school.

"We've had this conversation before, Martin. That's my father's money, not mine." Jordan wiped her hands on a towel they kept under the counter, brushing off the dust from the wine bottles. She gestured to the store. "*This* is mine." There was obvious pride in her voice. She was the sole owner of DeVine Cellars and business was good. Really good, in fact—certainly better than she'd ever projected at this point in her ten-year plan. Of course, she didn't make anywhere near the 1.2 billion her father may or may not have been worth (she never confirmed specifics about his money), but she did very well for herself on her own merit. She made enough to pay for a four-thousand-plus square foot house in the upscale Lincoln Park neighborhood, to treat herself to fine hotels when she traveled, and she still had plenty of money left over for great shoes. A woman couldn't ask for much more.

"Maybe. But you still get into any restaurant you want," Martin pointed out.

"This is generally true. Although I do have to pay, if that makes you feel any better."

Martin sniffed. "A little. So are you going to say yes?"

"Am I going to say yes to what?" Jordan asked.

"To Cal Kittredge."

"I'm thinking about it." True, there was the slight excess of smoothness to think about. But on the upside, he was into food and wine, and he *cooked*. Practically a Renaissance man.

"I think you should string Kittredge along for a while," Martin mused aloud. "Keep him coming back so he'll buy a few more cases before you commit."

"Great idea. Maybe we could even start handing out punch cards," Jordan suggested. "Get a date with the owner after six purchases, that kind of thing."

"I detect some sarcasm," Martin said. "Which is too bad, because that punch-card idea is not half bad."

"We could always pimp you out as a prize."

Martin sighed as he leaned his slender frame against the bar. His bow tie of choice that day was red, which Jordan thought nicely complemented his dark brown tweed jacket.

"Sadly, I'm underappreciated," he said, sounding resigned to his fate. "A light-bodied pinot unnoticed in a world dominated by big, bold cabs."

Jordan rested her hand on his shoulder sympathetically. "Maybe you just haven't hit your drink-now date. Perhaps you're still sitting on the shelf, waiting to age to your fullest potential."

Martin considered this. "So what you're saying is . . . I'm like the Pahlmeyer Sonoma Coast Pinot."

Sure, exactly what she'd been thinking. "Yep. That's you."

"They're expecting great things from the Pahlmeyer, you know."

Jordan smiled. "Then we all better look out."

The thought seemed to perk Martin up. In good spirits once again, he headed off to the cellar for another case of the zinfandel while Jordan returned to the back room to finish her lunch. It was after three o'clock, which meant that if she didn't eat now she wouldn't get another chance until the store closed at nine. Soon enough, they would have a steady stream of customers.

Wine was hot, one of the few industries continuing to do well despite the economic downturn. But Jordan liked to think her store's success was based on more than just a trend. She'd searched for months for the perfect space: on a major street, where there would be plenty of foot traffic, and large enough to fit several tables and chairs in addition to the display space they would need for the wine. With its warm tones and exposed brick walls, the store had an intimate feel that drew customers in and invited them to stay awhile.

By far the smartest business decision she'd made had been to apply for an on-premise liquor license, which allowed them to pour and serve wine in the store. She'd set up highboy tables and chairs along the front windows and tucked a few additional tables into cozy nooks between the wine bins. Starting around five o'clock on virtually every night they were open, the place was hopping with customers buying wines by the glass and taking note of the bottles they planned to purchase when leaving.

Today, however, was *not* one of those days.

Outside, the snow continued to fall steadily. By seven o'clock the weathermen amended their predictions and were now calling for a whopping eight to ten inches. In anticipation of the storm, people were staying inside. Jordan had an event booked at the store that evening, a wine tasting, but the party called to reschedule. Martin had a longer commute than she did, so she sent him home early. At seven thirty, she began closing the store, thinking it highly unlikely she'd get any customers.

When finished up front, Jordan went into the back room to turn off the sound system. The store felt eerily quiet and empty without the eclectic mix of Billie Holiday, The Shins, and Norah Jones she'd put together for the day's soundtrack. She grabbed her snow boots from behind the door and had just sat down at her desk to replace the black leather boots she wore when the chime rang against the front door.

A customer. Surprising.

She stood up and stepped out of the back room, thinking somebody had to be awfully desperate to come out for wine in this weather. "You're in luck. I was just about to close for the . . ."

Her words trailed off as she stopped at the sight of the two men standing near the front of the store. For some reason, she felt tingles at the back of her neck. Perhaps it had something to do with the man closer to the door. Her eyes immediately fell upon him—he didn't look like her typical customer. He had chestnut brown hair and scruff along his angular jaw that gave him a dark, bad-boy look. He was tall, and wore a black wool coat over what appeared to be a well-built physique.

This was no Italian-loafer wearer. Unlike Cal Kittredge, this man was good-looking in a rugged, masculine way. There was something a bit . . . rougher about him. Except for his eyes. Green as emeralds, they stood out brilliantly against his dark hair and five o'clock shadow as he watched her intently.

He took a step forward.

Jordan took a step back.

A slight grin played at the edges of his lips, as if he found this amusing. Jordan wondered how fast she could make it to the emergency panic button underneath the bar.

The blond man, the one wearing glasses and a camel-colored trench coat, cleared his throat. "Are you Jordan Rhodes?"

She debated whether to answer this. But the blond man seemed safer than the tall, dark one. "I am."

He pulled a badge out of his jacket. "I'm Agent Seth Huxley, this is Agent Nick McCall. We're with the Federal Bureau of Investigation."

This caught her off guard. The FBI? The last time she'd seen anyone from the FBI had been at Kyle's arraignment.

"We'd like to discuss a matter concerning your brother," the blond man continued. He seemed very serious about whatever it was he needed to tell her.

Jordan's stomach twisted in a knot. But she forced herself not to panic. Yet.

"Has Kyle been hurt?" she asked. In the four months her brother had been in prison, there already had been several altercations. Apparently, some of the other inmates at Metropolitan Correctional Center figured a wealthy computer geek would be an easy mark. Kyle assured her that he could hold his own whenever she asked about the fights during her visits. But every day since he'd begun serving his sentence, she'd worried about getting that phone call that said he'd been wrong. And if the FBI had sent two agents to her store during a blizzard, whatever they had to tell her couldn't be good.

The dark-haired man spoke for the first time. His voice was low, yet smoother than Jordan had expected.

"Your brother is fine. As far as we know, anyway."

Jordan cocked her head. That was an odd thing to say. "As far as you know? You make it sound like he's missing or something." She paused before folding her arms across her chest. *Oh . . . no.* "Don't tell me he's escaped."

Kyle wouldn't be so stupid. Well, okay, *once* he'd been that stupid, actions that had landed him in prison in the first place, but he wouldn't be that stupid again. That was why he'd pled guilty instead of going to trial. He'd wanted to own up to his mistakes and accept the consequences.

She knew her brother better than anyone. True, he was a technology genius, and assuming there was a computer anywhere within reach of the inmates, he could probably upload some code or virus or whatever that would spring open the cell doors and release all the prisoners in a mad stampede. But Kyle wouldn't do that. She hoped.

"Escaped? That's an interesting thing to say." Agent McCall looked her over. "Is there something you'd like to share with us, Ms. Rhodes?"

Something about this special agent rubbed Jordan the wrong way. She felt as though she were facing off against an opponent holding a royal flush in a game of poker she didn't realize she'd been playing. And she wasn't in the mood to play games with the FBI right then. Or ever. They'd charged her brother to the fullest extent of the law, locked him up at MCC, and treated him like a menace to society for what, in her admittedly biased opinion, was simply a really bad mistake. By someone with no criminal record, she noted. It wasn't like Kyle had *killed* anyone, for heaven's sake, he'd just caused a bit of panic and mayhem. For about fifty million people.

"You said this is about my brother. How can I help you, Agent McCall?" she asked coolly.

"Unfortunately, I'm not at liberty to fill you in on the details here. Agent Huxley and I would prefer to continue this conversation in private. At the FBI office."

And she would prefer to say nothing at all to the FBI, if they weren't dangling this bit about Kyle over her head. She gestured to the empty wine shop. "I'm sure whatever it is you have to say, the chardonnays will keep it confidential."

"I never trust a chardonnay," Agent McCall said.

"And I don't trust the FBI."

The words hung in the air between them. A standstill. Agent Huxley intervened. "I understand your hesitancy, Ms. Rhodes, but as Agent McCall indicated, this is a confidential matter. We have a car waiting out front and would very much appreciate it if you came with us to the FBI office. We'd be happy to explain everything there."

She considered this. "Fine. I'll call my lawyer and have him meet us there."

Agent McCall shook his head. "No lawyers, Ms. Rhodes. Just you."

Jordan kept her face impassive, but inwardly, her frustration increased. Aside from her general dislike of the FBI because of the way they'd treated her brother, there was an element of pride here. They had come into *her* store, and this Nick McCall person seemed to think she should jump just because he said so.

So instead, she held her ground. "You're going to have to do better than that, Agent McCall. You sought me out in the middle of a blizzard, which means you want something from me. Without giving me more, you're not going to get it."

He appeared to consider his options. Jordan got the distinct impression that one of those options involved throwing her over his shoulder and hauling her ass right out of the store. He seemed the type.

Instead, he pushed away from the bar and stepped closer to her, then closer again. He peered down at her, his brilliant green-eyed gaze unwavering. "How would you like to see your brother released from prison, Ms. Rhodes?"

Stunned by the offer, Jordan searched his eyes cautiously. She looked for any signs of deceit or trickery, although she suspected she wouldn't see anything in Nick McCall's eyes that he didn't want her to.

A leap of faith. She debated whether to believe him.

"I'll grab my coat."

Three

THE DRIVE TO the FBI office took longer than expected given the weather. The roads were terrible, but the SUV made the eight-mile journey without too much trouble. Comfortable behind the wheel despite the ice and snow, Nick took his eyes off the road long enough to steal a glance in the rearview mirror at the passenger in the backseat.

Jordan Rhodes. A billionaire heiress, riding in the backseat of his Chevy Tahoe. Not the way he typically capped off a workday.

She stared silently out the window. Her blond hair fell past the shoulders of her black coat, and she absentmindedly brushed a stray lock out of her eyes. She wore a cream cashmere scarf around her neck—at least he guessed it was cashmere—and matching gloves.

He'd seen photographs of her before, even beyond those Huxley had included in his highly thorough presentation. Given the wealth of her family, and the public's general interest in her brother's case, nearly every paper, television, cable, and Internet media outlet had extensively covered Kyle Rhodes's arrest and guilty plea. Nick recalled seeing several photos of Jordan and her father walking in and out of the courtroom at Kyle's side.

Objectively speaking, Nick knew she was stunning. No doubt, the long, blond hair, svelte figure, and Caribbean blue eyes would appeal to many a man. With her obviously expensive coat and wholly impractical-for-snow high-heeled boots, she reminded him of the ultra-chic, designer-clad Manhattanites he'd occasionally come across back in his New York days.

Not his type.

First of all, he preferred brunettes. And curves. And women without direct relations locked up in a maximum-security prison. Or an inheritance that rivaled the gross national income of a small country. That kind of wealth had to make a person . . . weird. Probably snobby and flashy, too. The impractical high-heeled boots seemed to be confirmation of this.

From the tight set to her jaw, he could tell that she knew he was watching her.

She didn't seem to like him very much. He was not particularly troubled by this. The beauty of this assignment was that Jordan Rhodes didn't have to like him. Huxley was going to be her date at Eckhart's party—he could be the one to work his charm routine. Assuming Huxley had a charm routine.

Nick's responsibility, on the other hand, was simply to secure Jordan Rhodes's cooperation. And to do that, he had to resolve a few unanswered questions first.

"So how's the wine business these days?" he asked, breaking the silence.

Jordan turned her head away from the window and met his gaze in the rearview mirror. "You don't need to make small talk with me, Agent McCall. I realize this isn't a social call."

He shrugged. "What can I say? I'm not much for uncomfortable silences."

"What's your position on uncomfortable conversation?"

Nick had to check his grin at that. Christ, she was a sassy one.

"This is some weather we're having," Huxley said, quickly interjecting to keep things light. "Good thing you've got four-wheel drive, Nick."

"True," he agreed. "Although a Chevy Tahoe can't be nearly as fun to drive as a Maserati Quattroporte."

Jordan stared at Nick with a mixture of surprise and annoyance. "You know what kind of car I drive?"

"I know lots of things. Trust me, I have files worth of annoying small-talk questions I can ask as we creep through this blizzard at ten miles an hour. I figured the subject of wine seemed the most innocuous."

She sighed, as if resigned to her fate. "The wine business is good."

"I'm curious: who's your typical customer?" he asked. "Do you get a lot of hard-core collectors or more locals from the neighborhood?"

"I get all types. Some people are just beginning to dabble in wine and looking for a comfortable place to learn more. Others are more experienced drinkers who like to come in and relax while sampling the wines we have open. Then there's a third group, who I would describe as serious collectors."

As Nick had guessed, she relaxed when discussing the subject of wine. Good. "I don't know much about wine myself. I did hear a story a few weeks ago about some collector from Chicago who spent over two hundred and fifty thousand dollars on a case of wine." He turned to Huxley. "Can you believe it? Two hundred and fifty thousand." He checked back in the rearview mirror. "You're the expert, Ms. Rhodes—in the wine world, what does one get for a quarter of a million dollars?"

"A 1945 Chateau Mouton-Rothschild."

"Wow. You came up with that awfully fast. I take it you heard about the auction, too?"

"Actually, I helped that particular collector locate the wine," she said. "I knew it was going to auction and that he would be interested."

"The guy had a strange name . . . I think he owned a restaurant or something."

Huxley looked over at Nick but remained silent, having realized that their interrogation of Jordan Rhodes had begun.

"Xander Eckhart," Jordan said.

"Must be nice having customers who buy a quarter million dollars worth of wine."

For a brief moment, she loosened up a bit. "Unfortunately, that sale went to Sotheby's," she said with a smile. "But, yes, Xander is a good customer."

And therein lay the question, Nick thought. *Just how good of a customer?* "I take it you know him well?"

"Well enough, I suppose."

"How well?"

There was a pause, and he saw the stiffening in Jordan's posture the moment she clued in.

"You want to know about Xander. That's what this is about?" she asked.

"Yes."

She appeared genuinely shocked. "Why would you be investigating Xander?"

Nick ignored the question, shifting into interrogation mode. "How would you describe the nature of your relationship with Eckhart?"

She seemed to weigh her options before answering. While sitting in the backseat of an SUV, in the middle of a blizzard, with two armed FBI agents in front, she didn't have many. "Xander has been a regular customer of my store for a few years. I often handle special orders for him, expensive or rare wines you can't get through a distributor."

"Have you had any interactions with him outside the store?" Nick probed.

"Perhaps I really should call my lawyer. I'm suddenly finding myself very uncomfortable with this situation, Agent McCall."

He caught her eye in the rearview mirror. "Why would talking about Xander Eckhart make you uncomfortable?"

She adjusted her position in the backseat, crossing one leg over the other. "Why don't you spare me the interrogation and just get to the point?"

"Outside the store, do you see Eckhart socially?"

"Occasionally. We know some of the same people, so from time to time I'll run into him at a party or at one of his restaurants. And every year I attend a charity fund-raiser that he hosts at Bordeaux. The party is this weekend, as a matter of fact."

"Is that the full extent of your personal relationship?"

She locked eyes with him in the mirror. "What else would there be to our relationship, Agent McCall?"

"Do you have any sort of intimate connection to Eckhart?"

Her voice was smoky in the darkness of the backseat. "Just a deep appreciation for good wine."

She turned away from him and stared out the window once again. Nick got the message, loud and clear: *Conversation over.*

When they arrived at the FBI office, he parked the car in the spot closest to the entrance of the glass and steel midrise building. The parking lot was virtually empty—with the snowstorm, nearly everyone had gone home for the evening. With a nod, he indicated to Huxley that he would get Jordan. He stepped out of the car and opened the back door.

Jordan hesitated before sliding across the seat. She stepped down from the SUV—one high-heeled, leather-booted leg first, then the other. Because Nick held the door open, they stood close to each other.

Thick snowflakes fell around them and tangled in her hair. Her voice was low, her tone as cold as the air. "The next time you want to know something, Agent McCall, don't bother to sweet-talk me first. Just ask."

"I assure you, Ms. Rhodes, when I sweet-talk a woman, she knows it." He held out his hand, being polite. "You're not going to get far in those boots."

She ignored his hand. "Watch me." She turned in her heels and walked away from the car, heading through the semi-plowed, snow- and ice-covered parking lot toward the entrance of division headquarters.

So help him, she didn't slip once.

Huxley stopped at Nick's side. "You could've given me a sign that you planned to question her in the car. Why not wait to bring up Eckhart at the office?"

"I wanted to catch her off guard. We needed to make sure she wasn't one of the flavors of the month."

"You think it's a good idea to piss her off like this? We're about to ask her to work with us."

"She'll cooperate." Of that, Nick had no doubt. He'd known it about thirty seconds after walking into her store, when he saw the anxious look on her face when they'd first mentioned her brother.

Has Kyle been hurt?

Jordan Rhodes may not have liked *him* very much, but she was obviously concerned about her brother. At the end of the day, that was all that mattered.

THE TWO AGENTS led Jordan to a conference room on the eleventh floor and told her to make herself comfortable while they "retrieved a file." She suspected this was FBI code for something shady, but wasn't exactly sure what. All she knew was that after Agent McCall's not-so-innocent questioning during the car ride over, she had her eye on him. Two of them, in fact.

She removed her coat, scarf, and gloves, and brushed the snow off her boots. Yes, fine, as McCall had annoyingly pointed out, her Christian Louboutins weren't exactly hardy, all-weather footwear. And back at the store, when she'd grabbed her coat from the back room, she had thought momentarily about changing out of them. But the snow boots she'd bought last November—not having any idea she'd be in this predicament—were hardly business appropriate. The way she saw it, there were some matters of style that simply needed to take precedence over practicality, and right at the top had to be the rule that said one did not wear black dress pants and pink Uggs to a meeting with the FBI. Not anyone who didn't want to look like a jackass, anyway.

Jordan took a seat at the conference table. She watched

the blizzard that raged outside the floor-to-ceiling windows, dreading the snow she'd have to shovel when she got home. Perhaps she should look into getting one of those power snowblowers, she mused. Or a man. Either could be quite handy in inclement weather. Then again, snowblowers took up a lot of garage space, and she generally liked to keep at least a three-foot buffer around the Maserati. Not to mention, most of the men she met presumably had even less interest than she did in shoveling snow—they likely would hire someone else to do that kind of thing. The downside to dating Italian-loafer types, she supposed.

Maybe she needed to find more of a guy's guy. One of those men who could start a fire with two sticks, could change a flat tire with one hand tied behind his back, and wasn't afraid that a snow shovel would scuff his cashmere-lined leather Burberry gloves.

The door flew open and in walked Nick McCall.

Someone, however, who at least knew what a *razor* was.

"Sorry to keep you waiting, Ms. Rhodes," he said.

As Huxley followed Nick into the conference room, Jordan noticed that both men had shed their coats. She also saw that they were armed, catching glimpses of the shoulder harnesses and guns they wore underneath their suit jackets.

"What happened to your file?" she asked.

"Would you believe it? We couldn't find the darn thing," Nick said. "Guess we'll just have to march on without it." He gave Huxley a nod.

"Everything we're about to tell you is extremely confidential, Ms. Rhodes," Huxley began. "You can tell no one about the purpose of this meeting."

Easy enough for her to do, since *she* didn't understand the purpose of the meeting. "All right."

"You already know that this pertains to Xander Eckhart. For some time now, we've had him under investigation. We believe he's running drug money through his nightclubs and restaurants for an organized crime syndicate led by Roberto Martino. You may have heard about the recent indictments of Martino and the others in his organization." Huxley gave Jordan a moment to process all this.

"You seem surprised," Nick said.

She shot him a look. "Of course I'm surprised. I had no idea Xander was mixed up in anything like this. You're sure of this?"

Huxley nodded. "Yes. We've been watching Eckhart. We've seen him on several occasions with a man we know to be one of Martino's associates. They meet in Eckhart's office, which is located underneath the main level of his restaurant, Bordeaux."

"The one down the hall from his wine cellar, you mean," Jordan said.

Nick sat forward in his chair, interested in this. "You've been inside Eckhart's office?"

"Yes. Last year at his Valentine's Day party, he gave me a tour of the entire space at Bordeaux."

"How well do you remember the interior of the office?" Huxley asked. "Would you be able to describe it, tell us the placement of the furniture, that kind of thing?"

"I can certainly try," Jordan said. "Is that what this is about? You want me to describe Xander's office to you?" It seemed too insignificant for all the secret-agent rigmarole.

Nick shook his head. "Unfortunately, it's not that simple. What we want is for you to help *us* get inside Eckhart's office. This Saturday night."

It took her a moment. "You mean during the party?"

Nick folded his arms on the table. "How would you feel about bringing along an undercover agent as your date, Ms. Rhodes?"

Jordan leaned in to meet him halfway. "I think that depends on who the date is, Agent McCall."

Next to Nick, Huxley pushed up his glasses. "Me."

Jordan looked over, surprised. "Oh. Okay."

"Try not to look so relieved," Nick said dryly.

"Sorry. It's just that Agent Huxley seems more . . ." She searched for the right word.

"Like a fancy-wine type?" Nick suggested sarcastically.

"I was about to say 'pleasant.'"

"Actually, I have been doing a lot of research into wine for this assignment," Huxley interjected. "From what I've read, Eckhart has quite an impressive collection." He shot Nick a glance and cleared his throat. "Not that I'll be drinking that evening, of course."

From Huxley's nervous look, Jordan guessed that Nick held some sort of position of authority over the younger agent. Another of the FBI's questionable judgment calls. "So I bring you as my date, and then what happens?" she asked Huxley.

"I'll break away from the party at some point and plant small recording devices in Eckhart's office."

They made it sound so easy. Then again, to them, maybe it was. "Tell me how my brother fits into this."

Nick took the lead here. "The U.S. attorney has agreed to a reduction of your brother's sentence to time served. If you cooperate with us, her office will file the motion on Monday. While waiting for the court to rule, we can arrange to have your brother transferred to home detention."

Jordan studied both agents carefully. "What's the catch? There has to be one, if you're willing to give up Kyle. Several months ago, the U.S. attorney had a blast making a public spectacle of the case. His way of being tough on crime, I suppose."

"The *former* U.S. attorney made a public spectacle of your brother's case," Nick corrected her. "The new one has a different agenda."

"You need to be aware that with any undercover operation, there is some risk of danger," Huxley added. "We think we can minimize the risk, but nevertheless, you should take that into consideration."

"How long do I have to make my decision?" Jordan asked.

"I think we all know you've already made your decision, Ms. Rhodes," Nick said.

How Jordan wished she could tell him that he didn't know her half as well as he seemed to think he did. But unfortunately, in this case, he was right. "I have one condition. Kyle can't know anything about our arrangement. He'd worry too much about me."

"*No one* can know about this until it's over," Huxley emphasized. "To maintain the cover, everyone has to think I'm actually your date that evening." He blushed. "Not that I'm suggesting we need to—ahem—get romantic or anything."

Nick hadn't taken his eyes off her. "So we have a deal?"

Despite the fact that Huxley would be her date on Saturday night, Jordan couldn't help but think that she was about to get into bed with the devil.

A green-eyed one at that.

She nodded. "We have a deal."

AT THE END of the meeting, Jordan and Huxley made arrangements to meet on Thursday evening, which was Martin's night to close the shop. The plan was to go over the details for Saturday night then.

After they escorted her down to the lobby, Huxley turned to Nick. "Why don't I take Jordan home?" He smiled at her. "It'll give me time to learn more about my new date." He gestured to the snow falling steadily outside the windows. "I'm not parked as close as Nick, so I'll pull the car around front." That decided, he slid on his gloves and hurried off.

Leaving Jordan and Nick alone.

She eyed him warily, bracing herself for another irksome remark since those seemed to be his specialty. What he said instead surprised her.

"So I guess this is it."

"You won't be around for the big event Saturday night?" she asked.

"Oh, I'll be there," he assured her. "But I'll be parked a few blocks away from Bordeaux, in a van with our tech team, making sure the recording devices are working correctly. So if you do see me Saturday, that means something has gone very wrong with this undercover op."

A silence fell between Jordan and Nick. She tried to ignore the weight of his gaze, but found this impossible. "What?"

"I was just thinking that your brother is lucky to have a sister who's willing to do something like this for him."

Jordan brushed her bangs out of her eyes, not having expected an actual compliment from him. And yes, her screwup of a twin was *very* lucky. But the truth of the matter was, she knew he'd do the same for her in a heartbeat. "Kyle deserves a break." She saw the skeptical look on Nick's face and sighed. "Go ahead, Agent McCall. Whatever it is you'd like to say about my brother, I've heard it all before."

"I have two brothers myself, Ms. Rhodes. I understand family loyalty."

She waited for the rest. "But?"

"But your brother did break the law. About ten of them, in fact. He hijacked a global communications network and created widespread panic by causing an outage that affected tens of millions of people."

Jordan rolled her eyes. "You can cut the dramatic lingo, Mr. FBI. My brother hacked into Twitter and shut down the site after his girlfriend posted a link to a video of her fooling around in a hot tub with another guy."

"He crashed the entire site for two days. In the most advanced denial-of-service attack anyone has ever seen."

"It was *Twitter*. Not the Department of Defense's website, or the NSA's. That guy who shut down Facebook last year only got a fine and community service. But in this case, the U.S. attorney—sorry, the former U.S. attorney—argued to the judge that a fine wouldn't be harsh enough for Kyle because of my father's money. Too bad for Kyle that he and I don't live off my father's money."

Nick pointed. "Your ride's here."

Jordan paused midrant and looked through the windows. She saw Huxley's car out front. Another SUV, although this one was a Range Rover.

She turned back to Nick. "Tell me something. Are you trying to get a rise out of me, or does being this irritating come naturally to you?"

Nick's eyes flickered over her with amusement. "I suppose I may be trying to annoy you a little."

"Why?" Jordan asked in exasperation.

He seemed to think about this. "Maybe because I can. Quite easily, apparently." He took a step closer and studied her face. "I bet you need a few more people in your life who annoy you, Ms. Rhodes."

Actually, she had a twin brother in prison who handled

the job just fine. And as for Nick McCall's assessment, she'd gotten used to people making quick assumptions about her because of her father's wealth. Although they weren't typically so up-front about it. "Seriously, who *are* you?" she asked.

He smiled. "Good question. It changes every six to nine months."

Those were the last words he said before Jordan walked out of the FBI building and climbed into Huxley's car. When she looked back, she saw that Nick had already left the lobby.

"Ready to go?" Huxley asked.

Jordan turned toward the road ahead of her. "Definitely."

Four

JORDAN HURRIED TO catch the light at Van Buren Street, thinking that if she never again laid eyes on Metropolitan Correctional Center after next week, she'd be just fine. The building was an eyesore: an ugly, gray triangle that shot up over thirty stories high with tiny vertical slats for windows.

She visited Kyle every Wednesday, having worked out a routine with Martin that allowed for that. She'd been extremely appreciative that her assistant had made it to the store on time that morning despite the near foot of snow the Streets and Sanitation Department was still struggling to clear off the roads. Because her car was snowed in and taxis were always a rarity on bad-weather days, she'd had to ride the L train downtown, which took extra time. Since visitors were permitted at the prison on a first-come basis, she liked to arrive promptly at noon, the start of visiting hours.

Jordan checked her watch as she approached the building and saw that she was right on time. She pushed through the doors and entered the lobby. At least it was warmer than the frigid thirteen degrees outside; at a minimum, the prison had that going for it. At the front desk, she filled out a

Notification to Visitors form and handed it over to Dominic, the lobby correctional officer, along with her driver's license. Having visited Kyle every Wednesday for the last four months, she was familiar with the routine.

"So I'm halfway through season two of *Lost*," Dominic told her. Other than getting to see Kyle, the lobby guard and their chats about television shows were pretty much the only things Jordan liked about MCC.

"Wow, you really flew through that first season," she said.

"What's up with the Others?" he asked. "They're creepy."

"You'll find out in about another hundred episodes. Sort of."

"Aw, don't tell me that." Dominic handed back her driver's license. "Are you and your brother sure you're not missing a triplet? Because the resemblance is uncanny."

Jordan smiled. Ever since *Lost* had first aired, people had commented that her brother looked like a certain well-known character on the show—which Kyle *hated*. Probably for that reason, the prison staff and other inmates made sure to tease him about it as much as possible. Personally, she found the whole thing quite amusing.

"I'm pretty sure there's no relation," she said. Either that, or her father had some serious 'splaining to do.

Dominic gestured to her neck. "Don't forget to leave your scarf behind when you check in your things. I'll see you next week, Jordan."

Not if all goes as planned. She felt very covert, having secret knowledge of her deal with the FBI. She realized she needed to be careful not to show that around Kyle. Too often, he could read her like a book.

Per MCC rules, she checked her coat, purse, scarf, and gloves into one of the lockers behind the front desk. A second correctional officer escorted her and several other visitors into one of the elevators and rode with them to the centralized visiting room on the eighth floor. The elevators opened and she and the other visitors were led into a security clearance area. She passed through the metal detectors, waited for a third guard to unlock a heavy set of doors made of steel and bulletproof glass, then stepped into the visiting room.

She'd been surprised the first time she'd visited Kyle at MCC. Perhaps the consequence of too much television, she'd thought they'd be separated by glass and would have to talk through telephones. She'd been pleased to discover that the inmates were allowed to meet their visitors in a large common room. Sure, the entire time they had four armed guards watching over them, but at least she could sit down with her brother face-to-face.

Ignoring the bitter sludge they called coffee—a mistake from her first visit never again to be repeated—Jordan opted for bottled water from one of the vending machines. She chose a table in front of a window encased by metal bars and took a seat. As she did every week, she tried to mind her own business and avoided paying too much attention to the other visitors waiting at the surrounding tables, assuming they preferred some modicum of privacy as much as she did. Her mind wandered, knowing she had several minutes to wait while Kyle made it past his various security checks before he could be processed through to the visiting room.

Jordo—I fucked up.

Those had been the first words out of Kyle's mouth when he'd called her that fateful night five months ago. She'd had no clue what he'd done, but in the end it came down to one thing.

"Can you fix it?" she'd asked.

"I dunno," he'd groaned worriedly. There was a hard thumping sound, which she'd guessed was his head hitting the wall.

"Where are you? I'll come get you and we'll figure it out."

His words were slurred. "Tijuana. Gettin' verryyy drunk."

Oh boy. "Kyle. What did you do?"

His voice rose in anger. "I juz shut down Twitter, thaz what I did. The ho damn thing. The *hell* with Dani."

Jordan hadn't caught all of that, but she'd grasped enough to understand that her computer geek of a brother had done something very, very bad because of Daniela, his girlfriend.

Kyle had a knack for attracting the wrong kind of girl—meaning vapid, money-seeking, skanky ones—and, as Jordan ultimately came to find out through her brother's inebriated ramblings that night, Daniela the Brazilian Victoria's Secret model ultimately was no exception. They'd met in New York at a gallery exhibition for an artist who was a mutual friend. They dated long distance for six months, a record for Kyle. Then Daniela flew out to LA to shoot a music video—a great opportunity, she'd said, because she wanted to become an actress. Of course she did.

On the second day of the trip, she stopped calling Kyle. Worried, he left messages on her cell phone and at her hotel, with no response. Late on the fourth night, he finally got a reply.

Via Twitter.

@KyleRhodes Sorry not going 2 work out 4 us. Going 2 chill in LA with someone I met. I think U R sweet but U talk too much about computers.

Twenty minutes later, in her next tweet, Daniela posted a link to a video of her in Hollywood making out with movie star Scott Casey in a hot tub.

It was tough to say which bothered Kyle more, the fact that he'd been dumped over Twitter, or the fact that Daniela had no qualms about publicly cuckolding him. Given his wealth and her minor celebrity status, their relationship had been talked about in gossip columns in both New York and Chicago, and had been mentioned several times on TMZ.com.

Kyle worked in technology; he knew it would only be a matter of time before the video of Daniela and the A-list actor went viral and spread everywhere. So he did what any pissed-off, red-blooded computer geek would do after catching his girlfriend giving an underwater blowjob to another man: he hacked into Twitter and deleted both the video and her earlier tweet from the site. Then, raging at the world that had devolved so much in civility that 140-character breakups had become acceptable, he shut down the entire network in a denial-of-service attack that lasted two days.

And so began the Great Twitter Outage of 2011.

The Earth nearly stopped on its axis.

Panic and mayhem ensued as Twitter unsuccessfully attempted to counteract what it deemed the most sophisticated hijacking they'd ever experienced. Meanwhile, the FBI waited for either a ransom demand or political statement from the so-called "Twitter Terrorist." But neither was forthcoming, as the Twitter Terrorist had no political agenda, already was worth millions, and had most inconveniently taken off to Tijuana, Mexico to get shit-faced drunk on cheap tequila being served by an eight-fingered bartender named Esteban.

Late the second night, after an unpleasant encounter with a cactus to the forehead while bending over to throw up outside Esteban's bar, Kyle had a moment of semi-clarity. He stumbled to his hotel room and called Jordan, then, realizing the error of his ways, powered up his laptop computer. Determined to right his wrongs, he hacked into Twitter a second time and put a halt to his earlier attack.

Only this time, Kyle wasn't as careful. Drinking cheap tequila served by an eight-fingered bartender came with its price. And the next day, when a sober and chagrined Kyle flew back to Chicago, he found the FBI waiting on his doorstep.

Despite all the attempts by his lawyers to dissuade him, Kyle steadfastly insisted upon pleading guilty. He'd done the crime, so he would do the time, he said. Jordan had found this to be an admirable sentiment, albeit one that would essentially cost him a year and a half of his life.

The heavy double doors swung open, jolting Jordan back to reality. The very *real* reality of bulletproof glass, barred windows, and armed guards.

The inmates entered the visiting room single file. Jordan watched as the first two men spotted their families and headed over to nearby tables. Kyle, her computer geek of a brother, was third in line.

His grin was the same every time she came to visit: part

embarrassed to see her given the circumstances, and part happy just to see her. He walked over in his orange jump-suit and blue tennis shoes as she stood up.

"Jordo," he said, his nickname for her ever since they'd been kids. Having obviously stolen all the tall genes from her upon conception, something she still hadn't forgiven him for, he leaned down to pull her into a hug. This and another brief embrace at the end of the visit were the only contact permitted.

"I've decided that orange becomes you," Jordan said teasingly.

He chucked her under the chin. "I missed you, too, sis."

As they took a seat at the table, Jordan saw some of the female visitors not-so-subtly checking Kyle out. In fifth grade, her girlfriends had begun handing her notes to give her brother after school, and the attention hadn't waned since. Frankly, the whole thing flabbergasted her. It was *Kyle*.

"Is it as bad out there as they say it is?" he asked. "From my six-inch window, it looks like we got hit with one hell of a storm."

"It took me nearly an hour to shovel the sidewalk this morning," Jordan said.

Kyle brushed his neck-length dark blond hair off his face. "See? That's one of the positives of being in prison. No shoveling."

Her brother had long ago set the rules regarding their visits. Jokes about being in prison were expected and en-couraged, sympathy was not. Which was good for both of them, considering her family had never done particularly well with the mushy and sentimental stuff.

"You live in a penthouse condo and haven't shoveled snow for years," she pointed out.

"A deliberate choice I made because of the trauma of my youth," Kyle said. "Remember how Dad used to make me shovel the whole block every time it snowed? I was eight when he came up with that plan—barely taller than the shovel."

"And I got to stay inside making hot chocolate with

Mom." Jordan waved off the retort she saw coming. "Hey, it was good for you—it built character." She paused for a moment, taking in their steel-barred surroundings. "Maybe Dad should've made you shovel the next block over, too."

"That's cute."

"I thought so."

An inmate shouted at them from across the room. "Hey, Sawyer! *Sawyer!* When are you gonna introduce me to your sister?"

An annoyed look crossed Kyle's face as he ignored the voice.

"Yo! Sawyer!" The inmate was quickly silenced by the approach of an armed guard.

Jordan made no attempt to hide her grin. "I think someone's trying to get your attention."

"I don't answer to that name," Kyle growled.

"Maybe if you would just cut your hair," she offered faux-sympathetically.

"*Fuck* Josh Holloway," he nearly shouted in frustration. "I've worn my hair like this for years."

"Getting a little loud over here, Sawyer," a guard warned as he passed by their table.

Jordan watched, amused, as her brother simmered at a low boil. "But the hair worked for Sawyer, because they were roughing it on the island. Although I think there had to have been some sort of salon or spa in the Others' camp. I mean, they performed surgeries on people; I would assume they could've rustled up a decent pair of scissors for a haircut somewhere—"

"I swear if you don't let this drop, I'll ban you from my visitation list."

She laughed at the likelihood of *that* ever happening. "You've been stuck to me like gum on the bottom of my shoe since birth. What would you do without my charming wit to cheer you up every week?"

She peered up as an inmate in his midthirties stopped at their table. As soon as he spoke, she recognized the voice of the man who'd been yelling across the room.

"So you're the sister." He looked her over appraisingly.

and smiled, managing to look harmless enough despite the black snake tattoo coiled around his right forearm. "Help me out with an introduction, Sawyer—let's do this proper."

A guard called over from across the room. "I'm not telling you again, Puchalski. No talking to the other guests." With a regretful look over his shoulder, the inmate shuffled off.

Jordan turned back to Kyle. "I take it Dad was here on Monday?" Unless something urgent came up, her father was as regular a visitor to MCC as she was.

"Sounds like business is better. I think the fallout is finally subsiding," Kyle said, referring to the fact that their father's company had not surprisingly taken a hit the previous financial quarter. Strange, how people tended to get ticked off when the vice president of a computer software corporation—and the CEO's son—was indicted and imprisoned for hacking.

Jordan was about to answer when Kyle turned in his chair to get more comfortable. She noticed something— a faded yellow bruise along the left side of his jaw. She looked down at the table and saw the telltale cuts on the knuckles of his right hand. "You got in another fight."

"It's no big deal."

"Doesn't look that way to me. Let me see that." She reached out and touched his chin to get a better look.

"Jordan, you know you can't—"

Just like that, the guard stood beside their table. He frowned at Jordan. "Sorry, ma'am, no contact."

She pulled back her hand. "Sorry." She took a deep, steadying breath. Normally, she handled the whole prison routine as well as could be expected, but every once in a while it got to be a bit much. Like when she couldn't even check to see if her brother was hurt.

"What happened this time?" she asked Kyle after the guard left.

"Just some talk that got out of hand," he said dismissively. "Some people have nothing better to do around here than run off at the mouth."

"Kyle, you're smarter than that."

"That's what Mom said to me when I came home after fighting Robbie Wilmer in the sixth grade. My first black eye."

"Well, since Mom's not here, you need to hear it from someone else."

"I'm not trying to get in trouble, Jordo." Kyle looked her in the eyes. "But this isn't Jane Addams Elementary School. There are different rules here, and if I want to survive the next fourteen months, I've got to play by them."

How tempted she was right then to tell him about the deal she'd made with the FBI. *Not another fourteen months. Just one more week.* But she kept her mouth shut. "Did the fight get you in trouble again with the guards?"

"A little disciplinary segregation never hurt anyone. You were about to say something else right then."

He really did know her too well. "I was going to yell at you some more, but decided it would be a wasted effort."

"Why do I think there's something you're not telling me?"

"Because you . . . have a lot of time on your hands these days so you look for mysteries where there are none?" she suggested.

"Or maybe I'm just really insightful. And if you're hiding something from me, Jordo, I'll figure it out."

"Thanks for the warning, Mr. Insightful. If only you could use your 'insight' to keep yourself out of prison from now on, *that* would be helpful."

Kyle squeezed her hand. "Aw, I'm so glad you came, sis. You have no idea how much I enjoy these little visits of ours. Ah . . . crap."

The guard was back at their table.

Kyle took his hand off hers. "I know, I know. No contact."

Jordan peered up at the guard. "What's with all the rules? You'd think we were in prison or something."

The guard's stoic face remained unchanged as he turned and walked away.

Jordan turned to Kyle. "Seriously, I don't even get a smile for that? Tough crowd."

Kyle looked around at the inmates in orange jumpsuits and armed guards. "Really? I hadn't noticed."

She caught his eye and smiled. But she was more careful this time not to let her thoughts show.

Just one more week, Kyle. Hang in there.

Five

"SO HOW'S KYLE doing?"

Jordan poured three glasses of wine and handed one each to Melinda and Corinne. "You know Kyle. He says he's fine." She set the wine bottle off to the side and picked up the third glass for herself. "But judging from the bruise on his face and the cuts on his hands, I'd say that his definition of 'fine' differs from mine."

She and her two friends had met at DeVine Cellars after the store closed, and were seated at a table near the racks of sparkling wine and champagne. As per their usual routine, Jordan provided the wine, and Melinda and Corinne brought dinner and dessert.

"He got in another fight?" Melinda asked. "What's the deal with this prison? Don't they have any guards there, or are the inmates running the asylum?"

Corinne was a bit more tactful. "Can't they separate Kyle from the guys giving him a hard time?"

"Kyle says he doesn't want special treatment. He thinks it will go away if he doesn't back down, like it's some kind of rite of passage. He told me that if these guys were 'serious' about hurting him, they'd use a weapon." Jordan swirled her glass, letting the wine open up. "I can't believe the current upside of my thirty-three-year-old brother's life is that his fights don't involve *weapons*."

She saw the concern on Melinda and Corinne's faces. "Sorry. Enough about me and my family problems. Let's talk about something else. What's going on with you guys?"

As they ate, the three of them chatted about work. Both Melinda and Corinne were teachers: Corinne worked at a public high school in the one of the poorest districts in the city and Melinda taught musical theater at Northwestern University, where the three of them had gone to undergrad.

Melinda took another sip of her wine and tipped her glass to Jordan. "This is really good. You said it's a merlot?"

"From South Australia. A 2008 Marquis Phillips."

"I like how fruit forward it is."

Jordan was impressed. "Look at you, breaking out the wine terminology." She dabbed her eyes with a napkin, feigning tears. "It's like seeing a child take her first steps. I'm so proud."

Melinda threw a napkin at her. "Just remind me to grab a bottle before I go. I want Pete to try it. He still won't touch merlot because of *Sideways*."

Jordan heard it all the time. Poor merlot had been disparaged in the film and still hadn't fully recovered its reputation. "I'll straighten Pete out the next time I see him."

"That reminds me—the five of us are still on for dinner next Saturday, right?" Corinne asked.

"Yep. But first let's talk about this weekend. Any special plans for Valentine's Day, Jordan?" Melinda asked.

Jordan paused midsip at the question. *This weekend? No special plans, really. Just helping the FBI infiltrate the lair of a wealthy restaurateur who launders money for a notorious drug cartel. You?*

Corinne chimed in. "Isn't this the weekend of Xander Eckhart's party?"

"Yes." Jordan held her breath in a silent plea. *Don't ask if I'm bringing anyone. Don't ask if I'm bringing anyone.*

"So are you bringing anyone?" Melinda asked.

Foiled.

Having realized there was a distinct possibility the subject would come up, Jordan had spent some time running through potential answers to this very question. She had decided that being casual was the best approach. "Oh, there's this guy I met a few days ago, and I was thinking about asking him." She shrugged. "Or maybe I'll just go by myself, who knows."

Melinda put down her forkful of gnocchi, zoning in on this like a heat-seeking missile to its target. "What guy you met a few days ago? And why is this the first we're hearing of him?"

"Because I just met him a few days ago."

Corinne rubbed her hands together, eager for the details. "So? Tell us. How'd you meet him?"

"What does he do?" Melinda asked.

"Nice, Melinda. You're so shallow." Corinne turned back to Jordan. "Is he hot?"

Of course, Jordan had known there would be questions. The three of them had been friends since college and still saw each other regularly despite busy schedules, and this was what they did. Before Corinne had gotten married, they talked about her now-husband, Charles. The same was true of Melinda and her soon-to-be-fiancé, Pete. So Jordan knew that she, in turn, was expected to give up the goods in similar circumstances. But she also knew that she really didn't want to lie to her friends.

With that in mind, she'd come up with a backup plan in the event the conversation went this way. Having no choice, she resorted to the strategy she had used in sticky situations ever since she was five years old, when she'd set her Western Barbie's hair on fire while trying to give her a suntan on the family-room lamp.

Blame it on Kyle.

I'd like to thank the Academy . . . "Sure, I'll tell you all about this new guy. We met the other day and he's . . . um . . ." She paused, then ran her hands through her hair and exhaled dramatically. "Sorry. Do you mind if we talk about this later? After seeing Kyle today with the bruise on his face, I feel guilty rattling on about Xander's party. Like I'm

not taking my brother's incarceration seriously enough." She
bit her lip, feeling guilty about the lie. *So sorry, girls. But this
has to stay my secret for now.*

Her diversion worked like a charm. Perhaps one of the
few benefits of having a convicted felon of a brother known
as the Twitter Terrorist was that she would never lack for
non sequiturs in extracting herself from unwanted conversation.

Corinne reached out and squeezed her hand. "No one
has stood by Kyle's side more than you, Jordan. But we
understand. We can talk about this some other time. And try
not to worry—Kyle can handle himself. He's a big boy."

"Oh, he definitely is that," Melinda said with a gleam in
her eye.

Jordan smiled. "Thanks, Corinne." She turned to Melinda,
thoroughly skeeved out. "And, *eww*—Kyle?"

Melinda shrugged matter-of-factly. "To you, he's your
brother. But to the rest of the female population, he has a
certain appeal. I'll leave it at that."

"He used to fart in our Mr. Turtle pool and call it a 'Ja-
cuzzi.' How's that for appeal?"

"Ah . . . the lifestyles of the rich and famous," Corinne
said with a grin.

"And on that note, my secret fantasies about Kyle Rhodes
now thoroughly destroyed, I move that we put a temporary
hold on any further discussions related to the less fair of the
sexes," Melinda said.

"I second that," Jordan said, and the three women clinked
their glasses in agreement.

Jordan took a sip of her wine, breathing a sigh of relief.
Three more days—that's all she had to make it. Then everything would be back to normal.

Six

IT IS A truth universally acknowledged that an FBI special agent in possession of great skill and talent is likely to engage in trash talk every now and then.

Nick—being possessed of said skill and talent—was, on that Thursday night, partaking in this practice, along with his coworker Jack Pallas, Davis's supposed other "top" special agent. The two of them had just finished working out in the state-of-the-art gym located on the building's second floor that was open twenty-four/seven. Some agents fell out of shape after graduating from the Academy, but not in Davis's field office. He held his agents to high physical standards and, as he bluntly told everyone in their welcome-to-Chicago speech, expected to see their asses in the gym.

Sweaty in their T-shirts, Jack and Nick grabbed towels from the shelf as they entered the locker room. They'd completed a seven-mile run on the gym's indoor track only moments earlier. While subtly trying to outpace and outdistance each other, they'd caught up on various odds and ends that Nick had missed during the six months he'd worked undercover on Fivestar. Eventually, their conversation turned to the arrests of Roberto Martino and the other members of his organization, and the investigation into Xander Eckhart.

"I hear you're taking orders from Seth Huxley nowadays," Jack said as they edged their way through the crowded locker room. The end of the workday, not surprisingly, was the gym's busiest time, with most agents squeezing in a workout before heading home. "How's that going?"

"If by 'taking orders' you mean providing my much-learned undercover expertise as a favor to our boss, then I'd say it's going great." Nick feigned confusion. "What I've been trying to figure out is why Davis had to bring me in on this case in the first place. I could've sworn another agent was already running the Martino investigation . . . Oh, wait—that would be you, Jack."

Jack took a seat on the bench in front of their lockers. "I've been a little busy these days. Thirty-four arrests in the last four months, McCall. That's a new record for me."

Nick stripped off his damp T-shirt, baring his chest. "Try twenty-seven arrests in the last *week*. That's a new record for the office."

"You're still seven arrests behind me, buddy."

Not for long, if Nick had anything to say about it. "It'll only be five after Eckhart and Trilani."

Jack scoffed at this. "Eckhart is a money-laundering case. Anything from Financial only gets you half a point." He stood up and peeled off his own T-shirt, revealing several scars, electrical burns, and a bullet wound on his chest.

Having worked on and off with Jack for several years, and given how they were both regulars at the gym, Nick had seen the other agent's scars before—souvenirs of the two days Jack had been tortured by Roberto Martino's men. Two days where he'd given them absolutely nothing in exchange. The scars were a quick reminder not only of the pride Nick felt in being a special agent in one of the toughest FBI field offices in the country, but also of the grudging respect he had for Jack. All trash talk aside, they understood each other's commitment to the job.

Davis wasn't getting any younger, and when he retired

as special agent in charge, either Nick or Jack likely would be asked to fill the position. Neither was entirely sure he wanted it, although the satisfaction that would be derived from beating out the other for the job provided strong motivation to at least consider the possibility.

Nick ignored the scars on Jack's chest, as was expected. He stripped off the rest of his clothes and slung a towel around his hips. "You know, it's interesting what you said a moment ago about taking orders. From what I hear, you've been taking a lot of orders yourself these days. From the new U.S. attorney." Actually, what he'd heard from several sources around the office was that Jack had been assigned to protect the new U.S. attorney as part of a murder investigation and had dived off a three-story stairwell to save her life. Also according to these sources—who had spoken only on condition of total anonymity—the two were now living together and Jack had subsequently "mellowed" a bit from his former days.

"We all take orders from the U.S. attorney around here," Jack said. "She is something." The corners of his mouth turned up as he slid out of his running pants.

Nick stared at him in astonishment. "Was that actually a smile? Shit, Pallas—all these years we've been working together, I wasn't even sure you had teeth."

"It's part of this whole softer side Jack is trying out," said a voice from around the corner. A younger, well-built African American man strolled over from the showers. Like Jack and Nick, he was naked except for a towel knotted around his waist. "It's kind of nice, actually—he barely ever threatens to kill people anymore." The young agent reached over the bench in the center of the aisle and stuck out his hand to Nick. "I'm Jack's partner, the inimitable Sam Wilkins," he said by way of introduction. "I've seen you around the office the past few days."

Nick shook his hand. "Nick McCall. You're the new guy from Yale, right? I've heard about you. People say you've got a wardrobe that rivals Huxley's."

"Who's got a wardrobe that rivals mine?" Huxley came

around the corner in a towel and—big surprise—Polo shower shoes. He took his glasses out of his locker and put them on. He spotted Wilkins. "Oh. Hello . . . Wilkins."

"Hello, Huxley," Wilkins replied coolly.

Nick pointed between the two of them. "You boys have a problem?"

"No problem," Huxley said. "Just a little friendly school rivalry."

"Not so much a rivalry," Wilkins corrected. "I'd call it more a mutual understanding between the two of us that Huxley here went to the *other* Ivy League law school; the one that follows behind Yale in the rankings."

"And also a mutual understanding that Wilkins here went to a law school that, while theoretically Ivy League like Harvard, teaches its students wholly impractical classes like Law and the Butterfly," Huxley noted.

With a chuckle, Jack mumbled under his breath to Nick. "It's like watching the preppy, well-bred versions of you and me trash-talking." He headed off to the showers.

Huxley looked offended by this. "I'm not *that* preppy." Naked except for his shower shoes, he took out a pair of neatly ironed boxer briefs from his duffle bag and pulled them on.

Nick decided to redirect the conversation. "So how did your meeting with Jordan Rhodes go today?"

"Fine. We got together at her house and went over the details for Saturday. If anyone at the party asks how we met, we're going to say that I'm a customer of her store. I know enough about wine to be able to pull that off without a problem. And I have to tell you—we couldn't have picked a better person to help with the op. Jordan was able to give me a detailed description of Eckhart's office. I'm not anticipating having much trouble getting the bugs placed quickly."

"You'll have to figure out a way to sneak away from the others," Nick pointed out.

Huxley slid on a light blue dress shirt. "Already got it covered. Jordan is going to pull Eckhart aside and talk to him about some special wine she's been trying to locate for him. While he's distracted, I'll slip away from the other guests and make my way to the office."

He gave Nick a knowing look as he buttoned his shirt. "Look, I know Davis asked you to babysit me on this." He held up his hand. "I get it, it's my first undercover op. But trust me, I've spent three months working on this case—no one wants Saturday night to go smoothly more than I do. I'm ready for it."

From the sound of things, Nick couldn't disagree.

TWENTY MINUTES LATER, Nick crossed the parking lot to his SUV, unlocked the door, and climbed in. Damn, it was cold. Six years had taught him that New York had nothing on Chicago in terms of bitter winters. He started the car and let it warm up for a few minutes. He was just pulling out of the parking lot when his cell phone rang, the sound carrying through the speakers via the Bluetooth system in his car. Nick checked the caller ID on the radio display.

Lisa.

He hadn't spoken to her in six months, since before he'd begun the Fivestar investigation. Frankly, he hadn't planned on speaking to her again. Sure, they'd had a couple of fun nights, but he'd made it clear from the beginning that there wasn't anything serious between them. Still, he didn't want to be rude and ignore her.

He answered the phone. "Lisa, hello."

A woman's earthy voice sounded through the speakers. "I heard you were back in town."

"Got your spies out?" Nick teased.

"Maya said you picked up carryout from Schoolhouse Tavern the other night," Lisa said, referring to the waitress who'd rung up his order.

"Right, I forgot that she teaches part-time at your yoga studio."

"She says you look exactly the same."

"It hasn't been *that* long, Lisa."

"Six months."

"Well, I told you it would be a while before you heard from me." *If ever.*

"But now you're back. Any chance you're free tonight?" she asked invitingly.

Nick sensed that this was the moment where he needed to politely—but firmly—make a clean break from Lisa. Actually, he thought he'd done that six months ago.

From the start, he'd explained to Lisa the same thing he explained to every woman he got involved with: he didn't do relationships. Working undercover for months at a time virtually precluded the possibility. Right now, he was focused on his job, and he liked being focused on his job. He'd been working undercover jobs for six years now, and he was good at it. While he reported to Davis, he generally handled his cases the way he wanted, which suited him well.

When he was a kid, Nick had seen the look of relief on his mother's face every time his father walked through the door after one of his police shifts. Unlike his father, however, there were many nights, and weeks, and months, when he didn't come home at all. He may have been focused on his career, but at least he knew not to inflict his unpredictable lifestyle on someone else.

"Lisa, look—we talked about this before I went undercover. This was just a casual thing," he said.

"But I thought we had fun together."

"We did. But I've got a few things going on with work, and some personal days I plan to use after that, so this isn't a good time for me."

Lisa's voice turned suspicious. "There's someone else, isn't there? You don't have to lie about it."

"There's no one else. I'm just not in a position to give you what you're looking for."

The phone went silent for a moment. As much as Nick tried to be a stand-up guy about these things, sometimes women got a little pissed when they realized that—hot sex notwithstanding—he'd really meant it when he'd said that he wasn't looking for a relationship.

"Fine. But being by yourself all the time is going to get lonely, Nick," Lisa said. "When that happens, you remember the good times we had together. And give me a call."

She hung up.

Nick exhaled in relief and made sure the call had disconnected. That hadn't been too bad. When he didn't call Lisa back, she'd move on. After all, it had been just *sex*. No sweet nothings, no endearments, no promises of the future. Soon enough, she would realize that she could get a better deal elsewhere.

He had just exited off the highway at Ohio Street when his cell phone rang again. He glanced over and checked the caller ID.

Shit.

He quickly backtracked, thinking about how long it had been since their last conversation, and realized he undoubtedly had another pissed-off woman on his hands. Perhaps this was one of the reasons he preferred to stay undercover. No accountability.

Bracing himself, he clicked the button on the steering wheel to answer. "Ma—I was just about to call you."

"Right. I could be dead and you wouldn't even know it."

Nick grinned. Despite being perfectly healthy and fit at almost sixty, his mother issued frequent proclamations about her death and the ways in which people would inevitably wrong her in it. "I think Dad, Matt, or Anthony would probably call me if that happened."

His mother, the illustrious Angela Giuliano, who had once disappointed every smitten, fiery Italian man of marriageable age in Brooklyn (as the story was frequently told to Nick and his brothers) by allowing the strong, silent, and decidedly non-Italian John McCall to drive her home from the Moonlight Lounge on a fateful New Years Eve thirty-six years ago, snorted in disagreement. "What do your brothers know? They both live less than fifteen miles from this house, and your father and I never see them."

Nick happened to know that both of his brothers, as well as practically every living relative in New York on his mother's side of the family, had dinner at his parents' house at three o'clock every Sunday afternoon, no exceptions. His father had long ago accepted the weekly Italian invasion as the price one paid for marrying into the Giuliano family.

As happened every time he spoke to his parents or his brothers, Nick felt a pang of guilt. He was more independent than his two younger brothers, and in that sense, the thousand-mile separation from his parents wasn't entirely a bad thing. But still, he sometimes missed those Sunday dinners. "You see Matt and Anthony every week. You see everyone every week."

"Not everyone, Nick," his mother said pointedly. Then her voice changed and turned warmer. "Well, except for this upcoming weekend."

Nick paused at this. It could've been a trap. Perhaps his mother suspected something was up with her birthday and was fishing for information. Although it was surprising that she'd come to him—she usually went after Anthony, who had the secret-keeping skills of a four-year-old.

"Why? What's happening this weekend?" he asked nonchalantly.

"Oh, nothing much. I just heard something about a sixtieth birthday party your father and you boys are planning for me."

Fucking Anthony.

"And don't go blaming Anthony," his mother said, quick to protect her youngest. "I'd already heard about it from your aunt Donna before he slipped."

Nick knew what her next question would be before the words left her mouth.

"So? Are you bringing a date?" she asked.

"Sorry, Ma. It'll just be me."

"There's a surprise."

He pulled into the driveway that led to the parking garage of his condo building. "Just a warning, I'm about to pull into the garage—I might lose you."

"How convenient," his mother said. "Because I had a really nice lecture planned for you."

"Let me guess the highlights: it involved me needing to focus on something other than work, and you dying heartbroken and miserable without grandchildren. Am I close?"

"Not bad. But I'll save the rest of the lecture for Sunday.

There's going to be a lot of gesturing on my part, and the phone doesn't quite capture the spirit."

Nick smiled. "Shockingly, I'm looking forward to it. I'll see you Sunday, Ma."

Her voice softened. "I know how busy you are, Nick. It means a lot to me that you're coming home."

He knew it did. "I wouldn't miss it for the world."

EARLY SATURDAY MORNING, Nick received yet another call.

He opened his eyes and saw that it was still dark outside. He rolled over in bed and peered at the clock on the nightstand. Five thirty-eight A.M.

He reached for his phone and checked the caller ID. Huxley.

Today was the big day, and Nick could certainly appreciate the junior agent's enthusiasm. Huxley had every right to be excited about his first undercover operation.

Just not at 5:38 A.M.

He answered the phone, his voice low and rough with sleep. "At this hour, somebody better be dead, Huxley."

There was a tortured groan on the other end of the line. Nick sat up in bed. "Huxley?"

A weak voice answered.

"No one's dead. But I think I might be close."

Seven

NICK RANG THE bell to Huxley's wood-frame duplex. As he waited on the front steps, he took a look around. Despite the blizzard that had hit earlier that week, the steps, walkway, and front sidewalk were shoveled pristinely. The yard had not one speck of litter, and the evergreens in front of the porch were shaped in a neat row of perfect triangles.

Definitely Huxley's place.

He rang the bell again and waited a few more seconds before trying the door. Huxley had said to come in if he didn't answer, in the event he was indisposed. Nick pushed open the front door and entered the quiet house cautiously. He instinctively reached for the gun holstered in the shoulder harness underneath his jacket, then caught himself. From the sound of things, whatever had gotten ahold of Huxley could not be stopped by bullets.

Nick paused in the entranceway. "Huxley? You alive?" There was a staircase to his left leading upstairs, and a dark hallway in front of him. No lights appeared to be on anywhere inside the place. He checked the bathroom to his right. Empty.

Then came a feeble voice. "In here."

Following the voice, Nick cut through the hallway, the soft thud of his footsteps on the hardwood floors the only sounds in the house. The hallway opened into a spacious great room and kitchen area that looked like something out of a Pottery Barn catalog. There, he spotted Huxley.

Or at least, what he *thought* was Huxley.

The well-groomed agent he was used to seeing in three-piece suits and sweater vests sprawled facedown across the beige sectional couch, with one hand limply clutching a garbage can on the floor next to him. Far from a three-piece suit, he was dressed in a navy sweatshirt and checkered flannel pants. Strangely, he wore only one sock.

Nick slipped off his coat and came around the couch. Huxley weakly lifted his head. His eyes were glazed, and the hair on the left side of his head shot up into the air in a blond Mohawk.

"I wouldn't get too close," Huxley warned. The effort of holding up his head proved too much, and his face fell back into the pillow.

Nick took a seat on the far opposite end of the sectional. "Wow. You look awful." He peered more closely. "What's going on with your hair?"

Huxley spoke into the pillow, his voice muffled. "The stomach pains came on when I was in the shower. I had to get out ASAP. Mid-shampoo."

Nick nodded. "And the missing sock?"

"In the laundry. I puked on my foot."

"Oh."

With painstakingly slow movements, Huxley rolled himself over. He groaned and his head lolled against the pillow. "The good news is, I haven't thrown up for twelve minutes. Before that I only made it nine."

"I don't think it's like labor contractions, Seth. Whatever you've got doesn't look like something that will pass quickly. Could it be food poisoning?"

"Doubtful. I have a fever. One hundred and two."

"The stomach flu, then."

"It appears so."

Before Nick could say anything further, there was a knock at the door.

Huxley closed his eyes. "That's probably Jordan. I called her right after you and left a message saying we had a problem."

Oh, they had a problem, all right. A couple of them. For starters, Eckhart's party was that night and his partner clearly wasn't anywhere near up to par. Second, there were about five thousand jokes Nick wanted to make about Huxley's hair, and he wasn't sure he could hold back much longer.

"I'll get the door." Nick cut through the hallway, working through their options. He grumbled to himself, realizing that they only had one at this point. This was *supposed* to be a simple assignment. A consulting job, Davis had promised. And now he was stuck.

He said a few Brooklyn-flavored curse words under his breath as he opened the front door.

Nick blinked at the sight of the woman standing before him. He'd expected to find the stylishly dressed and designer-clad sophisticate he'd met five nights ago. Instead, Jordan stood on the porch wearing a black ski jacket, black body-hugging leggings, and pink snow boots. She had her long hair pulled back in a high ponytail, with a few layers framing her face. She wore not a speck of makeup, had rosy cheeks from the cold, and her blue eyes sparkled in the winter morning sun.

Interesting.

This was a new side to Jordan Rhodes. Without the designer clothes, it was a good thing for him that she was still blond with ne'er-do-well relations, or he might be in danger of thinking she was quite cute. And given that his role in the Eckhart investigation had just expanded about tenfold, he didn't need to be distracted by cuteness right then.

Seeing him standing in Huxley's doorway, her eyes widened in surprise. "Agent McCall."

Nick raised an eyebrow. "Nice boots."

She leveled him with a glare. Apparently the boots were a taboo subject.

"You said that if I saw you today, it meant that something had gone really wrong with the undercover operation," she said.

He stepped to the side of the doorway. "I think you should probably see for yourself." He shut the door behind her, and they stood in the small entranceway. "But I warn you—it's a little disturbing." He led her down the hallway and into the living room, where the death-warmed-over version of his partner lay on the couch.

"Oh my gosh, what happened?" Jordan asked.

Shivering, Huxley mustered a faint smile. "I guess I look as bad as I feel."

"It's mostly the hair," Nick offered diplomatically. "It's . . . ridiculous."

"I can't deal with a comb right now. Too heavy." Huxley sighed wearily. "I'm a little under the weather," he explained to Jordan.

"That seems to be putting it mildly," she said. "You're shaking—are you cold?"

"It's the fever."

She spoke under her breath to Nick. "Is there a reason he's wearing only one sock?"

"He puked on his foot."

"Oh." She turned back to Huxley. "Can we get you another sock? Maybe a blanket or something?"

Huxley sat up, looking pained by the effort. "That's okay," he groaned. "I'm heading upstairs. If you two would excuse me . . ." He clutched his stomach. "I think this is going to be a rough one."

Jordan watched as Huxley clung to the railing and dragged himself upstairs. When she heard a door shut, she turned back and saw that Nick had moved into the kitchen. She followed him and watched as he began opening cabinets, searching for something.

"I know Huxley. He has to have it somewhere," he muttered to himself. "Ah—got it." He shut the cabinet door and held a bottle out to Jordan.

Hand sanitizer.

"Don't say I never got you anything," he said.

Despite herself, Jordan smiled. "Thanks," she said, taking the bottle from him. She poured an extremely generous amount onto her hands and made a mental note to touch as little as possible inside the house.

Upstairs, she could hear the faint sounds of Huxley groaning. "Should we do something?" she asked Nick.

"I think he'd probably prefer to be alone right now."

She nodded. She said the words first, needing to get it out there. "He's not going to make it to the party tonight, is he?"

"No, he's not. And that's a shame, because I know how badly Huxley wanted this. But he's shivering, he looks terrible, and he can't stay out of the bathroom for more than twenty minutes."

Jordan felt bad for Huxley. Aside from his obvious physical discomfort, she knew how much he'd put into this investigation. But selfishly, she had other issues on her mind at that moment, like the fact that this had been her one chance to get her brother out of prison. "Does this mean we're scrapping the plan for tonight?"

Nick leaned against the counter opposite her, stretching out his tall, leanly muscular body. He wore a navy crewneck sweater, jeans, and a gun harness that made him appear even more dangerous than he had that first night in her store. She took note of his strong, angular jaw, which was once again dark and stubbled.

It wasn't the *worst* look she'd ever seen on a guy. She wouldn't go as far as to say she liked it or anything, but she supposed some women found this sort of overt . . . manliness attractive.

"We're not scrapping the plan," he said. "This may be our only chance to nail Eckhart. But this development with Huxley means we need to make certain adjustments."

"Such as?"

His green eyes held hers. "Looks like you've got yourself a new date this evening."

Balls.

"I had a feeling you were going to say that, Agent McCall."

He shook his head. "No more Agent McCall. From this point on, I'm Nick Stanton, a self-employed real estate investor," he said, referring to the cover story they'd planned to use with Huxley. "I own several multiunit apartment buildings on the north side of the city that I rent out mostly to college students and recent graduates. We met when I came into your store to buy a bottle of wine for my property manager, Ethan, who just got engaged to a girl named Becky, an advertising executive originally from Des Moines who used to live in one of my buildings. You helped me pick out the perfect bottle of wine, and I was so entranced that I didn't pay any attention to what I bought." He scratched his jaw, putting on a show of trying to remember. "What kind of wine was it again, sweetie? Something French I'd never heard of."

Jordan noticed that he was going off the script a little. "A gamay?"

Nick snapped his fingers. "A gamay—that's it."

"With Huxley it was a carménère from Chile. And he picked it out."

"Well, Huxley knows a lot more about wine than I do. Since I don't have time to learn, my character is going to be more of a novice." He grinned. "Your character finds this refreshing in contrast to all the stuffy wine snobs you usually meet."

"But my character probably won't emphasize that fact tonight, since most of those stuffy wine snobs will be at this party," she threw back.

The two of them looked over as Huxley stumbled his way into the living room and sank onto the couch.

"I overheard you talking. You'll take my place, then?" he asked Nick.

"It's our only option at this point."

Huxley shook his head dejectedly. "Three years working for the FBI and I've never had to take one sick day. Today of all days, this happens." He leaned back against the pillows and looked Nick over. "You're going to need a suit."

"I have several suits," Nick said, appearing offended.

Huxley did not seem impressed. "A *real* suit." He held up his hand, cutting off Nick's objection. "No offense, but Men's Wearhouse or whatever isn't going to cut it tonight.

You want to blend, remember? Every person at the party will be checking out the guy walking in with Jordan Rhodes. You need to look like someone they would expect to see her with."

"*Hey*. I would date a guy who wore a suit from Men's Wearhouse," Jordan said indignantly.

Nick sized her up. "Huxley's right. I better get a new suit."

Jordan folded her arms across her chest, on the defensive. "You two are way off base with these assumptions about me."

Nick turned to face her, taking the bait. "Okay, I'll eat my words right now if you can honestly say that you've dated anyone in the last three years who wore a suit from Men's Wearhouse."

Jordan stared him in the eyes, wanting to prove him wrong like nothing else.

But.

She sniffed reluctantly. "Just to be clear, it's not a criteria I have. True, I tend to meet mostly men who have white-collar jobs. And if they want to spend their money on expensive suits, well, that's their business."

Nick shrugged. "You don't have to explain yourself to me, princess."

Jordan's eyes widened in surprise. She stepped over to him, pulling herself up to her full five foot five inches. "Listen, I don't know who you are, or where you came from, but nobody's calling anybody a *princess* around here."

"Brooklyn."

"Excuse me?"

"I'm from Brooklyn." The edges of Nick's lips curled up in a grin. "Your majesty."

Jordan stared him in the eyes for another moment, and then turned to Huxley. "Doesn't the FBI have some sort of top-secret vitamin shot they can give agents in these circumstances? Something that can get you up and running by tonight? Anything?"

"Sorry. I'm afraid you're stuck with Nick."

Lovely.

"Trust me, I'm not exactly thrilled about it, either," Nick said. "No offense, but being cooped up in a van for seven hours sounds more fun than hanging around with some elitist wine crowd." He glanced at his watch and swore under his breath. "We don't have a lot of time to pull this all together. Now that I'm taking your place, I need to find a backup man and get him up to speed," he said to Huxley. "And I need to go shopping, too."

He was so bent out of shape about the darn suit. Because of that, Jordan was tempted to hold her tongue and let him figure things out by himself. But like it or not, for Kyle's sake, the two of them were in this together. So she pulled out her cell phone.

"I'll take care of the suit." She scrolled through her contacts list, found the person she was looking for, and dialed.

A man's voice on the other end answered. "Please tell me you're coming in to shop. We've been dead this whole week because of the blizzard."

Jordan smiled. Two years ago she'd discovered Christian, a personal shopper at the Ralph Lauren store, and he'd never let her down no matter what the fashion emergency. "Are you working this morning? I need a man's suit. Fast."

"No problem. I'm at the store already."

"Perfect. He doesn't have a lot of time to shop, so do me a favor—pull some suits in advance. Shirts and ties, too. Nothing too trendy, something classic. I need a size . . ." She looked expectantly at Nick.

He didn't look thrilled that she was taking charge, but he didn't object either. "Forty-four long."

She repeated the information to Christian, who sounded intrigued.

"You've never sent me a man before," he said. "This forty-four long must be special."

"Oh, he's special all right. And he'll be there in fifteen minutes."

"Wait," Christian said before she hung up. "I'm dying here, Jordan. You've got to give me something. Who is this mystery man?"

She hesitated for a second, then realized she had to bite the bullet and start the lies at some point. Might as well cut her teeth on Christian.

"His name is Nick. He's . . . my boyfriend."

ON THEIR WAY out, Nick held Huxley's front door open for her. "Boyfriend, huh? I didn't realize we had taken things to that level."

"Oh, I'm sorry—this is my first undercover operation," Jordan said. "I'm a little unclear about the rules. Are we seeing other people in this fake relationship?"

He followed her down the steps to the sidewalk. "You expect me to make this decision on the spot? I'm a man, Jordan; I can't be pressured into these kinds of things."

She flashed him a sweet smile. "Lucky for you, it will all be over soon. Tomorrow you can have a fake freak-out over commitment issues that will lead to our fake breakup. After that, I think our characters will need some very real time apart." She began walking toward the street.

Nick caught her by the sleeve of her coat. "I think we need to make sure we're clear on something. You may be used to ordering your personal assistants around, or the minions at your wine store, but this is my investigation now. Which means that I'm in charge here—only me."

She pulled out her cell phone and cocked her head innocently. "Should I cancel the suit, then?" When he glared at her but said nothing, she smiled. "I'll take that as a 'Thank you, Jordan. I appreciate you helping me out in a pinch like this.'"

She headed in the direction of her car, but Nick caught her by the sleeve again. "Where are you going? You're coming with me to the Ralph Lauren store."

"Why would I go?"

"Because I've got about eight hours to make sure this undercover op is successful, and you need to fill me in on everything you told Huxley on Thursday. Particularly the description of Eckhart's office."

Jordan pushed up the sleeve of her coat and looked at

her watch. "It's after nine. We'll be cutting it too close if I go downtown with you. I'm supposed to open my store at ten and I need to go home and change first."

"Can't you get someone to cover for you?"

"Unfortunately, no," she said. Martin and Andrea—one of the two associates who worked at DeVine Cellars—were both set to cover the store that evening while she was at Xander's party, and her other sales associate, Robert, was out of town that weekend. Plus, they were having a closeout sale on several wines her distributors were unloading at bargain prices and she needed to get shelf talkers in place before the store opened. "Is there another time we can talk?"

Nick looked over at her car. "Does that Maserati come with Bluetooth?"

For over a hundred grand, about the only things it didn't come with were ejector seats and a parachute. "Yep."

"We'll do this by phone. I have your number."

Of course he did.

They separated at the street and climbed into their respective cars. Immediately after starting hers, Jordan pushed the button that warmed the tan leather seats. Like good wine and great shoes, heated seats on a February morning were at the top of her most-prized list of luxuries. She let the car idle for a minute before easing it out of its tight parking spot. Heading in the same direction as Nick, she took the one-way side street toward Lake Shore Drive and caught up with him at a stop sign.

She saw him glance at his rearview mirror, spotting her behind him. A few seconds later, her cell phone rang. When she answered, his whisky-rich voice came through the car's speakers.

"So I've been thinking about your question. My character has decided he doesn't want to see other people."

"What made you change your mind? Let me guess—the Maserati."

He chuckled. "Our cover story is that my character has been smitten from the moment he met you. He's not about to let another man get anywhere near you."

"Your character sounds a little possessive. Is this something my character should be worried about?"

They came to a stop at the light that would take them onto the Drive. Nick's voice was low, even smoother than the car's engine. "I think your character secretly likes it. You've been dating boring, uptight guys for too long. You've been looking for something different."

Jordan looked sharply at the SUV in front of her. "I think your character presumes too much."

His eyes caught hers in the rearview mirror. "Does he?"

The light turned green, and they drove off in opposite directions. As Jordan headed north, away from downtown and with Nick's car safely out of sight, she decided it was time to change the subject. "What do you want to know about the layout of Xander's office?"

"As much as you can tell me."

As she sped along the Drive with the gray expanse of Lake Michigan on her right, Jordan filled him in on as much as she remembered. She finished the call with Nick just as she pulled into her garage. She hung up and sat in her car for a moment, thinking about his comment.

You've been looking for something different.

Presumptuous words. Very presumptuous. But she couldn't help but wonder if there was any truth to them. Pushing the thought from her mind, she opened the car door and hurried into her house. There was one thing, at least, she knew without a doubt.

It was far too cold to be sitting outside thinking about Nick McCall.

THIRTY MINUTES LATER, suit in hand, Nick walked along Michigan Avenue toward the parking garage where he'd left his car. He made a phone call.

It was a truth universally acknowledged that FBI agents in possession of great skill and talent, even those who frequently engaged in the practice of trash-talking, understood that there were times when all bullshit needed to be set aside in order to get a job done.

This was one of those times.

After two rings, another agent answered Nick's call.

"Pallas."

"It's McCall. I've got a problem."

"The Eckhart op?"

"You got it. Huxley's out with the flu."

"What do you need?"

"Backup in the van."

"I'm on it."

"Meet me at the office in ten minutes."

"Yep."

Nick hung up the phone, mentally running through his checklist. Ridiculously overpriced Ralph Lauren suit? Sixteen hundred dollars, all of which had better be reimbursed by the Bureau. Backup man? Technically free, although he'd be hearing about this from Pallas for a long time. Nabbing the moneyman of the city's most notorious gangster while infiltrating an exclusive wine tasting?

Priceless.

Eight

AFTER A TEN-MINUTE pit stop at home to change her clothes and throw on some makeup, Jordan hurried out the door and walked the three blocks to DeVine Cellars. The streets were relatively quiet since most stores and businesses hadn't opened yet. Her cell phone buzzed loudly in her purse. She saw that it was Christian and answered.

"You couldn't at least send me a metrosexual to work with?" he asked.

She grinned at that. "How did the shopping go with Nick?"

"We survived. That's about all I can say. You should've seen his expression when he saw the colors of the ties I'd pulled to go with the suit. He told me that where he comes from, men don't *do* boysenberry. I shudder to think such a place exists."

"Boysenberry? You *are* lucky you survived. Thanks, Christian. I appreciate your help." Jordan made a mental note to send him a bottle of wine from the store.

"Feel free to send me all the suit-buying customers you want. And I think you'll be pleased with the results." His tone turned sly. "Happy Valentine's Day, Jordan. I have a feeling it's going to be a good one for you."

Right, she thought as she hung up the phone. Because Nick was her *date*. And of course any woman spending Valentine's Day with a date who looked like Nick was guaranteed a night of endless great sex.

Hot, scruffy-jawed, throw-me-down-on-the-table, mind-blowing sex.

Probably with dirty words.

Perhaps not a horrible way to spend Valentine's Day, she conceded. But it wasn't in the cards for her.

Jordan let herself into the store and hung her coat in the back room. She changed out of her snow boots and turned on the lights and music. She loved opening the store—that time of day more than any other was when it truly felt like hers.

Mornings were typically slow until about eleven, so she had a good hour to put out the shelf talkers and signs for the closeout sale, do inventory, and clean up. She doubted, however, that much cleaning would be necessary. Martin had closed the night before, and he tended to be as much a neat freak as he was a wine snob. Not an unwelcome quality in an assistant manager.

She checked the sales receipts from the night before and saw that they'd had a good night. In addition to regular sales, they'd added four new customers to their wine club.

The wine club was something she'd started two years ago. As often as customers asked for her and Martin's recommendations, it had seemed to be a worthwhile endeavor. Each month, she and Martin selected two wines with a combined value ranging from one hundred to one hundred and fifty dollars. She'd hesitated at first at the price, and had asked Martin whether they should consider offering more budget-friendly wines. She'd worried that at those prices, people wouldn't be willing to sign up for memberships.

"If I pick it, they will come," Martin had whispered dramatically.

She'd given him six months to prove he was right.

He had been.

With nearly eight hundred members, the wine club was a huge success. They sometimes took a gamble with the wines they chose—excellent in quality, but often from boutique, lesser-known wine makers. And Martin, a traditionalist, always insisted on choosing one Old World wine, despite the fact that research indicated consumers preferred New World wines because of their user-friendly labels. Yet no one in the wine club had complained thus far.

"They love you. Seriously, when are you going to open your own store and run me out of business?" she'd teased Martin one day.

"It's not me. It's you," he replied matter-of-factly.

"Hardly—you deserve the credit. If it had been up to me, this wine club would've been ninety percent California cabs. Ten-dollar New Zealand sauv blancs in the summer."

"And you still would've had eight hundred members," Martin said. "Let's be honest, Jordan. Rich people like what other rich people like. They buy the wines I pick because *you* tell them to."

She had immediately opened her mouth to object—the conversation was sounding far too *The Emperor's New Clothes* for her tastes—but part of her suspected that Martin wasn't entirely off the mark. Market share–wise, she knew a vastly greater proportion of wealthy Chicago wine buyers frequented her store. She may have been financially independent, but her father's money was there nevertheless, and with that came a certain level of fascination from others.

"You're sort of like the Paris Hilton of wine," Martin had offered.

She'd nearly keeled over in horror.

"If you promise to never, *ever* make that analogy again, I'll let you pick two Old World wines for next month," Jordan had said.

Martin had rubbed his hands together eagerly. "Can I make one of them a Brunello di Montalcino?"

"You always say the quality of the Brunellos is erratic."

"And for a lesser man, that might pose a problem," Martin had said. "I'm telling you, Jordan, with your name and my impeccable taste, I think we can really go places with this store."

So far, he hadn't been wrong.

Nine

NICK PARKED HIS car a half block from Jordan's house and walked the short distance in the cold. He opened a tall wrought-iron gate and stepped onto a front patio and garden area.

He had assumed her home would be nice—very nice—and hadn't been incorrect. The brick house stood two and a half stories above the ground, with elegant Juliet balconies curved around the arched glass windows of the main level. A large brick and limestone balcony, part of what he guessed was the master suite, looked over the front patio from the second floor.

As he climbed the stairs to the front door, he caught himself wondering if Jordan's father had bought the house, or if she made enough money to afford it on her own. Not that it was any of his business, he was just . . . curious.

He rang the doorbell and could hear its melodic chime through the door. When a minute or two passed without an answer, he reached up to ring the bell again.

The door flew open.

"Sorry," Jordan said breathlessly. "Zipper problems."

Nick tried not to show any reaction as he just . . . stared. From where he stood, he saw no problems whatsoever.

The deep purple fabric of her dress hugged all the curves of her slender frame. She wore her hair up, and a few errant blond chunks swept across her smoky-lined, ocean-colored eyes—eyes that sparkled even more radiantly than the diamonds in her ears.

She braced one arm against the door frame. "That's the longest you've gone without talking since we met, Brooklyn. I take it you like the dress."

Busted.

Nick regrouped. "Don't get too cocky. I was just trying to figure out where we're going to stash a microphone in that thing."

Jordan stepped aside as he entered her house and shut the door behind him.

Nick's eyes nearly fell out of their sockets.

My God, the back of her dress . . . it dipped invitingly low, practically begging him to stare at her ass.

"What's this about me wearing a microphone?" she asked.

He blinked cluelessly. "Excuse me?"

"You said I'm wearing a microphone?" she prompted him.

Right. The microphone. Undercover op. "It's just a precautionary measure. I want to be able to hear you and Eckhart talking while I'm downstairs in his office." Nick reached inside the pocket of his suit jacket and pulled out a wireless, quarter-inch-sized microphone. "Happy Valentine's Day."

Jordan examined it curiously. "I can't believe how small it is."

"It picks up voices from fifty feet away, even through clothing. All you need to do is tuck it inside your bra." His eyes went to the V of her neckline. "Assuming you're wearing a bra with that dress."

"Nope. Just Band-Aids over my nipples."

Six years working undercover for the FBI, another five years on NYPD vice, but damn if Nick had a clue how to handle that predicament.

Jordan grinned. "I'm kidding." She twirled her finger. "Turn around."

He complied. *Don't think about her nipples. Don't think about her nipples.*

He was thinking about her nipples.

"Are you done yet?" he asked brusquely. Perhaps things would go faster if he lent her some assistance . . .

"I think I've got it," Jordan said from behind him.

Nick turned around and watched as she adjusted her neckline, making sure her bra was hidden once again.

She straightened up and faced him. "What do you think? Good?"

His eyes roved over her. *Good* was putting it mildly. But instead of answering, he gestured to the door. He'd seen the car waiting for them out front, and it was time to go. "Ready for this?"

Jordan took a deep breath. "No. But I'll do it anyway."

BECAUSE OF ALL the wine they'd be offered at Xander's party, Jordan had rented a Town Car for the evening. It was what she did every year, and Nick had emphasized that it was important for her to stick to her routine as much as possible.

Sitting in the backseat next to him, she tried to ignore the butterflies in her stomach. She officially was about to take part in an undercover sting operation, and an excess of nerves could only hinder her objectives tonight. Previously, the closest to danger she had ever come had been the time a drunk, homeless man wandered into her store and knocked over a display of syrah before passing out on the floor. Really, though, the only danger had been that she would step on a piece of glass or stain her shoes as she cleaned up the mess, as the man had been so inebriated he hadn't woken up after his dramatic entrance. And Martin had been there to protect her, standing over the man with a loaded bottle of Côtes du Rhône until the police had arrived.

Jordan looked at Nick, who she suspected was carrying

something far more powerful than a Côtes du Rhône. Although where he could fit a gun in that perfectly tailored suit was anyone's guess.

He'd shaved for the evening, and centered in his chin was a small cleft she hadn't noticed before. The back of his dark brown hair brushed against the collar of his coat—he'd gotten a haircut as well.

When he had arrived at her house, there'd been a moment when she'd been struck by how refined and handsome he looked in his dress coat and suit. He would blend in at Xander's party without any problem. Interestingly, however, she thought she liked him better with the scruff and jeans. Thank God he annoyed her a good ninety-five percent of the time they were together, because she had absolutely no intention of being *attracted* to Nick McCall. Stanton. Whoever the heck he was that night.

He caught her looking at him just as the car pulled up in front of Bordeaux. The driver got out and walked around the car to Jordan's door. Nick studied her carefully, as if gauging her mood.

"So this is it." She tried to sound nonchalant, but there was a slight shake to her voice. The driver opened the door and she shivered when the cold, February air rushed into the car.

Nick leaned forward to address the driver. "We'll need just a moment." He pulled the door shut to give them some privacy.

He spoke quietly. "Jordan, look at me."

She did, and he held her gaze.

"You'll be fine. Trust me."

She nodded, finding comfort in his steady tone. "Okay."

Then he put his hand on her chin and moved closer—*wait, was he going to* kiss *her?*—and she felt the warmth of his breath against her neck as he whispered in her ear.

"But if anything goes wrong tonight, find the red-headed bartender. She's a friend."

Jordan's eyes flew open. *Wrong?*

She didn't have time to ask what could possibly go

wrong, because Nick pushed open the door and the driver automatically reached for her hand. So she put on her game face and stepped out of the car. Nick followed, and together they walked to the restaurant's front door and stepped inside.

Jordan had been to Bordeaux several times before, but the elegant décor continued to impress her. Soaring eighteen-foot ceilings, crystal chandeliers emitting a warm glow, and creamy silk wall panels all gave the place a light, airy feel. To their right, across the dining room, was a cream-lacquered arch that led to the VIP wine bar. On the opposite end of the dining room was an outdoor terrace that overlooked the river and another bar, which Xander maintained at comfortable temperatures via heat lamps in the winter months. According to the plan, she would invite Xander to join her for a drink on the terrace to discuss a wine she'd located for him, and that was when Nick would make his move.

She and Nick checked their coats with the hostess and made their way into the restaurant. Jordan immediately spotted several guests she knew, but hesitated before heading over. *Just one more minute.* That's all she wanted before she introduced her "date" to the world, and this game of theirs became very real.

Nick seemed to read her mind. "Why don't we get a drink?" He caught the eye of a waiter passing by.

"Cristal?" the waiter asked, offering them each a flute. Jordan took note of the bottle as he poured—a 2002 Louis Roederer Cristal rosé. As always, Xander had spared no expense.

Focus on the wine, she told herself. Nick had the challenging part of this assignment, not her. Over the course of the next few hours, she didn't need to do much except smile her way through several glasses of the beverage she'd spent the last several years becoming a semi-expert on.

Nick eyed his drink skeptically after the waiter left. "Conveniently, when you invited me tonight, you failed to mention there would be pink drinks."

She felt some of the tension leave her. She hadn't known what to expect with the whole pretending-to-be-dating routine, but so far it seemed to be business as usual between them. "It's a rosé."

This appeared to register with him. "Oh, like white zinfandel. My grandmother used to drink that."

Thank God Jordan hadn't taken a sip of her champagne, or she would've just choked on it. "First rule of the evening: never, ever mention white zinfandel around this crowd. Or things could get ugly very quickly." She lifted the champagne flute to her nose and instinct took over. She closed her eyes and inhaled, smelling baked apples, almonds, and dried fruit. She took a small sip, letting the champagne dissipate in her mouth before swallowing. The flavors flirted in her mouth, light and coy.

She opened her eyes and noticed that Nick was watching her closely.

"Good?" he asked.

That was an understatement. "Try it."

"I don't do pink drinks." He cocked his head. "Think you're ready to take on the wine bar yet?"

Jordan got the message—they needed to keep moving. "Sure. Let's see what Xander has in store for us tonight."

Together, they made their way to the private room. The wine tasting had begun, and the bar was loud as guests discussed their drinks. Nearly immediately, Jordan noticed the redhead bartender, presumably the "friend" Nick had alluded to earlier. She was attractive, and not at all what Jordan expected an FBI agent to look like. For a moment, she caught herself wondering just how good a "friend" the woman was to Nick. Then she remembered that was none of her business.

"Just starting?" the redhead asked as they approached the bar. She gave away no sign that she recognized them.

Jordan noticed that the bartender's curly hair was styled in a way that covered her ears. To hide an earpiece perhaps? Curious, she made a note to ask Nick about that later. "We'll take whatever's first."

"So how does this work?" Nick asked after the bartender set a glass in front of each of them. "This is my first tasting."

"Hmm, a wine-tasting virgin," Jordan said. "There's so much I could teach you."

"Just keep it simple, Rhodes. The basics."

"Okay, here's my prediction for tonight: unless Xander plans to break some rules, we'll start off with a couple light-bodied whites, move on to a chardonnay, then switch glasses and start with the reds. That's where the fun really happens."

Nick grabbed one of the tasting menus from the bar. "All right. Let's see how good you are. Call the first one."

"A sauvignon blanc," Jordan guessed. "Likely one from the Loire Valley. Then a Riesling, a pinot gris, and a California chardonnay."

He looked impressed. "Not bad."

She shrugged. "I know my way around a tasting."

"Except you screwed up the chardonnay."

Surprised, Jordan took a look at the menu. In the past, Xander had always picked a California chardonnay, but this year's selection was from Burgundy, France.

"Interesting, don't you think?" said a man to her left.

Jordan turned and saw Rafe Velasquez, co-owner of a lucrative hedge fund based out of Chicago. Like her, he was a regular of the party. She greeted him with a smile. "Hello, Rafe." She looked around the room. "Where's Emily?"

"She decided to stay home—most reluctantly. Our youngest has been fighting the flu all week, and she didn't feel comfortable leaving him with the nanny. I think something's going around. Everyone I talk to these days is sick."

Jordan thought back to Huxley, sprawled across the couch with his blond Mohawk. Something was going around all right, and it wasn't pretty. Turning to Nick, she made the introductions. "Rafe Velasquez, Nick Stanton." As the two men shook hands, she breathed a sigh of relief. She'd made it through the first intro without screwing things up.

"So you must be proud of yourself," Rafe said to her.

She cocked her head in confusion. "Meaning . . . ?"

Rafe pointed to the wine menu. "The reds?"

"I haven't gotten that far yet—I'm still stuck on the fact that Xander didn't go with a California chardonnay."

"Forget the chardonnay—check out the cabs."

Jordan's eyes skimmed over the menu. She pulled back in surprise when she read the names of the two cabernets Xander had chosen for the evening.

"What do you make of that?" Rafe asked slyly.

She didn't answer immediately. She had a feeling she knew what Rafe was suggesting, but it couldn't mean . . . well, *that*.

"Looks like somebody has a secret admirer," he said.

Nick frowned, suddenly very interested in their conversation. "I think I'm missing something here."

Rafe explained. "At last year's party, Xander, Jordan, and I got into a discussion about his red selections. See, Xander always picks Screaming Eagle as his cabernet—which is a fantastic wine, don't get me wrong. But Jordan jokingly said that if he ever wanted to shake things up, she'd be happy to give him some suggestions. So Xander asked what *her* favorite cabernets are."

Nick turned to Jordan. "What did you tell him?"

"I . . . may have mentioned the Vineyard 29 estate cab," she said.

Nick checked out the tasting menu. "That's on this list."

Yes, it was.

"And she also said that she was a huge fan of the Quintessa meritage. Which I completely agree with, by the way," Rafe said.

Nick checked again. "That's also on this list."

Yes, it was.

Nick's eyes narrowed. "So to be clear: two of the five red wines on this highly exclusive list are ones that *you* said are your favorites?"

Well, when he put it that way . . . Now on the defensive, Jordan felt the need to point something out. "I do own a wine store, you know. This is likely a professional compliment, not a personal one."

"Are you sure about that?" Nick's green eyes probed hers intently.

Before answering, Jordan thought through her recent interactions with Xander. Nothing jumped out at her as abnormal, no conversations she could immediately recall that signaled any particular interest in her. Sure, Xander came by the store often, but so did a lot of her regular customers. And he flirted with her from time to time, but Xander flirted with everyone. He was a notorious womanizer and constantly dated women he met in his clubs—usually leggy brunettes under the age of twenty-five. Being blond, five-foot-five if she stood really straight, and thirty-three years old, Jordan met none of his criteria.

But now that she was specifically thinking about it . . . there had been that one slightly odd conversation—five months ago, right before Kyle had been arrested, and just after she'd gotten back from a trip to the Napa Valley. Xander had dropped by the store, and she'd filled him in on some of the new wines she'd discovered.

"Must be a tough life, going to the Napa Valley several times a year on business," Xander had teased her as he perused the store's shelves.

Jordan had chuckled as she handed him a glass of a new pinot noir she'd just opened, not disagreeing with him. "Oh, and you have it so bad. You go wherever you want, whenever you want." She should know, he bragged about his exotic trips whenever he visited the store.

Xander took the glass of pinot from her. "Yeah, but Napa's different. That's not the kind of place you want to go alone. You should be with someone who can appreciate the experience." He took a sip of the wine. "It's good."

"A waiter recommended it to me. I liked it so much I had two cases shipped back here."

Xander followed her over to the bar. "Where did you stay while you were out there?"

"Calistoga Ranch. Have you been?"

"No. But I've heard good things."

"It's amazing," Jordan said. "I stayed in a private lodge overlooking a canyon. Every morning I had breakfast on the deck as the sun came over the hills, and at night I sat under the stars drinking wine."

"Now tell me that wouldn't have been better with someone else there." Xander folded his arms across his chest, as if daring her to contradict him on this. He wore a crisp black designer shirt with the top two buttons undone, charcoal gray pants, and a brand new Jaeger LeCoultre watch. He was a good-looking man, but he had a certain air about him that occasionally rubbed Jordan the wrong way. He seemed very eager to show off his money, particularly around her.

Because he was such a good customer, she smiled, humoring him. "Maybe next time. There'll be plenty more trips to Napa for me. I already have one planned for the beginning of March."

"Why wait until then?" Xander pulled out his cell phone. "I can have us booked first-class in two minutes."

She laughed. As if she could drop everything right then and hop on a plane. "I wish it were that easy." She grabbed a couple bottles of the pinot and carried them to a bin near the front of the store.

"Jordan."

The serious tone in Xander's voice stopped her. She looked over her shoulder and saw that he had the oddest expression on his face.

"Is something wrong?" she asked.

Just then, Martin strolled into the room, having finished checking inventory in the cellar. "I think we should order another case of the Zulu. People have been going crazy for South African wines—oh, Mr. Eckhart, I didn't realize you'd stopped in." He paused and looked between them. "Am I interrupting something?"

Jordan thought she saw a flash of irritation in Xander's eyes. But then it was gone, and she assumed she'd imagined it. Xander liked talking to Martin; the two of them had very similar tastes in wine. She saw no reason why he would be bothered by her store manager's presence.

Xander waved off the question. "No interruption. Just enjoying this new pinot." He gestured to his glass. "What's the price point?"

"Thirty dollars a bottle." Jordan continued to watch for any sign of the tension she'd seen on his face a moment ago. But there was nothing—he appeared as relaxed as always.

"I might have to start carrying it in my restaurants," he said.

The three of them discussed the wine's Robert Parker rating, and Martin's belief that it had been unfairly undervalued because of Parker's preference for big, bold reds. Shortly after that, Xander had left and Jordan didn't give a second thought to that one odd moment.

But now, with the advantage of hindsight, she perhaps had a different take on the conversation.

Now, she couldn't help but wonder if Xander had been interested in more than a new pinot that day. She'd assumed he'd been joking about the trip to Napa, but maybe not. Shortly after that conversation, Kyle had been arrested, and her life had fallen into complete chaos. She'd dropped out of the social scene and had taken a break from dating.

Perhaps Xander had been lying in wait since then. Holding off for a more appropriate time to reveal his feelings. Like tonight, with his "Homage to Jordan" wine list.

She locked eyes with Nick.

"We . . . may have a problem."

Ten

A PROBLEM.

Not the words Nick wanted to hear right then. No agent in the middle of an undercover assignment wanted to hear those words.

He smiled politely at Rafe. "Could you excuse us for a moment? I need to have a word with my date."

Without further ado, he took Jordan by the hand and pulled her off to the side of the room. He braced one hand on the wall next to her and peered down into her eyes. "Honey, before we came to this party, you might've mentioned that the host had the hots for you."

She stared back up at him, not looking particularly intimidated. In eleven years of law enforcement, Nick had made many a suspect sweat under the duress of what he knew was an impressive don't-fuck-with-me face, yet she didn't so much as bat an eye. Granted, none of those suspects had been wearing a knockout dress with a slit nearly down to the ass, so perhaps the don't-fuck-with-me face wasn't in top form right then.

"I didn't know myself, *darling*," she said. "And we still don't know that for sure. But let's say for argument's sake that Xander has more than a professional interest in me. Will that be a problem for you?"

Her words were careful and well chosen. To anyone who might be listening, it would seem as though she was merely placating a jealous lover, not an FBI agent who was a little cranky to be first learning of this development in the midst of an undercover op.

"I can handle it." In some senses, Nick supposed, Eckhart's attraction to Jordan could be a good thing. He doubted she would have much trouble convincing him to step away with her for a drink. Still, he was eager to keep things moving. They needed to mingle. Drink some wine. Plant a few wireless recording devices. The usual social obligations.

"We should rejoin the others," he said.

"Wait." Jordan put her hand on his arm, stopping him before he turned away. Her eyes were clouded with concern. "I'm sorry if I put you in an awkward position tonight. I honestly didn't know until I saw the wine list."

She looked so genuinely troubled right then, Nick couldn't help what he did next. He reached out and touched her chin. "Don't worry, Rhodes. I've got this." He grinned. "I think there's a glass of wine with your name on it at the bar."

"For five thousand dollars a head, there better be a lot more than one."

"Now I see why no one drives to this party." He took Jordan by the hand, turned around, and—

—Nearly ran into Xander Eckhart, host of the party and Nick's target for the evening.

"I always thought it's because parking is a bitch around here," Xander said in response to Nick's comment. Despite his light tone, his eyes were cold as he stuck out his hand. "Xander Eckhart."

Nick shook his hand, squeezing a little harder than was necessary. "Nick Stanton."

"I see you're here with Jordan."

"I am."

Jordan moved to his side. "Xander, I wondered when we'd see you. You've outdone yourself tonight, as always."

Xander broke the stare down with Nick long enough to turn his attention to Jordan. He took in her appearance. "As have you, Jordan. I'm flattered you made it. I know you've been keeping a low profile because of everything that happened with your brother. In fact, I was surprised when my secretary told me that you called this week to add a guest to your RSVP. I didn't realize you were seeing anyone."

Nick linked his fingers through Jordan's. "The late RSVP was my fault. I had originally made plans to be out of town this weekend. But when I realized it was Valentine's Day, I rescheduled my trip to be with Jordan. Couldn't miss out on the most romantic night of the year, could I?"

"Yes, that would've been a real shame," Xander said dryly.

"Nick and I were just discussing the wines on the tasting menu," Jordan interjected. "It looks to be a fantastic night."

"I suppose you could say that I'd been hoping to make a memorable impression this Valentine's Day. Certain recent developments, however, make me wonder if I've overshot a little." Xander gestured between them. "So I'd love to hear how you two met."

"At Jordan's store," Nick said.

"Oh, are you a wine man, Nick?"

"Can't say I am. I know white and red."

Jordan winked at him. "And now pink."

Nick smiled. True. "And now pink."

Xander looked between them. Whatever he saw, he didn't seem to like it.

"Will I sound overeager if I say I can't wait to see what you have in the cellar?" Jordan asked Eckhart. "You're always full of surprises, Xander."

Nick had to admit he was impressed. Not too many civilians could pull off acting this naturally in an undercover job, particularly in front of someone they knew was laundering money for a drug cartel.

Her suggestion worked like a charm.

"Who am I to make such a beautiful woman wait?" Xander gestured to an open door on the opposite end of the wine bar. "I'll take you down there myself. Follow me."

* * *

ECKHART LED THEM through the door and down a free-standing glass staircase. "Since this is your first time, Nick, I'll give you the fifty-cent tour."

Actually, the FBI had already paid five thousand dollars for that privilege. "I appreciate that, Xander."

"Given the value of my collection, I normally keep that door upstairs locked," Xander told him. "But I trust my guests tonight. Most of them, anyway. And with the others, I trust the six-foot-five, two-hundred-and-fifty-pound security guard I've got stationed downstairs."

As they descended into the lower level, Nick quickly understood the reasons for Eckhart's security system. He'd studied the blueprints of the building, and had been aware that the wine cellar took up a large portion of the space. But neither the blueprints nor Jordan's descriptions had prepared him for the sheer magnitude of the wine cellar he faced now. Or rather, the wine *cellars*.

They stood before three rectangular glass chambers, each approximately twenty-five feet long and ten feet wide. Through the floor-to-ceiling glass panels, Nick saw rows upon rows of what he knew, through Huxley's report, to be over six thousand bottles of wine stacked horizontally on slotted ebony wood shelves. Glass doors, several inches thick and flanked by elaborate security panels, guarded each of the three chambers of the cellar.

"Reds; whites; champagne and dessert wines," Xander said, pointing out the three chambers of the cellar. "Different storage temperatures for each, obviously."

Obviously.

"Over three million dollars in wine," Xander continued, making no attempt to disguise his pride. "Granted, a lot of that is for the restaurant. My own personal collection is worth roughly a million."

Nick resisted the urge to ask how much of that collection had been bought with Roberto Martino's drug money. "It's certainly a lot of wine."

A crowd of about ten people mingled near a door to their right, which Nick knew from the blueprints led to a private tasting room. A robust man in his early forties came over and greeted Jordan enthusiastically.

"Jordan—perfect timing. I need you to settle something. True or false: two years ago at this party, you and I were talking right here when a drunk guy, somebody's date, came out of the bathroom with his fly open and his tweed blazer tucked into his pants like a shirt. And he spoke to us for five minutes without ever noticing."

"Very true. He slurred something about how he'd never been drunk in his life because he had such a high tolerance for alcohol."

The man proudly turned back to the group at the door. "See? I told you. Can I steal you away for a few minutes?" he asked Jordan. "I need you to convince these guys that I'm not making this up."

With a glance in Nick's direction, she smiled politely. "Sure."

Nick watched her walk away, as did Xander. Then the two men turned and faced each other.

Xander didn't waste any time before launching the first salvo. "So. You didn't mention what you do for a living, Nick."

"Real estate."

"Are you a builder?"

"An investor. I rent out residential properties, mostly to college students and recent graduates."

"Real estate has really bottomed out these past few years, hasn't it?"

"Luckily not rental property, Xander. With everyone staying in school these days because they can't find a job, I'm turning people away."

Xander laughed haughtily. "Who would've thought the low-income housing market could be so lucrative?"

"Me."

A silence followed.

"Mind if I give you a piece of advice, Nick?"

About a hundred not-so-polite responses came to Nick's

mind, including one he favored about where, exactly, Eckhart could stick his advice, but for the sake of the undercover operation, he held his tongue. Causing a scene or being tossed out by a six-foot-five, two-hundred-and-fifty-pound security guard was not in the FBI's best interests. So he kept his sarcasm in check. Mostly. "I'm all ears."

Xander sounded smug. "Jordan may find you diverting for now, but how long do you think that's going to last? I see men like you all the time in my clubs and restaurants. You can put on the suit and look the part, but you and I both know that she's way out of your league. It's just a matter of time before she realizes it, too."

Nick pretended to think about this. "Interesting advice. But from what I can tell, Jordan's been doing a pretty good job by herself of deciding who is and isn't in her league." He grabbed Eckhart's shoulder and squeezed. "Have a drink, Xander—you sound like you need it."

He walked away, leaving Eckhart standing alone in the corner.

"Everything okay?" Jordan asked as he approached.

"Just getting acquainted with our gracious host," he said. "Now, what does a person have to do to get a drink around here?"

She cocked her head. "Follow me."

Jordan led Nick into a private tasting room adjacent to Xander's cellar that had a cozier feel than the rest of the lower level. Although guests were free to come and go all night, several had planted themselves in the leather armchairs that faced the lit fireplace, knowing that this was where the truly exceptional stuff was served. A man in his forties and wearing a suit—the sommelier Xander had hired for the evening—stood behind the bar pouring small amounts of wine into crystal glasses. A bulky security guard dressed in all black stood near the back of the room, discreetly out of sight yet there nevertheless.

Jordan brought Nick over to the bar and caught the eye of the sommelier, the same one Xander had hired for the party the past couple of years.

He grinned as he came over. "Ms. Rhodes! I was hoping

you'd be here tonight. I've been saving something special for you. A 1990 Chateau Sevonne."

A '90 Sevonne. Sweet Jesus, her heart began to race.

"Did you just gasp?" Nick asked as the sommelier poured their glasses.

Jordan tried to play it cool. "I don't think so."

"I'm pretty sure I heard it."

"Okay, maybe there was a *tiny* gasp," she conceded. "Because the 1990 Chateau Sevonne is supposed to be extraordinary. Thrilling. Breathtaking."

"Sounds orgasmic," Nick said with a wicked gleam in his eyes.

The sommelier made a hasty retreat.

Jordan gestured in his direction. "Very nice—you chased him away before he could tell us about the wine."

"Does it matter?" Nick asked skeptically. "At the end of the day, doesn't it all pretty much taste the same?"

She shook her head. "Truly, Nick. I don't even know where to begin with you."

He leaned confidently against the bar, baiting her with his grin. "Giving up already?"

She looked him up and down, debating. Then she picked up the two glasses the sommelier had poured and handed one over. "Not yet." She stopped Nick, her hand on his, when he tipped his glass to take a sip. "Uh-uh, virgin. With wine like this, a little foreplay is required."

He eyed her over his glass. "Foreplay?"

"Absolutely." Time for Wine Tasting 101. "So here's how this works. When tasting a wine, as opposed to casual drinking, there are four basic steps you need to remember: sight, smell, taste, then spit or swallow."

Nick paused at that last part and cocked his head. "And your personal preference on the latter would be . . .?"

"Only lightweights spit."

His right eye twitched.

Jordan raised her glass, fully into teacher mode now. "So the first step is sight."

Nick gave his glass a quick once-over. "Looks like wine to me. Check."

She shook her head. "No, tilt the glass and hold it over the white tablecloth." She demonstrated, holding her glass at a forty-five-degree angle. "You want to look at both the center of the wine, to determine its intensity, and the edge of the wine, to check its hue."

"And why am I doing this?"

"The wine's color can tell you a lot about whether it's a youthful wine or if it's showing signs of age." She continued her demonstration. "Then swirl the glass and watch how quickly the wine filters down after it stops moving. The slower the wine's legs flow down the glass, the higher the alcohol content in the wine."

"You know, by law they have to print the alcohol content right on the label. That could be a good clue, too."

"Perhaps we should save all questions and comments until the end of the tasting ritual."

He shrugged. "Fine by me. I'm as eager as the next guy to get to spit or swallow."

She *so* was going to regret giving him that as ammunition. "Next up is smelling the wine."

"This sure is a lot of foreplay." Nick peeked over the bar. "Don't they have any wines back there that are into quickies?"

Jordan struggled with that one, the edges of her mouth twitching. *Don't laugh. It'll only encourage him.* She marched on. "You want to swirl the glass to release the aromas of the wine, then bring it up to your nose and smell." She watched his technique, and corrected, "Don't hold the glass to your nose for too long—your olfactory senses will fatigue and you won't be able to pick up the different aromas."

Another skeptical look. "Olfactory fatigue?"

"Just try it again," Jordan said. "And this time, tell me what you smell."

Nick did as she asked. "I smell wine."

Jordan smiled reassuringly. "I used to say the same thing when I first started out. It takes a while to develop a nose for wine, to be able to distinguish the different aromas."

"Okay, Ms. Expert, what do you smell?"

"Sorry. No hints until you taste it for yourself," she said.

"Now, when you take a sip of the wine, suck in some air—that will open its flavors. Then swish it around your mouth before swallowing. Normally, I'd say you could spit it out if you want, but this wine costs fifteen hundred dollars a bottle. If you spit it out, about twenty people here will drop dead of a heart attack."

She lifted her glass, ready to taste the wine, when she saw the look of shock on Nick's face. "What?"

"Fifteen hundred dollars a bottle?" he repeated.

"Yep." She held up her glass. "Cheers." She took a sip of the wine and went through the whole routine: sucking, swishing, and swallowing. She felt the heady rush, the liquid warmth that flowed through her body, and the feeling of bliss that built and peaked and then slowly ebbed. And finally, the light-headed, flushed feeling. The afterglow.

Orgasmic, indeed.

She opened her eyes and saw Nick staring at her.

"I feel like I need a cigarette and a shower after watching that." His eyes seemed warmer than usual. "Tell me."

"Tell you what?"

"Whatever it is you would normally say after drinking that wine."

"I'd talk about how it felt in my mouth and what it tastes like," she said.

His gaze fell to her lips. "And?"

"It felt large and smooth. A real mouthful."

"Are you kidding me with this?"

Jordan laughed at his expression. "No, I'm serious—that's how I would describe the wine. I can't help it if one might read certain connotations into it. Wine is a very sensual thing."

Rafe Velasquez approached them. "What do you think of the Sevonne? It's a real mouthful, isn't it? Big and smooth."

"So everyone keeps telling me," Nick grumbled.

"He's new to wine," she explained.

Rafe gestured to Jordan. "Ah, well. You're certainly in the right hands tonight."

At that moment, she noticed Xander making his way toward the door, about to leave. Time for her to make her move.

"If you two would excuse me, I see Xander heading upstairs. I need to steal him away to discuss business. Will you be okay on your own?" she asked Nick.

His demeanor was so casual she almost thought he didn't catch that This Was Her Signal.

"I'll be fine," he said. "I'm sure I can find some way to amuse myself while you're gone."

Rafe slapped him on the shoulder. "Don't worry, Jordan. I'll make sure he stays out of trouble."

"Thank you, Rafe, that's very nice of you," she said, thinking she'd have a good laugh over that one later. She turned back to Nick. "I'll see you in a few minutes, then?" The plan was that he would come upstairs and find her on the terrace when he'd finished planting the recording devices.

His eyes held hers, calm and steady as ever.

"Before you know it."

Eleven

JORDAN SAW XANDER climbing up the glass staircase and called after him. "Xander—wait."

He turned around on the steps. "Jordan. Enjoying yourself tonight?"

"At your party? Always." She stopped on the step below him and gestured to her wineglass. "The Sevonne is fantastic, by the way. I like all your selections tonight."

"I paid attention to the ones you recommended last year."

"I'm flattered. And speaking of fabulous wine, there's something else you might be interested in."

"What's that?"

Jordan moved up a step to stand next to him. "A 2000 Château Pétrus."

Xander's eyes brightened with interest. "Tell me more."

"One case, going to auction through Sotheby's."

"Where and when?"

Hong Kong in April, but she didn't tell him that yet. She was about to act coy, which was something she really didn't want to do, but it seemed like the easiest way to make sure Xander stayed out of Nick's way. She took a deep breath and dove in. "Join me for a drink on the terrace, and I'll tell you everything."

She screwed it up.

Her voice came out sounding too high, her words too quick. Still, she kept outwardly calm and waited as Xander considered her offer for what seemed like an eternity.

Finally, he tipped his glass to hers. "What are we waiting for?"

He gestured for her to lead the way. When her back was to Xander, Jordan finally began to breathe again, wondering how anyone survived undercover work. Thirty minutes into her first—and last—assignment and she'd nearly broken out in hives. She needed to be smoother, especially once she and Xander got onto the terrace.

For better or worse, she was on her own now.

NICK WAITED FIVE minutes after Jordan left the room. He listened politely to the guests around him, drawing as little attention to himself as possible as they discussed tannins and nuances and structure and all sorts of other mumbo jumbo that didn't hold his attention half as much as when Jordan talked about wine. When he finished his glass of Chateau Some-Fancy-French-Crap, he asked Rafe where the bathrooms were located.

"Down the hallway, on the right-hand side," Rafe said.

Of course, Nick had already known that. He excused himself and left the room. He walked past the bathrooms and kept going toward the staircase. If anyone spotted him, he was simply a guest who had gotten lost in the cavernous lower level after having a couple of drinks.

He paused on the other side of the staircase, at the edge of the hallway that led to Xander's office. Satisfied that no one was around, he moved on. The first door on his left was a storage room; the next door, on the right, was a massive utility room that housed the building's heating and cooling systems. When he reached the door at the end of the hallway, he grabbed the handle and turned.

Locked.

Obviously, he'd expected this, but it had been worth checking nevertheless. Nick reached underneath his jacket and shirt to the small pouch he had strapped to his hip. He pulled out a lock-pick set. One of the benefits of playing a criminal for six months was that he'd refined certain illicit skills, and he doubted that Eckhart's simple deadbolt lock would give him much trouble. Being careful not to leave any sign of tampering behind, he twisted a flat, skinny torque tool into the lock while applying pressure. Then he used a pick to push up the lock pins one at a time. When the last pin was in place, he turned the torque tool like a key.

Voilà.

Nick stepped inside the office. He shut the door behind him and locked it. Then he reached into the inside pocket of his jacket and put a tiny receiver into his right ear. "Jack. I'm in."

Pallas's voice came through without any interference. "Sounds like you and Eckhart are getting along swimmingly."

At least he knew that the microphone strapped to his chest, which had been active since he and Jordan had arrived at the party, was working. "Eckhart is lucky I'm being such a gentleman tonight. Otherwise, I'd be tempted to throw my coat over his head, toss him in the back of the van, and show him what happens to people who get mouthy with FBI agents."

"And people say I have a dark side," Jack said. "At least you're learning a thing or two about wine. Good to hear you're making such an effort to improve yourself."

"Does the U.S. attorney know how much you like spending your Saturday nights eavesdropping on private conversations?" Nick asked.

"The U.S. attorney knows exactly how I like spending my Saturday nights."

Nick grinned at that. Then he surveyed the room, getting down to business. Eckhart's office was just as Jordan had described it: an oversized mahogany desk, two walls of built-in bookshelves, a file cabinet in the southwest corner of the room (which he checked—locked), and two leather armchairs centered by a coffee table. Five recording devices should cover the space easily.

His eyes moved to two electric sockets, low on the walls, that were immediately visible, and the glass light fixture on the ceiling in the center of the room. All great places to start. Another bug underneath the coffee table, and a fifth one attached to the bottom of Xander's desk, and they should be good to go.

Nick pulled a small screwdriver out of his lock-pick set. "Are you guys ready?"

"Ready," Jack said in his ear. "As soon as you get the first bug in place, we'll do a sound check."

Two nights ago after Bordeaux had closed, Reed and Jansen, the tech guys in the van with Jack, had attached a small receiver with an antenna to one of the air-conditioning units outside the building. The receiver would transmit the signal from the recording devices inside Eckhart's office over a several-block radius, which allowed them to park the van with the monitoring equipment farther away from the restaurant to reduce visibility.

Nick took the first recording device out of his suit pocket, ready to rock and roll. "Is Agent Simms hooked in?"

"I'm here," whispered Agent Simms, the "bartender" working in the VIP room. "I've got a visual on Eckhart and Rhodes. They just came up the stairs."

"Why am I not linked in to Jordan's mic, Jack?" Nick asked impatiently. He wanted to be sure he could hear her conversation with Xander. Both for the security of the assignment and just . . . because.

"We're working on it," Jack said. "We're dealing with eight different frequencies between the microphones on you three and the bugs. All right, Reed says you should be able to hear Jordan and Eckhart now."

"SO HOW DID you find out about the auction?" Xander asked as they cut through the VIP room. "I haven't heard anything about a case of 2000 Pétrus coming up for sale."

"I have my ways," Jordan said with a hint of mystery.

Actually, it wasn't so mysterious; a friend of hers from Northwestern worked in the wine department of Sotheby's and often gave her advance notice of big-ticket wines before they were entered into their catalog.

She and Xander stopped at the bar for their drinks.

"How can I help you, Mr. Eckhart?" asked the redhead bartender. Her eyes momentarily held on Jordan.

Xander gestured for Jordan to go first. "What'll it be?"

"Tough choice. You know I have a fondness for both the Vineyard 29 and the Quintessa."

"Close your eyes. I'll surprise you," he said.

Jordan wondered how she would handle this situation were she *not* involved in a covert sting operation with the FBI. Here she was at the party with another man, yet Xander was obviously flirting with her. Ultimately, she realized, she didn't have the luxury of handling the situation as she might have normally. Keeping Xander preoccupied was her focus right then. So she obligingly closed her eyes.

She heard Xander whisper something to the bartender.

"This is going to be a trick, isn't it? You're going to pour me a glass of a ten-dollar wine to see if I can tell the difference," Jordan said.

"Like I would ever serve a ten-dollar wine," Xander scoffed. "Okay. You can open your eyes now."

She did, and saw Xander holding two glasses of red wine.

"Shall we?" he asked, with a nod in the direction of the terrace.

Several guests watched them curiously as they made their way out of the VIP room and through the main lounge. As soon as they stepped onto the terrace, Jordan felt the rush of cooler air as it swept over her bare shoulders.

"Over here," Xander said, leading her to a heat lamp perched near the balcony that overlooked the Chicago River.

All the other guests were inside, and Jordan suddenly wondered if anyone could see them. She took some comfort in the fact that Nick could at least *hear* her.

Xander handed her one of the glasses. "Happy Valentine's Day." He clinked his glass to hers.

"Thank you." Jordan took a sip of the wine, tasting the

dark red fruit, rose petals, chocolate, and chili powder. "It's the Vineyard 29."

"You're good," Xander said.

"It's one of my favorites. I should recognize it by now."

"How many people know enough about wine to appreciate how fantastic this one is?" Xander stood against the railing, stretching one arm in her direction. "I guess a better question is, how many people can even afford this wine to know how good it is? You and I are similar in so many ways, Jordan."

Hmm . . . not so much. First, she generally didn't associate with infamous criminals. Twin brother excepted. Second, she usually tried to avoid being a *snob*, a character trait Xander seemed to have fewer qualms with.

Changing the subject, she looked out at the water and the backdrop of the Chicago skyline at night. "The view is great out here."

Xander moved closer to her, his eyes holding on her face. "Yes, it is." He reached out and brushed a stray lock of hair behind her ear.

Uh-oh.

Jordan debated how to finesse her way through this predicament. She hoped that Nick was moving his ass as fast as humanly possible down there in Xander's office, because the situation up *here* on the terrace was starting to get awfully damn sticky. Normally she'd be giving Xander the polite version of her "Back off, buddy" speech, having no desire to fan the embers of affection of a man who was in cahoots with notorious gangsters. But given the parameters of the evening, she needed to stick it out a bit longer.

Kyle, dear brother of mine, if you so much as get a parking ticket after this, I'll call you Sawyer *for the rest of your life. Oh—and I'll also tell Dad about the time you broke Mom's rocking chair playing WrestleMania with Danny Zeller and blamed it on the dog.*

"You flatter me, Xander," Jordan said, subtly putting a few inches of space between them. "But I've seen pictures of that model you're dating. She's beautiful."

"Come on, Jordan. You know you're gorgeous," he said.

"And if your date hasn't told you that ten times tonight, he's an idiot."

"My date probably wouldn't be too pleased if he knew we were having this conversation right now."

"Yet still, you asked me out here."

"To talk about the Pétrus."

Xander dismissed this. "You could've sent me an e-mail about the Pétrus. You wanted to talk to me alone tonight. And I think I know why." He moved his finger to the side of her face and stroked her cheek.

"Xander," she said in a calm tone. "I'm sorry if you misunderstood my reasons for asking you to come out here. But I'm with Nick tonight." She reached up and removed his hand from her face.

Convicted felon of a brother or not, this money-laundering asshole was not touching her again.

At her rebuff, Xander's expression took on a harder edge.

"Excuse me, Mr. Eckhart?"

Jordan started at the unexpected sound of the woman's voice. She turned and saw the redhead bartender/FBI agent standing a few feet from them, in front of the doorway that led to the restaurant.

"Yes?" Xander asked, obviously annoyed with the interruption.

"We're nearly out of the zinfandel. I was wondering what you would like us to open in its place?"

Xander frowned. "That's impossible. There should be more than enough. Excuse me for a moment, Jordan." He strode over to the bartender and pulled her aside to speak privately.

Jordan turned her back to them. Facing the river, she gripped the railing and exhaled in relief. She had a feeling a certain special agent was watching out for her from his post in Xander's office. She glanced down at her chest, feeling the microphone stashed safely in her bra.

"Nice save, Brooklyn," she whispered under her breath.

Xander and the bartender took a few minutes to wrap up their conversation, and then she left. He walked over to Jordan, shaking his head. "No clue what that was all about. This is my fifth year throwing this party. I *think* I know how much wine to order. I kept telling her there were extra cases of all the wines in the storage room, but she insisted we were out of the zin. Then suddenly, she tells me that she realized she forgot to check the racks behind the door." He rolled his eyes. "Fucking airhead. I'm firing her after tonight."

That airhead is listening right now, Jordan thought. *And she is going to have a* lot *of fun arresting you in the not-too-distant future.*

Xander resumed his place by her side at the railing. The interruption seemed to have calmed his earlier response to her rejection. "So. Where were we?"

"We were talking about the Pétrus," Jordan said.

He shook his head. "Uh-uh. We were talking about us."

"Xander, there is no us."

"There should be. I've wanted to say that for a long time. Seeing you here with Stanton shows me what a fool I've been for not saying it earlier."

"But that's the problem, Xander. I am here with Nick."

"It'll never last between you two."

She pulled back. "Why would you say that?"

He gave her a get-real look. "Don't you think you should be with someone more on your own level?" He put his hand on top of hers and ran his thumb over her fingers. "Jordan, Nick Stanton is a nobody."

"A nobody who's going to throw your ass into the river if you don't get your hands off my date."

What struck Jordan, as she looked over at the sound of the voice, was that the Nick she saw standing to the right of them was not the devil-may-care, always-ready-with-a-quip man she knew.

This man was angry.

Nick's expression was dark and intimidating. His voice, however, remained calm. "You have guests who are looking for you, Eckhart."

Xander shifted. After a moment of studying Nick, he seemed to decide that a quick departure was the safest course of action. "We can finish our conversation later, Jordan," he said coolly. He passed by Nick as he walked to the door. "You are really starting to annoy me, Stanton."

Nick didn't blink. "Good. By the end of the night I hope to finish the job."

Xander's scowl deepened as he turned and left the terrace.

Nick watched him leave before turning his attention to Jordan. He looked her over, his voice softening. "Are you all right?"

"Yes." She exhaled as he walked over. "That got a little too close for comfort for a moment there." She gestured to his face. "What's with the look?"

"It's my don't-fuck-with-me face."

Jordan nodded, impressed. "It's not bad."

"Thanks." Nick smiled slightly, and the tension seemed to lift as the darkness left his face. He raised an eyebrow. "You handled yourself well."

Yes, true, she pretty much rocked this assignment. Except for the part where she'd nearly broken out in hives. And that little bit at the end there, when Nick sort of had to rescue her from Xander.

Jordan chose her words carefully, just in case anyone was listening. "Were you able to find some way to amuse yourself while I was up here?"

Nick tucked his hands into his pockets and shrugged casually. "I found a few things to divert my attention."

She couldn't help but smile. He always seemed so effortlessly confident, as if nothing fazed him. "That's good."

As they stood there, each taking in the other, an uncharacteristic silence fell between them. A cold breeze blew over Jordan's shoulders. With their assignment now complete, she realized that her work with the FBI was nearly over. At the end of the night, she and Nick would go their separate ways. Later, someday, she would have one heck of a story to tell her girlfriends.

Tough to say what she would tell them about Nick. Probably, she'd talk about how he annoyed her a good eighty-seven percent of the time they were together.

"You're shivering. We probably should get back inside," he said.

"We probably should." Jordan's eyes held Nick's for another moment, then she finally turned and began to walk toward the door that led inside the restaurant. She heard Nick clear his throat pointedly and glanced back over her shoulder.

He held out his hand, waiting. "Sweetie?"

Right. In a couple of slow strides, Jordan crossed the distance between them and slid her hand into Nick's. His grip was warm, firm, and strong. She caught the satisfied expression on his face. "You're enjoying yourself quite a bit this evening, aren't you?"

He laughed, tilting his head in acknowledgment.

"More than I'd thought, Rhodes. I'll give you that."

Twelve

FROM A CORNER in the far end of the VIP room, Xander Eckhart stood in a circle of his friends. He watched as Jordan and Stanton walked in and made their way over to the bar. When she smiled at something Stanton said, Xander's eyes narrowed.

Out of the corner of his eye he spotted Will Parsons, one of Bordeaux's two managers. "Excuse me for a moment. I need to check on something." Xander stepped away from the group.

"Seems like the night is going well so far," Will said when he approached.

Sure, Xander thought. Except for the part where he had to watch some jerk-off who owned rental property and didn't know the first thing about wine get cozy with the woman who was supposed to be with *him* tonight.

"I need you to call Gil Mercks for me," he said, referring to the man they often used for what one might consider "sticky" situations. "Tell him I need to see him immediately. He should go around to the back door and call me on my cell phone when he gets here. It's important the guests don't see him."

Will sounded surprised. "You need Mercks tonight? Is there a security issue? I just checked the cellar and spoke to the guard. He wasn't aware of any problem."

If there was one thing Xander didn't like, it was people who asked too many questions. "It's a personal matter. Just call Mercks and tell him to get here as soon as possible."

XANDER WAITED DOWNSTAIRS in his office. Mercks had left him a message, letting him know that he was five minutes from Bordeaux. He appreciated the notice, having needed a few minutes to slip away from the many guests who wanted to corner him and gush about the wine. Normally he basked in such adoration, but not tonight.

He eased back in his desk chair and ran his hand through his hair. For five months he'd foolishly waited to make a move on Jordan. He'd had his chance that afternoon in her store, when they'd talked about her Napa trip, but her damn assistant had cock-blocked him. Then her brother had pulled his Twitter stunt and she'd become consumed with family matters. After a few weeks had passed without the right moment arising, and then a couple months, he had decided to create the perfect moment himself—at his party. Wine was *their* thing, after all, a passion they shared. Jordan would know what he'd been trying to tell her when she saw the tasting menu, without him even having to say the words.

So much for the best-laid plans.

Xander had the business side of his life nailed down. He was the top restaurant and nightclub owner in Chicago, and a year ago he'd set some things in motion to expand far beyond that. With the very private assistance of the notorious—but powerful—Roberto Martino, he planned to take on the big four scenes in the nightclub industry: New York, Las Vegas, Los Angeles, and Miami. In exchange for mixing Martino's drug money into the cash flow of Bordeaux and his other clubs and restaurants, Martino—through a tangled web of dummy corporations—financially backed the projects Xander had in development. That included the properties he had purchased in Los Angeles and New York, clubs that were set to open this summer, as well as a sixth restaurant in Chicago that he planned to renovate and reopen the following spring.

Sure, in exchange he had to deal with Trilani and the annoying cash drop-offs and accountings for all money running through his various clubs. And, of course, there was the small problem that what he was doing for Martino was illegal. But Xander had never been afraid to bend the rules when it came to business—in fact, some would claim that he was downright ruthless—and in his opinion, the payoff was worth skirting around a few federal laws. The way he saw it, the world was his oyster, and he planned to slurp it down with a bone-dry Sancerre.

His personal life, on the other hand, had not been blessed with the same abundance of riches.

He was a picky man. Sure, he'd fucked plenty of the gorgeous women who came to his clubs and restaurants, but that was just mindless sex. To date, he'd only come across one woman who he considered his equal, both with her business savvy and her love of wine, and that was Jordan Rhodes.

And the half billion dollars she stood to inherit one day sure as hell sweetened the pot.

With that kind of money at his fingertips, he wouldn't need Roberto Martino's financial backing—an arrangement he certainly didn't plan to continue indefinitely. Which meant that Jordan Rhodes, and that beautiful, incredible inheritance of hers, was definitely a cause worth fighting for. And the first step in any battle was to know one's enemy.

Xander's cell phone rang, interrupting his thoughts. "You're outside?" he answered.

"At the back door," Mercks said.

"I'll be right there." Xander left his office, being careful to make sure no one was around. He could hear the voices of his guests carrying over from the other side of the staircase. Luckily, the back door was at the far end of the hallway in the opposite direction of his wine cellar and tasting room, which meant that nobody should see him with Mercks.

He punched the code into the security panel next to the back door, silently deactivating the alarm. When he opened the door, Mercks stepped inside. He was an average-looking man with glasses and nondescript thinning brown hair. He wore a gray overcoat and appeared entirely innocuous. Xander supposed that was the point.

"This is a little unusual, Eckhart," Mercks said. His glasses fogged from the warm air. He took them off and wiped them with the edge of his scarf.

Xander gestured for Mercks to follow him. "This couldn't wait. Follow me and I'll explain." Inside his office, he gestured for the private investigator to have a seat in one of the leather chairs next to the coffee table.

"Parsons said this was some kind of personal matter," Mercks led in.

"Yes." Needing to return to the party before he was missed, Xander got straight to the point. "There's a man here who has become a problem. His name is Nick Stanton."

"What kind of problem?" Mercks asked.

"He's with the woman I was supposed to be with tonight."

Mercks nodded. "Ah. And what can I do to help?"

"I want you to follow him. I want to know everything there is to know about him."

"Done," Mercks said without batting an eye. "What do you know so far?"

"Not much. He says he's in real estate. Rental property. Time is of the essence with this. I need you to dig up whatever dirt you can before he and the woman get too close. That's why I asked you to come here tonight—I want you to start following him now."

"I've got a guy who can be waiting outside in five minutes," Mercks said. "Just two things we need to be clear on before we get started: first, this kind of surveillance and background check isn't going to be cheap."

Xander waved this off. "Money's not a problem. Not when it comes to this woman."

"Second, there's always a chance I might not find anything on this guy. For all you know, he's a boy scout."

Xander thought back to the dark expression on Nick's face when he'd found him on the terrace with Jordan.

"This guy is no boy scout," he assured Mercks. "You'll find something. There's always something."

Thirteen

NICK HATED TO admit it, but Huxley had been right.

All evening, people studied him curiously. They went out of their way to engage him in conversation, and—with the exception of Eckhart—made polite inquiries about him and Jordan without crossing the line into being intrusive or rude. Mostly, they wanted to know how they'd met. After all, if *she* liked him, that was good enough for them.

This philosophy carried over into wine, he noticed. People waited to hear her reaction to a wine before commenting themselves, and then almost always vocalized a similar opinion. Perhaps her palette was simply that good, but he suspected the consensus also had something to do with the fact that others viewed Jordan with no small degree of fascination. She was smart, beautiful, ridiculously wealthy (or at least she would be one day), and her family recently had been plagued with a very public scandal. In any setting, this would make her a person of interest. In the staid circles of the Chicago wine community, it made her a star.

Nick watched as she spoke to a couple in their midthirties, wondering if she realized how much influence she held. If pressed, he would have to admit that she was turning out to be not what he'd expected when they'd first met. He kept waiting for her to display some sign of weirdness and/or snobbery, but so far she seemed relatively, well, normal. A somewhat irritating conclusion to arrive at, given how much he hated to admit that he'd been wrong.

"So how did you and Jordan meet?" the man standing across from Nick asked.

How Nick wished he could shake things up, considering this was the sixth time he had been asked that question in the last half hour. *Interesting story, actually. We met in her wine store, when I offered her a deal to get her brother out of prison in exchange for cooperating in a covert FBI investigation.* "It was just one of those things," he began, launching into their now familiar tale of romance. "I'd dropped by Jordan's store to buy a bottle of wine for my property manager. He'd gotten engaged over the weekend and I thought I should—" He frowned when he felt his cell phone vibrating inside his blazer. He reached into his pocket and pulled it out, apologizing. "Sorry. I need to check this for work."

He looked at the number on the caller ID and instantly knew.

Something was wrong.

He caught Jordan's curious look. "It's Ethan. I should grab this."

She nodded—understanding there obviously was no Ethan—and managed an affectionate smile. "Of course."

Nick stepped out into the hallway, away from the others. He answered his phone with a casual tone. "Ethan, I'm surprised to hear from you. Don't you ever take a night off?"

Jack answered, short and to the point. "You've picked up a tail. Someone is going to follow you and Jordan home tonight."

Nick's jaw tightened. "Any idea how that happened?"

"Eckhart's making a play for Jordan. He hired a guy to follow you and dig up whatever dirt he can on Nick Stanton."

Just what they needed. "I'll have to call you back to discuss this further," Nick said. "But obviously, this changes our position in the matter."

"There is some good news," Jack noted.

"What's that?" Nick asked.

"At least we know the bugs in Eckhart's office are working."

HAVING PICKED UP on the "Ethan" code, Jordan was impatient for answers.

Nick did a great job of maintaining the charade with everyone else, but she noticed a subtle change in his demeanor after the mysterious phone call he'd received.

Xander's party was typically an event she looked forward to every year, but on this night she counted the minutes until she and Nick could leave without bringing attention to themselves. A long two hours later, they made their way to the waiting Town Car and settled into the backseat. As soon as the driver shut the back door, Jordan opened her mouth, needing to know *something*.

Nick put his hand on her leg, just above her knee, and squeezed. He held her gaze and shook his head in a barely noticeable gesture. *Don't.*

She closed her mouth and watched him for some further sign.

The driver climbed into the car and looked at them in the rearview mirror. "Back to your house, Ms. Rhodes?"

"Yes," Nick answered for her. He turned back to Jordan and acted as if nothing was amiss. "Did you have a good time tonight?"

Jordan may not have had a clue what was happening, but she understood that she needed to play along with the small talk. "I did. You?"

"I found my introduction to the wine scene very interesting. And speaking of interesting, remember that project Ethan and I have been working on? I got an e-mail from him this evening with some unexpected news. I'll show it to you."

He handed his phone to Jordan. When she took it, she saw a warning typed onto the screen:

WE'RE BEING WATCHED
FOLLOW MY LEAD

A chill ran down her back. Watched by *whom?* And why? She handed Nick back his phone, her heart suddenly racing. "That *is* unexpected news." She fell quiet, not sure she could keep the tremor out of her voice.

Nick did something unexpected. He reached out and covered the top of her hand with his. "I'm on it." The steadiness of his gaze confirmed just that. "Trust me."

Jordan took a deep breath, realizing that she did trust him. She didn't know Nick all that well, and frankly didn't like—well, mostly—what she did know, but she had no doubt that he could handle whatever problem was thrown their way. So she left her hand where it was, covered by his.

When the Town Car finally came to a stop in front of her house, she resisted the urge to immediately jump out. Instead, she waited with forced patience as the driver handed her a clipboard with a bill for her to sign. She quickly added in a tip, scrawled her signature, and gave him back the clipboard. "Thank you."

"Any time, Ms. Rhodes."

She opened her door and stepped out of the car without waiting for the driver—a minor breach in Town Car etiquette, but she had more important things to focus on than playing the part of the pampered rich girl. Being followed by unknown villains and engaging in domestic espionage tended to put one's priorities in perspective.

She met Nick at the sidewalk—he'd gotten out of the car as soon as she had—and he took her arm and led her toward her house. She saw him look casually past her, to the street.

"Keep walking at a regular pace," he said low in her ear. "We're just a regular couple, coming home from a party."

"Could you please tell me what's going on?" she whispered back.

"A car turned onto the street and parked a few houses down. The driver turned off the car but didn't get out. People don't usually sit in cars with the heat off on cold nights like this." He opened the front gate and led her toward the stairs. "You're rushing, Jordan."

Yes, true, she had picked up the pace. She began heading

up the steps to her front door. "It's thirteen degrees outside," she whispered impatiently. "And we're supposed to be on a date on Valentine's Day, remember? Maybe my character is simply eager to get to the hot sex part."

Nick caught her at the top of the steps and pulled her closer. "That's not a bad idea."

Jordan's heart began to race faster. "What are you doing?" she asked breathlessly.

His eyes burned into hers, brilliant green in the moonlight, and there was no mistaking his intentions. "It is our cover, after all."

"You're going to kiss me *here*? Now?" she whispered.

He raised his hand to cup her cheek. "Yes. So make it look good, Rhodes."

Without another word, his mouth came down on hers.

At first, the kiss was light and teasing as his lips gently brushed against hers. It took Jordan a half second to respond, but then she realized something: he was playing with her. Trying to take control with his whole I'm-in-charge, Mr. FBI Agent routine.

The hell with that, she thought. If there was going to be kissing involved in this undercover operation, she was going to do it right.

She slid her arms around Nick's neck and pressed closer. She parted her lips and kissed him back, softly melding their mouths together. She felt him freeze—ha, ha, he hadn't been expecting that—then suddenly—

—He was kissing her. *Really* kissing her. And . . . *wow*. With his hand still holding her cheek, his tongue circled around hers in hot sweeps that made her breath catch. They kissed until the cold February air turned warm around them and crackled with electricity. She sank her fingers into Nick's hair, and had to fight back a gasp when he moved her backward and pinned her firmly against the front door.

Without breaking the kiss, he grabbed for the small silver purse that dangled from her wrist and rummaged inside. He pulled her keys out, reached past her hip, and fumbled with the lock. She felt the door give, and in a breathless bundle they stumbled inside the house.

Nick slammed the door behind them, and neither of them moved. He trapped her between his arms, his lips barely an inch from hers as he stared down into her eyes. "Do you kiss all your fake boyfriends like that?" he asked raggedly.

"Considering you're the only fake boyfriend I've ever had, yes," she panted. When he waited for her to say more, she put on her best innocent face and tried to sound nonchalant. "What? You told me to make it look good, so I did."

Nick's phone rang from inside his coat, interrupting them.

WITH THE DISTRACTION of the ringing phone, Jordan slid out from under Nick's arms and walked into the kitchen. He watched her leave, noticing that she touched her fingers to her lips as she turned the corner. He could still feel his own lips there, could still taste the intoxicating flavor of her. He might've known zilch about cabernet, pinot, and all the other wine varietals, but her kiss was something he'd have no problem describing: luscious, rich, and tantalizing.

His phone rang again.

Right, he had work to do. A minor undercover assignment he was supposed to be focusing on. He pulled his phone out and saw that it was Pallas calling. "We're back at Jordan's house," he answered. Thank God the microphone taped to his chest was well out of range of the receiver, or the guys in the van would've gotten an earful moments ago. "Tell me everything."

As Pallas filled him in on the details of the conversation they'd intercepted between Eckhart and Mercks, Nick slid off his coat, loosened his tie, and unbuttoned his shirt. He ripped the microphone and tape off his chest. "We were followed here by a black sedan," he said after Jack finished. "I wasn't able to get a look at the driver. Are you still in the van?"

"I left Reed and Jansen there. I just arrived at the office, and we're working up a full profile for you as we speak," Jack said. "Davis is on his way. He wants you to call in."

Thirty seconds later, Nick had his boss on the line.

"Pallas filled me in on everything," Davis said. "I'm still trying to decide who's going on my shit list for this mess."

"Xander Eckhart is at the top of mine," Nick said.

"Well, I can't yell at him," Davis grumbled. "How about Huxley? He's been working this up for months; he's the one who picked Jordan Rhodes. A heads-up that there's a romantic connection between her and Eckhart would've been appreciated."

"There's no romantic connection," Nick said. "Don't blame it on Huxley—we had no way of knowing this was going to happen."

"You know what it means now that Eckhart has someone following you."

Yes, he did. Nick had known what it meant the moment Pallas had called him at Eckhart's party. "It means that I'll be playing the part of Nick Stanton longer than expected."

Davis paused. "Obviously, you can't go to New York tomorrow."

Nick pinched between his eyes. "I know."

"I'm really sorry, Nick. I roped you into this and now you won't be able to make your mother's party."

"It comes with the job. You know that, Mike—you did this for years."

"I did. And I also know that after a while, it takes its toll. Six years of nearly back-to-back undercover assignments is a long time. If you weren't so good at it, I would've reassigned you already."

But he was good at it. Nick changed the subject. "What do we know about this Mercks guy Eckhart has following us?"

"We ran a background check and cross-referenced him in our database. He owns a private investigation firm in the Loop. Seems to have a lot of wealthy clientele."

"Any connections to Roberto Martino?"

"None that we've found. He might be nosy and highly inconvenient, but I don't think he poses any threat."

Nick was relieved to hear that. That last thing he'd wanted was anyone connected to Roberto Martino camped outside Jordan's house.

"There's one final matter we need to discuss," Davis said. "Jordan."

"You understand what this development with Eckhart means in terms of her continued involvement in the investigation?" Davis asked.

"Yes."

"Does she?"

"Not yet," Nick said. "I'll explain everything to her as soon as we hang up."

"She's not going to like it."

No, she isn't. And it wasn't exactly a conversation Nick looked forward to, but he had a job to do and this was part of it. He and Davis discussed a few outstanding matters related to the investigation, his boss wanting to be certain they were on the same page. Then Nick hung up and went into the kitchen, ready to be the bearer of bad news.

Fourteen

JORDAN STOOD AT the counter while she waited, checking her e-mail on her iPhone. She did this more out of habit than interest, since the only person she wanted to hear anything from right then was Nick.

She set the phone off to the side when he walked into the kitchen. Her eyes lingered momentarily on the shirt buttons he'd undone at his throat. He'd loosened his tie, too, and wore the shirt casually open-necked, giving her a peek of smooth, tan skin.

She refocused. Bad guys outside her house. Not good. "Now can you tell me what's going on?"

"Your friend Xander is causing all sorts of problems." Nick told her about the private investigator Eckhart had hired to follow him.

Jordan sank into one of the bar stools. "I just assumed Xander was flirting with me, like he does with everyone else. I didn't think he was actually serious. In my defense, the entire time I've known him, he's never dated any woman over the age of twenty-five. I assumed that was some kind of rule of his."

"Apparently, he's willing to break the rules in your case,"

Nick said. "And now we deal with it. Which brings me to my next point: since I'm being followed, I can't go back to my place tonight. Obviously, there can't be any connection between Nick Stanton and Nick McCall. Which means I'm stranded here."

Jordan raised an eyebrow. "I see."

"Just for tonight," he told her. "By tomorrow morning my office will have worked out alternate arrangements."

She checked her watch. "It's after midnight already. You FBI guys move fast."

"We have to, given our predicament. That is, unless our characters were thinking about moving in together." He grinned. "I didn't think we were ready for that step yet."

"I think that's good thinking on your part. What happens after tomorrow?"

"Well, see, that's where things get a little interesting," Nick said. "Now that I'm being followed, we can't give Eckhart a reason to suspect that anything is off. Which means that until we get the evidence we need through the electronic surveillance, I have to remain undercover. So for the time being, I'll continue to be Nick Stanton, a real estate investor who rents properties to college kids and people in their early twenties. And who also is . . . dating you."

It took a moment for this to sink in.

"We have to pretend to be dating?" Jordan asked. "As in, for more than just tonight?"

"Yes."

She couldn't help but feel as though she'd been given the bait-and-switch routine. "My agreement with the FBI was a one-shot deal. Now you're changing the game on me."

"Xander Eckhart changed the game," Nick emphasized. "On all of us. Trust me, if we had known about his interest in you, we never would've come to you with this deal."

Jordan bit her lip, still feeling guilty about that.

"I'm not blaming you," he said. "I'm just trying to explain why we're in this position. After tonight, it will look odd if you and I are never seen together again. And not looking odd is the number one rule in undercover work."

"Okay. Let's say that I agree to this. How long would we have to pretend to be dating?" Feeling thirsty, she got up and walked over to one of the cabinets. She pulled out two glasses. "Water?"

Nick nodded yes. "I can't give you an exact time frame, although I don't expect it to be very long. A week? Maybe a little longer? However long it takes for us to get the evidence we need through the bugs in Eckhart's office."

Jordan filled both glasses with water from the refrigerator, then set one in front of him. "So walk me through this. What would I have to do as the supposed girlfriend of a real estate investor who rents properties to college kids and people in their twenties?" She took a sip of her water.

"You'd need to have lots and lots of sex with me."

Jordan choked on the water and began coughing.

Nick blinked innocently. "No good?"

Her watering eyes undoubtedly lessened the effect of her glare.

Nick smiled. "The answer is that we need to act, from all outward appearances, as if we're a real couple. Xander thinks that you like me enough to spend five thousand dollars to bring me to his party, and that I'm similarly smitten enough to cancel work plans to be with you on Valentine's Day. If that was all true, what would you do next?"

"I don't know . . . I'd probably start by calling my girl-friends and meeting them for brunch tomorrow to tell them all about you," Jordan said.

"There you go."

She pointed for emphasis. "No way. You need my help, and . . . well, I agreed, so I'll help you. But it stays between us. No bringing my friends and family into this."

Nick thought this over. "All right. To the extent we can reasonably keep your friends and family isolated from this, I'll go along with that. It's not like I want to lie to them, either." He turned oddly serious. "Speaking of family, there's something else I have to tell you. And you're not going to like it."

Not exactly Jordan's favorite lead-in. "What?"

He rubbed his hand over his jaw and sighed. "You're *really* not going to like it."

"Okay, now you're making me nervous."

He looked her dead in the eyes. "We can't release your brother on Monday."

The words fell like stones between them.

Jordan said nothing for a moment. On this subject, there would be no jokes or bullshit between them. "Tell me the truth: did you ever intend to release Kyle, or did you simply make that up to get me to take you to Xander's party?"

"Releasing your brother was always part of the plan," Nick said. "And it still is. Just not yet. Now that Eckhart has his eye on you and me, we have to proceed cautiously. Letting your brother inexplicably walk out of prison four-teen months ahead of schedule could lead the wrong person to ask the right questions."

"You didn't worry about letting Kyle out early before."

"Before, you didn't have a man sitting in a car outside your house, watching us and running background checks on me."

Jordan folded her arms across her chest. "Maybe so. But my brother and I are getting the raw end of this deal. Kyle is the reason I agreed to help you. I've done everything you asked. I've even agreed to continue to pretend to be your girlfriend, which goes well beyond the original plan. And now that it's time for the FBI to uphold its end of the deal, conveniently, there's a problem."

"I understand your frustration, Jordan," Nick said quietly. "Trust me, this is not an ideal situation for anyone."

His subdued tone took the fight right out of her. And knowing Nick, that had been his intent. She was angry and annoyed—with him, even though the rational part of her realized this wasn't his fault; with the FBI in general; with Xander; even with Kyle. But mostly what she felt right then was tired.

She ran her hands through her hair. "I think I should show you where you'll be sleeping tonight. It's getting late."

* * *

AFTER LEADING NICK to the guest bedroom, Jordan left him with a polite nod good night. He heard her retreating footsteps on the hardwood floors of the hallway, then a quiet click as she shut her bedroom door.

Clearly, she wasn't happy about the news concerning her brother, and Nick couldn't say he blamed her. She *was* getting the raw end of the deal with the FBI, but sometimes that was how things went. That's why they'd chosen her, after all. With her brother's freedom at stake, she wasn't going anywhere—no matter how unhappy she was that they'd changed the terms of their deal. The special agent in him knew all this and was glad the operation hadn't completely tanked because of the curveball Eckhart had thrown at them that evening.

The man in him, however, felt like shit.

Nick closed the door and checked out the guest bedroom. His eyes skimmed over the king-sized bed with its plump, welcoming pillows and silk blue comforter. Through a doorway on his right, he found a private bathroom designed in creamy marble and well stocked with virtually every toiletry imaginable. It certainly beat the eight-by-eight-foot cell he'd slept in as part of his last undercover assignment.

Getting comfortable, he slipped off his suit jacket and made one last call for the night.

"So? Is Jordan on board?" Davis asked.

"Of course. Eckhart's not going to slip away that easily. But there's a catch." Nick eased onto the bed. "I'm calling in that favor you owe me. The one that just tripled in magnitude because of this mess you roped me into."

Davis sounded surprised. And a little suspicious. "What kind of favor?"

"Do we still have Agent Griegs in play?" Nick asked.

"Yes. Why?"

"This will involve him, too."

Davis sighed. "I'm not going to like this favor, am I?"

"Probably not," Nick said. "But I debated between this and having you call my mother to explain that it's your fault I can't make it to her sixtieth birthday party. You pick.

But I should warn you: my mother is Italian. *New York* Italian, which is like being five hundred percent Italian."

Davis swore under his breath. "The hell with that. I'll get ahold of Griegs."

Fifteen

NICK WOKE UP the next morning not immediately recognizing his surroundings. An occupational hazard. When he felt the silk comforter brush against his bare chest in a caress, he remembered.

Jordan.

He wondered how angry she'd still be that morning. If he were an introspective person, one of those in-touch-with-hidden-emotions types—aka a *woman*—he would probably take note of the fact that it was much harder to blow off her dislike of him than it had been merely six days ago. And, if he were an introspective person, he might also ask himself what he'd been doing by calling in that favor with his boss last night.

Thank goodness, then, that he wasn't such a person.

Because if he were, he would also have to tell himself to shut up and stop asking so many damn questions. He had an assignment to focus on.

He sat up and listened for any sound outside the guest bedroom, wondering if Jordan was awake. He checked the clock on the nightstand, saw that it was just past seven A.M., and figured she was still asleep after the late night they'd had.

He yanked the comforter off and made his way into the bathroom. He sped through his shower routine and threw on the shirt and pants he'd worn the night before, having no other options. Despite its other luxuries, Palazzo Rhodes didn't come with a spare set of men's clothes.

He looked in the mirror and decided to skip shaving. For anyone who might be watching from a black sedan out front, Nick Stanton had just spent the night rolling around in bed with a smart, sexy woman and undoubtedly had better things to do this morning than shave.

Nick Stanton was a lucky SOB.

Nick *McCall*, on the other hand, had work to do, starting with a few phone calls. Including one in particular he dreaded.

He went downstairs to the kitchen, found an expensive-looking espresso maker that appeared wholly unused, then poked around and saw no other machinery in the house capable of producing caffeine. This brought about a round of grumbling about damn fancy rich types and their damn fancy gadgets as he sat down at the counter and called in to the office.

"We've got a condo for you in Bucktown," Davis told him. "1841 North Waveland, unit three-A. It'll work well for you—two bedrooms and an office, top amenities. Nice enough that it won't raise any suspicions."

"Can't have Jordan Rhodes's boyfriend slumming it now, can we?" Nick grumbled.

"I wasn't thinking so much about the girl, more that a successful property investor such as yourself wouldn't be slumming it," Davis said. "What's gotten into you this morning, sunshine?"

Nick grunted. Damn pesky questions. "Just haven't had my morning coffee, boss."

"Perfect. Because you and your girlfriend are going to make a run over to Starbucks so we can drop off your new house keys. There's one located a couple blocks from Jordan's house, at the corner of Barry and Greenview. Pallas will meet you there at ten—you know the drill. Got car keys for you, too—you'll find a Lexus waiting in the parking spot of your new condo."

"Sounds like I'm moving up in the world."

"As they say, you are the company you keep," Davis quipped.

When Nick hung up with his boss, he checked his watch. It was nearly nine A.M. in New York, which meant he had only a short window to catch his mother before she left for church. He steeled himself and dialed the phone number. Heck, he already had one woman mad at him that morning because of his job; he might as well make it two.

His mother picked up on the second ring.

"Happy birthday, Ma," he said.

"Nick! What a surprise to hear from you," she said in an overly dramatic tone. She lowered her voice to a whisper. "Hold on—let me go into the other room."

There was a pause, then she came back on the line. "Okay, the coast is clear. Your father still thinks I don't know about the party. Are you at the airport? You should call Anthony or Matt to pick you up—tell them to bring you right over. Who knows how long it's been since you've had a decent meal? I've already got a pot of sauce on the stove."

Nick closed his eyes. She was making his favorite—penne arrabiatta. Just shoot him now.

No sense in delaying the inevitable. "Ma, there's no easy way for me to say this, but . . . I'm not coming today. They put me on a new undercover assignment, and there's been an unexpected development that means I can't get to New York. But as soon as the assignment's over, I'll visit for a whole week. I promise."

He waited. He could practically hear her thoughts.

Your promises aren't worth very much these days, are they?

And it would be the truth.

"I understand," she finally said. "I know how hard you work, Nick. Your job comes first. You do what you need to do."

He tried to explain as best he could without getting into

details. "This wasn't something I planned. The case was supposed to end last night. You know that if there was any way I could make it today, I would."

"Don't worry about it," his mother said in a short tone. "The family will be disappointed, but I'll explain it. Frankly, I don't think anyone will be too surprised you're not coming." She made some quick excuse about needing to finish getting ready for mass, told him to call soon, and hung up.

Nick set his cell phone down on the counter and blew out a ragged breath. Plain and simple, that sucked. He would've preferred she'd just yelled at him—that he could handle. But hearing the disappointment in her voice was tough.

He heard Jordan clear her throat from the doorway. He looked over, not having realized she was there.

She shifted awkwardly. "I overheard your conversation when I was coming down the stairs." She walked over and took a seat in the stool next to his. "Your mother's birthday is this weekend?"

Nick nodded. "Her sixtieth. My family planned a big party for her."

"She was born the year after my mother. My mom would've been sixty-one this June." She hesitated before continuing. "She died in a car accident nine years ago. Maybe you knew that already."

Actually, he had known that from the file Huxley had pulled together. Jordan had been in business school at the time of her mother's car accident. "Yes."

"Granted, I'm a little biased when it comes to the subject of mothers. But I would've given anything to have been able to throw a sixtieth birthday party for mine." Jordan held his gaze. "I'm sorry you couldn't make it home this weekend." She rested her chin in her hand and sighed. "What can I say? Xander's an asshat."

Nick blinked, then laughed. And something pulled tight in his chest when he realized that was exactly what she'd intended. "I didn't realize billionaire heiresses were allowed to say *asshat*."

With a slight smile, she glanced at him sideways. "You don't know a lot about billionaire heiresses, do you?"

"No." Although he did know one in particular who looked awfully cute in her jeans and long-sleeve navy T-shirt that made her eyes seem impossibly more blue.

Suddenly uncomfortable, Nick looked away and cleared his throat. He shook off the feeling and changed the subject. "We need coffee." He pointed to the high-tech espresso maker. "Think you can skip the homemade stuff and go for a Starbucks run? I have to get my new house keys from another agent who will be there at ten. I was thinking you could be the contact person for the drop-off."

Jordan's eyes widened. "Ooh, that sounds very cloak and daggerish. How will I know who to get the keys from? Some sort of secret code word?"

"Don't worry. He'll find you."

Just then, the doorbell rang.

Jordan looked at Nick, and he gave her the same look right back.

"Are you expecting someone this morning?" he asked.

"No. Are you?"

Neither of them moved, and the doorbell rang again. Twice in quick succession.

"Whoever it is, it sounds like he or she isn't going away." Nick stood up and pulled his gun out of the harness at his calf. He tucked it into the back of his pants, where it was more accessible. "Stay close to me while I check this out."

Jordan gestured to the gun as she followed Nick to the front door. "Take it easy there, cowboy. I don't want you blowing a hole through some poor guy asking for donations for Greenpeace."

"Door-to-door solicitations when it's fifteen degrees outside?" Nick asked. "I don't think so."

The doorbell rang a third time.

Nick gestured to the door. "You have a library, a wine cellar, an espresso machine that looks like it could launch a space shuttle, and yet no peephole. Personal security isn't a priority for you?"

"I have another security measure that works just fine," Jordan retorted. "It's called an alarm system." Using the panel on the wall next to the door, she deactivated the security alarm before unlocking the deadbolt. She glanced over at Nick, who had moved to her side and stood behind the door.

He nodded.

Jordan opened the door and—

—Panicked.

Melinda stood on the doorstep, shivering. "Geez, took you long enough to answer. Let me in—it's freezing out here."

Before Jordan could say anything, Melinda brushed past her and stepped inside. As her friend unwrapped her scarf, Jordan peeked over her shoulder and saw Nick standing behind the door. He shrugged helplessly.

She leaned against the door, keeping it open so that she could block Melinda's view of Nick. Hopefully, whatever the reason behind this untimely visit, they could keep things short and quick. Without her moving an inch from that spot.

"So here's the question," Melinda led in. "Who's Tall, Dark, and Smoldering?"

Jordan gestured nonchalantly with her free hand, the one that didn't have a death grip on her front door. "I'll go with Gerard Butler in *300*. Or that naked guy from the first *Sex and the City* movie."

Melinda pointed. "Good answers. But neither is correct to-day." She pulled a folded newspaper out of her oversized purse. "This just in from Anne Welch's Scene and Heard col-umn in the *Sun-Times*, the weekend roundup." She read out loud from the paper. "'Millionaire restaurateur Xander Eck-hart's annual charity fund-raiser at uber-swanky restaurant and nightclub Bordeaux raised over a hundred thousand dollars for Children's Memorial Hospital and proved once again the place to be seen by Chicago's social elite.'"

She held up her finger for emphasis as she read the next part. "'Gorgeously attired in an amethyst-colored backless dress, wine entrepreneur Jordan Rhodes, daughter of billion-aire Grey Rhodes and sister of the illustrious Kyle Rhodes, who made headlines worldwide five months ago when he . . .' " Melinda cleared her throat. "Well, I think we can skip over that part, Twitter, prison, et cetera, et cetera. Ah, here we go: 'Ms. Rhodes attended the party with an unknown man who sources describe as tall, dark, and smoldering. Sources also say that the couple appeared quite close. Here's hoping, for all our sakes, that this Rhodes twin is luckier in love than her brother.' "

Melinda refolded the paper and stared expectantly at Jordan. "So I repeat: who is 'tall, dark, and smoldering'?"

Jordan swore to herself—potently vile, offensive curse words that undoubtedly were not in the vocabulary of most billionaire heiresses. She knew that Melinda would never, ever in a million years let this go until she had some answers. The jig was officially up.

She pushed the door closed, revealing Nick.

He grinned and held out his hand in introduction. "Nick Stanton."

"Interesting." Melinda's eyes went wide as she slowly shook his hand. "Melinda Jackson." Coming in at a flat five feet tall, she let her gaze travel up and up before she got to Nick's face. She seemed to take particular note of his unshaven jaw and casually untucked dress shirt.

She turned to Jordan with a grin that spoke volumes. *Somebody got la-id.* "Now I know why it took you so long to get to the door."

"Nice, Mel. We were simply . . ." Jordan looked at Nick for help.

"Trying to start her espresso machine," he offered.

Melinda raised an eyebrow. "Is that what you kids call it nowadays?"

"Did you come here this morning solely to harass me about my date?" Jordan asked.

"Actually, after reading the paper, I came over to drag you out to brunch. I didn't realize the *date* was still going. So tell me all about yourself, Nick. I'm eager for the details, since Jordan is being so circumspect these days."

Nick opened his mouth, but Jordan promptly cut him off. She had to set *some* rules here: no lies, or as few as possible, to her friends and family. "Actually, Mel, we'll have to take a rain check on the meet and greet. Nick and I were just about to run out. Can I call you later?"

Melinda studied her suspiciously. "You're acting awfully odd. What's going on here?"

Nick came to her rescue. "It's my fault. I roped Jordan into coming with me to meet a friend for coffee. My sneaky way of keeping the date going." He slid his arm around Jordan's waist and pulled her close.

"Aw, aren't you two just the cutest?" Melinda smiled at Nick. "Some other time, then. Oh, I know—Jordan should bring you to dinner at Corinne's on Saturday. That way you can meet everyone at once."

Jordan shook her head. No way, no how—that would mean lying to her friends all evening. "Oh, unfortunately, Nick already has plans for Saturday." She spun around to face him, which put her body smack up against his firm—really firm—chest.

Wow.

She pled with her eyes for him to play along. "You know, that thing you mentioned earlier that you have to do. On Saturday."

"You mean that meeting with the developer I told you about," Nick said without hesitation. "The one who's building the new apartment complex in Old Town for me."

She could've kissed him right there. Handy, these undercover FBI agents, when one needed a lie on the spot.

Jordan turned back to Melinda with a reluctant shrug. "Darn developer." She patted Nick affectionately on his cheek. "Doesn't he know how much I want to show off this tall, dark, and smoldering guy to all my friends?"

Nick threw her a look that said she needed to shut up. Fast.

Jordan clapped her hands together, not disagreeing with that. "So. I don't mean to rush you out, Mel"—of course she did—"but Nick and I really should get going."

She somehow managed to get her friend out without any more deceit or trickery, and shut the door behind Melinda with a groan. "I hate that I had to lie to her like that. Thanks for helping me out when she invited you to dinner on Saturday. This secret-agent stuff is not my thing."

"Just hang in for twenty more minutes and then you can be free of all secret-agent responsibilities for the rest of the day." Nick pointed in the direction of the door. "Starbucks. My treat."

"Are you *sure* I don't need a code word or something?" Jordan asked. "Maybe we should have one just in case."

"You'll be fine, Rhodes. Trust me."

ON THEIR WAY to Starbucks, Jordan noticed that Nick kept a watchful eye out as they walked the few blocks from her house—presumably checking to see if they were being followed. How surreal that this was her life now, she thought. Making up a fake boyfriend, lying to her best friend, and looking out for shady private investigators who had been hired by a money launderer.

Ah, to go back to simpler times, when she was merely the sister of the world's most infamous Internet terrorist and daughter of a billionaire.

Nick held the door open for her when they arrived at Starbucks. She hurried into the coffee shop, savoring the warmth inside and the anticipation of getting her much-needed caffeine fix. She checked out the other customers, looking for anyone who might be their FBI contact. She shivered, a combination of nerves and excitement, and decided that she'd become quite the badass these days. *She* had an FBI contact.

Nick hadn't told her anything about how this drop-off would go down, so she followed standard protocol and acted normal. She ordered her drink at the counter. "I'll take a tall, one-pump, sugar-free vanilla soy latte please."

Nick seemed to find her order amusing. Of course he did.

"Just a grande coffee for me," he said.

Jordan stepped to the side to wait for her drink to be called, when someone bumped her from behind.

A firm hand on her shoulder steadied her. "Sorry. My bad," said a man's voice.

"No worries." She glanced up at the man with nearly black hair who smiled apologetically as he left the coffee shop. She pulled her cell phone out of the pocket of her coat. Not unexpectedly, she had a text message from Melinda:

CALL ME LATER—I WANT ALL THE DETAILS ABOUT NICK.
BTW, HE'S SEX ON A FUCKING STICK.

Subtlety always had been one of Melinda's strengths.

Jordan tucked the phone away when her drink was called. Nick walked over with his coffee.

"Ready?" he asked.

She cocked her head, confused. "Don't we have that thing you need to take care of?"

"Already done." Nick took her gloved hand in his and leisurely led her out of the store. To anyone watching, they were just an average, everyday couple getting coffee on a Sunday morning.

Jordan studied him as they stopped at the street corner outside Starbucks. Finally, she caught on. "The guy who bumped me."

"Yep. The keys are in your left coat pocket."

"Son of a bitch, that's good."

Nick grinned confidently. "I told you, Rhodes. This is what we do."

NICK DROPPED JORDAN off at her house and told her that he'd call her later. Not seeing the black sedan that had followed them the night before, nor anyone else who looked suspicious, he decided they could forgo the aren't-we-the-loving-couple good-bye kiss. As he strode down her front steps, he caught himself momentarily wishing they *had* been followed.

The introspective side of him—which luckily didn't exist—would've had a field day with that one.

Halfway down the block, he spotted his car, still parked on the street where it had been all night. He kept right on walking—he couldn't risk that someone would see him driving it and trace the license plate. He headed to the nearest intersection to hail a cab, making a mental note to arrange to have someone from the office pick up his car and bring it back to his condo. His real condo.

He found a cab easily and gave the driver the address that would be his home for the next week or two. He checked his phone and listened to two messages from Huxley, who apologized profusely for forcing him into the assignment and screwing up his plans to fly to New York. Although Nick appreciated the messages, they weren't necessary. No one had forced him into anything, and he had no doubt that every other agent in the Chicago office would've made the same decision he had. It was part of the job they'd all signed up for. If he'd expected to be pampered and coddled through his undercover assignments, he would have gone to work for the CIA.

His phone rang just as he was tucking it back into his coat. He saw that it was his brother, Matt, and answered. "I had a feeling you'd call."

"Anyone ever tell you that you're a douchebag?"

Nick grinned at the inside joke. Back when he and his brothers were younger, they'd once gotten carried away and "accidentally" tossed three footballs through Tommy Angolini's second-floor apartment windows after he'd claimed during recess that Scottish douchebags couldn't throw for shit. Tommy had been wrong on two counts: first, in not knowing that they were only *half*-Scottish douchebags, and second, in doubting the athletic prowess of the McCall brothers.

Not surprisingly, that bit of good-natured fun had put an end to any trash talk from Tommy Angolini, but also had royally pissed off their father. A sergeant on the NYPD at the time, he had rounded up Nick and his brothers, brought them down to the Sixty-third Precinct, and locked them up in an empty jail cell.

For six hours.

Needless to say, after that the McCall brothers had all developed a healthy appreciation for the benefits of being law-abiding ten-, nine-, and seven-year-olds. The only person more traumatized by the lockup had been their mother, who'd spent the six hours crying, refusing to speak to their father, and making lasagna and cannoli—three helpings of which she'd practically force-fed each of her sons immediately upon their homecoming from the Big House.

"The last person who called me that watched while three footballs crashed through his living room windows," Nick said.

"Seeing how you can't seem to find your way to New York to save your life, I'm not too worried," Matt shot back. "You'd better be saving the world from a biological weapons attack or foiling a plot to assassinate the president."

"Nope. That's next week's agenda."

"Seriously, Nick—you couldn't even make it to Ma's party? We've been planning this for months."

Feeling like a major asshole, Nick distracted himself by looking out the rear window of the cab and keeping an eye out to see if he was being followed. "I know. But something came up that made leaving impossible. I'll figure out some way to make it up to Ma. How bad is she taking it?"

"She says she's not FedEx-ing you any more arrabiatta sauce," Matt said.

Nick whistled. His mother had to be *really* pissed if she was threatening to cut off food. "That is bad."

"Unless you suddenly announce you've got a girlfriend or you're getting married or something, I think you're going to be on her shit list for a while." Matt chuckled. Being the middle child and peacemaker of the family, he didn't hold grudges for long. "She's getting crazy with this grandchildren stuff, you know. If I so much as mention that I'm having drinks with a woman, she's on the phone with Father Tom, asking what days the church has free for a wedding."

"Unfortunately, there's no imminent announcement on my end, so I'll be in the doghouse for a while." Nick oddly caught himself wondering what his mother would think of Jordan. Tough to say whether the billion-dollar inheritance or the convicted felon of a brother would freak her out more. Not that it mattered. "I'm planning to come out there as soon as I finish this project with work. If Ma won't let me in the door, think I can crash with you?"

"Sure. And don't worry about Ma," Matt said. "I'll tell her there's a new cute assistant DA that I ran into at the station. That should distract her for a while from your sorry-ass excuse for a son."

"Thanks. And out of curiosity, did you actually run into a new cute assistant DA?"

His brother sounded sly. "Better than cute. You know I'm a sucker for a woman in high heels and a power suit. Hey—Anthony wants to talk to you next. Here he is."

Nick heard muffled sounds as Matt handed the phone over, then his youngest brother came onto the line.

"Hey—anyone ever tell you that you're a douchebag?"

And so it went.

Sixteen

AFTER THE EXCITEMENT of the weekend, it felt strange for Jordan to return to her normal routine on Monday. All day at the store she was on edge, waiting for something to happen, some problematic development in the case: Xander had discovered the recording devices in his office; Mercks had clued in to Nick's real identity; the FBI, for whatever reason, had decided to call the whole thing off.

It didn't happen.

By Tuesday night, it was fair to say that she was essentially back to her normal routine, with one notable addition: Nick called to check in every night at nine thirty when she got home from DeVine Cellars. Through him, she learned that Xander and Trilani had met that morning, which meant first and foremost that Xander wasn't suspicious—yet—and second, that the FBI was on their way to getting the evidence they needed to make the arrests.

"If this keeps up, you won't be stuck with me for long," Nick said teasingly. Then, for the third evening in a row, he asked if she had noticed anything unusual during the day.

"You keep asking that," Jordan said. "Trust me, you'll be

the first person I call if anything seems out of the ordinary. I have no lofty ambitions of being a hero in all this."

"Just keeping an eye on you, Rhodes."

The next day, Jordan fought the downtown traffic and headed back to MCC. *So much for last week having been my final visit,* she thought as she rode up the elevator.

She and her brother got their usual table, right in front of the grimy, bulletproof window covered with steel bars. Nothing but the best seat in the house when visiting Kyle Rhodes.

He laid into her the moment he sat down. "Who's Tall, Dark, and Smoldering?"

Jordan's mouth dropped open. "Shut up. You've been reading Scene and Heard?"

Kyle gestured to the bars. "What else am I supposed to do in this place?"

"Repent. Reflect on your wrongdoings. Rehabilitate your criminal mind."

"You're avoiding the question."

Yes, she was. Because her brother was number two on the list of people she really, really didn't want to lie to, right after her father. "It's no big deal. He's just a guy I brought to Xander's party." Who, yes, happened to be tall, dark, and smoldering. Allegedly. And who *occasionally* made her smile, when he wasn't busy getting under her skin. Like an itch she couldn't scratch. Or a tick.

"For five thousand dollars a head, I doubt he's 'just a guy,'" Kyle said.

Suddenly, their friend Puchalski, the inmate with the black snake tattoo, was at their table. "So who's this tall, dark, and smoldering jerk?" he asked Jordan, seemingly affronted.

Jordan held out her hands. "Seriously, does everyone read Scene and Heard in this place?"

Puchalski gestured to Kyle. "I snagged it from Sawyer here while he was reading the financial section. I've got to keep up with current events." He winked. "I won't be in this place forever, you know."

"You will be if you don't shut your yap and start following the rules, Puchalski," a guard warned as he passed by.

The inmate scuttled off.

Kyle picked up where they'd left off. "So now the big secret's out."

Jordan glared at her brother, who apparently had decided to be more annoying than usual on this particular subject. "Yes, it's true—I had a date. Ooh, shocking." Then she thought of something. "Wait, does Dad know about the gossip column?"

"He didn't mention it when he visited on Monday. I doubt he reads Scene and Heard." Kyle eased back in his chair, rubbing his jaw thoughtfully. "This is an interesting situation, Jordo . . . What's it worth to you to keep this information under wraps? Because I'm going to need some income when I get out of this place, and I hear that wine business of yours is really taking off."

"Get real. You owe me."

Kyle sat up, indignant at that. "For what?"

Jordan folded her arms on the table. "Sophomore year. You took Mom's car out of the garage in the middle of the night—without a license—to drive over to Amanda Carroll's. Dad thought he heard a noise when you tried to sneak back in, so I distracted him by saying that I'd seen a strange person in the backyard. While he was looking out my bedroom window, you crept by and mouthed, 'I owe you.' Well, now I want to collect."

"That was *seventeen* years ago," Kyle said. "I'm pretty sure there's a statute of limitations on IOUs."

"I don't recall hearing any disclaimers, expirations, or caveats at the time."

"I was a minor. The contract's not valid."

"If you want to weasel your way out of this, I suppose that's true." Jordan waited, knowing she had him. Despite the impression one might get from the orange jumpsuit, her brother was quite honorable. And he always kept his word.

"Fine," he grumbled. "I finally get some dirt on you, Ms. Perfect, for the first time in thirty-three years, and it's wasted."

He grinned. "Good thing that trip to Amanda Carroll's was worth it, or I'd be pretty pissed about this."

Jordan made a face. *Way* too much information. "I'm hardly perfect. I'm just a lot better at not getting caught than you." She took in their surroundings. "Maybe I should've given you a few pointers."

Kyle nodded approvingly. "Nice one."

"I have months and months worth of this material," Jordan said. "I figure I better get it in while . . . it's still fresh in my head."

Whoa. She needed to be careful—she'd almost slipped there.

"You were about to say something else." Kyle eyed her suspiciously.

Truly, she was the *worst* secret-agent-accomplice-type person ever.

BUT ON THURSDAY, Jordan's brief respite of normality came to an end.

At the store, they had a pickup party for their club members, and the place was packed with customers. Robert and Andrea, the two sales associates, had a steady stream of people at the register, while Martin and Jordan worked behind the bar and around the room, pouring and telling people about the additional wines they'd opened for the night. When they finally closed the shop at nine thirty, a half hour after the usual time, Jordan was exhausted but satisfied. Sales from the tasting had been good—not surprisingly, one of the best times to sell wine to people was after they'd already drunk a few glasses of it.

They were organizing the store—Martin cleaning up, Jordan organizing the sales receipts, and Andrea drying glasses as Robert washed—when Jordan heard her cell phone ringing. She walked into the back room to grab it.

"Why haven't you been answering your phone?" Nick demanded when she answered. "I've been trying to reach you all night."

"I had sixty people in the store until just a few minutes

ago. I didn't hear it ringing and couldn't have answered it even if I had."

"I'm in my car, two minutes from the store. When I get there, you and I are going to have a talk about your lack of vigilance with your cell phone."

"No—wait." Jordan shut the door so the others couldn't hear. "Look, Nick, I'm beat. We had a pickup party tonight, I've got three employees in the store, and I don't have the energy to do the whole pretending-to-be-dating thing in front of them. Plus, you sound like you're raring to go over this, and as much as I normally enjoy being lectured after a long day of work, I'm wondering if we could just save that for another time. As in, you know, never."

Nick didn't say anything at first. When he finally answered, his voice had a note of suspicion to it. "What's a pickup party? Sounds sketchy. And it definitely sounds like something my girlfriend shouldn't be attending."

"It's a party where club members pick up their wine. Not people."

He sounded somewhat appeased. "Hmm. Just as long as no one's putting their keys in a fishbowl or anything."

Jordan smiled. "How 1970s of you. I think it's wrist watches now, not keys."

"I don't even want to know how you know that." Nick paused. "Seriously, how do you know that?"

"I saw it on Oprah." Jordan took a seat at her desk. "What's the emergency, anyway? I assume there is one, if you were trying to reach me all night."

"Someone's been following me all day."

She turned serious. "Do you think we're in trouble?"

"No, I actually think this is a good sign," Nick said. "Eckhart's investigator must be getting desperate, not having been able to dig up any dirt on me. But since he's watching, we need to make sure everything looks on the up-and-up."

"And that means . . . ?"

"That you and I are going on another date. The weekend starts tomorrow. With as much as Nick Stanton likes you, he'd want to see you again. Soon."

"Nick Stanton doesn't play the usual relationship games. I think I like this guy. Hold on a second and I'll see what I can do." Jordan checked the calendar on her phone. "How about lunch on Sunday? I usually take a half-hour break once Martin gets in."

Nick sounded insulted. "You're trying to push me off to a Sunday *day* date? That's the lowliest of all weekend dates— where you slot the scrubs who barely beat out doing laundry. I want a Friday or Saturday night date. Period."

The Great Oz had spoken.

"Sorry, but this Friday I'm having dinner with my father. And as you already know, on Saturday I have plans with my friends," Jordan said. "But if it'll make you feel better, I could bump you up to Sunday evening, after the store closes."

"There's a man who's been watching my every move for the last eight hours, Jordan. He's going to wonder what's going on when Nick Stanton, who supposedly has a girl-friend and a regular life, sits at home alone on a Friday and Saturday night. The FBI didn't magically produce friends for me as part of this cover. Other than my fake house and my fake office, there aren't too many places I can go because I can't risk anyone recognizing me. *You* are the part of this assignment that makes everything look normal. So it's either dinner with your father on Friday, or Saturday with your friends. You pick."

Jordan bit her tongue, knowing he was at least partially right. Still, for a fake boyfriend, he was awfully bossy. "Fine. You can pick me up on Saturday night and I'll take you to dinner with my friends. I'll tell them your work meeting was canceled or something."

"See? Was that so hard?"

Yes, because now she had to lie to three more people she cared about, but she'd worry about that later. "Just be at my house at seven."

WHILE DRIVING BACK to his condo—with a guy on his tail—Nick's cell phone rang a few minutes after he finished talking to Jordan. He saw that it was Huxley, who Davis had assigned to be the liaison on the favor Nick had called in.

Finally. Nick had been expecting this call all day. "I was thinking you might've forgotten my number," he said as he answered.

"Sorry for the delay," Huxley said. "Griegs isn't easily accessible, given the circumstances."

True. "So what's his assessment of the situation?" Nick asked.

"That Kyle Rhodes isn't exactly Mr. Popularity with some of the inmates at MCC. He's already been involved in several altercations. It doesn't sound like he's the instigator, but the guards have started putting him in disciplinary segregation nevertheless. Probably hoping that will pacify anyone who thinks he's getting special treatment because of his money."

For the first time, Nick sympathized with Kyle Rhodes. Being sentenced to prison for a crime he'd willingly committed was one thing, but being thrown in disciplinary segregation merely for defending himself was another. "But Griegs will keep an eye on him?"

"He says he'll try. But he told me to warn you that there's probably not much he can do. Apparently, Rhodes isn't exactly helping the situation—he defends himself when threatened. Griegs says it's just as likely that Rhodes will end up injuring somebody else during a fight. Either way, it's not a good situation."

"No, it's not." That wasn't the report Nick had been hoping for. "Kyle Rhodes sounds like a ticking time bomb."

"And if he explodes, Jordan Rhodes will pull out of this deal," Huxley said. "You got any ideas how to keep her brother under control?"

"I always have ideas, Huxley. We'll talk soon."

Seventeen

"SO TELL ME about your friends."

Jordan looked over at Nick. He'd insisted upon driving, even though she had wanted to take a cab. Given the circumstances, meaning that the evening counted as a work night for him, he said he didn't plan to drink much. Which was a shame, because she'd brought along some great wines and had been planning to take another shot at making Nick a non-scoffer. She might not get another chance, after all. Things seemed to be progressing well with the surveillance of Xander, which meant that their dating charade wouldn't last much longer.

"Well, you already met Melinda," she said. "She'll be there with her boyfriend, Pete."

"What does he do for a living?" Nick asked.

"He writes operas. That's how he and Melinda met—they're both in musical theater."

Nick eyed her skeptically. "They're not going to burst into song or anything during dinner, are they?"

"That depends on how many bottles of wine we've gone through."

Nick muttered something about men from Brooklyn not *doing* musical theater. "What about the other couple?"

"Corinne is a high school teacher and her husband, Charles, is a lawyer."

This, at least, seemed to meet with his approval. "Sounds more my speed."

"Do try to get along with everyone, sweetie," Jordan said. "Remember that we're in that stage of our relationship where you're trying to impress me by getting to know my friends."

"I've never been very good at that stage." Nick thought about this. "Actually, I've never been at that stage."

"I'm sure you can handle one night of it. Just do whatever it is you normally do on a date."

Nick looked over with a devious sparkle in his eyes.

"Other than that," Jordan said.

Charles and Corinne lived with their son in a three-bedroom bungalow in Andersonville, a quaint, charming neighborhood a few miles north of downtown Chicago. As they climbed up the steps to the front porch, Jordan saw Nick look over to their right. She heard a car approaching down the block at the same moment she felt his hand move to her waist.

She waited until they were at the front door and spoke quietly. "Are we being followed again?"

"Yes."

She rang the doorbell and took a deep breath, preparing herself for the next episode of the Nick and Jordan show.

NICK PLASTERED ON a charming grin just as the door opened. A woman with straight, jet black hair greeted them with a cheerful smile.

"Hey, guys." She held the door open and introduced herself. "I'm Corinne. It's so nice to meet you, Nick. We've heard . . . well, honestly we've heard nothing about you. Jordan's been oddly quiet about this whole thing. Melinda's been telling everyone that you're some kind of spy or secret agent."

Jordan tripped over a child's boot and would've fallen if Nick hadn't caught her in his arms. He shot her a look. *Stay cool.*

Corinne apologized to Jordan and kicked the boot out of the way as Melinda and a man with sandy brown hair and a medium build came out of the kitchen. "Don't take it personally," the man told Nick with a chuckle. "Mel thinks everyone's a spy or secret agent these days. She's addicted to watching *24* on DVD." He shook Nick's hand. "Pete Garofalo."

Melinda punched Pete in the shoulder. "I didn't say I thought he was a spy, I said he looked James Bond-*esque* with the five o'clock shadow and the dress shirt and pants."

A second man, wearing a red and white checkered apron, called out to Jordan and Nick from the kitchen, throwing in his two cents. "From what we heard, it sounds like Melinda caught you two at an inopportune time on Sunday morning. Something about how long it took you to answer the door?" He grinned cheekily as he held up a pair of salad tongs, greeting Nick. "I'm Charles, by the way."

Corinne scolded her husband from the doorway. "Charles Kim—what kind of host are you? At least let the new guest take off his coat before we begin embarrassing him."

Melinda was still stuck on the *24* thing. "And I don't see you grabbing the remote away from me when that countdown clock starts chiming," she said to Pete. "Unless it's to get a quick check of the scores on Monday nights."

Nick's ears perked up at the mention of scores. *Sports.* Now there was a topic upon which he could wax poetic. "Too bad Monday night football is over," he lamented to Pete. "But there's always basketball. Who are you eying for the Final Four?"

Pete looked mildly embarrassed as he gestured to Melinda. "She's, um, referring to the scores on *Dancing with the Stars.*"

"He likes it when they do the paso doblé," Melinda threw in.

"The dance symbolizes the drama, artistry, and passion of a bullfight. It's quite masculine," Pete said.

"Except for the sequins and spray tans," Melinda added.

Pete clapped his hands together, ignoring this. "How about you, Nick? Are you a fan of the reality television performing arts?"

Nick threw Jordan a look, trying to decide if his character was so smitten that he needed to feign an interest in *any* topic that involved sequins and spray tans that did not also involve cheerleaders.

She stood up on her toes and whispered in his ear. "Don't worry. It's like a bottle of wine that needs to breathe. They mellow out after about an hour or so."

DINNER WENT SMOOTHLY enough, particularly because Jordan's friends turned out to be a warm, welcoming group. Nick felt satisfied that to an outside eye—or eight of them— he and Jordan appeared to be simply a normal guy and girl on a date on Saturday night.

From time to time throughout dinner, he studied Jordan curiously. He was having a hard time sizing up what, exactly, was "normal" for her. A week ago, she'd been entirely in her element at Eckhart's fund-raiser, chatting it up with the crème de la crème of Chicago society while wearing a designer dress and drinking wine that cost more than what many people earned in a week. On the other hand, she seemed just as comfortable with her friends, wearing jeans and a sweater and eating homemade pizza in a house that looked like a Toys "R" Us had exploded inside it.

She surprised him. He could handle anything Xander Eckhart threw at him; was unfazed by money laundering, undercover ops, fake identities, fake condos, offices, and cars, and private investigators who followed him around the clock and watched his every move. But Jordan had managed to throw him off guard more than once already, and Nick knew that could be a dangerous thing.

A prime example was that kiss neither of them acknowledged.

Despite being much shorter in duration and objectively far more pleasant than any other assignment he had been given, this was one undercover investigation he looked forward to wrapping up. Quickly. Before anything got . . . messy.

Shifting his attention away from Jordan, Nick turned to Charles, the lawyer, who sat on his right. The two of them spoke about Charles's criminal defense practice, with Nick being careful not to give away the fact that he obviously knew a lot more about the justice system than the average real estate investor.

"Does your firm handle a lot of high-profile cases?" he asked. He hadn't recognized the name of the firm when Charles had mentioned it earlier, but Chicago was a big city with a lot of lawyers.

"We get our fair share," Charles said. "I mean, nothing as high-profile as the Roberto Martino trial. Not that my firm would represent the likes of him." He lowered his voice. "At one point, we talked to Jordan's brother about handling his case, but he decided to go with a different firm. Which is a shame, given the way things turned out. I mean, Kyle gets eighteen months over at MCC for a crime that hurt no one, yet it took years for the FBI and U.S. Attorney's Office to get their acts together and arrest one of the most notorious crime lords in the country. That's our federal criminal justice system at work."

"Charles." Corinne reached over and squeezed her husband's hand with a meaningful look in Jordan's direction. "You know she worries about Kyle. Let's not bring that up tonight." She smiled. "Maybe you could tell us how you and Jordan met, Nick."

All conversation at the table stopped.

Frankly, Nick was surprised it had taken this long for someone to ask. Out of the corner of his eye, he saw Jordan take a nervous sip of her wine. He knew this was the part of the evening she'd dreaded, the part where they told more lies to her friends.

Perhaps he could help her out with that.

"Jordan and I met two weeks ago, at her store," he said. "On the night of the big snowstorm."

Pete chuckled. "You really must've been jonesing for wine to go out in that mess."

Nick reached across the table and linked his fingers through Jordan's. "I think Fate had a higher purpose for bringing me to her store that night." He winked at her. *I've got this.*

Melinda melted. "That's so sweet."

"Then what happened?" Corinne prompted.

Nick faced Jordan's friends. For her sake, he'd tell the truth—perhaps not the whole truth—but at least nothing but. "Well, I asked Jordan a few questions, some quips were exchanged, and I distinctly recall her making a sarcastic comment about chardonnay. I can't tell you exactly what happened from there, but five days later I found myself at Xander Eckhart's party drinking pink champagne."

Her friends laughed. Charles raised his glass. "That's how it happens, Nick. A cute smile, a few clever words, and five years later you're watching *Dancing with the Stars* on Monday nights instead of football."

"Hey, don't knock it until you've tried it," Pete said indignantly.

As the group teased Pete, Nick felt Jordan squeeze his knee underneath the table.

She spoke softly as she held his gaze. "Thank you."

It took far more effort than it should have to make his tone sound as cavalier as always.

"Any time, Rhodes."

MELINDA AND CORINNE struck fast, cornering Jordan in the kitchen while she opened a bottle of Moscato d'Asti she'd brought to go with dessert.

"About your mystery man," Melinda led in. "I think he really likes you."

"I agree. This one has the legs to be around awhile," Corinne said. "And I like *him.* Which, of course, is the most important thing."

"*We* like him," Melinda emphasized.

Jordan set the corkscrew on the counter, their enthusiasm making her feel like an even bigger jerk than before. Of course they had to go and like Nick. Although she couldn't say she blamed them—he was laying on the charm a little thicker than usual tonight.

"I hope it seems like he likes me," she said, trying to walk a fine line of truth with her words. "Isn't that what's supposed to happen when people date?" She reached into the cabinet behind her and grabbed six champagne flutes.

"It's funny, though. It almost seems like he's trying to hide it. Like how he kept sneaking looks at you during dinner," Melinda said.

Corinne pointed. "I saw that, too!"

Jordan turned around. "I didn't notice any unusual amount of looks." She thought about this for a moment. If Nick had been looking at her, she supposed it was just part of the role he was playing that night.

"I like how he calls you Rhodes," Corinne said.

"It *is* my name."

"Yeah, but it sounds affectionate when he says it. Playful."

"Flirty," Melinda agreed.

"Naughty," Corinne said.

The two of them burst into giggles.

Oh boy. Jordan took a sip of the moscato, thinking she was going to need a second round pronto if Melinda and Corinne continued the post-dinner debriefing much longer. She tried to diffuse their interest without giving anything away. "Look, Nick is a complicated person. Perhaps we should let this one simmer for a while before we read too much into his every move."

Melinda leveled her with a stare. "Jordan. You don't have to pretend around us. It's okay to admit that you like this guy."

She shifted uncomfortably. "Well, I brought him here tonight. That speaks for itself, doesn't it?"

Both Corinne and Mel waited expectantly.

Jordan caved and gave them what they wanted, sensing there would be no moving on—and no peace for the rest of the evening—until she did so. "All right. Sheesh. I like the guy, okay?" She waited for the sinking feeling that would come with the knowledge that she'd just told her friends another lie.

It didn't happen.

She must've been getting better at this secret-agent-accomplice thing than she'd realized.

Eighteen

"WHAT DO YOU mean, you haven't found anything on Stanton?" Xander demanded to know. "You must not be looking hard enough." If Mercks thought he was paying four hundred dollars an hour for piss-poor surveillance, he had another think coming.

It was Sunday morning—over a week since Mercks had begun his assignment. They were back in Xander's office, where he conducted all of his business. With the security system he'd installed to protect his cellar, it was the one place he always felt secure.

"Trust me, we've been looking." Mercks was seated in one of the chairs in front of Xander's desk. "First we started with the basics: Nick Stanton has no criminal history, good credit, and a clean driving record. He owns a condo in Bucktown valued at just under a half million, and pays his mortgage on time. Between checking and savings accounts, stocks, mutual funds, convertible securities, and bonds, he's worth about another million. No outstanding debts, no unusual draws from his bank accounts.

"Next we moved on to personal information: he's an only child, both parents are deceased. No ex-wives or kids, at least none that we could find. He grew up in a midsized town just outside of Philadelphia, and went to Penn State. Majored in management through the College of Business. Nothing remarkable in his academic records. Came to Chicago about a year after he graduated and has lived here since."

"What about his job?" Xander asked. "This real estate business or whatever that he owns."

Mercks nodded. "Stanton is the sole owner of a real estate investment company that owns rental properties. He's got a small office in Lakeview that appears to be staffed with two other employees, at least from what we've seen. Stanton gets to work every morning by eight thirty, leaves at six. Takes a half-hour lunch around one, seems to favor Jimmy John's. Not sure if he likes turkey or roast beef—that didn't seem necessary to the report."

Xander scowled, not appreciating the humor. "And his relationship with Jordan?"

"We've been tailing him ever since your party, just like you asked. He spent that night at her house, and then they went for coffee in the morning. He saw her again yesterday evening—they had dinner with some of her friends who live in Andersonville. He brought her back to her house around midnight and spent about twenty minutes inside before he left."

"He didn't spend the night?" Xander asked.

"Maybe she had a headache."

"Maybe she's getting bored with him."

Mercks shrugged. "You can decide for yourself. We've taken photos of the two of them together." He tossed a manila envelope onto the desk. "They're chronological."

Xander pulled out the photographs. The first one in the stack was of Stanton and Jordan on the night of his party, judging from the purple dress he saw peeking out from underneath her coat. They were kissing on her front stoop and looked far from bored with each other.

He leafed through the remaining photos. Jordan holding hands with Stanton as they came out of a Starbucks. Stanton with his arm around her waist, whispering something in her ear as they waited on the front porch of an unfamiliar house, presumably her friends' place. The final image was of Stanton, leaving Jordan's house as she watched from the doorway.

"That last photo was taken last night," Mercks said.

Xander put the photographs back into the envelope and set them off to the side. "I'm not convinced. And let me tell you why. I know a lot of people in this city, and I've been asking around about Nick Stanton. No one's ever heard of the guy. So I'm supposed to believe that this nobody, who knows nothing about wine, comes out of the blue and just so happens to walk into Jordan's store and sweep her off her feet? I'm not buying it."

"People meet like that all the time," Mercks said.

Xander jabbed his forefinger on his desk for emphasis. "People don't meet *Jordan Rhodes* like that all the time. Her father has one point two billion dollars. *Billion*. I'm calling it now—this thing is some kind of setup. Stanton's after her money. He's probably a con artist or something."

He pointed at Mercks. "You stay on Stanton until I say otherwise. There's more to this story. I can feel it."

THE FOLLOWING DAY in his fake office, Nick eased back in his desk chair. He grinned, amused with this latest report. "So Eckhart thinks I'm a con artist who's after Jordan's money. Good. That should keep him distracted for a while."

He'd called Huxley after listening to the recording of the conversation. His partner had been stationed in the van a couple blocks from Bordeaux every day since he'd recovered from the stomach flu. Over the course of the past week and a half, they'd developed a good working relationship: Huxley listened live from the van to Eckhart's conversations, then e-mailed for Nick's review the digital audio files, along with notes of the minute and second markers for any conversations that were particularly relevant to their investigation.

Huxley took the day shift in the van, and they had two additional agents working the evening and early morning

shifts—including Agent Simms, who, per Eckhart's promise, had been fired from her bartending position the day
after his party. The agents covering the second and third
shifts similarly sent over audio files for Nick's review,
although thus far there'd been very little substantive evidence gathered through the recording devices during those
hours.

They'd recorded a second conversation between Trilani
and Eckhart, and this was good progress for their case. None
of it, however, was particularly thrilling work. But Nick
needed something to do while working at his fake office, and
this kept him busy enough. Thus, they carried on: Huxley,
holed up in a van seven days a week, weeding out hours
upon hours of Eckhart's tedious wine, nightclub, and restau-
rant-related conversations, and him, stuck in a stuffy office
five days a week with two interns pretending to be "Ethan"
the property manager and "Susie," his office assistant.

Nick peered through the glass pane that separated his
private office from the front office where the two interns
worked. At least they were able to work remotely from their
laptop computers, so the façade wasn't a total waste of Bureau resources. Still, he could only imagine the excited
looks on their faces when Davis had approached them with
the chance to work undercover. A boring office job probably had not been what they'd had in mind.

"As long as you and Jordan keep Eckhart fooled about
your supposed relationship, we should be fine," Huxley
said. "Still, I'll feel better when we're finished with the
surveillance and can be done with this whole thing."

Nick ran his hands through his hair, in agreement with
that sentiment. The situation with Jordan was starting to
seem too real for his comfort. This normally would be the
point when he, sensing a possible attachment, would back
away from the situation. But with her, he was trapped. Con-
sequently, all he could do was carry on as usual, being that
guy who didn't let things become real, who was always
handy with a quip but didn't have feelings deeper than that.

Because he didn't. Undercover agents didn't allow themselves to become attached to a case or anyone involved with it.

He wasn't complaining—he'd signed on for this. He'd worked hard to get where he was, and being the best undercover agent in the Chicago field office was a major accomplishment. It was his specialty, the thing that differentiated him from the other agents in the office. Without that distinction, he'd be just another guy with a badge, a gun, and cool facial scruff. Hell, he'd be Pallas.

That alone was more than enough motivation to get his head back in the game.

"You and me both, Huxley," he told his partner. "The faster we can wrap this up, the better. For all of us."

Nineteen

JORDAN FEIGNED A pleasant smile for her customers. "What do you think?"

The couple, in their late twenties, looked at each other. "I like it," the woman said, swirling the two-ounce pour of chardonnay.

"I like it, too," the man agreed. "It's not as buttery as a lot of chardonnays I've tasted. Let's get a bottle."

"Perfect." Jordan rang them up. Then she headed over to one of the tables in the corner, where a group of women in their early forties were drinking wines by the glass. "How are you ladies doing? Can I answer any questions about the wine?" When she had finished there, she moved to the next table, then to the racks where a few additional customers were browsing, before hurrying back to the bar to ring up one of her regulars.

"Busy tonight," he noted.

Jordan bagged up his four bottles. "Can't complain." Actually, she could complain—quite easily, in fact—but she wouldn't. Not around customers, anyway.

The stomach flu had struck DeVine Cellars.

Both of her sales associates had been out sick since

Monday, which meant that she and Martin had to divide all the shifts between the two of them. Normally this wouldn't be a problem, but she had visited Kyle that morning, per usual, so Martin had opened the store and she had to work the evening shift—by far the busiest time—alone. As such, she'd been running around almost nonstop since five thirty, hadn't eaten, hadn't even had a chance to go to the bathroom, and was feeling more than a little crabby.

But not in front of the customers.

She plastered on another smile as she made her way around the bar and scooted toward the back hall. It looked as though everyone was content for the next thirty seconds, so this was her chance to make a run for it.

The chime on the front door rang.

Son of a bitch. If one more friggin' customer came through that friggin' door before she'd had a chance to pee, somebody was going to get a corkscrew up his—

She hurried around the corner to check the door and barreled right into a tall, hard body.

Nick.

He caught her in his arms. "Whoa. Looks like somebody missed me," he said in a teasing tone.

Jordan pleaded with her eyes. "Please help me."

His expression turned serious. "Anything. Name it."

"Oh, thank you." Jordan put her hands on Nick's hips and turned him around to face the rest of the store. "Stand here. Make sure that nobody steals anything or sneaks a glass of wine." She took a step down the hallway before glancing back. "And don't touch anything." She hurried to the bathroom before her eyeballs turned yellow and floated out of her skull.

When she returned, she found Nick still at his post.

He pointed to the door. "Is it okay that these two guys came in with a wheelbarrow and took off with a couple crates of wine? They only took the pink stuff, so I figured no one would kick up much of a fuss."

"Ha, ha." Jordan scooted around him and slid behind the bar. "Thanks for keeping an eye out. What are you doing here, anyway?" She checked herself, aware there

were others around. "I mean, this is such a pleasant surprise. Sweetie."

Nick shrugged. "I worked late this evening and was about
to drive home when I was overcome with the sudden urge to
see my girlfriend."

Code for being followed, Jordan guessed. "I'm closing in
twenty minutes. We could grab something to eat after that."

Nick checked his watch. "You haven't eaten dinner yet?
It'll be after nine thirty before you get out of here."

She threw him a charming smile. "Nine *twenty* if I have
help cleaning up the store from my sweetheart of a boyfriend." She saw a customer approach the bar on the opposite end and left Nick grumbling to himself. A few minutes
later, when she came up for air, she noticed that he was
gone. She looked around the store, not seeing him anywhere, but didn't have time to focus on that until after the
last customer had left the store.

Jordan shut the door and locked it with a flourish. She'd
survived.

No offense to all her wonderful customers, whose business she appreciated so much, but she thought they'd never
get the hell out. She drew the shades on the front windows
and looked around the store.

Crap, it was a disaster.

She heard a knock on the door. She walked over, ready
to tell whoever it was that the store was closed for the day.
Instead, she saw Nick through the glass. She unlocked the
door and let him in.

He was *still* grumbling. "You're already too skinny," he
said gruffly. "If my mother saw you, she would handcuff
you to the kitchen table and make you eat lasagna for a
week." He held up two bags from Portillo's. "I didn't know
if billionaire heiresses preferred hot dogs, burgers, or Italian beef—I'll skip the obvious joke there—so I got one of
each."

Jordan went weak in the knees at the sight of the red and
white striped bags. Chicago dining at its finest. "Please tell
me you have cheese fries in there," she whispered.

"Yep."

She nearly ripped the bags out of his hands. "You are a god."

They chose a table nestled between the wine racks. As Nick unpacked the food, Jordan grabbed an open bottle of zinfandel and poured herself a glass.

"You?" she asked.

He raised an eyebrow. "Wine with cheese fries? No thanks."

"Wine with everything. Because wine means the responsible part of the day is over." After finishing her pour with a flourish, Jordan checked out her options and decided that billionaire heiresses liked burgers best with their cheese fries. She sighed happily as she took a seat, getting off her feet for the first time in hours. She took a bite of her burger and actually moaned.

Nick gestured with his Italian beef sandwich. "That tops your reaction to the wine we had at Eckhart's party. The Château Seville or whatever."

"Sevonne. And nothing beats burgers like this. When I was a kid, we used to get Portillo's almost every Saturday night." She took another bite and closed her eyes. "God, I haven't had this in years."

When she opened her eyes, she saw Nick watching her intently. "What?"

"It's just . . . when you eat and drink, you make these faces that are—" He stopped himself and exhaled. "Never mind. What were we talking about?"

Jordan pointed to her burger. "Food. Wine."

He nodded. "Right. So wine means the responsible part of the day is over, huh? That's catchy. You should put that on a bumper sticker and slap it on the Maserati."

She smiled. "I'll keep that in mind."

Nick took a sip of his soft drink. "What got you interested in wine, anyway?"

Jordan dipped a French fry into the cheese sauce. "My mom. She was really into wine. When I was in high school, my dad had a skybox at the United Center, and during the summer, he and Kyle would go to Bulls games on weekday nights. He offered to take me, too, but sports"—she made a face—"not really my thing."

"A travesty."

"I'd say the same thing about you always passing up good wine."

"Hmm." Nick didn't look convinced.

She continued on with her story. "So on those nights, my mom and I would go out to dinner. She called them our girls' nights out. She'd let me have a glass of wine with dinner—which, of course, made me feel extremely grown-up. I wasn't allowed to tell my dad or Kyle about that part. The wine was our secret, something just my mom and I shared."

She smiled at the memory before taking another sip of wine.

"I'm sorry she never got to see this place," Nick said gently. "I'm sure she would've been very proud."

Jordan nodded and felt her eyes sting. She cleared her throat and kept things light. "It's just because I look so good in comparison to Kyle. He's currently setting the bar very, very low for the Rhodes twins."

Nick laughed. "I think you look pretty good in comparison to anyone."

Jordan pulled back in surprise. "Wow. Was that actually a compliment?"

He paused midchew, as if just having realized what he'd said. He took a moment, finished chewing, then shrugged. "Sure. Even I can give my fake girlfriend a compliment when the role requires it." He winked. "And you should hear me when I whisper sweet nothings."

"I'm sure it's a real treat." Jordan reached for another fry and dipped it into the tub of melted cheesy goodness. "What about you? How did you end up at the FBI?"

"Well, that goes back to the time I was ten years old and thrown in jail," Nick said.

She laughed. *"Ten?* Oh, Nick, you little troublemaker. What did you do?"

"My brothers and I broke a couple of windows after this kid called us douchebags. My father, who was an NYPD sergeant at the time, brought us down to the stationhouse and locked us in a cell for six hours. Scared the crap out of us."

"I bet," Jordan said with a smile. "Sorry. I'm sure it was quite a traumatic experience."

Nick stole the cheese fry out of her hand. "Keep mocking me, and I'll eat every one of these."

She put on a serious face. "I'm listening."

"When we got home that night, my dad set my brothers and me down and told us that his actions reflected on the New York Police Department, and that our actions reflected on him. And that he hoped, from that point on, that we would conduct ourselves in a manner that honored the badge he wore." He paused. "I remember thinking that someday I wanted to have a job that I was just as proud of. And that stuck with me. So I joined the NYPD straight out of college. I liked it enough, but after five years I felt like I wanted more. Which brought me to the FBI. After I graduated from the Academy, they transferred me to Chicago. That was only supposed to be for three years, but I like it here. Having a little bit of distance from my family is not entirely a bad thing."

Jordan swirled the wine in her glass. "What do they think about you working all these undercover assignments?"

Nick chuckled. "You should hear my mother go on about it." He adopted a thick New York accent. "'My son, the FBI agent, you think he has time to call with all those big, important cases they assign him to? I could be *dead* and he wouldn't know it.'"

Jordan laughed, enjoying these rare insights into the real world of Nick McCall. Until now, he'd been somewhat of a mystery. "I bet you miss them all."

He shrugged. "Sure. Although I try to keep that fact from my brothers. Our relationship is more of the sarcastic, annoy-the-crap-out-of-each-other type."

"Oh, I think I know the kind," Jordan said. Her relationship with Kyle wasn't exactly defined by expressive sentimentality, either.

When they had finished eating, Nick offered to help her clean up the store.

"You don't have to help me out," she said. "I was just kidding about that earlier."

"And let you do all the hard work? If anyone's watching, my character needs to look like a helpful and supportive boyfriend."

She tossed him a dishtowel. "In that case, your character can get to work on all these dirty wineglasses."

Between the two of them, they cleaned up the store quickly. Nick had parked out front, and he drove Jordan the four blocks to her house, where he insisted on walking her to the door. Per usual, she saw him check out the other cars parked on the street.

"Were we followed?" she asked.

"Actually, I don't think so," Nick said. "We're in the clear."

"Oh, good." Jordan stopped at the top of the steps. As they stood in the moonlight on her front stoop, it struck her that this had been the first evening she'd spent truly alone with Nick. No private investigators watching them, no friends, no Xander Eckhart and company. Just them.

Almost like an actual date.

"Thanks for dinner and for helping me out tonight." She paused, struck by the truth of what she was about to say next. "I had a really good time."

Nick seemed amused by her surprise. He moved up another step, joining her at the top of the stairs. "You don't have to sound so shocked. I'm not all bad, you know."

"Maybe just *mostly* bad," Jordan teased.

Nick cocked his head, considering this. "Mostly bad . . . I guess that's progress."

They stood very close, Jordan noticed. As in, end-of-the-date, do-I-invite-him-inside close. Which made no sense, considering this arrangement between her and Nick was all a charade.

They both fell silent for a few seconds. The night, the street, and everything else suddenly felt very still. Finally, Jordan gestured to her house. "I should probably get going inside. Subzero temperatures out here and all."

Nick pointed to his car. "Right. And I need to get home. Have to get up bright and early for my fake job."

"Okay, then."

"Great."

Neither of them moved.

"So I guess I'll see you later," Jordan said. She turned to go—if for no other reason, her feet were beginning to freeze in her boots and pretty soon she wouldn't be able to move.

Nick caught her hand. "Jordan."

He said her name so quietly, if it hadn't been for the relative silence of the night, she might have missed it. When she turned around, his eyes were looking into hers as if searching for something.

Then just like that, the moment was gone. He gave her a curt nod, his expression unreadable once again. "I'll call you later." He dropped her hand and strode down the steps without looking back.

Twenty

THE NEXT MORNING, Jordan spent her first hour at the store doing inventory and placing orders with her distributors for the following month's wine supply. She was leaving for Napa Valley on Friday, a trip she'd planned months ago. While she generally tried to make it out to wine country three or four times a year for business, she was particularly excited about this trip—she had an appointment to visit a new winery whose debut cabernet she was considering for the store's wine club.

Plus, she needed the weekend away, from Chicago, FBI undercover assignments, and everything else. A few days alone would do her some good, get her back to thinking clearly again. Maybe get her to stop wondering whether Nick had wanted to kiss her last night.

Somehow, she'd blurred the line in her head between what was real and fake in their situation. But a *real* date would've kissed her last night, not given her a token "I'll call you later" before hightailing it off her front porch. Yet here she was, still thinking about him.

Jordan did a mental headshake, forcing herself to focus on work. Wanting to make up for the extra shifts she had to burden her staff with during the time she'd be in Napa, she had scheduled herself to both open and close the store that day. Luckily, Andrea was feeling better and was set to come in at one o'clock, which meant that Jordan wouldn't have to work the evening shift alone again.

After placing orders, she posted on the store's Facebook page about the special they were running through the weekend: buy three reds, get the fourth half off. Then she turned to her favorite project—paying bills. She cringed at the gas bill and cursed the ridiculous cost of keeping a large store warm in the winter. Apparently, the folks at Peoples Gas thought she had a half-billion dollars at her disposal.

A little heiress humor.

Shortly before noon, the chime on the door rang as the first customer of the day walked in. Jordan looked up from the bar and smiled at the woman, an attractive brunette wearing a North Face coat and yoga pants that showed off her fit, curvy physique.

Either on her way to or from the gym, Jordan guessed. "Can I help you?"

The woman seemed to ponder this question for a moment. "I'm just looking for now." She looked around the store, as if checking to see if anyone else was around.

Jordan wondered if Martin had finally found a woman who appreciated a light-bodied, bow-tie-wearing pinot. "Take your time. If you have any questions, let me know."

The woman paused. "Actually, the hell with it. I do have a question." She stalked over to the bar. "Is it serious between you and Nick?"

The question, completely unexpected, caught Jordan off guard. "I'm sorry?"

"Nick McCall. Is it serious between the two of you?"

Jordan took a moment to respond, thinking carefully about her answer. "I know a Nick Stanton, but not a Nick McCall." She looked the woman over. "I'm sorry—I didn't catch your name."

"Lisa. And the name of the guy who was in your store last night is Nick *McCall*. Trust me—I would know. I know Nick very well."

Reasonable reaction or not, Jordan caught herself bristling at the implication. "If you know Nick so well, why do you need to ask me if things are serious?"

Lisa shifted uncomfortably, seeming to hedge a little. "I haven't heard from him for a couple weeks. Then I happened to see him yesterday in his car. I followed him here and thought I'd catch him inside the store, until I spotted you two through the door. You looked cozy."

Apparently, the Nick and Jordan show was picking up viewers every day. "I think this is a conversation you need to have with Nick, not me."

Lisa laughed at that. "Maybe you don't know him that well after all. Because if you did, you'd know that you don't ask Nick questions. It's part of his whole no-strings-attached, I-don't-*do*-relationships routine." She raised an eyebrow. "Or hasn't he given you that speech yet?"

Hearing the other woman's words, Jordan felt it. A pang of disappointment, strong enough that she had no choice but to acknowledge it.

Nick didn't do relationships.

It should've meant nothing. Of course he hadn't given her any such speech—there'd been no reason for him to. Because, just like she'd thought, any connection between them was imaginary.

With that in mind, she managed to maintain a nonchalant air in front of Lisa. This was her store, and no one was going to make her look like a fool in it. "You don't really expect me to tell you what Nick and I talk about, do you?" she asked coolly.

"Oh . . . I get it. You haven't slept with him yet, have you?" Lisa smiled smugly. "Listen, honey, I hate to be the bearer of bad news, but you'll hear his speech soon enough—right before he fucks you. It's part of his code or whatever. Trust me, *lots* of women have been down this road with Nick."

Jordan pretended to think this over. "Thanks for the tip, Lisa. This all has been very informative. Particularly the creepy part where you said you followed Nick and stood outside my store watching us." She pointed to a wine display. "Hey—you know what *I* like to do after stalking an ex-boyfriend? Pour myself a nice glass of petite syrah. And you're in luck, because we're having a sale on reds to-day . . ."

ACROSS THE STREET, Mercks's investigator, a man named Tennyson, froze with the camera in his hands when the door to DeVine Cellars flew open. The brunette in yoga pants stormed out, looking pissed. She crossed the street, heading straight toward the car he sat in.

Tennyson panicked. On a whim, he'd decided to follow Jordan Rhodes to see if she gave them something. Anything. Because after eleven days of tailing Stanton, they'd come up with nothing of any significance to report to Eckhart. By now he was familiar with Stanton's routine: the guy wouldn't leave his office for lunch until one o'clock, which meant he had plenty of time to kill.

At first, tailing Jordan Rhodes had seemed to be no less boring than following Stanton. Tennyson had parked his car across the street, and using the zoom on his camera, he could see into the wine store through the front windows. Rhodes made a lot of phone calls, worked at the bar on her laptop computer, and rearranged wine bottles. Really exciting stuff.

But then the brunette with the bombshell figure had shown up, and things had gotten interesting.

Tennyson initially had assumed that the brunette was a customer, and from what he could tell through the camera lens, Jordan Rhodes had assumed that, too. But then the brunette had said something that had made Rhodes tense, and Tennyson had begun paying closer attention. No clue what either woman had said, but from their rigid body language, he personally had been hoping for a cat fight. Then Rhodes smiled, gestured to some wine bottles on the bar, and the brunette stormed out.

Tennyson quickly tossed the camera onto the passenger seat beside him and covered it up with the backpack filled with snacks, water, and cigarettes he always kept on hand during a surveillance. He grabbed his cell phone off the dash and pretended to make a call.

The brunette pulled out her keys and pushed the unlock button, and the lights on the car in front of him blinked. So far, she hadn't noticed him. Tennyson watched out of the corner of his eye as she yanked a cell phone out of her coat pocket and dialed. He'd had a smoke in the car a few minutes earlier, and had cracked the window open to get some fresh air. As such, he was in a perfect position to hear her end of the conversation as she approached her car. It sounded like she was leaving a voice mail message for someone.

"Hello, Nick McCall, or should I say, Nick *Stanton*, whoever the hell you are today—I'd assumed you hadn't called because you were on another undercover assignment, not because you had your dick stuck in some skinny blond bitch. I thought you told me this wasn't about another woman? Guess you lied about that. And why am I not surprised? It's what you do for a living, after all. Lie to people."

The remainder of the brunette's tirade became muffled as she climbed into her car, then she slammed the driver's door shut and everything went quiet.

Tennyson sat in his own car—motionless—still holding the phone in his hand.

Ho-ly fuck.

After the brunette drove off, he made a call of his own.

"Mercks. You are not going to believe this. I think I've got something on Stanton. I mean, I've fucking *got* something. We need to run another background check. This time on the name Nick McCall."

Twenty-one

AT EIGHT O'CLOCK that evening, DeVine Cellars was hopping. Thursdays often were the store's busiest nights, as people liked to get their wine situations settled before the weekend. Tonight was no exception.

Andrea pulled Jordan off to the side. "There's a Nick Stanton on the phone for you. He says it's important."

"On my cell phone?"

"No, the store phone."

"Thanks, Andrea." Jordan went into the back room and picked up the extension. "Hello?"

Nick did not sound pleased. "I've been calling your cell all day."

"I got your messages; I just haven't had a chance to call you back."

"We need to talk about Lisa," he said.

"There's not much to say other than what I already told you in my message." She'd called Nick after Lisa had exited the store in a snit—no clue why that might be—and left a message saying that he might want to keep his eye out for semipsycho, yoga-pant-wearing ex-girlfriends.

"I'm sorry she approached you at your store. That was

way out of line." He paused. "What did she say to you, exactly?"

"Well, she asked some questions about us," Jordan said. "Then there was some talk about your no-relationship policy. How you always tell the women you get involved with that you don't date anyone seriously."

There was a long silence on the other end of the line.

"Oh."

So it's true, Jordan thought.

Nick exhaled raggedly. "Look, Jordan—I can't leave the office right now because I'm working on something that'll take another hour. But we need to talk. I'll come by the store as soon as I'm free."

She tried to sound flip. "There's really nothing to talk about. After all, it's not like you owe *me* any explanations. Although my character was somewhat surprised to learn that you're one of those guys with lame commitment issues."

So much for flip.

Nick paused. "I have a good reason for being one of those guys, you know."

Please. "Those guys always have their reasons." Jordan could hear the noise from all the customers outside. "I need to get going. I've got a store full of customers."

"No, Jordan, we have to—"

There was a knock on the door, and Andrea stuck her head in. "Sorry. There's a customer out front asking to speak with you."

"Unfortunately, sweetie, I really have to go now," she said to Nick. "I'll call you back later." She hung up the phone before she said anything else she'd regret.

With a deep breath, she plastered on her best smile, determined to focus on work. She turned back to Andrea. "Thanks. Did this customer say what he or she wants to speak to me about?"

"*He*. A very good-looking he," Andrea said with a grin.

Jordan tiredly rose from her chair. "Please tell me it's not Xander Eckhart." She definitely was not in the mood to deal with that situation right then.

"It's not Xander. This guy says you owe him a case of wine."

Curious, Jordan followed Andrea out of the back room. The store was crowded, and nearly all the tables were filled with customers drinking wine. She spotted the mystery man, sitting by himself at a table near the dessert wine and champagne section.

He eyed her appraisingly as she walked over. "Jordan Rhodes. Good to see you again."

She stopped before him and smiled. "Cal Kittredge. It's been a while."

AN HOUR LATER, Nick swore under his breath, cursing the lack of parking spots in front of DeVine Cellars. He found one a block away, parked the car, and climbed out. He was a man on a mission tonight, and his target was Jordan Rhodes. Whether she wanted to or not, they needed to talk.

He strode up to DeVine Cellars just after nine o'clock. He peered through the front window, knowing he'd likely see her closing the store.

Bingo.

His eyes followed as she walked over to the bar in her black silk shirt, slim-fit skirt, and high heels. Before going inside, he allowed himself a few seconds to watch her as she grabbed a bottle of wine and carried it over to a table in the corner.

She really was gorgeous. Any man would be lucky to—

Nick stopped midthought, suddenly catching sight of the *guy* she was with. Medium to tall build, model-perfect brown hair, with a scarf wrapped around his neck despite the fact that it was seventy degrees inside the store.

Obviously a douchebag.

Jordan poured wine into two glasses sitting on the table. She set the bottle down and took a seat in the chair opposite the douchebag. He said something she apparently found amusing, and then he picked up the bottle and filled her glass even more.

Nick watched as Jordan sipped her wine and made The Face—the seductive, the-hell-with-wine-you-should-see-what-I-look-like-having-sex face. At least that was how he interpreted it.

Watching her with a predatory gaze, the douchebag grinned. Apparently, he had a similar interpretation of The Face.

Something inside Nick snapped.

That was *his* fake girlfriend in there. Sitting at the table where they had just shared cheese fries the night before. And if she thought she could throw scorching hot sex-looks to any pansy-ass scarf-boy who wandered into her shop, she had another think coming.

He had a look of his own to show the douchebag.

It was time to break out the don't-fuck-with-me face.

JORDAN SET DOWN her glass and closed her eyes as the flavors of the wine enveloped her. "Mmm, I needed that."

"Long day?" Cal asked.

"Very." She glanced around the store. She'd let Andrea leave a few minutes ago, as amends for the extra shift she would have to put in over the weekend. She was relieved to see that things appeared to be in relatively decent shape.

Cal seemed to read her mind. "What if I stuck around and helped you close the store? Then we could check out that new Thai place I was telling you about. It's BYOB, so pick any wine you want." With a grin, he gestured to the wines on the shelves behind them. "It's on the house."

"How generous of you." Jordan swirled her wine. "But I think I'm going to have to pass on Thai."

"Does this have anything to do with Tall, Dark, and Smoldering?"

While grumbling to herself about the ridiculous Scene and Heard column, Jordan thought about the best way to answer Cal's question. "The situation with Tall, Dark, and Smoldering is . . . complicated."

"How complicated?" Cal asked.

You wouldn't believe it if I told you.

The chime on the door rang, and a cold gust of wind

blew in. Jordan looked over and was surprised to see Nick standing in the doorway.

He wore his dark overcoat and a formidable scowl. With his eyes trained on her and Cal, he strode over to their table. "Looks like I'm just in time for last call." Wasting no time, he held out his hand to Cal. "Nick."

"Cal Kittredge."

"Nice to meet you, Cal. The store's closed."

Jordan shot him a look for his rudeness. "Nick."

He held up his watch and tapped it. "See? Nine o'clock."

Cal looked from one to the other. "I get the feeling I've stepped into the middle of something here."

Nick smiled mock-pleasantly. "Yes. And here's your chance to step out of it." He grabbed Cal's coat off the back of his chair and handed it over.

Jordan glared at him. "You can't be serious."

"As a heart attack, sweetie. We need to talk."

She turned back to Cal. "I am so sorry about this. You really don't need to leave."

Cal held up his hand and stood up. "No worries, Jordan. It's probably better that I go. We can talk later when I come back for the wine."

Nick's scowl deepened at that.

Jordan stood up from the table, brushed past Nick, and followed Cal to the door. She went for a joke, trying to cover her embarrassment. "Not the way DeVine Cellars usually treats its customers. I guess I should've warned you that it's 'Take a Tall, Dark, and Scowly Guy to Work' day."

"Remind me about that day next year. I think I'll stay home," Cal said. After a quick good-bye, he was gone.

Needing a moment to calm down, Jordan locked the door and pulled down the shades on the front windows. No need to let any random passerby see that she was about to have a very real argument with her jackass of a fake boyfriend.

When she'd composed herself, she turned around to face Nick. "I cannot believe you just did that."

He had taken off his coat and set it over a chair, an indication that he planned on going nowhere. He leaned back against the table and folded his arms, his light gray sweater pulling tight across his broad chest. "Oh, I'm sorry. Did I interrupt something between you and your customer?"

"Yes, you did interrupt something. It's called a *conversation*. And aside from being a customer, that was Cal Kittredge from the Food and Wine section of the *Tribune*. People in my business don't usually piss him off by throwing him out on his ear."

"I didn't realize he was so important to you," Nick said sarcastically.

Jordan glared at him. "What has gotten into you tonight?"

Nick pushed away from the bar and closed in on her. "I'll tell you what's gotten into me. How do you think it would look if anyone was watching you tonight? They'd see my supposed girlfriend having drinks with another guy."

Of course, Jordan thought. The *investigation*. The only thing he cared about.

"Why was he here anyway?" Nick asked. "Are you . . . interested in this guy?"

She stalked away from him. "I don't have to answer that."

He followed her. "Yes, you do. It could be relevant to the undercover op."

Jordan whirled around. "Oh, blow your undercover op out your ass. I didn't ask any questions when your ex-girlfriend waltzed into my store and told me about the numerous women you've screwed. And how you don't give a damn about any of them because you don't *do* relationships. So the same rule goes for you: no questions. Which means that if I want to have drinks with Cal Kittredge, or any other man, that's *my* business, not yours."

She put her hands on Nick's chest and shoved. *Take that.*

He didn't budge.

Instead, his hand clamped down on her wrist and he pulled her closer. "The hell it isn't," he growled. "I'm making it my business."

His mouth came down on hers and he kissed her. His hand swept to the back of her head as he claimed her lips, rough and possessive. Jordan was pissed off and fired up, and she grabbed his sweater to push him away, but . . .

God, yes.

Instead of pushing, she clutched his sweater and pulled him close. He kissed her until she was breathless, then pulled back and peered down at her with blazing green eyes.

"There. See if the douchebag can kiss you like that," he rasped, his tone both angry and satisfied.

Jordan's cheeks flushed hot, flamed by fury. "I bet there are plenty of douchebags around who can kiss me like that."

"Then I'll have to work harder to stand out from the crowd." Nick grabbed her again.

They slammed against the brick wall next to a shelf of wine bins. Nick's mouth slid down to her neck, and Jordan felt as though her legs melted right there. She had to stifle a moan when his stubbled jaw scraped against her skin.

Rough. Just like she'd imagined it.

"I shouldn't be doing this," she murmured against his ear. "I don't even like you seventy-five percent of the time."

His voice was a silky, hot caress. "But what do you think about the other twenty-five percent?" Not waiting for an answer, his hands slid up the front of her shirt and gripped the collar. He pulled impatiently, and the first button popped open. Then the second.

He pushed back and took in her now exposed bra. His eyes moved to her face and he heatedly held her gaze. He popped open the third button while she watched.

"You could tell me to stop," he said huskily.

Yes, she could.

When she remained silent, he yanked harder and popped open the fourth and last buttons at the same time. She felt the rush of cool air against her heated skin as he captured her mouth with his. While his tongue swirled around hers, he pulled down one of the cups of her bra, groaning deep in his chest when her breast spilled free.

"Nick," she breathed.

He lowered his head and teased one of her nipples with his tongue. She threaded her fingers through his hair, loving the feel of the thick, soft layers.

He yanked down the other cup of her bra, so that both of her breasts were pushed up for his mouth. He groaned when she arched forward eagerly against the brick wall. "God, Jordan, you are so fucking hot."

For you, she nearly blurted out. She bit her lower lip and closed her eyes when his tongue twirled around the peaked tip of her other breast. He slid one of his hands up her thigh, underneath her skirt, and her body trembled with anticipation. He nipped the tight bud of her nipple at the same moment he slid his hand into her panties and cupped her. She gasped, overloaded by the sensation.

He slid a finger inside her and moved it in and out in a deliciously slow motion. He added another finger, then brushed his thumb against her clit, teasing her until her legs were shaking.

"Do you want this?" His lips swept over hers as he continued the exquisite torture with his fingers. "I want to hear you say it. No more games, no more sarcasm. Just the truth."

She didn't need to think—she already knew the truth. Maybe she was a fool to keep going in spite of everything Lisa had said about Nick. But she'd have to be a bigger fool to let some stranger's jealous words dictate how she led her life. She'd make her own decisions about Nick—and have no one to blame but herself for the consequences.

She pulled back to meet his eyes. "Take me home."

Something happened.

She saw it on his face—his expression softened. The tough exterior, the walls, the mask he wore as an undercover agent melted away, leaving just him. He said her name and kissed her again, and she met his mouth eagerly. No holding back now, they peeled away from the wall and made their way to the back room.

Nick held her face in his hands, his gaze hot and possessive. "If I take you home, I'm staying. All night."

Jordan nodded. "And I expect lots of dirty words."

He laughed, then stroked her cheek with his thumb. "Seriously, Rhodes. They broke the mold with you."

She smiled as he leaned down to nuzzle her neck. Melinda and Corinne were right—she did like the way he said her last name.

Her cell phone rang from the back room. Which she ignored, of course.

But when the store phone rang next, she felt Nick go still.

"Ignore it," Jordan said in a throaty voice. "Let me grab my coat and we'll be out of here."

The store phone stopped ringing. Her cell phone started up again.

Nick swore, shaking his head furiously. "I can't believe I did this. I cannot believe I fucking did this." He peered down at her, suddenly very serious. "You need to answer your phone, Jordan."

She reached for him. "Whoever it is can wait. I'm busy right now."

"Actually, it can't wait. It's . . . probably someone calling to tell you that your brother was just stabbed in prison."

Jordan's heart stopped. She pulled her hand back. "*Why* would someone be calling to tell me that?"

Nick checked his watch. "Because about ten minutes ago, your brother was stabbed in prison." He held up his hand when he saw the look on her face. "He's fine. I promise. But you should take this call. If it's your father, I don't want him to panic. I can only imagine what they're saying on the news."

"The news?" She pushed him away from her. "What the hell did you do to my brother?" She quickly adjusted her bra and pulled at her shirt, holding it closed with one hand as she headed for the back room to answer her ringing cell phone.

Nick caught up with her in the hallway. "I know you're freaked out. But right now you need to trust me. If it's your father on the phone, tell him that you spoke to an ER intake nurse at Northwestern Memorial who said that Kyle is okay."

She swallowed. "Kyle's in the emergency room?"

Green eyes held hers steadily. "Just tell your dad that he's okay."

Another leap of faith.

She pulled her wrist out of Nick's grasp, hurried to the back room, and yanked her cell phone out of her purse. She glanced down and saw her shirt gaping open, bra exposed.

Lovely.

She answered her phone. "Dad."

"Jordan—have you seen the news?"

No, sorry. Been busy making out with my fake boyfriend against a brick wall. "About Kyle, I know. I was just about to call you."

Her father exhaled, as if relieved he didn't need to break the news to her. "All I know is what they're saying on TV— that he was stabbed during some kind of fight. They took him out of MCC in an ambulance and brought him to Northwestern Memorial. I've been trying to get ahold of somebody who knows something. Anybody."

Jordan held Nick's eyes while answering her father. "I just got off the phone with an intake nurse in the emergency room. She told me that Kyle is going to be okay."

"Oh, thank God. Then why did they take him out of MCC?" he demanded to know.

A little improvisation was required here. "The nurse said she couldn't give me any details over the phone." She propped the phone against her shoulder, freeing her hands so she could button up her shirt. "I'm getting in the car now, Dad. I'll meet you at the hospital. But everything's going to be okay."

"I believe it when you say it, kiddo. I . . . think you would know if something was wrong with Kyle. You two always know." He cleared his throat. "I'm on my way to the hospital, too. I was having dinner at a friend's in Evanston, but I'll be there as fast as I can."

After Jordan hung up the phone, she stared at it for a moment. "I just lied to my father. That was the one line I hadn't crossed in all of this."

Nick came up behind her and rested his hands on her

shoulders. "You weren't lying when you told him your brother is okay. He *is* okay."

She shrugged away from him. "Tell me what's going on. Why is Kyle in the emergency room?"

"The story being run in the media—which they believe to be true—is that Kyle was stabbed by another inmate during a fight that broke out at lockdown," Nick said.

Jordan fought back the panic that rose in her throat. "And the truth?"

"The truth is that your brother was barely nicked by an undercover agent in a carefully orchestrated operation that now provides us with a plausible excuse to remove him from MCC."

Her head was swimming. "Wait—is Kyle in on this?"

"Of course not," Nick said matter-of-factly. "That hasn't changed—no one can know about our arrangement until the Eckhart investigation is over."

Our arrangement. Right. "You should've told me."

Nick held up his hands. "I know—I fucked up. Big time. I saw you with the douchebag and then you and I started arguing, and . . . then we were doing a lot more than that. I just forgot about everything else. I'm sorry."

Jordan exhaled, not able to process the "everything else" part right then. Making sure her brother was okay was priority number one. "I need to get to the hospital."

Nick held her eyes. "Can I come with you?"

She shook her head. "My dad will be there. He'll want to know who you are, and I'm not ready to have that conversation." Frankly, *she* didn't know what was happening between her and Nick. She certainly couldn't explain it to her father.

In response to her answer, Nick's expression turned more businesslike. He nodded. "Of course. You should be with your family."

He left after that, and Jordan stayed in the back room until she heard the chime ring against the door. She took a moment to collect herself, then grabbed her coat and headed to the hospital.

Twenty-two

XANDER SURVEYED THE dark, seedy interior of the bar, thinking he definitely wasn't going to find a decent glass of wine in this place.

Why Mercks had suggested they meet at this shithole was beyond him. Then again, everything about the text message he'd received earlier that day from Mercks had been odd.

WE NEED TO TALK. NOT YOUR OFFICE—LINCOLN TAVERN ON ROSCOE AT 10 P.M. DON'T SPEAK TO ANYONE ABOUT THIS.

First, it was strange that Mercks had sent him a text message—they'd never communicated by that method before. Second, why couldn't they meet at his office? They always met in his office. The place was a fortress.

Xander found a table near the back of the bar and took a seat, hoping to go as unnoticed as possible. God forbid he was recognized and anyone found out he'd set foot in this place. The mortification would kill him—if whatever skeevy brew they had on tap didn't kill him first.

"No wine list?" he asked sarcastically when a middle-aged waitress with bleached hair approached his table. A far cry from the sleek, pretty young things who waited tables and tended bar at his clubs and restaurants. "I'll take a gin and tonic. Clean glass, please."

He ignored the waitress's look as she headed back to the bar. He shrugged out of his coat, set it carefully over the back of the chair next to him, and glanced at his watch. He frowned when he saw that Mercks was late. He'd hoped to make this a quick meeting, whatever it was about. He wanted to make it back to Bordeaux before the eleven o'clock crowd rushed in. Thursdays were always good nights for them, and he loved being at Bordeaux, watching, mingling, and proudly soaking it all in.

He lived the good life—hell, the great life. And the icing on the cake would be Jordan Rhodes. With her money, his knowledge of nightclubs and restaurants, and their mutual passion for wine, they could be an unstoppable team. She was perfect for him—she just needed to see it. Hopefully Mercks had some positive news on that front.

A few minutes later, Mercks finally showed up. "Sorry. Traffic on the Drive was worse than I'd expected." He set a black leather shoulder bag on the chair next to him. "My usual," he said to the waitress when she approached.

"You come here regularly?" Xander looked around, appalled. "Why?"

"Because nobody asks any questions here."

"Of course they don't. They've got about three working brain cells between them." Xander pointed to a man slumped over the bar. "I don't think that guy's even alive."

"Don't worry about them. Focus, instead, on the question *you* should be asking," Mercks said.

Xander scowled. He never liked games. "What question is that?"

Mercks said the words with emphasis. *"Who is Nick Stanton?"*

Xander sat forward, interested. "You found something? I knew it. No one's that clean. He's a con artist, right?"

"I suppose you could say that's true, in a sense." Mercks pulled a file out of his briefcase and set it on the table. "See for yourself."

Xander opened up the folder and saw a photograph on top. As unexpected as the image was, it took him a moment to process what he was seeing: Nick Stanton wearing a bulletproof vest over a long-sleeved T-shirt and jeans, standing in front of a blue and white squad car as he spoke to two uniformed policemen. It appeared to be some kind of crime scene. The squad car had the letters *NYPD* blazoned prominently across the side.

He looked up at Mercks, confused. "I don't get it. Stanton was a New York cop?"

"Nick *Stanton* doesn't exist—that's a fake identity," Mercks said. "Nick *McCall*, on the other hand, used to be a member of the vice department of the NYPD. He spent five years there before leaving and going back to school. At a small academy in Quantico, Virginia."

Xander's body went cold.

"He's FBI?" he hissed.

"Yes."

Xander jabbed the picture with his finger. "This man, who was at *my* restaurant, drinking *my* wine, is a fucking Fed?"

"Yes. It was hard to find anything recent on him—I suspect he's been working undercover for a while. But we do know that he graduated from the Academy six years ago before moving here."

"So why was he at my party?" Xander asked.

Mercks leveled him with a look. "I think you can answer that better than I can."

There was a moment during which neither man said anything, and Xander wondered how much Mercks knew about his dealings with Roberto Martino. He'd thought he'd taken enough precautions to keep Martino a silent, hidden partner in his businesses, but perhaps that information wasn't as much on the down-low as he'd believed.

The fact that the FBI had sent an undercover man to crash his charity fund-raiser appeared to be confirmation of this.

"Whatever you're involved in, Eckhart, the Feds know," Mercks said quietly.

In a haze, Xander stood up from his chair. "I've got to go."

He pulled out his wallet and threw down a bill without looking at it. "Don't speak to anyone about this." He started to walk away from the table, then stopped and looked back, realizing something. "Jordan. Was she in on this?"

Mercks shook his head. "No clue. The guy I had following McCall caught the aftermath of some catfight she had with another woman. Jordan must have used the name Nick *Stanton*, because the other woman seemed confused by this. We overheard her say his real name when she left him a message. Sounds like the two of them don't see eye to eye on who's dating the real Nick. So it's possible that Jordan has no idea what's going on and that McCall has been playing her all along."

Xander's words dripped with ice. "Find out. I want to know if she's the one who did this to me."

Twenty-three

ON THE DRIVE to the hospital, Jordan caught a news report on a local radio station that informed her, in matter-of-fact terms, that Kyle Rhodes, son of billionaire computer software magnate Grey Rhodes and infamous cyber-terrorist— "It was *Twitter*, people!"—had been stabbed by another inmate and transferred to Northwestern Memorial Hospital. According to the report, "unnamed sources" at Metropolitan Correctional Center had released a statement confirming only that the prison had taken certain measures deemed necessary to ensure the safety of one of its inmates who had been the target of violence on multiple occasions.

Hearing that, Jordan curled her fingers around the steering wheel. She reminded herself of Nick's promise that her brother was fine.

When she arrived at the hospital, she stopped in front of the valet stand, not wasting time with the parking garage. The valet in his early twenties eyed the Maserati in awe as she stepped out of the driver's seat.

"Nice," he told her.

She quickly handed him the keys. "Just keep it under eighty." She hurried through the sliding doors of the emergency room, trying not to think of the last time she'd rushed there after getting a frantic call from her father. That call had been about her mother's car accident, and by the time she had arrived at the hospital, it had been too late.

Jordan pushed the memory from her mind. *Not this time.* She walked to the front desk, where a young receptionist greeted her with a polite smile.

"I'm here to see my brother, Kyle Rhodes. He was brought in about a half hour ago."

The receptionist's eyes widened. "Oh, yes—he passed right by here. He was kind of hard to miss, with the orange jumpsuit and the two prison guards following the stretcher."

"Stretcher?" Jordan inhaled unsteadily. "Did he seem, you know, okay?"

The receptionist's face brightened as she got That Look women often got around Kyle. "He seemed angry about the stretcher, but other than that, he looked fine. Although he did have the top part of his jumpsuit pushed down, with a bandage on his left arm. He was wearing only a T-shirt, but I didn't see any blood on it or anything. Just that tight, white T-shirt. Very tight. Muscle-hugging, I'd say . . ."

Her voice trailed away as she stared off dreamily.

Jordan rolled her eyes. "He used to stick Skittles up his nose and shoot them into our mother's flower pots. He called it 'target practice.'" She snapped her fingers, trying to bring the woman back to reality. "So come on—where is he?"

The receptionist came out of her daze. "Right. Sorry." She punched something into the computer. "They moved him up to room 360-A." She pointed. "Elevators are down the hall and to the left."

IT WOULD BE hard to miss Kyle's room, considering it was the one with two armed prison guards standing out front. Jordan recognized one of them as her buddy from her visits to MCC, Mr. Cranky with all the rules.

He raised an eyebrow as she approached. "Girl-Sawyer . . . we were wondering when you were going to show up."

Jordan stopped before him. "Does this mean we're friends now?"

He gestured to their surroundings. "Different setting, different rules."

"How's my brother?"

"A little riled up. Mostly pissed about the stretcher." He pointed to the door behind him. "The doctor is checking him out now. You can go in if you want," he said with a kinder tone than usual.

"Thank you." Jordan paused, thinking she saw a spark of knowing in Mr. Cranky's eyes. She wondered how much the prison guard knew about her deal with the FBI, and if that had anything to do with his sudden change in attitude. She tabled that issue and pushed open the door to Kyle's room.

Her brother was sitting upright on an examination bed, with the orange jumpsuit pushed down around his waist and a bandage on his forearm. His other hand was handcuffed to the side of the bed. He argued with the doctor who hovered over him with a needle.

"A tetanus shot? You guys carried me in here like an invalid for a *tetanus shot?*" He scowled.

"Ignore him. He's always been a baby about shots," Jordan said from the doorway.

Kyle looked over and grinned. "Jordo."

The doctor seized on the distraction and promptly stuck him in the shoulder with the needle.

"Son of a—" Kyle half shouted in surprise. "That hurt more than the damn fork."

"You'll probably have some soreness at the injection site for a couple days," the doctor said, not looking sorry at all. He stuck a Band-Aid on Kyle's shoulder. Jordan smiled when she saw that it had Elmo faces on it. Such a tough guy, her brother.

She walked over to the table, thinking she must've heard him wrong. "Did you just say that you were stabbed with a fork?"

"Yes, I was stabbed with a fork," Kyle grumbled.

The corners of Jordan's mouth twitched. "I see."

Kyle beckoned with his hand. "All right. Let's just get it over with."

"Salad or regular?"

"You know, I didn't stop to measure it as it was going into my arm," Kyle said sarcastically. "Fucking Puchalski."

Jordan's mouth dropped open, and she barely noticed as the doctor left the room. "Puchalski? The harmless bald guy with the snake tattoo?" *He* was the undercover agent on the inside?

Inconceivable.

Kyle threw out his free hand in exasperation. "I know— he and I always got along fine. Then tonight during lock-down, we were in line heading back to our cells and he starts up again with the Sawyer crap. So I told him to drop it, like I've told him a hundred times before, and he just *loses* it. Grabs me by the collar, tackles me to the ground, and starts yelling that he can call me whatever the hell he wants. Then he pulls a fork out of his shoe and does this."

He shifted and lifted the bandage with his handcuffed hand, revealing four red—and pretty damn tiny—puncture wounds. Jordan squinted. "Is there something I'm supposed to be looking at there?"

Kyle made a face. "Very funny. It stung like a bitch. For at least . . . two or three minutes." He saw her staring at him and cocked his head. "What?"

Jordan said nothing. Instead, she reached out and did something she hadn't been able to do in four months. She hugged her brother hard and held on for as long as she wanted. "I'm just glad to see you're okay."

"Don't be getting all mushy on me now. You know the rules," Kyle growled. But he squeezed her back tightly with his free arm.

She felt tears of relief spring into her eyes. "Different set-ting, different rules." She pulled back, and quickly brushed at her eyes. "Mr. Cranky the prison guard told me that."

"Did he also happen to tell you why they brought me to this hospital?" Kyle asked. "Because I sure as hell can't fig-ure it out."

There was a voice to their left.

"They brought you here because I asked them to."

An attractive woman with long brown hair and wearing a gray pin-striped suit stood in the doorway. She walked over and shook hands with Jordan and Kyle.

"Cameron Lynde, U.S. attorney," she said in introduction. She folded her arms across her chest and studied Kyle. "So what do we do with you now, Mr. Rhodes? I've been getting all sorts of reports that you're having problems at MCC."

Kyle brushed his hair off his face defensively. "Nothing I can't handle."

"Six fights in the last four months—and now this attack. You're a PR disaster waiting to happen," Cameron said.

Jordan threw Kyle a look. "You only told me about four fights."

"It's *nothing*," Kyle said to both of them.

The U.S. attorney appeared to mull this over. "I don't like it. With the media's interest in your case, if something happened to you at MCC, my office would take a lot of heat."

"Your office didn't seem too concerned about my well-being four months ago," Kyle said.

"I think it's safe to say that the *former* U.S. attorney had a very different agenda than I do," Cameron said. "You've served four months of hard time—harder than many others. Perhaps we can look into an alternate arrangement."

"Thanks, but no thanks. I don't want to be shipped off to another prison—the same thing will just happen there." Kyle pointed begrudgingly to Jordan. "Plus, if you take me out of Chicago, I'd miss my annoying sister's cheery visits."

Jordan nearly got teary-eyed again. That may have been the nicest thing her pain-in-the-ass brother had ever said to her. She put her arm around him. "He's the gum I can't scrape off the bottom of my shoe," she explained to the U.S. attorney.

Cameron laughed. "I have a friend like that." She turned back to Kyle. "I wasn't talking about moving you to a different prison. I was thinking more along the lines of home detention."

The door opened again, and a tall and well-built man wearing jeans and a corduroy blazer walked into the room. He carried a backpack in one hand. Jordan recognized him as the FBI agent who'd "accidentally" bumped into her at Starbucks and slipped Nick's keys into her coat pocket. But if the agent recognized her—and she was sure he did—he gave away nothing.

"Agent Pallas. Perfect timing," Cameron said.

"Are we all set?" he asked.

"I was just about to explain to Mr. Rhodes how this will work." She turned back to Kyle. "This is Special Agent Jack Pallas—he's going to fit you with an electronic monitoring device that you'll wear around your ankle twenty-four hours a day. Inside the device is a GPS transmitter that will tell the supervising probation officer in charge of your parole where you are at all times. You'll be able to work, and will be permitted to leave your residence for preapproved purposes like doctor's appointments, court appearances, things of that nature. Your probation officer will go over the specifics of the arrangement with you."

Kyle held up his hand, confused. "Probation officer, parole—what are you talking about? I have twelve more months of incarceration to serve."

"Not anymore. You're going home, Mr. Rhodes."

Agent Pallas moved to Kyle's side. He took keys out of his pocket and unlocked the handcuff with a *snap*.

Kyle stared at his free hand for a moment, then peered up at Cameron with a confused expression. "I don't understand. Why would you do this?"

Of course, three people in the room knew the true answer to that question. But Jordan maintained her poker face, as did the U.S. attorney.

"Because it's the fair thing to do, Mr. Rhodes. That's the best answer I can give you," Cameron said. "One thing, however—for appearances' sake, I think it would be best if you spent tonight at the hospital. And I'd appreciate it if you would keep a low profile over the next couple weeks."

"Not a problem. It's not like I have an active social calendar these days," Kyle said.

"Sit back and put your left leg on the table," Agent Pallas told him. He unzipped the backpack and pulled out a black ankle monitor.

Kyle lifted the leg of his jumpsuit. "I don't know what to say," he said to Cameron. "Thank you, I guess. It's good to see they've replaced Silas Briggs with someone who's a little more reasonable." He grinned. "Not to mention, someone with a much prettier face."

Agent Pallas snapped the ankle monitor on, and Kyle yelled out in pain.

"Son of a bitch, you got some skin there!" he said to Pallas.

Cameron threw the FBI agent a look. "Jack."

He shrugged. "It slipped." He turned back to Kyle with a look that could wilt plants.

"Easy there, Wolverine," Kyle grumbled. "Put the claws back in—I meant no disrespect."

There was a knock at the door. Mr. Cranky the prison guard stuck his head in. "Hey—we've got a package for Sawyer."

"You're getting deliveries at the hospital already?" Jordan asked her brother.

Agent Pallas went to the door. He took the package from Mr. Cranky, which turned out to be a blue garment bag, and brought it into the room. He hung the bag on the back of the door, unzipped it, and did a quick check of the contents.

"Clothes? Did you arrange for that?" Cameron asked Jack.

He shook his head. "Must've been one of the other agents." He stole a glance at Jordan, and she knew.

Nick.

Cameron clapped her hands together. "Well. I'm sure you two don't want us hanging around any longer." She pulled a card out of her jacket pocket and handed it to Kyle. "This is the contact information for your probation officer. He'll be expecting you to call him tomorrow when you get home. Remember, we'll be watching." She joined Agent Pallas at the door, and paused before the two of them left. "And stay away from Twitter, Mr. Rhodes. For all our sakes." With an efficient turn of her heel, she was gone.

"Are they serious?" Kyle asked Jordan. "I can just walk out of here tomorrow?"

She shrugged innocently. "Looks that way." She pointed to the garment bag. "Let's see what's inside."

Kyle got up from the hospital bed and walked over to the bag. He unzipped it and pulled out jeans and a gray long-sleeved shirt. "Jeans." He fingered the material, turning quiet. When he finally spoke, his voice was thick with emotion. "Never thought I'd be so glad to see denim in my life."

He regrouped and threw Jordan a wry look. "Who'd have thought the FBI could be so thoughtful?"

She came over and rested her head against her brother's shoulder. *Or one agent in particular, at least.* "I think there's more to some of these FBI guys than meets the eye."

The door flew open and Grey Rhodes rushed in, looking harried despite his tailored sport coat and dark pants. He saw Kyle, exhaled in relief, and rested his hands on his knees like he might pass out from running. "You're here."

"Not for long." Kyle threw his arms out with a grin. "Starting tomorrow, I'm a free man."

Grey looked over at Jordan. "They didn't say he had a head injury."

Jordan smiled. "No, it's true, Dad. Kyle's been released from prison. And he was stabbed with a fork."

Her brother stared at the ceiling. "I'm going to be hearing about this for years, aren't I?"

"Kyle, dear brother of mine, you have no idea."

"EVERYTHING OKAY, XANDER?"

The question came from Will Parsons, who was once again on duty as general manager that night. Bordeaux was packed, as expected. Xander stood in the doorway between the main lounge and wine bar, a position from which he could see virtually the entire club. He wanted to watch for a few minutes. Soak it all in.

"I'm fine," he told Will. Of course, that wasn't true.

He was fucked. He should've been satisfied with being

the top nightclub and restaurant owner in the city. But a year ago, he'd gotten greedy.

Sure, he could say that no one refused Roberto Martino. And this was true—at least, no one refused Roberto Martino without suffering some very serious consequences. But Xander hadn't needed to be coerced; he'd been perfectly willing to have Martino invest in his businesses as a silent partner. And now, it seemed, he would pay the price for that.

"I'm heading down to my office. I don't want to be disturbed," he told Will.

Will nodded. "Of course."

Xander cut through the VIP wine bar and entered the security code on the panel next to the door that led to the lower level. As he descended the staircase and walked along the hallway to his office, he ran over the events of his wine tasting two weeks ago—the evening that Nick Stanton, aka Special Agent Nick McCall, had infiltrated the heart of his empire.

He wasn't a fool—he had a pretty good idea what McCall had been after that night. Access to his meetings with Trilani.

If it hadn't meant that he was so thoroughly screwed, Xander could almost admire the FBI's cleverness. Using Jordan Rhodes—either with or without her knowledge—to get into his office on virtually the only night such an act was possible took careful, intricate planning.

And now he was a dead man.

Roberto Martino would kill him for letting the FBI in—inadvertently or not. That was the price one paid for doing business with Martino—mistakes were not tolerated, particularly where money was concerned. Xander foolishly had assumed he was above any such mistakes.

He entered his office and took a seat at his desk. As he sat there, knowing that the room was undoubtedly bugged, the weight of the situation pressed down on him like an anvil. He had the FBI coming in from the front, gearing up to launch a full-fledged attack, and Roberto Martino behind him, ready to slit his throat at the first sign of trouble.

He pulled his cell phone out of his jacket and called Trilani, knowing he would get his voice mail. He heard the beep.

"Carlo," he said in a strained, weak voice. "We can't meet tomorrow. I've got the stomach flu, whatever that thing is that's been going around. Trust me, you don't want to get close to this. I should be fine by next week—let's meet Tuesday instead."

Xander hung up. *Got all that, you FBI pricks?*

Unable to resist, he quietly ran his hand underneath the desk, searching for the bugs. He found nothing. He got up and walked over to the bookshelves on the other side of his office and gave them a thorough once-over. Again nothing. He moved next to the coffee table and chairs in the corner of the room and felt around. He came up empty-handed yet again. Nick McCall apparently knew a thing or two about planting bugs in well-hidden places.

Then there was the issue of Jordan.

Xander remembered all too well how she'd pulled him away from the crowd and asked to have a drink with him on the terrace—allegedly to discuss the case of Pétrus going to auction. He didn't want to believe she had deliberately betrayed him. Maybe there was a part of him that simply didn't want to accept the fact that he so naively could have feelings for someone who had no problem stabbing him in the back.

As he'd told Mercks, he wanted to know what Jordan knew. And if it turned out that she had been involved with the FBI, she would pay for her betrayal.

That, at least, was the one part of this messed-up situation he could control.

Twenty-four

JORDAN LEFT THE hospital shortly after midnight. She stepped outside to retrieve her car from the valet, only to discover that there was no valet. A sign informed her that parking attendants were available until eleven P.M.—information that would've been helpful an hour ago.

She went back inside the hospital, handed her ticket over at the first-floor customer service desk, and retrieved her car key. The clerk directed her to the parking garage across the street.

"The valet leaves the unclaimed cars on level two," he said.

Braving the icy wind coming in off Lake Michigan, Jordan trudged dutifully across the street. At the elevator bank, she saw that each level had been assigned a famous singer and a song to help people remember where they'd parked. Level two, her stop, was Frank Sinatra. "Chicago," naturally.

Inside the elevator, she leaned her head against the wall tiredly.

Long day. Crazy day. First the unexpected visit from Lisa, then her angry argument with Nick, then the not-so-angry moments with Nick, then her brother had been stabbed (sort of) and released from prison.

She definitely was ready for Napa.

When the elevator arrived at her floor, she stepped out and spotted her car. She stopped in surprise when she saw Nick leaning against the Maserati, waiting for her.

Her heart skipped a beat.

An interesting fact, because she wasn't typically a heart-beat-skipping kind of girl.

"I didn't expect to see you here," she said.

He watched her approach. "I couldn't leave things the way they were between us. Hopefully you don't think I'm that big of an asshole."

Actually, she didn't think he was an asshole at all. She stepped closer. "You must be freezing from standing out here," she said softly.

He gestured to his car. "I've only been here for about a minute. I got out of my car when I saw the elevator coming up. Can we talk?"

Jordan pushed the unlock button on her key, and the Maserati's headlights blinked. "Have a seat." She walked around and slid into the driver's side of the car. Nick climbed into the passenger seat, his long legs and tall frame filling the space next to her.

She started the car and turned on the seat warmers—his first, then hers. He appeared both amused and touched by the gesture. "Thank you."

Warm air blasted all around them as the heat kicked in.

Jordan angled herself in the seat and, without saying a word, leaned forward to kiss him. A long, deep kiss.

"That was for what you did for my brother," she said when she pulled back.

His eyes shone like emeralds. "I told you I'd get him out of prison. It just took some creativity."

"But you didn't have to send him the clothes. That meant a lot to Kyle."

Nick ran a finger along her cheek, his voice husky. "We both know I didn't do it for Kyle."

She did know that. She slid her hands inside his coat and shifted closer to the warmth that radiated from him. "So tell me this, Nick McCall. Where do we go from here?"

Nick had been asking himself that very question all night. He went with the truth. "I have no idea." He tilted her chin up, wanting to look her in the eyes when he said this. "You know that my job makes things complicated. You've seen it firsthand. I go from identity to identity—gone on assignment for weeks and months at a time."

Jordan paused. "And?"

He cocked his head, not following her. "And . . . that's what makes things so complicated."

"No, I get that part. I'm just waiting for the rest. According to Lisa, you're supposed to give me this whole long speech. I've been feeling a little left out."

He chucked her under the chin. *Smart-ass.* "You're not getting the same speech everyone else does."

"Oh." She smiled, looking extremely pleased. "Good."

"That still doesn't tell us where we go from here."

Jordan sat back and stared at him for a long moment, as if debating something. "I'm going to Napa tomorrow, for the weekend. You could come with me." She raised an eyebrow. "It even works with your character. Nick Stanton would never let his girlfriend go to such a romantic place alone."

Now it was Nick's turn to fall silent. Not because he wasn't tempted as hell by the offer—but there was something else. "I don't know what you're really asking me here," he said candidly.

She considered this. "For now, I'm just asking if you want to spend the weekend with me in Napa."

An entire weekend alone with her. In a hotel room. Christ, he got hard just thinking about it. "A man would have to be a saint not to be tempted by that offer, Rhodes."

Sensing his hesitation, Jordan rested her elbow against the smooth, tan Italian leather of her seat. "I'm a big girl, Nick. And I've been fully briefed on your 'issues' with relationships, so you can consider me duly warned." She grinned mischievously. "Frankly, I don't think it'll matter. There's at least a fifty percent chance you'll annoy me so much on this trip that I'll be glad to see you go afterward."

Nick laughed at that and hooked his finger into her coat. He pulled her closer. "And if by some miracle I fail to accomplish that?"

Her voice was low and throaty, anticipating his kiss. "Then we'll deal with that when we get there."

Something in Nick's chest pulled tight. Xander Eckhart had been right about one thing: Jordan Rhodes *was* out of his league. Hell, she was out of everyone's league.

The aforementioned saint would probably walk away, knowing that a man with a job like his had no business getting in deeper with a woman like her. Because a saint would also know that whatever he could give Jordan, she would always deserve more.

So call him a devil. Because walking away from her right then was not something he could do. Instead, he slanted his mouth over hers, taking his time with this kiss. No need to rush now—starting tomorrow, she was his for two nights. Days, too. The possibilities . . .

"I should mention one thing," Jordan said.

"Hmm?" he said distractedly. His mouth broke away from hers to trail a path along her throat. The hell with wine—she reminded him instead of the smoothest, richest bourbon he'd ever tasted. And she was definitely making him burn.

"This is a business trip for me," she continued. "So you'll have to go to some wine tastings."

Nick swore, his mouth going still at her neck. "I knew there'd be a catch."

She laughed. "You'll live." She pulled back and cocked her head. "Can I ask you something? It's been bothering me all night."

"Fire away."

"*Puchalski* is a federal agent? That's some cover."

"We placed him inside MCC two months ago. His cell-mate is one of the leaders of a south side gang—somebody we think is responsible for a string of murders. We're hoping the cell-mate will get chatty and start bragging about his so-called accomplishments."

"How'd you convince him to go along with stabbing my brother? Poor Puchalski. He's probably in disciplinary segregation because of all this."

Nick snorted. "To get him into the right cell, we had to coordinate with MCC. The guards know who he is. Your friend 'Puchalski' will be just fine. He's probably hanging out in the warden's office right now, drinking beer and watching TV while *pretending* to be in disciplinary segregation."

"Well, I'm very impressed that you pulled it all off." Jordan smiled slyly. "You know . . . this special-agent thing is kind of sexy at times."

Nick grinned to himself. *Good.* Let the douchebag try to top that.

Twenty-five

XANDER HAD BEGUN to panic.

He was trapped in his home, under the guise that he was recovering from the stomach flu. Granted, his home was a three-bedroom, four-thousand-square-foot condo in the luxurious Trump International Hotel & Tower, so being trapped there wasn't exactly a hardship. But all that alone time had given him hours upon hours to reflect on the gigantic, steaming pile of shit the FBI had just dumped on his doorstep.

His first thought had been to shred every account statement, financial record, and tax document connected to Bordeaux and his other clubs and restaurants. Then he realized this would be a worthless endeavor—his accountants, the banks, and the IRS all had their own copies and records of everything he'd ever filed. Not to mention, he kept most of that information in his office at Bordeaux, and he certainly didn't want the FBI hearing him cleaning out his files. The one and only advantage he had right then was that no one except for Mercks knew he was onto them.

His second thought had been to turn himself over to the Feds and try to work out some kind of deal to testify against Martino. There was one problem with this: there was a hundred percent chance that Martino would try to have him killed before he ever got to testify, and about a ninety-five percent chance that he would succeed even if the Feds placed him under protective custody.

Not good odds.

Simply put, Xander didn't want to die.

It seemed strange to be thinking in those terms. Of course he didn't want to die; no one wanted to die. But in the last twenty-four hours, it had occurred to him that this was a very real, imminent possibility. And if Roberto Martino ever discovered that he had practically handed over the evidence of their money laundering to the FBI—for fuck's sake, he'd given Nick McCall a *tour* of the lower level—that death was not only going to be imminent, but extremely painful.

Just days ago, he thought he'd been on his way to being king of the world. His biggest concern had been a woman. What he wouldn't give to go back and freeze his life right there.

Xander stood in the kitchen, staring inside the massive subzero refrigerator that was stocked twice a week by his housekeeper—who he'd given the weekend off, using the flu excuse. At this point, he didn't trust *anyone*. He needed to force himself to eat, despite the constant gnawing, queasy feeling in his stomach. He had to keep his energy up so he could think.

His cell phone rang. He reached into his pants pocket, pulled it out, and saw it was Mercks. "What did you find out?"

"You mean other than what they're saying on TV?" Mercks asked.

Xander's mouth went dry. "They're talking about me on TV? Did the FBI make an announcement?"

"No, not you. I meant about Kyle Rhodes. It's everywhere—in the papers, on TV, on the Internet. How have you missed this?"

Xander headed for his library. How had he missed some irrelevant story about Kyle Rhodes? Because television sucked nowadays, that's how—all reality shows and hour-long dramas that introduced some mysterious event that was dragged out for seven seasons before coming to a wholly anticlimactic finale that explained jack shit. And while he normally read the paper, he'd been a little bit preoccupied with other matters over the last eighteen hours—primarily, how to keep himself alive and out of jail.

"Hold on—I've got the *Tribune* here somewhere." Sure enough, he found it on the desk in his library where he'd tossed it with his mail earlier that morning, tucked under the new *Wine Spectator*. He pulled the newspaper out and read the headline: "Twitter Terrorist Released After Stabbing."

"Rhodes is free?" he asked Mercks.

"Apparently, he was attacked in prison. The U.S. attorney released a statement saying that she agreed to permit him to serve the remainder of his sentence in home detention out of concern for his safety."

"And this interests me because . . . ?"

"I can't help but wonder if Kyle Rhodes was released because someone else paid his debt to society."

Xander felt the sickening betrayal in his stomach. "You think Jordan made a deal? Me for her brother's release?"

"I think that's certainly a possibility."

Xander fell silent for a moment. "Where is she now?"

"She drove to the airport this morning with McCall. Tennyson followed them inside the terminal and overheard them checking in. They caught a flight to San Francisco."

Xander knew Jordan—she and McCall weren't staying in San Francisco. He'd bet half a billion dollars they were in the Napa Valley instead. "I think you've told me everything I need to know." His mouth pulled tight. "I see no reason to follow her and McCall any longer."

"I know this wasn't the information you were looking for."

"You did your job, Mercks. Don't worry, you'll still get paid."

After Xander hung up, he paced through his penthouse like a caged tiger. He felt trapped, so trapped he could barely breathe. He ran his hand through his hair—for the first time since Mercks had laid the news on him about the FBI, he felt wild, out of control.

Goddamn Jordan Rhodes had sold him out.

"*Fucking bitch!*" He whipped around and threw his phone at a silver-framed decorative mirror hanging on the wall in the foyer. The glass shattered and fell in large shards to the travertine floor.

He stared at the broken glass and walked over. For the past eighteen hours, he'd had no one to focus his anger on other than himself. *He* had been the greedy bastard. *He*, like many people, had naively assumed that Martino and his organization were untouchable and beyond the reach of the law. Apparently the new U.S. attorney, with her so-called war on crime, had not received the memo: this was Chicago—corruption was *expected*.

And while he loathed the FBI, he wasn't surprised by their actions—they were pigs; this is what they did. He was no one to them, just a name on a case file. A target.

But Jordan knew him. Knew him well enough to be able to tease him about his favorite kinds of wine. Well enough to score an invitation every year to his exclusive party. Well enough to make him have feelings for her.

Xander picked the largest shard of glass off the tile. He ran his finger along the jagged edge and winced when it pierced his skin. A drop of blood popped through, cabernet red, and he stared at it, suddenly feeling more grounded and clearheaded than he had in days.

Twenty-six

"MAYBE I SHOULD drive the rest of the way. So you can take a break."

Jordan took her eyes off the road to look over at Nick. "We're five miles from the resort. I'm pretty sure I can make it."

"But these roads are very hilly. Winding. Wouldn't you feel more comfortable with me driving?"

"I've been doing just fine for the last three and a half hours."

Actually, Nick had been doing just fine, too. He'd rather enjoyed being chauffeured by Jordan during their drive from the airport. It had given him plenty of time to enjoy the gorgeous view: the long, blond hair pulled back in a sophisticated knot, the crisp white summer dress, the silk scarf wrapped elegantly around her neck, and the many inches of sleek, slender legs.

And the picturesque rolling hills dotted with white and pink blossoming flowers weren't half bad, either.

"But perhaps *I* would be more comfortable if I drove the rest of the way," he said. Clearly, she wasn't picking up on his subtle message.

Jordan pulled the car to a stop in the left turn lane of the divided highway, about to take them onto a side street that led into a canyon. She turned to face him. "Okay. What's going on? Why would *you* suddenly be more comfortable driving?"

"We're not supposed to stand out, remember? We're still undercover. And I suspect that ritzy places like this are accustomed to seeing the man driving the car. People are going to think I'm your assistant or something."

She pointed. "Now *that* would be a fun cover—let's do that one for a change. I get to be in charge, and you have to call me Ms. Rhodes all weekend."

"No."

"I'll even get you a little notepad, and you can follow me around taking dictation. And I'll make you drive ten miles to the nearest Starbucks to get me a latte, which I'll send back three times until you get it just right. Because that's what all the *rich* women do."

"You're joking about this."

"Of course I'm joking," Jordan said. "Otherwise, I'd have to take your comment seriously about the man needing to drive the car, and I'm in far too good of a mood to lecture you on the fact that sexual politics have changed somewhat since the 1950s."

"Speaking of the 1950s, has anyone ever told you that you look like Grace Kelly?"

Jordan relaxed, smoothing back her hair. "Actually, my grandfather used to say that. You're trying to change the subject, aren't you?"

"Definitely. In hindsight, that assistant comment probably wasn't so slick. I should warn you—I may have these momentary Cro-Magnon lapses from time to time. Bygones."

Jordan opened her mouth to say something, then shut it. She threw her hands into the air. "How do you always do that? You tiptoe right to the edge of thoroughly pissing me off, then somehow you sweet-talk your way out of it."

Nick grinned. "Aha. I told you when we met that you'd know if I was sweet-talking you."

Jordan stared out the front windshield, shaking her head.

"Seriously, I must've killed somebody's prized goat or something in a former life. And this is my penance."

He laughed. "Oh, admit it. You love it."

"That's the penance part. My slow descent into madness."

Seeing the grin curling at the edges of her lips, Nick leaned forward in his seat to kiss her. "Aw, you say the sweetest things." And he wouldn't have it any other way.

They continued their drive, and as the trees grew even thicker, he began to wonder about this resort she was taking him to. They turned a corner, and she veered the car onto a one-lane street that took them over a narrow bridge.

"What's the name of this place we're staying at?" He realized how odd it was that he needed to ask. Since they'd landed in San Francisco, Jordan had been calling the shots. Both the FBI agent and Cro-Magnon in him felt somewhat unsettled by this. *He* was used to taking charge of a situation—any situation.

With another glance at Jordan, he decided to go with the flow. For now. At the very least, it gave him a few more minutes to enjoy the view.

"Calistoga Ranch," she answered him.

"It seems off the beaten path," he said.

"It's meant to have a rustic, one-with-nature kind of feel," Jordan said. They drove around another bend, and then pulled into a clearing at what appeared to be the main lodge. Several cars lined the driveway ahead of them, and Nick did a quick tally: two Mercedes, one Porsche 911, a BMW 6 Series, and an Aston Martin.

Nick raised an eyebrow as Jordan parked their rental car behind the Aston Martin. "Rustic?"

"Well . . . call it 'rich-person rustic,' " she conceded. She opened her door and slid out of the car, all long, slim legs and heels and her golden blond hair shining in the warm California sun. In an instant, she looked like she belonged.

"Welcome back, Ms. Rhodes," said the valet as he took the keys from her. "Did you have a pleasant flight?"

"Very pleasant. Thank you."

"I'll load the bags into the cart while you check in." With an efficient nod, the valet took off.

Nick came around the car and took Jordan's hand. "The cart?"

"Cars aren't allowed on the resort grounds, so they shuttle us to and from our room in a golf cart."

"Rich-person rustic doesn't include walking?"

"Our room is a mile away. Uphill." She pulled him closer. "I know it's asking a lot, sweetie, but try to enjoy yourself. You might be surprised and actually like it here."

Nick took a look around. His first thought was that it was a good thing he hadn't taken a vacation in a while, because he definitely was going to need the extra cash to pay for his half of the trip. If Jordan thought he was letting her foot the bill, she could think again. Where he came from, men did not mooch off their girlfriends. Even their obscenely wealthy heiress girlfriends.

Girlfriend.

His left eye began to twitch.

Jordan looked over. "You okay?"

"Just a little pollen or something." He rubbed his eye for emphasis.

They entered a large, Western-style main lodge, where a front desk clerk greeted them. She seemed to recognize Jordan immediately, confirmed her reservation for a one-bedroom hillside lodge, and produced an actual set of keys. Apparently, rich-person rustic didn't include key cards, either.

Within minutes, they were in a golf cart, cruising along a small paved road with a thickly forested cliff on one side of them and a lake on the other. Along the way, they passed by several bungalow-style guest lodges set a good distance apart for privacy.

From behind his sunglasses, Nick studied the valet in the front seat of the golf cart. No more than twenty-three years old, the blond, tanned guy looked like he should be sitting on the beach in a lifeguard chair. Instead, he chatted animatedly with Jordan about a winery he'd recently discovered.

After a several-minute drive, the valet parked the cart at

the edge of a walkway that led up a hill. "You know the drill, Jordan. Gotta hoof it from here. I'll grab the bags."

"*I'll* grab the bags." Nick gave the valet a tip and a look that said that no further assistance, questions, comments, or wine chitchat was necessary. Jordan looked on with amusement, but said nothing as she led him up a path with stairs that led to a bungalow on a hill. She unlocked a gate, and they stepped onto a large covered patio complete with a fireplace, an outdoor living area, and an incredible view of the canyon below them.

She used a second key to unlock a glass door that took them inside the lodge and into a living room with a marble-surround fireplace and state-of-the-art entertainment center.

"So this is rich-person rustic." Nick set the bags down and looked around. Through the windows, he could see that the master suite was an entirely separate space on the opposite end of the patio. He walked back outside, cut across the deck, and opened the door to the bedroom. He took in the king bed covered with plush pillows and the dark cherry dressers and nightstands. Adjacent to the bedroom was a large stone and granite bathroom complete with two vanities, an oversized tub, and a combination steam/rain shower. French doors along one wall of the bathroom led to a private *outdoor* shower.

"Think it'll do?" Jordan asked from behind him.

Nick turned around, slightly embarrassed to have been caught gawking at their surroundings. He shrugged, taking on a nonchalant tone. "Sure. I've just never known anyone who could afford all this." He reached down and unstrapped the gun harness from his calf. He set it on the nightstand next to the bed, along with his wallet.

Jordan gestured to the gun. "Well, I've never known anyone who walked around with one of those strapped to his leg. So I guess this is something new for both of us."

Nick straightened up, the reality of the situation hitting him. Here he was: an FBI agent from Brooklyn, spending the weekend in wine country with a woman who would one day inherit a half-billion dollars.

He walked over to her. "What are we doing?"

She smiled slightly, as if she'd been wondering this herself. "I have no clue."

Nick peered down at her, standing close to, but not yet past, the point of no return. Jordan didn't move, just looked at him through half-lowered eyes. Waiting.

Without a word, he reached up and tugged her hair out of its knot. He watched as it spilled over her shoulders in blond waves, a wild contrast to the sophisticated dress, scarf, and designer high-heeled shoes she wore.

He stepped across the remaining space that divided them. "So what do billionaire heiresses like to do in the Napa Valley?"

She held his gaze. "Right now, probably the same thing as FBI agents from Brooklyn."

Enough said.

JORDAN KNEW, FROM the look in Nick's eyes when he scooped her up in his arms and plunked her down on top of the covers, that the time for jokes was over.

He pinned her hands in one of his against the comforter, then leaned down and kissed her, hot and demanding. She swirled her tongue around his, no playing around this time, and no teasing. When she arched against him, he released his grip and slid his hands down her arms. Then he continued over the swell of her breasts.

He grabbed hold of the V-neck collar and ripped her dress open.

She gasped against his mouth. "My, somebody is impatient."

His voice had a rough edge. "It's your fault. I've been thinking about getting you naked since the first time I saw you drink wine." He ran his thumb along her lower lip. "I've thought about a lot of things."

While holding his gaze, Jordan licked the tip of his thumb and watched as his eyes turned dark and smoldering. He pushed the dress down her arms and tossed it onto the floor, and the scarf around her neck quickly followed. Then he pulled back and looked at her.

Normally, she would've felt self-conscious, lying in her bra and panties with the bright light of the afternoon sun streaming into the bedroom. But then Nick ran one of his hands along her body, from her throat to her hip, and the undisguised wanting she saw on his face made her feel quite bold instead.

She kicked off her shoes and reached for his shirt. "Your turn."

He watched as she undid the buttons of his shirt. After she pushed it off him, he grabbed the bottom edge of his white T-shirt and pulled it over his head. He knelt above her, shirtless and stunning, his chest, arms, and stomach as toned and chiseled as a Roman god's.

He was gorgeous. Perfect. Jordan had known Nick had been hiding the goods underneath his clothes, but this went even beyond what she'd imagined.

Her voice came out in a near whisper. "And the rest?"

"If you insist."

With a devilish smile, he rose and stood at the foot of the bed. He kicked off his shoes, and then undid the button and zipper of his jeans. Without any hesitation, he shed his jeans, boxer briefs, and socks. He stood before her, unabashedly naked in the sunlight.

Propped up on her elbows, Jordan took in every inch of bronzed skin and sleek muscle, her eyes widening at the sight of his thick, hard erection.

"Think it'll do?" he teased, repeating her earlier question.

She crooked her finger and beckoned him back to the bed.

Nick lowered himself over her, his eyes lit with an emerald fire that made her heart pound. He skillfully snapped open the front closure of her bra with one hand and watched as her breasts tumbled free. "Now we're getting somewhere."

He eased her back onto the comforter and slid the straps of her bra over her shoulders. Jordan shivered with anticipation. "Nick," she whispered, needing him to kiss her. Their mouths came together, and she sighed when his fingers brushed across the tips of her breasts. He lowered his head, plumped up her breast, and pulled the nipple into his mouth.

With his other hand, he spread her legs and sank his hips between them.

She moaned and pressed instinctively against him as he worked his tongue across each of her breasts. She curled her fingers through his dark hair as hot flames licked at her stomach, and lifted her hips eagerly when he moved his hands to her hips and slid her panties off.

"I should slow down," he said huskily as he pulled one of her nipples into his mouth and sucked gently.

Slow down? "Not a chance, Brooklyn."

He smiled, and the stubble along his jaw scraped against her breast. "Now I'm definitely going to slow down."

He used his fingers to part the soft, wet folds between her legs, spreading her open, then he teased her with his forefinger for what felt like eternity. As her tongue tangled with his, she gasped when he slid a finger into her and began to move it in and out in a slow, smooth rhythm.

He whispered wickedly in her ear. "I love seeing the look on your face when I touch you. Maybe I should watch you come just like this."

Dirty words. Oh, he so did not play fair. But the Nick and Jordan show was a two-person show. She slid her hands over his well-muscled chest, her fingers brushing against the sprinkling of dark hair. She had two words for him. "Flip over."

His eyes flashed; apparently he liked that idea.

He grabbed her hips and rolled them over in one smooth move. She straddled him, settling his rock-hard erection between her legs, skin against skin. She heard the low rumble in his chest.

He definitely liked this idea.

Nick closed his eyes when Jordan bent down to kiss him. First his neck and throat, then she traced a path along his chest. Letting her take control had seemed like a fine idea thirty seconds ago, but now he wasn't so sure he could take too much more of her mouth on his—

Christ, she was going lower. She shifted her position, and she burned her way along his stomach with her tauntingly soft lips. He exhaled unsteadily when her tongue licked the trail of hair that started below his navel, and his cock throbbed in anticipation.

Go lower.

She wrapped her fingers around his engorged shaft and began to stroke. As she worked him with her hand, she kissed his hip, his inner thigh . . . and he opened his eyes to watch.

Go lower.

She gently licked the head of his erection.

She slid her tongue around the ridge, taking her time. She was tasting him, he realized, just like a wine. He groaned and tangled his fingers in her hair. "Jordan . . . put me in your mouth."

With a coy smile, she did just that.

He growled deep in his chest as she wrapped her lips around his cock. When she brought her tongue into the mix as well, his eyes nearly rolled back in his head. He gently palmed her head, to steady himself more than anything, and watched as she slid him deeper into her mouth. She wrapped her hand around the base, stroking him in a silky, fluid motion until he was pulsing with need.

He stopped her with his hand and pinned her with his eyes when she looked up. "Come here."

He saw the answer in the devious sparkle of her blue eyes. *No.*

While holding his gaze, she teased the head of his cock with her tongue, then slid him all the way back into her warm, wet mouth.

He nearly came right there.

Unable to resist, he watched as she continued with the delicious torture for several moments, and something about their eye-to-eye connection—and the fact that it was *her*—made it absolutely the hottest moment of his life. His tone was low and guttural. "Jordan."

Hearing the edge to his voice, she released him from her mouth and sat up, straddling him with his cock settled right between her legs. He slid his hands up and cupped her breasts, gliding his thumbs over her nipples. "Are you ready?" he asked, thinking he might spontaneously combust if he didn't get inside her right then.

"So ready," she said in a throaty voice.

Nick grabbed his wallet off the nightstand and pulled out a condom. He unwrapped it, placed it at the head of his cock, and took her hand, wanting her to do it. He cupped her ass as she rolled it over him. Then she leaned forward and rested her hands on his chest as he moved himself into position.

He kissed her as she lowered herself onto him, capturing her moan with his mouth as she stretched to accommodate him. When he was fully inside her, he clenched his jaw, straining against the overload of sensation. She felt so warm, so wet, and so fucking good, that his mouth just started *talking*. "Ride me, Jordan," he groaned. "Oh God, baby . . . love me."

She sat back and began sliding up and down on him. He held her hips, guiding her, moving her in a smooth, sensual rhythm, fighting the urge to go off at the sight of her naked above him in the bright light of day.

"Lean forward," he rasped. "I want one of those beautiful breasts in my mouth."

With a sharp inhale, she did as he asked. He took one of her rosy nipples into his mouth and flicked his tongue over it. Still riding him slowly, she let out a stifled cry, and he knew she was getting close. "Spread your legs wider," he whispered. When she shifted, he grabbed hold of her hips and held her steady. He took charge of their rhythm, thrusting up into her with smooth, deep strokes. She said his name again, urgently, and he knew she was at the edge. And he was right there with her.

She whimpered and closed her eyes, and that sound, plus the exquisite expression on her face, drove him right over. "Let me feel it, baby," he groaned. He kissed her as they both exploded, first her as she cried out, then he followed when he felt her tighten around him, pulling him deeper inside. They moved together, gasping and riding through the aftershocks, until she finally slowed to a stop and collapsed on his chest.

They lay there for a long time, skin to skin, hearts pounding.

After several minutes, she broke the silence. "That's the longest we've ever gone without talking." She perked her head up. "I didn't break anything, did I?"

With his finger, Nick brushed a lock of hair out of her eyes and tucked it behind her ear. "No."

She looked concerned when he fell quiet again. "Are you okay?"

"Definitely. Just thinking that it's never been . . ." He stopped awkwardly. Man, he sucked at this.

Her expression turned tender, a look that said she got it, as she leaned forward to cover his lips with her own.

"For me, either," she whispered softly.

Twenty-seven

JORDAN PEERED THROUGH the car window at the heavy wrought-iron fence that loomed before them. The gates bore a marble crest with an elaborate monogrammed *B*, the logo for Barrasford Estate winery.

Nick sat next to her in the backseat. "Nobody's answering. That's a shame. Guess we'll just have to head back to the resort." He snapped his fingers. Damn.

"It looks like the driver is speaking to someone on the intercom now. Oh—and the gates are opening. See, I told you they were expecting us," she said, nudging him.

"I'm excited. Really. How long do we have to stay?"

Jordan threw him a look. "It's a wine tasting, Nick. You're not exactly being tortured here."

"Anything that keeps me from being alone with you is torture, Rhodes."

She shook her head. "Ha—that's not going to work this time." She pointed. "Behind those gates is what's rumored to be a new cabernet that rivals some of the best in all of Napa and Sonoma. I *love* cabernet. I've been in the Napa Valley for"—she checked her watch—"two hours and thirty-eight minutes and I haven't had a drop of wine yet. Don't get me wrong, I love earth-shattering sex as much as the next girl, but right now we are going inside and trying that wine."

"What happens if I say no?"

"You can pretty much kiss spit or swallow good-bye."

Nick was out of the car in a flash.

Jordan watched with amusement as he walked around the car, opened her door, and held out his hand, all gentlemanly.

"Ms. Rhodes."

"Mr. Stanton." She slipped her hand into his, looking forward to the day when he was once again simply Nick McCall.

Their driver nodded at them as they passed through the gates. "Enjoy the wine. I've heard good things."

Jordan checked her watch. She and Nick were scheduled for a four o'clock appointment, the last tasting of the day. "We'll probably be about an hour and a half."

"Take your time," the driver said, with the easy grin of a man who was paid well by the hour.

With her hand in Nick's, they strolled through a beautifully landscaped Mediterranean-style courtyard with a fountain.

"Okay, tell me what I need to know about this place," he said.

"They're new—their first vintage will release next month. They're not a large vineyard, only about forty acres. They produce exclusively cabernet sauvignon. They're very eager to compete with the top wineries in the market, and at only a hundred dollars per bottle, have priced themselves well to do that."

Nick shot her a look. "Only a hundred dollars a bottle?"

"For the big boys of cabernet, that's not a bad price. If I can get them to lower their bulk rate, I plan to make them one of our May wine club wines. Assuming I like what I taste."

At the end of the courtyard, they came to a set of enormous oak doors—at least fifteen feet tall—that led into a two-story winemaking facility. The doors were open, and a professionally dressed woman in her late twenties greeted them warmly.

"Welcome to Barrasford Estates, Ms. Rhodes," she said.

Jordan smiled and shook her hand. "Call me Jordan. This is Nick Stanton."

"I'm Claire," she said, shaking Nick's hand next. "Follow me."

They made small talk, and Claire asked them about their trip while leading them through the wine production facilities. In sharp contrast to the warm Mediterranean style of the outside grounds, everything inside was modern and pristine stainless steel—except for the twelve massive French oak fermentation tanks that were roughly fifteen feet high by ten feet wide.

"Explains the size of the doors," Nick noted.

Claire nodded. "Moving those tanks in here was quite an adventure, I can tell you."

The tour of the facilities was shorter than many Jordan had been on at other wineries, and she wondered about that until Claire explained.

"We do things a little different here," she said. "We like people to see all stages of our wine-making process as it's actually happening, so we'll be showing you a short documentary film that covers everything from harvest to bottling."

She led them into a large conference room with one wall of floor-to-ceiling windows that captured a view of the valley and the Mayacamas mountain range. Claire invited them to have a seat at the marble-covered table, and opened a bottle of wine.

She explained as she poured two glasses. "So this is our estate cabernet—which will make its debut this coming May. The grapes were harvested two and a half years ago, then the wine was aged for eighteen months in oak barrels." She handed Jordan and Nick each a glass. "Enjoy the wine while you watch our film. I'll be back in fifteen minutes and would be happy to answer any questions you might have."

After Claire left, Jordan swirled her glass, releasing the aromas of the dark red, fragrant wine.

"This is more formal than I'd expected," Nick said. "Are all wine tastings like this?"

"It varies. Some take you on a tour of the facilities or bring you out to the vineyards. Others are more casual and you just pull up a chair and drink. Barrasford Estate apparently has a movie." She took a sip. The wine was lush and full, exactly what she liked in a cabernet. "Now that's a mouthful." She winked at Nick as the lights in the room dimmed and a screen dropped down from the front of the room.

After the film ended, Claire came back and asked what they thought of the wine. Jordan had explained who she was when she'd made the tasting appointment, so they knew she was there on business. She praised the wine and raised the idea of introducing it to her store's club members.

"Your cab would be slightly outside my usual price point, but I'm hopeful we can work something out given the size of the order I would place," she said to Claire.

"I don't have the authority to handle any sort of negotiations with respect to price," Claire said apologetically.

"Of course." Jordan pulled a business card out of her purse. "That's all my information, if you wouldn't mind passing my card along to your sales director. You can tell her that my store's wine club has over eight hundred members who would be introduced to your wine with a recommendation from both my manager and myself. Between the two of us, I think we can get much of the Chicago wine community very excited about Barrasford Estate's upcoming release. What distributor do you use in the Chicago area?" By law, she wasn't permitted to buy wine for retail use directly from the winery, but if Barrasford used one of her regular distributors, they should have no problem brokering a deal.

"Midwest Wine and Spirits, I believe," Claire said.

Jordan nodded. "I work with them all the time." She pointed to the card. "I plan to finalize my May wine club picks during this trip, so ask your sales director to give me a call before the weekend is over if she's interested."

A few minutes later, Nick and Jordan were seated at a

table on the winery's open-air terrace. Several other groups, mostly couples, sat at nearby tables, and the atmosphere felt more casual and welcoming than the other parts of the tour.

Sitting across the bistro table with his dark sunglasses, facial scruff, jeans, and black button-down shirt, Nick looked decidedly bad-boyish for a wine tasting. Not that Jordan particularly minded. No offense to the guys she typically dated, but Nick blew them all out of the water.

"You drive a hard bargain," he said in reference to her negotiations with Claire.

She waved this off. "What I proposed is a good arrangement for everyone." A light breeze blew her bangs into her eyes, so she smoothed them back into the bun she'd pulled her hair into after getting dressed at the hotel.

"Do you think the sales director will contact you before Monday?" he asked.

"I think the sales director will contact me before we leave here today," she said confidently.

Nick studied her through his sunglasses. "That's a bold call. I guess we'll find out how good you really are."

Claire returned with a tray filled with six glasses of wine and a basket of crackers. First, she set down the two biggest glasses, one in front of each of them. "I brought you each another glass of our cabernet. As a comparison, I thought you also might like to try some barrel tastings from next year's vintage." She set two smaller tasting glasses in front of each of them. "So after we harvest the grapes and ferment the wine, we fly in a professional taster from France—the renowned Philippe Fournier—and set him up in a room with samples of wine from our twenty-eight different vineyard blocks. For three days, he tastes the wine and gives us recommendations on the percentage each of the samples should contribute to our final estate cab." She smiled. "Then everyone drinks and parties for two days, before we get back to work." She clasped her hands together. "So, are there any questions I can answer for you at this time?"

"I think we're good for now. Thank you," Jordan said.

When they were alone again, Nick leaned in and spoke

under his breath. "And the hundred-dollar-per-bottle question is: does any of that make a difference?"

"If people enjoy the wine enough to spend a hundred dollars on it, then sure."

He looked skeptical.

"You can't think of it as merely a beverage, Nick—every glass of wine is its own experience," Jordan said. "Approach it the same way you might approach, say, a new relationship."

He looked even more skeptical now. "A relationship?"

Jordan picked up her glass of cabernet. "Sure, think about it. You start by looking at the wine. That's your first impression. You ask yourself, 'Does this look good to me? Am I interested in finding out more?' Then you get a little closer to the wine. You try out its aromas, and if it's something you like, your body reacts instinctively, begins to hum with the anticipation of going further. You let the wine begin to tease you, draw you in, seduce you. You're close at this point to getting a taste, but you're not there yet. Maybe you hold out a little longer, delay that final gratification, keeping yourself right at the edge for as long as possible. And finally, when you get to the point that you just can't wait anymore, you taste. You give yourself over to the rush, the smooth, silky feeling of the wine, its flavors, its scent, and you taste again. And again. Until you feel that flush begin to build, that warm, tingly euphoric feeling that goes on and on, even after the last drop is gone, before you slowly float down on a cloud of bliss."

She tipped her glass at him. "Now that's what drinking wine is about."

Nick's expression remained unreadable, his eyes hidden behind the dark sunglasses. Then he looked over at Claire as she passed by their table. "I think we're going to need a second round."

She clapped her hands with delight. "Wonderful! Glad to hear you're enjoying the wine."

After she left, Nick took off his sunglasses and set them on the table. He picked up his glass and tipped it to Jordan. "All right, Rhodes. For you, I'll give it a real shot." He swirled his glass, smelled the wine like a pro, and took a good, hearty sip.

He closed his eyes for a moment, as if debating, then he looked at her. "Black cherry. And licorice."

Jordan's wine-geek heart nearly burst with pride. "I knew you had it in you."

A woman stopped at their table and introduced herself. "Jordan, hi. I'm Denise, the director of sales. Claire mentioned that you were interested in featuring our wine in your store? Let me grab a pen from the bar and we can talk specifics."

Nick nodded, impressed, as the sales director stepped away. "Nice job."

Jordan smiled. "I told you, Nick. This is what I do."

NICK PULLED JORDAN into his arms as soon as they got back to their bungalow. She felt a rush of excitement—and happiness—when he bent his head to kiss her. She'd caught the way he'd looked at her during the car ride back to the resort and had sensed he'd had other things on his mind than tasting more wine. Normally, she would've suggested having a sunset drink on the terrace of the resort's bar, but she was willing to bend a little . . . if he was, too.

He slid his hands to her waist as he kissed her neck. "So what's next on the agenda?"

Jordan closed her eyes and thought she definitely could get used to having Nick around for wine tastings if this was what she had to look forward to afterward. "I thought we'd keep it simple, order room service, and have dinner on the deck." It was a little chilly, but the fireplace would keep them warm. She didn't want to miss this chance to eat under the stars—now that she finally had someone to share Napa with, she planned to go all out.

"I like that idea," he murmured against her skin. He reached up and carefully undid the top button of her shirt-dress, seemingly more patient than last time. "But room service will take at least an hour. Which means that we have some time to kill before dinner."

Her thoughts exactly. "True. I was thinking I'd take a bath and relax for a while."

His hands stilled on the second button of her shirtdress. "Oh. Sure."

"I was also thinking that you could come with me."

Nick cocked his head. "Yeah . . . I'm not exactly a bath kind of guy." He got a wicked look in his eyes. "But there's always that outdoor shower."

Jordan shrugged nonchalantly. Nick McCall had a few too many rules—it was high time he started bending them. "Suit yourself. But if you change your mind, you know where you can find me." She slid out from his embrace and went over to the bar.

He followed her and leaned against the wall, watching as she poured herself a glass from the half-finished bottle Barrasford Estate had given them when they'd left. Feeling Nick's gaze on her, she headed across the terrace to the master suite. She hummed to herself as she went into the bathroom and began filling the tub. She set the wineglass on the marble ledge, adjusted the temperature of the water, and added some bath gel. She sipped her wine, letting the water run for a couple minutes before she walked back into the bedroom.

Each room of the bungalow had windows that vertically spanned three-quarters of the wall, which meant she could see across the terrace into the living room. Nick sat on the couch with the TV remote in his hand, watching a basketball game.

Jordan rolled her eyes.

Men.

He looked over and saw her watching him. She turned her back and innocently went about her business. While in front of the window, she unzipped her dress and let it fall to the floor.

She just so happened to be wearing a thong right then.

She kicked the dress aside. Next, she unsnapped her bra—possibly taking a moment longer than necessary to ease the straps off her shoulders—and dropped it to the floor as well.

Then she strolled into the bathroom, naked except for her thong and heels.

Inside the bathroom, she dug a clip out of her makeup bag and pulled her hair up. Then she stripped out of her underwear and heels and slid into the steamy water. She grabbed her wineglass, leaned her head against the back of the tub, and silently counted to ten.

She made it to six.

"You didn't say there would be bubbles." From the doorway, Nick frowned at the offensive white foam.

Jordan tried not to smile. "Agent McCall . . . imagine seeing you here. Change your mind about the bath?"

"I'm thinking about it." With his gaze trained on her in the tub, he stepped into the bathroom. He carried the open wine bottle and a glass in one hand.

Jordan watched as he set them both on the ledge of the tub. Without saying a word, he unhooked the gun harness strapped to his calf and set it on the bathroom vanity. Next, he pulled a condom out of his pocket and tossed it next to the wine bottle.

"I see you're packing heat again." She lifted one leg out of the bubbles and turned off the faucet with her foot.

Nick's eyes held on her bare leg, and then traveled up to her breasts that peeked out of the water.

"And *I* see that somebody believes she's calling the shots around here with this bubble bath power play." He stripped out of his clothes.

Jordan took another sip of wine—needing something to quench her suddenly parched mouth—as Nick stepped into the tub and lowered his naked body into the water. He grabbed her by the ankle and pulled her onto his lap, so that she straddled him.

"So is this your attempt to reassert your authority?" she teased.

He answered her with a kiss that fogged the bathroom mirrors. As their mouths moved together at a slow, languorous pace, her breasts felt tight and her nipples peaked, ready for his touch. When she instinctively began to rock forward on his lap, his thick erection settled right between her legs and pressed firmly against her sensitive skin.

Jordan's hand tipped—she'd forgotten about the glass she held—and the wine nearly spilled on Nick before she righted it. "Almost got you there." She reached over to set her glass onto the ledge.

He took it from her. "That gives me an idea." He pressed the rim of the glass against the swell of her left breast and watched her face as his intention sunk in.

Jordan sucked in a breath, the wine-geek in her doing battle with the woman who was very turned on. "That's . . . a really good wine."

"And I can't think of a better pairing." He tipped the glass, and a small stream of wine flowed down her breast, covering her nipple. "Maybe it's time I showed you how *I* like to taste wine."

She gasped as he lifted her breast to his mouth and sucked. He ran his tongue around the pebbled tip. "Mmm . . . I taste sassiness. And a lot of spice."

He reached for the glass and poured wine over her other nipple. He set the glass back down and pulled her breast into his mouth. With a quiet moan, she ran her hands over the flexed muscles of his shoulders and arms. She shifted in his lap, so that the tip of his erection was right at the warm, wet entrance between her legs.

He groaned and pulled his mouth off her breast. He dug his fingers in her hair, kissing her hard. "Don't tempt me, Jordan. You have no idea how much I want to be inside you with nothing between us."

He lifted her off his lap and plunked her into the hot, bubble-filled water. She saw that he had the don't-fuck-with-me look on his face. The bossy but ridiculously sexy version.

"Sit up on the ledge," he said.

She raised an eyebrow. "I'm not used to taking orders in the bathtub, Agent McCall."

"You better not be."

Smiling to herself over the possessive tone to his voice, Jordan moved to the edge of the tub. Perhaps, she decided, even a strong woman could acquiesce in interesting situations like these.

She lifted herself out of the water and sat on the ledge. The cool air gave her goose bumps as water dripped down her body and into the tub.

Another order. "Spread your legs."

Her body turned to jelly. "What happens if I say no?"

A confident grin played at his lips. "You won't."

Damn. So true.

As her body buzzed with anticipation, she slowly did as he asked.

Nick rose out of the water onto his knees, his white-hot gaze taking in her spread legs. The water streamed down his toned abs and muscular thighs, and his thick, engorged shaft jutted out from his body.

Jordan swallowed hard.

He grabbed the glass again, moved toward her, and tilted the rim to her navel. As she watched, he poured a small amount of wine down her abdomen. His voice was gentler this time. "Lean back."

Propped up on her elbows, Jordan closed her eyes and moaned when she felt his warm breath against her inner thighs. When his tongue parted her folds, her legs went limp, and she just . . . gave in. She felt his firm grip on each of her thighs, holding her open for him. She'd never felt so exposed, yet also unbelievably sexy, as he tormented her with his mouth until she was shaking. He brought her right to the peak, right to the point where she was saying his name nearly nonstop, when he stopped.

"No," she gasped.

His voice had a strained edge. "With you moaning my name like that, I'm going to fucking explode if I don't get inside you." He grabbed the condom off the ledge. "Turn around."

Clearly, they needed to have a talk about his dominant tendencies in sexual situations. Later. Much later.

Jordan lowered herself into the water and bent over the ledge, her elbows on the marble. She looked over her shoulder. "Like this?"

She watched him rip open the wrapper and roll the condom on. Then he moved behind her and gripped her hips to guide her bottom up, so that she was on her knees. "Like this."

"Who's making the power play now?" She just barely had enough wits for one last sassy comment before she felt his hard, hot, shaft nudging her open. She closed her eyes and moaned, her fingers splaying over the marble ledge as he slowly entered her from behind.

He leaned forward and kissed the nape of her neck. "Me. And you love it."

Twenty-eight

THE NEXT DAY, Nick found himself on yet another winding, tree-lined road, heading to yet another winery. Kuleto Estate winery, Jordan had said—which, of course, meant nothing to him. So in response, he'd made his usual grumpy noises of protest, although some of that was for show more than anything else. After last night, he'd mellowed—just a touch—on the subject of wine. It wasn't the *worst* thing a man could drink, he supposed. No doubt, he still preferred a good, stiff bourbon, but he'd begun to think that wine held a certain appeal under the right circumstances.

His mind flashed back to the image of Jordan lying on the bathtub ledge, moaning his name as she arched against his mouth.

And now he had a hard-on.

He looked over at the cause of his problem, sitting next to him in the backseat of the limousine she'd hired to drive them around for the day. Quickly, he realized that looking at Jordan wasn't going to help anything. She was all put together again, polished and stylish in her navy dress and heels, and all he could think about was mussing her up. In fact, if it were up to him, this particular billionaire heiress would stay good and mussed all weekend.

Of course, whenever it came to Jordan, things were *not* entirely up to him. "How long will this tasting last?" he asked her.

"Hours. It includes lunch."

He grunted his displeasure. She smiled in amusement, and the gesture was inconveniently contagious. He'd planned to act cranky for at least five more minutes.

Nick noticed then that the road had narrowed as it wound up the mountain. When the drop-offs on the car's right turned steep, he saw Jordan clutch the edge of her seat.

He slid his hand over hers. "You okay?"

"I hate this part of the drive."

"Then why are we doing it?"

"You'll see when we get there."

Twenty minutes later, the car pulled to a stop at the top of the mountain. The driver parked the car, stepped out, and opened Jordan's door. "I'll grab the basket out of the trunk and bring it into the winery, Ms. Rhodes. I'll make sure they put it in the refrigerator."

Nick followed her out of the car. "What basket?" His FBI antenna went up—the limo had been waiting when he and Jordan arrived at the main lodge after being driven from their room in the golf cart, so he had no clue what might be inside the trunk.

"I had the resort put together a picnic lunch for us," she said. "After the wine tasting, I figured we could grab a spot to eat, well, anywhere." She gestured to the view all around them.

He took his first good look at the place. While he might not have been the type to ooh and aah easily over scenery, even he could appreciate the sight before him. The winery overlooked sweeping views of vineyards, emerald green rolling hills, the valley, and a sparkling blue lake below. Down a short path stood an idyllic Tuscan-style villa surrounded by flowers, gardens, and lush, shady trees.

"What do you think?" Jordan asked.

While taking in the view, it occurred to Nick that the downside of always being in charge and setting the rules of his relationships—and he used that term very loosely—was that no one ever surprised him with things like this. Actually, no woman had ever surprised him before, period. He normally didn't give them a chance to. Yet here he was, unexpectedly standing on a hilltop in the Napa Valley with a woman who pretty much knocked him off his feet every time they were together. He'd be pissed about that if she didn't somehow manage to do it while putting a smile on his face.

Very sneaky.

The incredible view made him think of something he'd wanted to say to Jordan ever since they'd arrived in Napa. He put his hands on her waist and pulled her close, holding her gaze. "I think this whole weekend is amazing. But you know that I don't need any of these things, right? I'm here because of you—not for fancy resorts, or fireside dinners, or picnic lunches on a California hilltop."

She smiled and touched his face. "I know. That's what makes it even better."

A voice called out from behind them. "Jordan Rhodes."

Nick turned and saw a man with sandy brown hair walking over to them.

"Mike. So good to see you again," Jordan said.

"Look at you—gorgeous, as usual," he said. "I saw your name on today's appointment list. With a plus one, huh? About time." He shook Nick's hand. "You must be the plus one."

Nick returned the handshake. "Nick Stanton." The "plus one" was getting tired of using that name.

Mike gestured toward the villa. "Come on in—we're a little crowded this afternoon, but I think we can make some room at the bar."

They followed him inside the winery and walked into a noisy, cozy room. Guests drank wine at a long banquet table, at cocktail tables scattered along the walls, and at the large bar in the corner. A friendly black Labrador mingled

among the guests, quite content to be fed Brie cheese and
crackers under the tables.

Nick relaxed as he and Jordan settled into the last two
open chairs at the bar. This kind of wine tasting was much
more his style.

Mike slid two empty glasses in front of them. "Where do
you guys want to start?"

Nick thought about this. "Do you have anything in a pink?"

Mike eagerly grabbed a bottle from the back bar. "Actually, we have a gorgeous Rosato. Predominantly made from
cabernet and Sangiovese grapes, fermented in stainless steel,
then briefly in French oak, it's a lush, aromatic blend of wild
strawberries and blood oranges, full in the mouth without
being too heavy. Perfect for a sunny, spring day like this."

"Sounds delicious," Nick said. "I'll take everything but
that one."

LATER THAT NIGHT, Nick lay on his side, listening to
Jordan's steady breaths as she slept next to him. After spending a large part of the afternoon at Kuleto winery, and then
another hour at a smaller winery she'd wanted to check out
for her summer wine club selections, they'd stumbled back to
the bungalow and finally explored the outdoor shower. For
dinner, they'd made their way to the resort's restaurant, a
Pacific Northwestern–style lodge that sat on a lake nestled
against tall pine trees and mountains. They'd scored a table
on the deck and had talked as the sun set—about his family,
her family, about lots of things.

There was one topic they hadn't broached, however. The
subject of them.

In the morning, they would leave Napa and return to
Chicago, and then . . . Nick wasn't sure what would happen. For a guy who typically kept his relationships with
women easy and breezy, this was an odd position to be in.
He usually didn't think about the next step because, usually,
there was none. But Jordan Rhodes had walked into his life
and now here he was—staring at her in the dark, watching

her sleep. That was the type of thing a sentimental, introspective man did. Not him.

He, on the other hand, was a rational, logical kind of guy, and there were a few cold, hard facts staring him in the face. First, he'd known Jordan for three weeks. *Three* weeks. And they'd officially been together for only the last forty-eight hours of that. Second, taking the next step with her would mean one of two things: either they would spend long periods of time apart while he was on an undercover assignment, or he needed to consider a major change in his career.

The fact that he was even considering such a thing seemed crazy. One simply did not make that kind of decision after dating a woman for *forty-eight hours*.

But.

The alternative meant saying good-bye to Jordan as soon as the Eckhart investigation was over. And that just felt . . . wrong. He liked seeing her lying in bed next to him, and wanted to see her there more often. A lot more often.

In other words, he wanted it all—and that simply couldn't happen. So he had a tough decision to make.

There was another problem complicating this decision: he had no clue what Jordan was thinking. Sure, he knew she liked him, but not once had she talked about what would happen back in Chicago. Perhaps she didn't want to address the issue yet, or perhaps she simply didn't have any answers herself. Maybe she was just as confused as he was.

He'd always been a straight shooter with women. But this conversation, with this particular woman, unnerved him. Because—if he was being honest with himself—he knew that there was a part of him, a good part of him, that wanted her to ask the questions he'd always tried to avoid, wanted to hear her say the things he'd never given another woman a chance to say. Like that this weekend meant something more than just a weekend.

Jordan stirred and stretched out in her sleep. She rolled even closer, attempting to edge him out to a measly one-third of the king-sized bed. He couldn't help but smile while firmly holding his ground—even in her sleep she tried to take control.

She was smart and beautiful and successful, and probably the most remarkable woman he'd ever met. With all she had going for her, it was hard to see her ever lacking for—or needing—anything. And although he'd never want to change her strength and independence, some Cro-Magnon, club-swinging, plain-old greedy bastard deep inside nevertheless wanted to know that she needed *him*.

He'd come to the Napa Valley. He'd even semi-willingly gone to wine tastings—three of them. And he'd specifically told her that she wasn't getting his usual no-relationships speech. So the way he saw it, the next step was hers. Sure, she'd wined and dined him, but maybe that was par for the course for billionaire heiresses. So before he put himself out there any further, and thought about those career decisions he couldn't believe he was thinking about, he wanted something more from her. Unbelievably, for once he actually wanted to talk about feelings—but hell if he would be the one to bring it up first. He was a guy. He did have some pride.

Still, that didn't mean he couldn't *show* her how he felt.

Nick's eyes moved over Jordan, taking in the tank top and underwear she slept in. He shifted and slid between her legs, careful to keep his weight on his forearms as he kissed her throat and collarbone to wake her up. She sighed contentedly and smiled when she opened her eyes and saw him.

He brushed his thumb against her cheek—that smile got to him every time. "Hey, you," he said softly.

"I was dreaming about you." She wrapped her arms around his neck, pulling him closer. "But this is even better."

Pride or no pride, if he had been one of those sensitive types, he'd say he knew he was a goner right then.

Twenty-nine

THE NEXT MORNING, as he and Jordan packed their suitcases, Nick's phone rang with a call from his boss. This was not unexpected—in fact, he'd been waiting for this particular call all weekend. The one where Davis asked him what the hell he was doing.

"Good to hear from you, boss," Nick answered pleasantly. He stepped out onto the terrace and waited for the conversation to go downhill from there.

"What the hell do you think you're doing in the Napa Valley?" Davis demanded.

Bingo.

"Nick Stanton figured he should treat himself to a little R and R. The real estate market for rental properties is really booming these days."

"Don't give me any of that Nick Stanton crap," Davis warned. "Do I need to remind you that you're in the middle of an investigation?"

"An investigation in which my primary objective is to appear to be dating Jordan Rhodes. As such, I see no conflict with my present location. Not to mention, I've checked in with Huxley and the other agents on the team several times while I've been gone—Eckhart's been quiet this weekend, sick with the stomach flu. He's scheduled to meet with Trilani on Tuesday morning, and I'll be back in town well before then. Today, as a matter of fact."

Davis grunted. "Well, don't you have all the answers?"

"You'd expect nothing less of me, boss."

"I expect you to remember that you're an FBI agent, that's what I expect."

"Trust me, that fact hasn't slipped my mind once since I've been here," Nick said sharply.

Davis paused, likely surprised by his tone. He responded carefully. "All right, Nick. You seem to have things under control. I suppose you've earned a little leeway."

"Thank you. You're . . . not going to give me the touchy-feely speech about being your top agent again, are you?"

Davis chuckled. "No speeches. Just a question: violent motorcycle gang or insider trading?"

"Is this an opinion question? Generally, I frown on both."

"Good. Because one of them is going to be your next undercover assignment. Figured I'd let you pick. Personally, I'd go for the insider trading just for the cushy lifestyle. You'd be pretending to be a hedge fund trader, so we can probably get you something even better than the Lexus. Although Pallas made me promise that he gets to teach you how to ride a bike if you pick the motorcycle gang."

Despite the teasing, Nick remained silent. *Another assignment.* It was all happening so quickly.

"Still there, McCall?"

"Yes. Just thinking that this conversation seems a little premature. I'm not finished with the Eckhart investigation yet."

"According to Huxley, you guys are close. He seemed fairly confident we'd be able to wrap things up after Eckhart's meeting with Trilani on Tuesday. Do you disagree?"

Nick paused. "No."

"Glad to hear it. In addition to tying you up, I've had three agents practically living in a van outside Bordeaux for the last two weeks. The sooner we can finish this, the better," Davis said. "I know you've got your New York trip coming up, but as soon as you're back I figured we can start prepping you for your next case."

Nick knew this was how it worked. It was how he'd done things since he'd begun working undercover several years ago. He went from assignment to assignment and didn't think twice about it. But now . . .

He looked through the window and saw Jordan standing next to the bed, packing the white dress into her open suitcase.

Like it or not, it was decision time.

JORDAN WAS BEGINNING to get nervous.

Nick had been acting strangely ever since he'd received the phone call at the resort. It was just like the time he'd gotten the call from "Ethan" at Eckhart's party—she knew something was up. Sure, he'd put forth a good effort during the drive from Napa to the airport, and again during their flight home, but she could see it in his eyes.

She'd asked him twice what was wrong and had gotten nowhere. She'd begun to think she needed to break out some seriously badass interrogation tactics—and then realized she had no such tactics. Although he did respond well to the thong and high heels technique.

Something to keep in mind.

When they got back to her house, Nick left his suitcase by the front door and carried hers upstairs to her bedroom. Jordan waited in the kitchen, eying that suitcase by the front door and becoming more worried as she contemplated its meaning. If she was reading between the lines and speculating about Nick's mysterious behavior—something she didn't want to do, but since he wasn't *telling* her anything she had no choice—she would have to say that it didn't appear as though he planned to stay the night.

Suddenly, she had a bad feeling she knew why Nick was behaving so oddly. She had only asked him for a weekend, and now that weekend was over.

She heard him coming down the stairs and pulled herself together. She was overreacting, obviously. She had to be. He

liked her, and they'd just spent an incredible two days together. There was no reason to start getting all worried and
presumptuous now.

She threw on a smile when he entered the kitchen. "Thank
you for carrying that upstairs for me," she said, referring to
her suitcase.

"Just how many bottles of wine did you stash in there?"
he asked.

"Actually, it's the shoes." She tried to look casual. "So,
should we talk about this thing you've been avoiding all
day?"

Standing at the opposite end of the counter, Nick nodded.
"Yes. Sorry—I've been mulling a few things over in my
head." He took a moment, as if deciding where to begin.
"That call this morning was from my boss. He wanted to talk
about my next undercover assignment."

Jordan blinked in surprise. "Your next assignment? You
haven't even finished the one with Xander yet."

"Eckhart plans to meet with Trilani on Tuesday morning," he said. "I think we'll probably be able to wrap things
up after that."

Jordan's heart sank. *So soon.* Sure, she'd known the end
of the investigation was looming, but she hadn't realized it
was this close. "When do you begin your next assignment?
I assume you at least get some time off, right?"

Nick shook his head. "Not much. I'd planned to go to
New York to spend a few days with my family, and when I
come back my boss wants me to start getting up to speed on
the next assignment."

What about us?

Jordan caught the words just before they spilled out of
her mouth. Nick's expression was unreadable, and it occurred to her: perhaps she hadn't been overreacting to the
suitcase by the door. Perhaps, despite all the sweet words
and the really, really fantastic sex and her gut instinct, she'd
been wrong to think that her weekend with him had become
something more than just a weekend.

In other words, perhaps she'd just become a Lisa.

Nick hadn't made a single promise to her over the weekend. In fact, he hadn't once brought up the subject of what might happen once they got back to Chicago. For her part, she'd deliberately avoided the issue, not wanting to look too pushy or needy. Besides, she'd figured, *she* was the one who'd taken the first step and asked him to go to Napa with her. Which meant the next move was his.

And now he seemed to be making that move. Backward. Right out her front door.

Still, she wasn't ready to give up just yet. She kept her cool, resolved to hear whatever it was Nick had to say. Assuming he had something to say.

"What kind of assignment is it?" she asked. There—she'd even managed to pull off sounding casual.

He shifted uneasily. Not a good sign.

"I could choose either a motorcycle gang or insider trading," he said.

You could choose neither, she thought.

But she didn't say it.

Instead, she decided to try a different tactic. The hell with beating around the bush. "So where does that leave us?"

Nick hesitated, then dodged the question. "Where do you think that leaves us?"

What Jordan wouldn't do right then for those badass interrogation techniques. He was being far too cagey. Also not a good sign.

Still, she pressed on. Hell, she would make this as easy as possible for him—she'd even start him out. "I think that this was an incredible weekend." She paused, waiting for Nick to pick up from there. *Me, too, Jordan,* he could say. *And I want to keep it going. I don't care what it takes—we're fantastic together.* Something along those lines. Anything.

She stared at him expectantly. He stared right back at her. Undoubtedly the second longest amount of time they'd ever gone without talking.

Then . . . the strangest look of resignation came over his face. And he finally picked up where she left off. Except he didn't say what she'd wanted to hear.

"But we both knew it was just a weekend," he finished, his voice noticeably flat.

Jordan felt the ache—a sharp pang—cut through her. *It meant a lot more than that to me.*

But she didn't say that, either.

Instead, she put on a brave face. She was getting pretty good at telling lies these days; she could handle one more. "You said your job made things complicated. I suppose this is the complicated part."

Nick watched her closely with those amazing green eyes of his. "I'd been hoping, actually, that things wouldn't have to be so complicated," he said quietly.

Ah, she got it—he didn't want her to make this *awkward*. Probably the reaction he was accustomed to from all the other Lisas in his life. But she had her pride. As she'd told him before, she was a big girl. She wouldn't yell, she wouldn't cry, she wouldn't beg him to stay. But she needed him to leave.

Her eyes stung at the thought.

Now. She needed him to leave *now*.

"We're both adults, Nick. This doesn't have to be a long, drawn-out discussion. We had our weekend together, and now we've come back to the real world. You've got your job and all the trappings and rules that come with that."

He stepped toward her. "So that's it?"

Jordan guessed that he'd expected her to at least ask him to stay one more night. But every moment she spent with him would only make this harder. "I think it's probably better to make a clean break. Given the inevitable."

"The inevitable." He stood up straight and folded his arms across his chest. "I have to say, this was not how I saw this conversation going."

She cocked her head at that. "Well, is there any other option?" Although she kept her expression carefully neutral, inside she felt anything but. *Say you don't want to leave.*

Nick studied her for a long moment. "No, I guess not."

A silence fell between them.

"I think, all things considered, that it's best if you go now." Jordan forced herself to meet his eyes, then had to look away before he could read too much in her own.

He nodded. "Yeah, I think so, too." He edged his way

toward the front door, then paused. "Should I call you on Tuesday to let you know how things go with Eckhart?"

"Sure." Jordan followed him and watched as he grabbed his suitcase. The image of him leaving her place, suitcase in hand, would likely stay burned in her brain for a long time. But for now, she kept her chin up. All she had to do was keep it together until he walked out the door.

Nick rested his hand on the door handle, and when he looked at her one last time, what she saw surprised her.

His eyes blazed with anger.

"Well, Rhodes, thanks for the weekend," he said, his jaw clenched tight. "I'll be sure to send you a check for my half of the hotel room. Hell, maybe I can even write it off as a business expense."

Now that was a slap in the face. And Jordan was confused. Why would he be mad at *her*? "That's a little cold. You don't have to be an asshole about things."

His expression was incredulous. "*I'm* the asshole?"

She pointed between them. "Is there something I'm missing here? Because all I said was—"

"Don't bother, I heard you the first time," Nick said, cutting her off and yanking the door open. "I heard every word you said." He stormed out, slamming the door behind him.

Jordan stood in her living room, staring at the door in confusion.

Well.

No clue what *that* was all about.

Thirty

AFTER KYLE LET Jordan into his penthouse condo, a man dressed in a black tuxedo came around the corner and greeted her.

"Good evening, Ms. Rhodes." He held out his hand. "May I take your coat?"

"Of course. Thank you." Jordan handed over her coat and threw her brother a wry look when the man hurried off. "You hired a butler?" That would be *so* Kyle.

He slung his arm around her neck, half-hugging her, half-dragging her toward the dining room. "No, Dad brought in a waiter for dinner tonight. Hope you're in the mood for sushi, because he bribed the head chef from Japonais to cook for us."

Actually, she wasn't in the mood for sushi. Or any dinner, for that matter. For the last twenty-four hours, all she could think about was Nick. And thinking was all she'd been doing, since he hadn't returned any of her calls. She'd tried his cell phone three times and had left him messages. Not a word in response.

Given the way he'd stormed out of her house on Sunday night, it was obvious that they'd had some kind of misunderstanding. Clearly, they needed to work on their communication skills. An issue she intended to address with him as soon as he *called her back*.

For now, however, she had her family to deal with. This was her brother's homecoming dinner, the first time the three of them had gotten together since his release from prison and the hospital. "Sounds like Dad really went all out," she said to Kyle.

Grey was waiting for them in the dining room, with a glass of Scotch in his hand. He gestured magnanimously. "What can I say? How often does a father get to celebrate his son's release from prison?" His sharp blue eyes narrowed in on Kyle. "You better say 'only once.'"

Kyle held up his hands innocently. "Only once. I promise."

They took their seats at the dining table, which had been set with crystal stemware and china.

"Since this is a celebration of sorts, it's a good thing I brought something, too." Jordan handed a bag with her store's label to Kyle. "I figured it's been a while since you've had a decent glass of wine. So I thought long and hard about the perfect bottle for you."

Kyle looked touched. "Aw, Jordo, you shouldn't have. But I will gladly drink it regardless." He pulled out the wine bottle and checked out the label. He threw her a look. "Very funny."

Grey leaned forward. "What is it?"

Kyle set the bottle on the table to show him the label. "Orin Swift. The *Prisoner*."

Her father laughed, and Jordan smiled innocently. "It actually *is* one of my favorites."

As the waiter began to serve them sashimi and ahi tuna ceviche, Jordan and her father let Kyle guide them on how much, or little, he wanted to discuss his incarceration at MCC. Mostly, he talked about how he still couldn't believe he was out.

"Such a shame that I didn't get to say good-bye to my fellow inmates," he said sarcastically. "Actually, Puchalski was the only guy I liked. I still can't figure out what got into him."

As Jordan used her chopsticks to pick up a piece of hamachi, she decided it was best to get her brother off that topic as fast as possible. "Sounds like he just snapped."

"But why would he have a fork in his shoe?" Kyle mused. "That makes me think he was planning the attack, which doesn't make sense."

Let it go, Kyle. She shrugged. "Maybe he always keeps a fork in his shoe. Who understands why any of these felon types do what they do?"

"Hey. I am one of those felon types."

Grey tipped his glass of wine. "And who would've thought you would do what you did?"

"It was *Twitter*," Kyle mumbled under his breath.

"Maybe we should change the subject," Jordan suggested, sensing the conversation could only spiral downward from there.

"Okay. Let's talk about you instead," Grey said. "I never asked—how did Xander's party go?"

Now there was a potential land mine of a topic. "It went fine. Pretty much the same party as usual." *Except for a little domestic espionage.* She threw Kyle a look, needing help. *Change the subject. Fast.*

He stared back cluelessly. *Why?*

She glared. *Just do it.*

He made a face. *All right, all right.* "Speaking of wine, Jordo, how was your trip to Napa?"

Great. Leave it to her genius of a brother to pick the *other* topic she wanted to avoid. "I visited that new winery I told you about. We should have a deal this week so that my store will be the first to carry their wine in the Chicago area."

Grey's tone was casual. "Did you bring Tall, Dark, and Smoldering with you on the trip?"

Jordan set down her chopsticks and looked over at her father. He smiled cheekily as he took a sip of his wine.

"*You* read Scene and Heard, too?" she asked.

Grey scoffed at that. "Of course not. I have people read it for me. Half the time, it's the only way I know what's going on with you two. And don't avoid the question. Tell us about this new guy you're seeing. I find it very odd that you've never mentioned him." He fixed his gaze on her like the Eye of Sauron.

Jordan took a deep breath, suddenly very tired of the lies and the secret-agent games. Besides, she had to face the truth at some point. "Well, Dad, I don't know if you have to worry about Tall, Dark, and Smoldering anymore. He's not talking to me right now."

Kyle's face darkened. "Tall, Dark, and Smoldering sounds like a moron to me."

Grey nodded, his expression disapproving. "I agree. You can do a lot better than a moron, kiddo."

"Thanks. But it's not that simple. His job presents some . . . challenges."

That was definitely the wrong thing to say.

"Why? What kind of work does he do?" her father asked immediately.

Jordan stalled. Maybe she'd overshot a little with the no more lies promise. She threw Kyle another desperate look. *Do something. Again.*

Kyle nodded. *I'm on it.* He eased back in his chair and stretched out his intertwined hands, limbering up his fingers. "Who cares what this jerk does? Send me his e-mail address, Jordo—I'll take care of it. I can wreak all sorts of havoc on Tall, Dark, and Smoldering's life in less than two minutes." With an evil grin, he mimed typing at a keyboard.

Their father looked ready to blow a gasket. "Oh no—*you* do not get to make the jokes," he told Kyle. "Jordan and I make the jokes. You've been out of prison for four days and I seriously hope you learned your lesson, young man . . ."

As their father's lecture continued, Jordan smiled gratefully to her brother from across the table.

Kyle winked in reply. *No problem.*

SHE SHOULD'VE REALIZED, however, that she wasn't entirely off the hook.

"Do you want to tell me what that was all about?" Kyle asked as soon as their father left.

Jordan sighed. "I wouldn't know where to start." Something had been nagging her all evening. Yes, she was mad at Nick for not calling her back, but she'd begun to wonder if she maybe, possibly, shared just a *tiny* bit of responsibility for their fight.

She toyed with the stem of her wineglass absentmindedly. "Do you ever think we're not . . . open enough?" she asked Kyle. "With our feelings, I mean. I suppose we are kind of sarcastic sometimes."

To his credit, he neither laughed nor scoffed at the question. "Mom was always the expressive one. When she died, I think the three of us sort of fell into this routine." He smiled in a rare moment of sincerity between them. "But I think we get by well enough."

Jordan shared the smile. She thought her family did pretty okay, too. Federal incarceration excepted. "But what about with other people?"

Kyle shrugged at this. "I shut down Twitter after finding out that my girlfriend cheated on me. That seems pretty expressive."

"You could've just told her how hurt you were," Jordan said gently.

Kyle fell quiet in response to her comment. They'd talked a lot about the infamous Twitter incident, but not about the feelings that had caused it. She'd sensed that her brother barely wanted to admit to himself that there were any such feelings.

"Telling someone how you feel can be risky, Jordo," he finally said. "Once the words are out, there are no takebacks."

She didn't disagree with that. But if the alternative to gathering some courage and laying her feelings on the line was becoming an infamous Internet terrorist, perhaps it wouldn't kill her to be straight with Nick. Yes, he could've made things easier by not acting like a stubborn jerk, but nothing about Nick had been easy since the night they'd met. It was one of the things she liked about him. Eighty-two percent of the time.

She took a deep breath, ready to start by being honest

with herself. "Kyle . . . I think I screwed up." She held up a hand, qualifying this. "Partially. Tall, Dark, and Smoldering deserves a lot of the blame. At least half. Maybe two-thirds. Of course, he's probably sulking right now, thinking that *I'm* the only one who's wrong here. He's kind of frustrating that way. He gets under your skin, like a tick, or a burr, or a thorn, or . . ." She looked to her brother for help. "What else gets under your skin?"

"Scabies?" he suggested.

"Scabies? This is what you come up with?"

Kyle stared at her as if she was losing it. "I have no idea what you're talking about, Jordo. But I'll say this, if you think you screwed up, there's only one question—the same one you asked me five months ago: Can you fix it?"

Jordan sighed. "I'm trying."

Her brother's gaze was firm. "Try harder."

She glared at him. "*Okay*." Then after a moment, she nodded in concession. "Okay."

Thirty-one

DEVINE CELLARS WAS ready to go promptly at ten o'clock, and so was Jordan.

Nick still hadn't called her back, but this was okay. She was pumped, recharged, and if he didn't want to take her calls, that was just fine. She'd march down to that fake office of his and tell him how she felt in person. Hopefully, there'd be some corresponding indication that he returned her feelings, but she couldn't dwell on that. This was new territory for her—the whole mushy, expressive thing—and if she thought about it too much, she might chicken out and resort to her quippy, self-protective defaults. And look where that had gotten her.

She knew from her prior conversation with Nick that Xander was meeting with Trilani that morning, and guessed that Nick would be busy until later in the day. To preoccupy herself until then, she threw herself into the store's opening tasks. When she'd blown through all of those by 10:22, she looked around for something else to distract herself with. She was debating whether to alphabetize the wines in the store within each varietal type and geographic origin when the bell chimed against the front door.

Thank God, a customer. Jordan spun around, and her smile wavered before she caught herself.

Xander Eckhart walked into her store.

Jordan quickly hid her surprise. Obviously, Xander and Trilani must have rescheduled their meeting. Since she and Nick hadn't spoken since Sunday, she was out of the loop on these things.

She deferred to her now standard method of handling situations in which she was wholly clueless—she acted normal. Or at least tried to. "Xander. It's good to see you again. It's been a couple weeks."

"Since the night of my party." Not surprising given the cold temperatures outside, he wore a dark overcoat and black leather gloves.

"How have you been?" Jordan hoped she didn't sound as unnerved as she felt. She hadn't counted on seeing Xander again before . . . well, ever, actually. Perhaps this had been wishful thinking on her part—he was a regular customer of her store, after all.

You can do this, she reassured herself. She'd managed to maintain the friendly charade during his party; she could certainly handle some small talk while he perused the store. They were so close—the FBI was nearly finished with their investigation. She wouldn't screw things up now.

Still, there were tingles at the back of her neck. *Why wasn't he meeting with Trilani?*

She watched as Xander walked—without pausing—past the "New and Noteworthy" wine display at the front of the store.

He *always* stopped and checked out that display. The snob in him couldn't resist, couldn't stand the idea that there might be some notable wine out there that he didn't know about.

Jordan swallowed hard.

With as little movement as possible, she slid her hand underneath the bar and pushed the panic button.

"How am I doing?" Xander asked. "Truthfully, Jordan, not so great. Not so great at all."

"I'm sorry to hear that. Did something happen?"

As he approached, Jordan could see that his expression was stone cold.

"Actually, something did happen. I found out that someone I thought I could trust lied to me. Betrayed me." He stopped directly opposite her at the bar.

A long silence stretched between them.

"Just tell me *why* you did it," Xander finally said. "But I should warn you, Jordan—if I don't like your answer, things could go very badly for you."

He reached into his overcoat and pulled out a gun. "And I have a feeling there's a really good chance I'm not going to like your answer."

NICK PACED IN his fake office, waiting for his cell phone to ring.

He'd told Huxley to call as soon as Trilani arrived at Bordeaux for his meeting with Eckhart, but he hadn't heard a word yet.

While he paced, he tried not to think about Jordan.

As a guy, he knew that he wasn't supposed to admit these kinds of things, but this whole argument with her had completely freaked him out. Over the course of just a few days, he'd gone ballistic when he'd seen her talking to the douchebag, he'd called in every favor owed him to get her felon of a brother out of prison, they'd spent a whirlwind weekend in *wine country* of all places, he'd actually considered changing his job for her, and then they'd had a fight and he'd stormed out of her house feeling like he'd been used for sex.

Clearly, he wasn't himself these days.

And the only way he knew to get back to being himself was to cut off the problem. To push Jordan out of his life completely.

That made him freak out even more.

Somehow, with her sneaky ways, she'd managed to get inside him and screw up all his plans. He'd been perfectly happy with his life until she'd come along with her wine and her sassiness and her sparkling blue eyes and the way she always made him laugh. He would laugh at himself for being such a sucker . . . except he hadn't so much as cracked a smile since he'd left her house on Sunday.

It all had happened too fast. He'd always assumed that one day he'd get bored with undercover work and that he'd *slowly* transition out of bachelorhood when that happened. But *this*—this wild, heart-pounding, nerve-wracking, exhilarating, rollercoaster ride between him and Jordan—was nuts. Plain and simple. And here's what freaked him out most: if he was one of those sensitive, introspective types, he would say that the feelings he had for Jordan sure seemed a lot like love and he, Nick McCall, didn't *do* love.

Or hell, maybe he did.

Still pacing in his office, he added a whole slew of Brooklyn-flavored swears to that, most of which he guessed the average sensitive, introspective type wouldn't even know the meaning of.

The way he saw it, he had two choices. Plan A: keep avoiding Jordan and see if this heart-pounding, nerve-wracking feeling went away as quickly as it came. He remembered something he'd once overheard at a family party: his cousin Maria had been babbling on about her boyfriend problems and had said she'd read in *Cosmo* that it took a person one-half the length of a relationship to get over a breakup.

That didn't sound too bad, Nick thought. If he only counted the times they'd hooked up, he and Jordan had been together for three days. According to *Cosmo*, he should be over her in thirty-six hours.

He checked his watch. *Damn.* By his calculations, he was supposed to have moved on three hours and twenty-four minutes ago. Not a good sign.

Which brought him to Plan B: fuck *Cosmo* and accept the fact that this heart-pounding, nerve-wracking feeling was never going away. And deal with it. Plan B had one good thing going for it—it meant that he got to storm down to Jordan's store and tell her just how pissed he was that she'd messed up all his plans. He wasn't sure where the conversation would go from there, but he'd come up with something. Or maybe he'd simply scrap all the talking and kiss her until she remembered how boring her life would be hanging out with a bunch of douchebags wearing scarves.

Now *that* sounded like a plan.

Nick's cell phone rang, and he checked. Huxley. About time. But the news was not what he had expected.

"Looks like Eckhart skipped out on another meeting," Huxley said.

"Is he still sick?"

"No clue. There's been no communication by Eckhart from inside his office all morning."

Nick didn't like the sound of that. Eckhart had been very quiet over the past couple days. Since they'd assumed he had the stomach flu, this hadn't raised an immediate flag. But people who worked with Roberto Martino did not make a regular habit of blowing off his men. "I don't like that he's gone radio silent."

"You think he's onto us?" Huxley asked.

Nick swore under his breath. He didn't know how that could be possible, or what would've suddenly tipped Eckhart off, but he'd been involved in enough undercover investigations to know that if an agent had to ask whether his cover had been blown, then, yep—his cover probably had been blown. "We need to wrap this up ASAP."

"Do you think we got enough evidence to convict?"

"It'll have to be enough. I'll call Davis to let him know that we should proceed with Eckhart and Trilani's arrests." Nick's other line beeped, and he checked to see who was calling. "Speak of the devil. I swear, Davis either has ESP or taps on our phones. He always knows when this stuff goes down."

He clicked over to answer Davis's call. "I was just about to call you, boss. We've got a situation here with Eckhart."

Davis's voice sounded uncharacteristically terse. "What situation?"

Nick explained that Eckhart hadn't shown up for the meeting with Trilani. When he was finished, Davis's next question caught him off guard.

"Where is Jordan Rhodes right now?"

Nick didn't see why that was relevant right then. "I'm guessing she opened her store at ten. Why?"

"We picked up a call coming from the phone line at De-Vine Cellars. The line that connects to the alarm system," Davis said. "Somebody there pushed the panic button."

Jordan.

Nick already had his car keys in his hand and was running out the door. "I'm on my way."

JORDAN'S EYES HELD on the gun pointed at her.

She tried to keep her voice calm. "Xander. What are you doing?"

He tightened his grip on the gun. "Come around the bar. Slowly. And go shut the shades."

The store's phone began to ring. *The alarm company,* she thought. When she didn't answer, they would send the police over. Which meant she needed to keep Xander talking until they got there.

Getting her first good look at him, she saw that he hadn't shaved for several days. And there were dark circles underneath his eyes, eyes that regarded her with calculated fury. "I think you should put the gun away so we can talk about this."

"And I think you should shut your lying mouth. Go close the goddamn blinds."

Not being in a position to disagree, Jordan did as he asked. Xander kept the gun trained on her as she walked to the front windows and pulled down the shades, one at a time.

"And the one over the door," he ordered. He stood directly behind her and placed the gun against the back of her head. "Don't get any ideas about running."

Jordan closed her eyes, feeling the pressure of the barrel against her scalp. *Just keep stalling.* As she shut the final shade over the door, she looked hopefully for someone who might be walking by, someone she could possibly signal, but no luck.

She did a quick assessment in her head. She must've bought herself at least three or four minutes already. The police had to be on their way. After she finished drawing the shade, she heard her cell phone ringing in the back room.

"Lock the door." The gun dug harder against the back of her head.

She did as he asked.

"Now move back into the center of the room."

Jordan glanced around the store, at the wine bottles everywhere. Maybe she could grab one to use as a weapon and . . . risk being shot by the man who had a big-time ax to grind with her, a man who undoubtedly would be all too happy to have another excuse to pull the trigger.

Not the best plan.

She moved toward the middle of the store and turned around.

"Now we can talk without worrying about interruptions," Xander said.

More stalling. "Great. Maybe now you can tell me why you have a gun pointed at me."

"Drop the fucking charade, Jordan. I know everything. Your boyfriend, Nick McCall, works for the FBI. You brought him to the party so he could bug my office." Xander cocked his head, drawing closer. "It was when you asked me to join you on the terrace, wasn't it? Is that when he did it?"

"My boyfriend's name is Nick *Stanton* and he's in real estate," Jordan said steadily. "The night of the party, I asked you to join me on the terrace to discuss wine. That's all."

With his free hand, Xander backhanded her across the face.

Caught off guard, Jordan fell back and tripped on the leg of a display table. Her wrist cracked against the tile floor as she tried to break her fall.

Her eyes blurred from the sharp pain in her cheek and shooting down her wrist. She touched her face gingerly and winced. Holding her left arm against her body, she propped herself up with one hand and turned around to face Xander.

He stood before her with a satisfied glint in his eyes.

"Not so smug now, are you?" He knelt down to her. "Tell me the truth." Once again, he moved the gun to her head.

Given the circumstances, Jordan knew she needed to give him something. *When in trouble . . .* she went with her usual out.

"I did it for Kyle." Her voice was strained from the throbbing pain in her wrist as she began to tell her lies. "The FBI threatened me. They said they would make sure that he was denied any chance for early parole, and that they'd make his life a living hell at MCC." She looked at Xander as if pleading for him to understand. "He's my brother, Xander. I had no choice."

He seemed momentarily uncertain. Then the hard expression returned. "Bullshit. It's been all over the news— they let your brother out of prison. *That* was your deal."

"You think I'd be foolish enough to agree to leave Kyle in prison after they threatened him? I told them I wouldn't cooperate unless the U.S. attorney promised in writing to release him."

For a moment, Xander almost appeared to believe her.

At that point, Jordan would take any moment she could get.

Then he shook his head. "Nice try. But I don't think you'd shack up with McCall after he threatened your brother."

"Our whole relationship was a setup. Because of the bugs in your office, the FBI knew you were having Nick followed. They made me play along—told me I needed to pretend he was my boyfriend."

"And going to Napa with him—was that part of the setup, too?"

Jordan paused, not having realized Xander knew about that. "It was a previously scheduled business trip, and Nick thought it would look more convincing if he went with me."

She prayed that he bought it.

"I gotta hand it to you, Jordan—you're good," Xander said with a humorless laugh. "I almost believe you. But your days of playing me are over." He gestured with the gun. "This whole thing nearly worked out perfectly for you. You got your brother out of prison and snagged a boyfriend in the process. You even managed to work in the romantic trip to Napa you've always wanted. And you got it all at *my fucking expense*," he said through clenched teeth. He pressed the gun to her temple, his hand shaking.

Jordan closed her eyes. *Oh God*.

"You destroyed my life," he hissed. "I'll lose everything over this. My restaurants, my home, my wine collection—Martino's money has touched everything, and the Feds are going to take it all." He dug the gun harder into her skin. "I'll go to prison. *If* Martino doesn't get to me first. I'm a dead man, Jordan. Because of you."

As she lay on the floor of her store, trembling, Jordan realized that she hadn't thought about what would happen to Xander when the investigation was over. Maybe she hadn't wanted to. "Xander, I—"

"Don't." His hand shook. "You ruined me, and now I'm going to return the favor. I'm getting the hell out of here. Taking off to a faraway place that doesn't have an extradition treaty. I'll spend the rest of my life looking over my shoulder, worrying who will find me first—the FBI or Martino. Not the way I thought things were going to work out for me. But at least I'll have one thing: the satisfaction of remembering the look on your face when I pull this trigger."

He was desperate. Jordan could see the sweat beading along his brow and knew she was looking at a man at the end of his rope. So she pushed through the fear that threatened to overwhelm her and played her last card.

"My father will pay you anything you want," she blurted out.

Xander went still. She had his attention.

Then she heard voices outside the front door.

NICK PULLED UP in front of DeVine Cellars just in time to see two uniformed Chicago police officers approaching the door. They stopped a few feet from the store as he parked haphazardly along the curb. He jumped out of the car and quickly assessed the scene—noting the closed shades on the windows and door—and hurried to the back of his car to pop the trunk. He flashed his badge with one hand as the police officers came over, and reached for a midsized metal lockbox inside the truck.

"FBI," he said in a low voice, not wanting Xander to overhear them from inside the store.

"We received a call that you guys were on your way," the older cop said.

"Have you made contact with anyone inside?" Nick asked.

"Just got here seconds ago, right before you pulled up."

"We may have a hostage situation." Nick opened the lockbox with a key on his key ring, and heard another car pull up as he grabbed his spare gun and lock-pick kit. He glanced over his shoulder and saw a familiar Ford LTD Crown Victoria come to a stop behind him. He was closing the trunk of his car just as Jack Pallas and his partner, Wilkins, strode over.

Pallas wasted no time with preliminaries. He handed Nick a bulletproof vest. "What's the plan?"

Nick slipped the vest over his shirt. It went without saying that he was in charge. It was his investigation, and more important, Xander Eckhart had *his* girl in there. He'd be damned if anyone else tried to call the shots.

"I'm going in through the back door," he said. "Jack, you cover me. Wilkins—you guard the front." He nodded to the two uniformed cops. "They can serve as backup."

"I'll let you know when we're in," Jack said to Wilkins, pointing to the small receiver in his ear. Wilkins wore a receiver in his ear as well, and both men had transmitters wired to the collars of their bulletproof vests. "Don't move until you get my signal, Sam."

Wilkins pulled back the slide on his gun, ready. "We've got a second team on the way that'll be here in minutes," he told Nick. "You sure you don't want to wait?"

"We're not waiting." Nick took off toward the alley, with Jack following him.

They cut through the alley and stopped at the back door to DeVine Cellars. Nick saw that the lock was a standard dead bolt and prayed Jordan didn't have a chain on the inside of the door that would prevent quick and quiet access.

He glanced over at Pallas as he pulled out his lock-pick kit. "I'll take Eckhart. You make sure the scene is clear—it's possible that Trilani is in there with them." He got to work on the lock. He moved fast and steadily, but still it took time he worried they didn't have.

In his head, he kept playing over and over what might be happening inside Jordan's store. And he knew one thing: he was a fucking fool. His job, being the top undercover agent, his stupid pride—it all meant nothing. The only thing he wanted was to know that she was safe.

He gritted his teeth as he pushed the lock pins into place with the pick. "This can't be it. No way. There are too many things I need to say to her."

He didn't realize he'd spoken out loud until Jack answered him.

"You'll get your chance."

Nick stared the other agent in the eyes. "I better. And just so we're clear, depending on what I find inside, there's a good chance I'm going to kill this piece of shit."

HAVING HEARD THE voices, Xander's eyes darted to the front door. "Who's that?"

Please let it be the police, Jordan prayed.

They both watched the door for what felt like an eternity. When nothing happened, Xander slightly eased his grip on the gun. "Sounds like they're gone."

"Let's get back to the money," Jordan said, stalling once again. "My father could wire whatever you want in exchange for my release. Fifty million. A hundred. Wherever it is you plan to vanish, that will go a long way toward keeping you comfortable."

Xander's lips pulled back in a sneer. "There's only one problem: I couldn't touch that money. Thanks to you, the Feds are watching all my accounts."

"My brother shut down Twitter from a laptop computer in Tijuana, Mexico. Trust me—he and my father can manage to open a bank account wherever you want, under whatever name you give them."

Xander paused again. He sat up, hovering over her on his knees. Jordan saw his hesitation.

"The money will give you your life back, Xa—"

"Shut up!" He shoved her against the ground, and the back of her head banged against the tile. He wiped sweat off his brow with one hand, and his voice rose. "I can't think with all your talking! Just *shut up!*"

Jordan braced herself when she saw him draw back his other hand, about to hit her with the gun. She closed her eyes and pleaded silently—*please don't let it hurt too much—*

A gunshot rang out across the store.

Her eyes flew open.

Xander jerked back and dropped the gun to the floor. He clenched his shoulder, his arm hanging limply at his side from a perfectly aimed bullet. He saw something coming from the direction of the back door and his eyes widened in panic. He scrambled to his feet and quickly backed away from Jordan. He held up his hand defensively. "No, I didn't—"

Nick stormed toward Xander with a menacing look. "I told you to keep your hands off her," he said in a low growl.

He grabbed Xander by the throat and flipped him to the ground with one hand. He shoved his knee against Xander's chest, pinning him to the floor, and pointed his gun right between Xander's eyes.

"Who's out of his league now, asshole?"

Xander remained motionless and quiet, undoubtedly the smartest decision he had made all morning.

Nick stared down at him for a long moment, his expression icy. Finally, he looked over at Jordan. "Are you okay?"

She nodded. "Yes." Hearing the tremor in her voice, she cleared her throat. "I think so." She pushed herself up with one arm, holding her injured wrist to her chest.

"You're hurt." Nick shoved the gun against Xander, who half grunted, half whimpered. "Care to explain how that happened?"

"She tripped and fell."

"Now there's an original answer," Nick said disgustedly.

Someone approached from behind them. Jordan turned

and saw the agent who'd put the monitoring device on Kyle's ankle. Agent Pallas, if memory served.

"I checked the cellar," he told Nick. "No sign of Trilani or anyone else." He raised an eyebrow at Xander's position. "We're good here?"

Nick eased his gun off Xander's forehead with what seemed to be a great deal of reluctance. "Yes. We're good." With one hand, he caught a pair of handcuffs that Agent Pallas tossed over. He yanked Xander up by the lapels of his coat. "Please try to resist. It would make my day."

"Fuck you, McCall," Xander said. But he held his hands out complacently as Nick slid on the cuffs.

Agent Pallas walked over to the front door and unlocked it. "We're clear." Another FBI agent in a bulletproof vest and two police officers stormed into the store, guns drawn. Nick handed Xander over to the other agents, and then walked toward Jordan.

He bent down and took her hand. "Think you can stand?" he asked softly.

She was very aware of the five extra pairs of eyes on her, one pair of which belonged to the man who'd just held a gun to her head. "Get me out of here. Please."

Nick nodded. He helped her up, being careful with her wrist. He led her toward the door, stopping to address the younger FBI agent. "Did you call for an ambulance?"

"It's on the way," the agent said.

Nick looked at Xander, whose face was strained with the pain of the gunshot wound. "Get another one for him. Tell them to take their time."

As he led Jordan out of the store, she bumped her wrist against her chest and sucked in a breath at the flash of pain. "I think it's getting worse."

"It's the adrenaline wearing off," Nick said tersely. He led her over to his car and opened the door to the backseat. "You should sit here while we wait for the ambulance."

"Just a heads up: I might throw up in your car from the pain."

His eyes flashed, yet still there was no quip or sarcastic comment. He was acting very un-Nick-like.

"I can handle it," he said. After he'd gotten her settled, he stood up and did the weirdest thing.

He began to pace next to the car.

Jordan watched him go back and forth, all intense strides and furious turns. At one point, he ran his hands over his face and took a deep breath. Then he stopped abruptly and knelt down next to the car.

"Still think you're going to throw up?" he asked.

Jordan shook her head, baffled. "No."

"Good." Nick grabbed her by the back of the neck and kissed her.

Well, then.

She forgot all about the pain in her wrist.

Nick pulled back and looked her over, his face filled with worry. "One more second and he would've hit you with the gun. And who knows what else. When I think about what could've happened . . ." He gripped her shoulders determinedly. "I should've told you this earlier, Jordan. Now that I've got my chance, you're going to hear it whether you like it or not. You came into my life and messed the whole thing up and now I'm screwed. Because I'm in love with you. As in balls-out, head-over-heels, watching-*Dancing-with-the-Stars*-on-Monday-nights, wine-and-bubble-bath kind of love. Hell, I think I'd even wear a scarf indoors for you."

Jordan smiled, her eyes misty, as she touched his cheek. "That's the best kind of love."

She took a deep breath. "I have a few things to say myself. Mainly just one, actually. Don't take this next undercover assignment. Stay with me instead."

Nick's eyes pierced hers, refusing to let her off that easily. "Tell me why."

"Because . . . I love you." She exhaled. *No take-backs.* The words were out there forever.

And it felt great.

He pulled her against his bulletproof vest. "About time you said it," he said gruffly. "It's been three damn weeks." He kissed her, and just as his hand curled around the nape of her neck, someone behind them cleared his throat.

Jordan pulled back and saw a gray-haired man wearing a

no-nonsense, FBI-type suit standing next to the car. She also saw that the once-quiet scene outside her wine store was swarmed with FBI agents and police officers.

Oops.

"First Pallas and now you," the gray-haired man said, shaking his head at Nick. "It's like I'm running a goddamn dating service around here." He spun around. "Wilkins! Huxley!" he barked. "Next case that involves a single woman— you're up."

Standing at the sidewalk, Agent Wilkins pumped his fist excitedly. "*Yes.*"

Huxley adjusted his glasses with a grin, looking decidedly pleased.

"That was supposed to be sarcastic. I'm getting too old for this shit," the gray-haired man mumbled under his breath. He turned to Jordan with a smile. "Ms. Rhodes—I'm Mike Davis, the special agent in charge. I can't tell you how relieved I am to see that you're safe." He nodded approvingly at Nick before walking away. "Good work, McCall. As always."

Jordan thought of something. "Wait—how did you know I was in trouble?" she asked Nick. "The panic button calls the police, not the FBI."

"The day after Xander's party, I put taps on both your home and store phone lines," he said.

"I don't recall us having any discussion about you doing that."

Nick grinned cheekily, looking like his old self again. "I told you I was keeping an eye on you, Rhodes."

She heard the sound of an approaching ambulance. Her cue. "Not to play the needy girlfriend card or anything, but do you think you can come with me to the hospital? Because any minute, I'm going to freak out over the fact that I had a *gun* pointed at my head, and it's not going to be pretty."

She had no clue what she'd said, but from the sudden look of tenderness on Nick's face, it seemed to strike a chord with him.

He reached up and stroked her uninjured cheek. "If you need me, I won't leave your side. I promise."

Thirty-two

THEY MADE HIM leave her side.

Due to so-called hospital "policy" and "safety regulations" —aka a load of bullshit—they wouldn't let Nick accompany Jordan into the X-ray room. He was debating whether to pull out his gun or his FBI badge—figuring one of them ought to do the trick—when Jordan squeezed his hand.

"I'll be fine. Maybe you could try to round me up a Vicodin or something for my wrist?" she suggested.

He threw her a knowing look. "You're trying to distract me."

"Yes. Because I see you making the don't-fuck-with-me face. And if you start shooting people, they'll get bumped ahead of me in the X-ray line, and then I'll really be screwed."

With a glare at the hospital staff, Nick reluctantly headed out to the waiting room. To distract himself, he called Davis. "Any idea yet how Eckhart knew we were on to him?"

"He's not saying a word," Davis said. "Except that he wants to talk to a lawyer, of course. How's Jordan?"

"She's getting some X-rays taken. Her wrist is definitely broken; I don't know yet about her cheekbone. You can tell the U.S. attorney that I better see charges for assault, battery, and false imprisonment added to Eckhart's indictment." Nick paused. "And when I get back to the office, I want to speak with you privately. About the kind of work I'm going to be doing going forward."

Davis was quiet for a moment. "All right, McCall. Whenever you're ready."

Nick spotted two men he would've recognized anywhere enter the radiology department and hurry toward the check-in counter. "I've got to go, Mike. We'll have that talk soon." He disconnected his phone and watched as the younger of the two men gestured angrily at the clerk behind the desk.

Apparently, Kyle Rhodes didn't like being told he couldn't see Jordan, either.

Nick walked over. *Nice way to meet the family.* He'd seen the camera crews pulling up at DeVine Cellars as the ambulance had pulled away—someone had obviously alerted the media.

"Mr. Rhodes—if I could have a word with you, please. It's about Jordan."

Both Grey and Kyle turned around. Jordan's father looked the same as he did in *Time, Newsweek,* and the *Wall Street Journal,* with his distinguished silver and blond hair and tailored suit. Kyle, who was dressed in cargo pants and a dark gray sweater, looked ready to brawl with anyone who got in his way. An interesting contrast to Jordan, Nick mused. Sure, she was sarcastic, but she seemed far more cool and levelheaded than her twin brother.

Grey looked Nick over questioningly. His eyes held on the gun harness Nick wore over his shirt. "And you are . . . ?"

He held out his hand. "Special Agent Nick McCall. First off, you should know that your daughter is going to be fine." He saw both Kyle and Grey exhale in relief. "Jordan's been through an ordeal, but she is . . ." *Incredible. Strong. Smart. Gorgeous. Hot as a firecracker in bed.*

Probably better to keep that part to himself.

". . . quite tough," he finished.

Grey Rhodes shook his hand cautiously. "Thank you, Agent McCall. Yes, she is."

Nick gestured to an alcove where they could speak without

everyone's eyes on them. "Why don't we talk over there, where it's more private?"

The two men followed him. "They're saying on the news that my sister was attacked in her store," Kyle said once they were alone. His concern for Jordan was etched in his face. "Does this mean the FBI is investigating the case?"

"It's more complicated than that. Jordan was attacked by a man named Xander Eckhart, a local businessman. You may know of him. There was a struggle, and she suffered a broken wrist and a bruised cheekbone. Eckhart had a gun, but Jordan was able to stall him until we arrived at the scene."

Kyle and Grey exchanged shocked looks.

"But Xander and Jordan are friends," Grey said. "Or certainly close acquaintances. She attends his charity fund-raiser every year."

"This was a jealousy thing, wasn't it? I'll fucking kill Eckhart," Kyle said. "I've been to his clubs a few times, and he always asks me about her." He turned to his father. "I bet it's because he saw her at his party with this new guy—Mr. Tall, Dark, and Smoldering or whatever. The jerk-off who isn't talking to her."

It took all of the jerk-off's undercover skills not to react to that. "It wasn't because of jealousy," Nick said. "Not directly, anyway. Eckhart attacked Jordan because she was cooperating with the FBI in an undercover investigation in which he was the target. Eckhart somehow learned of Jordan's involvement in the investigation and wanted revenge."

"An undercover *FBI* investigation?" Grey repeated. "How could my daughter help you with something like that?"

"We needed access to an office that Eckhart keeps in the lower level of Bordeaux. The party was our only opportunity, so Jordan agreed to bring along an undercover agent as her date."

Grey's eyes were steely cold. "That sounds very dangerous, Agent McCall."

"It sure does." Kyle took a step closer to Nick. "Five months ago, I got a nice taste of the courtesies the FBI extends to the Rhodes family. So let's cut the bullshit. What kind of threats did you bully my sister with to get her to cooperate in your investigation?"

Normally, Nick didn't take too kindly to hotheaded ex-cons who invaded his personal space. But this particular hotheaded ex-con happened to share DNA with his girlfriend, so he was willing to play nicer than usual. "I didn't threaten your sister, Kyle."

"Oh, I suppose she decided to help you out of the kindness of her heart," he said sarcastically.

"If you want to know Jordan's reasons for helping us, I suggest you ask her yourself."

"Trust me—I plan to." Kyle's voice rose as he pointed to the corridor that led to the X-ray rooms. "Because my sister is in there with a broken wrist, and from what I'm hearing, she narrowly escaped being killed. All because the *FBI* put her in the line of fire. So I'd like to know why she would ever agree to help you unless—"

He stopped as a look of realization crossed his face. "No." He pointed emphatically. "Do *not* say that she did this for me."

Nick didn't have to say anything else.

Kyle took a step back and ran his hands through his hair. He said nothing for a moment. Then he wiped his eyes as he looked up at the ceiling, shaking his head. "Goddammit, Jordo."

Grey cleared his throat and looked pointedly at Nick. "I'd like to know more about this undercover agent who posed as my daughter's date. The ubiquitous Tall, Dark, and Smoldering."

Nick put on his best meet-the-parent smile. "I generally prefer to go by Nick."

Kyle did a double take. "*You?* You're the jerk-off dating my sister?"

"Is that a problem?"

"Um, yeah. It kind of is," Kyle said dryly. "Because the last FBI agent I met nearly snapped my ankle off putting on a monitoring device. And the two agents before that threw me in prison. So no FBI agents are sniffing around my family. Period."

Nick folded his arms across his chest, not worried in the slightest. "In what alternate reality do you think Jordan's going to let *anyone* make decisions for her?" He gestured to the doors that led to the X-ray rooms. "But you should go give her that speech right now. She could use a good laugh, and that ought to do the trick."

"My God, he's as sarcastic as she is," Kyle muttered under his breath to Grey.

Hearing that, Nick knew he was in.

With the Rhodes clan, that was the ultimate stamp of approval.

JORDAN SAT ON the examination table, holding up her wrist to check out her new fiberglass cast. "How long do I have to wear this?" At least her cheekbone wasn't broken. Although thanks to Xander, she'd have a heck of a bruise for the next week.

"Six weeks," the resident told her. "And make sure you keep the cast as dry as possible. I'd suggest baths."

Jordan thought about the last bath she'd taken. Probably best to keep the tub free of a certain FBI agent, if dry was the goal.

"I've written you a prescription for Vicodin for the pain. And if your arm gets itchy, you can point a hairdryer on the cool setting down the cast," the doctor continued. "If that doesn't work, try Benadryl."

After running through the rest of her discharge orders, the doctor left. Jordan was attempting to gather up her purse, coat, and the hospital paperwork she'd collected when she heard a familiar voice from the doorway.

"Already trying to do everything by yourself. Imagine that."

She turned around and saw Kyle. He walked over and took everything out of her hands and set it on the examination table.

"You're here," Jordan said in surprise.

"Dad's here, too. We rushed over when we heard that you'd been attacked in your store." Kyle pulled up his pant leg and gestured to the monitoring device around his ankle. "Here's a funny thing—I thought this device was supposed to alert the parole department if I go outside certain set boundaries. So the whole time I was out there in the waiting room, I kept thinking a team of U.S. marshals would come storming in with guns blazing. But nope—nothing." He gave the ankle monitor a solid knock and shrugged. "You know, Jordo, I'm beginning to think the darn thing doesn't work."

Jordan leaned against the examination table. She had a feeling she was going to need that Vicodin quickly, to make it through this conversation headache-free. "All right. How much do you know, and how much do you only think you know?"

Kyle pointed at her. "I know *everything*. Like the fact that you are the most foolish, stubborn, overprotective . . . all-around best fucking sister in the world." He grabbed her and pulled her into a huge bear hug. "If anything had happened to you, I never would've forgiven myself," he said against the top of her head. "Why did you do it? I told you I was handling things in prison."

Jordan thought about how best to explain. "You know the panic you felt when you heard I'd been attacked at the store?"

"Yes. It sucked."

"Well, I felt something like that every day you were at MCC."

"Aw, shit, Jordo." He squeezed her tighter.

She winced. Not that she didn't want to prolong the lovely brother-sister moment, but her arm was pinned against his chest. "Kyle . . . the wrist. Help."

He pulled back and grinned sheepishly. "Sorry. How long do you have to wear that cast, anyway?"

"Six weeks."

"Oh, that blows. I bet your arm is going to be all shriveled and puny when they take it off."

And so the lovely brother-sister moment was over.

"Thanks," Jordan said. "Did you say Dad was here, too?"

Kyle threw her a you-are-so-busted look. "Why, yes, he

is. He's out in the waiting room, grilling Tall, Dark, and Sarcastic."

Jordan's mouth formed a silent *O*. She *was* busted. "You've met Nick?"

"Yep, we've met, all right. He was kind enough to inform me that I have absolutely no say in whether you two date."

"Well, you don't."

"You know, you all could at least pretend that my opinion makes a difference." Kyle shot her a sideways glance. "You like this guy, don't you?"

Jordan couldn't keep the smile off her face. "Yeah, I like this guy. He rescued me from a crazed man with a gun, he makes me laugh, and he calls his mother *Ma*. I'd say he's a keeper."

NICK HAD SURVIVED the grilling from Jordan's father about the honorability of his intentions, and he'd told her that he'd loved her without so much as an eye twitch. Now there was only one thing left to do to make the relationship official.

He used the controls on the car steering wheel to dial his cell phone. It felt good to be back in his real car, and a few minutes ago it similarly had felt good to be back in his condo. He'd stopped there to pick up a few things after dropping Jordan off at her house. Her friends, and Martin, had heard the news about the attack and had descended upon the house in a chaotic, concerned swarm. With them there, Nick had felt comfortable enough leaving Jordan for a quick trip.

She'd asked him to stay at her house for a while—teasingly saying she needed an assistant while she got used to the cast on her wrist—and he'd agreed. Frankly, he'd planned to stay with her all along. Now that she'd sucked him into this boyfriend thing with those tricky feminine wiles, she'd better believe that he was going to do it right.

The person on the other end of the line answered after

three rings. Her tone was dry. "So you do remember this phone number. Imagine that."

Nick grinned. Some things never changed. "Does this mean you're speaking to me again?"

His mother sniffed reluctantly. "I suppose. They still keeping you busy at the Bureau? Working on any important cases?"

Nick felt a tug of emotion. Sure, his mother could be a lot to handle at times, but her pride in the work he did never wavered. "Actually, I just made an arrest today. Took down a hotshot restaurant owner in an investigation that's connected to the Roberto Martino case you've probably read about in the papers. Which means that my undercover assignment is over."

"Do you know what they'll assign you to next?"

"No clue. But I'm going to ask to be taken off undercover work."

His mother's shock could be heard through the speakers. "You're giving up undercover work? Why?"

Nick took a deep breath and braced himself for the interrogation. "Well, Ma, see . . . there's this girl."

Silence.

He checked to make sure the call hadn't been dropped. "You still there, Ma?"

A sniffle.

"You can't be crying already," he said. "I haven't told you anything about her yet."

"It doesn't matter, Nick," his mother said through her tears. "Those are the three words I've been waiting thirty-four years to hear."

Thirty-three

AROUND SIX O'CLOCK the following evening, at the
end of Nick's first day back in the office, he knocked on
Jack Pallas's door and stuck his head in. It'd been a long
day, complete with an arrest and paperwork and statements
pertaining to Eckhart (shooting a suspect, even a dickhead
one, had its bureaucratic drawbacks), and he was ready for
a break.

Pallas eased back in his chair and beckoned with his hand.
"All right. Let's do this."

"We found Trilani holed up with one of his ex-girlfriends
in a studio apartment on the south side," Nick said. "With
Eckhart, that makes twenty-nine arrests for me in the last
four weeks."

"I'm still winning at thirty-four."

"I wouldn't count on holding that lead for long." Nick
cocked his head. "You free to grab a drink? I'm buying."

Pallas regarded him curiously. "Sure, as long as it's not
some trendy wine bar. I heard about the crowd you're running with these days."

"Does the U.S. attorney know you spend your workdays
listening to office gossip?"

Jack grinned in satisfaction. "The U.S. attorney is thrilled that there's finally someone else for this office to gossip about."

They headed out to a sports bar located across the street from the FBI offices. They ordered their drinks and discussed work for a while, mostly the Eckhart investigation and the upcoming Martino trial. Having worked undercover for so long, Nick realized that he'd missed the camaraderie between agents that arose when one was in the office on a regular basis.

Which brought him to the reason he'd wanted to speak to Jack. He'd figured out a potential way to manage his own cases and remain at the top, yet still be with Jordan every night. Or at least, the vast majority of them. "So I told Davis that I want to take a break from undercover work," he led in.

Jack took a sip of his Grey Goose on the rocks. "I wonder why that might be."

"Let's just call it an adjustment of priorities." Nick saw no reason to beat around the bush about this next part. Pallas was a good guy, and an excellent agent. "There's more. You and I both know that Davis has been thinking about retiring. I told him today that when that happens, I'd like to be considered for the special agent in charge position. I wanted you to hear it from me first. Thought you might be eying the job, too."

Jack considered this. "I've given it some thought," he admitted. "But politically, I doubt it would go over well if the special agent in charge of Chicago and the U.S. attorney of the same district were involved in a personal relationship." His expression was one of pride. "And since Cameron got there first, it looks like I'm adjusting my priorities, too." He paused. "Plus, I hear that people think I'm cranky." He rubbed his jaw, musing. "Not sure why that is."

"Maybe it's all the brooding and glowering."

"No one complains when you break out the don't-fuck-with-me face."

"True. But I have natural charm that wins people over." Nick turned serious again. "So we're good?"

"Nick McCall, special agent in charge." Jack slapped him on the shoulder. "I suppose there are worse things that could happen to this office." His eyes moved up to a television on the wall behind Nick. "Now there's a sight I never get tired of seeing."

Nick turned around to look. On the television, U.S. Attorney Cameron Lynde was holding a press conference about Xander Eckhart's arrest, the hostage situation at DeVine Cellars, and the connection to the Roberto Martino trial. The two agents watched as Cameron easily fielded the reporters' questions. Then the news piece cut to video footage of the hero of the day, "billionaire heiress and businesswoman" Jordan Rhodes. On the screen flashed an image of Jordan, looking as sleek and sophisticated as ever despite the cast on her wrist, as she stepped out of the Maserati.

Jack leaned over. "Ever get the impression that these women are way out of our league?"

"I shot the last guy who said that to me."

"And people say *I'm* cranky."

Nick chuckled as his eyes turned back to the television screen. As it turned out, he didn't care whose league Jordan was in. All that mattered was that she was his.

FOUR DAYS LATER, Nick sat on the oversized couch in Jordan's media room. Facing her, he placed a small black box in her hands and said three words. "Let's do this."

She looked down at the box, then back up at him. "This is a really big step, Nick."

"I'm ready."

"Are you sure? After this, there's no turning back."

"I want to make it official." He nodded at the box. "Come on—the suspense is killing me."

"All right. Just don't say I didn't warn you." Jordan pointed the small black remote control at the television. Three more clicks, and Nick heard the words that would seal his fate forever.

"*LIVE! It's Dancing with the Stars!*"

Jordan settled in next to him on the couch as the parade of

"stars" sashayed their way down a grand staircase and onto the screen. She glanced over to see his reaction. "Hanging in there?"

Nick stared at the television.

There were no words.

"It's . . . even worse than I'd imagined," he whispered. "Is there a reason none of these men have buttons on their shirts?" Horrified, he took in the spray tans. The sequins and feathers. The caked-on makeup and the plunging necklines. And those were the *guys*. He pointed. "Is that dude wearing eyeliner?"

Jordan patted his knee affectionately. "It's not too late. There's probably a basketball game on somewhere."

Nick eyed the remote control that sat on the coffee table in front of them. It was tempting. But he'd promised.

He turned his attention back to the screen, so shocked and awed by the foreign sights and sounds that he barely noticed when Jordan got up from the couch and headed over to the wet bar behind them. He heard her open a bottle and pour a drink. Then she wrapped her arms around him and placed a glass in his hand.

"Here. Maybe this will help."

Nick looked down, expecting to find a glass of wine. Instead, he saw a familiar amber-colored liquid in a rocks glass.

Bourbon.

"You are a god," he said to her.

Jordan smiled. "I even carved out a slot in my wine cellar for the bottle."

Nick set the rocks glass on the coffee table and pulled her into his lap. "A whole slot? Now that's the sign of a serious relationship." He kissed her, biting her lower lip teasingly. When she opened her mouth to his, he pulled her closer and slipped his hands underneath her shirt. He closed his eyes as her lips traced a path along his neck.

Her voice was throaty and seductive. "You know, I think it's really sexy that you'd watch this show just for me."

Ding!

Just like that, a light clicked on in Nick's head. He opened his eyes and grinned knowingly. "Oh, *now* I get why guys watch it." He exhaled in relief, his faith in men restored. *Whew*.

Jordan smiled at his reaction. "And all was right with the world."

Nick peered down into her teasing eyes as she lay snug in his arms.

Indeed it was.

Loved *A Lot Like Love*?
Don't miss the next Julie James romance,
featuring Kyle's story,

Read on for a special preview of

Just the Sexiest Man Alive

by Julie James

One

TAYLOR DONOVAN MAY have been new to Los Angeles, but she certainly recognized a line of bullshit when she heard one.

It was 8:15 on a Monday morning—frankly, a bit early, in Taylor's mind anyway, to be dealing with this latest round of nonsense coming from her opposing counsel, Frank Siedlecki of the Equal Employment Opportunity Commission. But hey, it was a gorgeous sunny morning in Southern California and her Starbucks had already begun to kick in, so she was willing to play nice.

Frank's call had come in just as Taylor had pulled into the parking garage of her downtown L.A. office building. After answering, she had let her opposing counsel go on for several minutes—without interruption, she might add—about the righteousness of his clients' position and how Taylor and her utterly nonrighteous client should consider themselves lucky to be given the chance to make the whole lawsuit go away for a paltry $30 million. But at a certain point, one could only take so much nonsense in one Monday-morning phone call. Luscious Starbucks or not.

So Taylor had no choice but to cut Frank off mid-rant,

praying she didn't lose the signal to her cell phone as she stepped into the lobby elevator.

"Frank, Frank," she said in a firm but professional tone, "there's no way we're going to settle at those numbers. You want all that money, just because your clients heard a few four-letter words in the workplace?"

She noticed then that an elderly couple had gotten into the elevator with her. She smiled politely at them as she continued her phone conversation.

"You know, if the EEOC's going to ask for thirty million dollars in a sexual harassment case," she told Frank, "at least tell me somebody was called a 'slut' or a 'whore.'"

Out of the corner of her eye, Taylor saw the elderly woman—seventy-five years old if she was a day—send her husband a disapproving look. But then Frank began rattling on further about the so-called merits of the plaintiffs' position.

"I have to be honest, I'm not exactly impressed with your case," she said, cutting him off. "All you've got is a sporadic string of some very minor incidents. It's not as if anyone slapped an ass or grabbed a boob."

Taylor noticed that the elderly couple was now subtly but quickly moving away from her, to the opposite end of the elevator.

"Of course I'm not taking you seriously," she said in response to her opposing counsel's question. "We're talking about thirty million dollars here!" Instead of shouting, her voice had a laughing tone, which experience had proven to be far more infuriating to her opponents.

Not seeing any reason to waste another minute, she summarized her position with a few simple parting thoughts.

"Frank, this case is a publicity stunt and a shakedown. My clients did nothing illegal, and you and I both know I'll have no problem proving that to a jury. So there's no reason to discuss your ridiculous settlement offer any further. Call me when somebody sees a penis."

Taylor slammed her cell phone shut for emphasis. She slipped the phone into her briefcase and smiled apologetically at the elderly couple. They had their backs pressed against the elevator wall and were staring at her, mouths agape.

"Sorry about the whole 'penis' thing," she said, trying to make amends. "I guess I get desensitized to it." She shrugged innocently as the elevator announced its arrival at the twenty-third floor with a high-pitched ding. She glanced over at her grandparently co-riders one last time.

"It's an occupational hazard."

Taylor winked.

And with that, the elevator doors opened and she stepped out onto the busy office floor that awaited her.

TAYLOR LOVED THE sounds of a bustling law office. The phones ringing off the hook, the furiously righteous conversations that spilled out behind closed doors, the printers busily shooting out fifty-page briefs, the mail carts wheeling by as they dropped off court orders—this was all music to her ears. They were the sounds of people working hard.

And no associate—or so Taylor hoped the senior partners agreed—worked harder than she did. From the moment, now seven years ago, she had first set foot in the Chicago office of Gray & Dallas, she had done her best to make sure everyone knew she was an associate who was going places. And now the firm had sent her to Los Angeles to litigate a highly publicized class-action sexual harassment case involving one of the nation's most upscale department stores. She was fully aware it was a test to see exactly what she was capable of.

And she was more than ready.

That morning, Taylor strolled through the hallway to her office, gliding by her secretary's desk just as she had done every morning for the past two weeks since coming to Los Angeles.

"Good morning, Linda. Any messages?"

Linda sprung to attention at her desk. There was something about Taylor that apparently made others around her feel as though they needed to look busy.

"Good morning, Ms. Donovan," Linda replied efficiently.

"You do have one message—Mr. Blakely would like to see you in his office as soon as you're available."

Taylor paused briefly. That was odd—she hadn't planned to meet with Sam that morning.

"Did he say what it's about?"

"Sorry, no, Ms. Donovan."

Taylor headed into her office as she called back a message to Linda. "Call Sam's secretary and let him know I'll be there in five minutes."

Then she poked her head back out the door and smiled at her new assistant.

"And Linda, remember—it's *Taylor*."

TAYLOR COULDN'T HELP but pause in the doorway to admire Sam's office before knocking to announce herself. It was a gorgeous corner office with a massive cherrywood desk and matching bookcases, plush cream carpet, and floor-to-ceiling windows covering two walls.

To her, the richly decorated partner's office constituted far more than a mere status symbol designed to impress clients and other lawyers. It was an indication of true success. And one day, in the hopefully not-too-distant future, she would have such an office of her own—the sign that she had accomplished the one primary goal of her adult life.

Years ago, Taylor's parents had made sacrifices in order for her to get where she was standing on that Monday morning. Growing up in Chicago in a decidedly blue-collar neighborhood, her three rambunctious and not particularly academically oriented older brothers had gone to the local boys' Catholic high school. Taylor, it was first assumed, would similarly go to the local girls' school. But after seeing their only daughter's remarkably high grade-school aptitude test scores, Taylor's parents decided that she deserved the best education money could buy, even if that meant spending money they didn't have. So, in order to make the annual eighteen-thousand-dollar University of Chicago Lab School tuition payments (while still supporting four kids), her parents took out a second mortgage on their house and her father sold the 1965 Corvette Stingray convertible he had been restoring in the garage.

Deeply appreciative of these sacrifices, Taylor promised her parents that they would never regret the investment they had made in her education. This was a promise that guided her all through high school and college, and eventually on to Northwestern Law. It was a promise that still motivated her to this day. After law school graduation, Taylor had chosen to work at Gray & Dallas for the simple reason that it was the top-ranked law firm in Chicago and one of the best worldwide. It gave her a sense of pride to be part of such a machine.

And she would do whatever it took to succeed there.

Fortunately for Taylor, unlike so many of her law school classmates who had turned to the practice of law because med school was too hard and took too long to make any money, or out of family pressure, or because they simply couldn't think of anything better to do, she genuinely loved being a lawyer. From the moment she'd conducted her first mock cross-examination in her law school trial advocacy class, everything felt like it clicked into place.

And so, as she stood in the doorway of Sam's plush partner's office, she couldn't help but smile not only in admiration but also in anticipation of what she hoped was soon to come.

One day, Taylor vowed silently to herself. One day.

She straightened her suit and knocked on Sam's door. He looked up from his computer and smiled warmly in greeting.

"Taylor! Come on in."

She took a seat at one of the chairs in front of Sam's desk. In the style of all shrewd attorneys, the guest chairs were positioned six inches lower than Sam's own, giving him the advantage of looking down on his visitors.

"Settled in yet?" Sam inquired.

Taylor grinned guiltily at the question, thinking of the unpacked boxes scattered along the hallway outside the living room of the two-bedroom apartment the firm had rented for her. "Almost."

"Moving's a pain in the ass, isn't it?"

"It keeps me busy when I'm not here."

Sam studied her. "Yes, I've seen you burning the midnight oil already. You should take some time to settle in before your case gets going full throttle."

Taylor shrugged determinedly. For her, there was no speed other than full throttle. And Sam Blakely—the head of the litigation group in Los Angeles—was a man she very much wanted to impress.

"I just want to hit the ground running, that's all."

Sam had sharp, fox-like facial features that became even more pronounced as he grinned approvingly at Taylor's all-business style.

"Then tell me how the case is going."

Taylor eased back in her chair as she gave Sam her summary. "It's going very well. We have the call for our motions in limine this week—I think we'll be able to keep out nearly half of the EEOC's evidence. And one of their lawyers called me this morning to discuss a settlement."

"What did you say?"

Taylor tilted her head coyly. "Let's just say they understand we're not interested."

Sam chuckled. "Good. Keep me posted, and don't hesitate to stop by if you need any guidance."

Taylor nodded agreeably, appreciating Sam's hands-off approach to their case. So far since she'd come to L.A., he had been more than happy to let her take the ball and run with it—a management style she thrived under.

She assumed that would be the end of their meeting. But instead of dismissing her, Sam shifted in his chair as if he had more to say.

"Something else on your mind, Sam?"

His body language right then seemed a little . . . odd. She didn't know Sam all that well yet, so she couldn't read him like she could the partners back home in Chicago. She waited as Sam eased back in his chair and stared at her with a poignant pause, creating the dramatic buildup for whatever he was about to say. Like so many trial attorneys Taylor had come across, Sam appeared to believe in acting out his entire life as if in front of a jury.

"Actually, there is another matter on which I was hoping to get your assistance," Sam began carefully. "I know we only have you on loan from Chicago for the harassment case, but this wouldn't be a full-time assignment."

Taylor was intrigued by this lead-in. She was already working nights and weekends, so she figured this mystery assignment had to be a great opportunity if Sam thought she should squeeze it into her schedule.

"Is it a pro bono matter?" she asked.

Sam leaned back in his chair as he considered this question carefully, like a trapped witness at a deposition. "Well . . . not exactly. I'd call it more of a favor."

Taylor's bullshit radar instantly went into high alert. So-called "favors" for partners generally meant wasted non-billable hours preparing a bar association speech or researching the DUI laws of Natchitoches, Louisiana, to help out a wayward-but-good-hearted nephew.

"What kind of favor?" Taylor asked, although she already knew exactly what Sam's response would be. "It's a very interesting situation . . ." he'd begin. All partners described the criminal activities of their ne'er-do-well relations as "interesting situations."

Sam leaned forward in his chair. "It's a very interesting situation . . ." he began.

Bingo.

Taylor tried to appear enthusiastic as he continued.

"It's a favor to one of the partners here, Bill Mitchells," Sam said. "I'm sure you're familiar with him—he's head of the tax group. One of his clients asked him for a favor."

Taylor could barely keep from rolling her eyes. Great— *client* criminal relations. The only thing worse than the spoiled prep-school offspring of rich partners was the spoiled prep-school offspring of *insanely* rich CEOs. She steeled herself for the rest of Sam's pitch.

But what he said next surprised her.

"As you likely are aware, Bill does tax work for most of the big names in Hollywood. One of his clients, an actor, is about to start filming a legal thriller. He's asked to work with one of our litigators to get a feel for how real lawyers act in the courtroom. You know, demeanor, where to stand, those kinds of things."

Sam paused once again for dramatic effect. This provided Taylor an opportunity to digest what he was saying.

Babysit an actor when she was just three weeks from trial? Preposterous.

It had to be a practical joke. Ha ha, yank the chain of the new associate from the Midwest who thinks everyone in Los Angeles is obsessed with celebrities.

Taylor smiled and shook her finger at Sam to let him know she was in on the gag.

"I'm guessing you're joking."

But Sam's face turned serious, and he gave her that "what's the problem?" look partners give associates when assigning a three-month document review.

He wasn't joking.

Balls.

"Let's be honest, Taylor," Sam said in his best we're-all-buddies-here tone. "I'm not going to put a partner on this. I've got better uses for those of us that bill out at eight hundred dollars an hour." He winked at her. In public and around clients, partners loved to put on a big show of feigning embarrassment over their ridiculous billing rates. But behind closed doors, they were a source of great pride.

"However, it's an excellent client development opportunity," he went on, "so I need an associate who will make a good impression. You."

Taylor folded her hands in her lap and thought quickly of the best way to graciously decline Sam's offer. She knew he meant the opportunity as a compliment, but working with some prima donna actor on his overly melodramatic "You can't handle the truth!" courtroom scenes was hardly her idea of serious lawyering.

So she flashed Sam her best soft-rejection smile.

"Sam, I'm flattered. But don't you think one of the associates from this office would be better suited for this kind of project? I'd hate to waltz in here as the new girl and steal their opportunity to work with a Hollywood actor."

That didn't sound half bad, she mused. Apparently, she had a bit of a flair for acting herself.

But then Sam topped her with his trump card.

"Well, Taylor, Chicago assures me that you're the best litigation associate this firm has. If that's true, then don't you think it should be you representing us?"

A direct challenge to her skills as a lawyer. Taylor's kryptonite.

She sighed, having only one answer to that.

"When would you need me?"

Sam grinned victoriously, looking ever fox-like once again. "Thursday."

For a brief moment, Taylor saw a possible way out of this situation. "Oh . . . that's too bad," she said. "I have to argue those motions to compel on Thursday." She snapped her fingers. Damn.

But Sam was not about to let her off so easily.

"And as much as I know it will kill you to miss a chance to be in court, I'm sure you can get someone else to cover it." Then he folded his hands politely, indicating that the discussion was over.

And so Taylor stood up to leave. She gave Sam her best team-player, I-couldn't-be-more-thrilled-to-squeeze-this-shit-into-my-schedule grin.

"No problem, Sam, I'll work it all out."

She turned to leave and had made it all the way to the door before she realized something. She glanced back over her shoulder.

"I didn't even think to ask—who's the actor?"

Sam peered up distractedly from his computer, having already turned his attention back to $800-per-hour work.

"Um . . . Jason Andrews."

And with those words, Taylor's hand slipped just the slightest bit on the doorknob.

She turned back toward Sam, trying to appear nonchalant. "Really. I see."

But unfortunately, her initial reaction had not gone unnoticed. Sam's face turned serious as he rose from his desk and crossed the room to her.

"You know, Taylor, I told his manager that your reputation in this firm is that you can go head-to-head with any man. And win." Sam paused meaningfully and stared down at her like an army drill sergeant.

"Do *not* get starry-eyed on this," he lectured firmly.

Taylor's eyes narrowed at the mere insinuation. After Daniel, her days of being starry-eyed, dreamy-eyed, or any other-eyed over any man, celebrity or not, were finished.

Sam was right; she was more than capable of going head-to-head with any man. She had, essentially, been raised that way. Growing up, her father, a police sergeant, worked double shifts and her mom, a nurse, often worked overtime, so Taylor had frequently found herself being watched by her three older brothers. And in their minds, the only way to handle being stuck after school and on weekends with a girl was to pretend that she was, in fact, a boy. (Albeit one who had pigtails.)

One of Taylor's favorite movies was *A League of Their Own*, and in that movie Tom Hanks's character had a line that had always resonated with her: one of his girl ballplayers was crying after he had chewed her out for missing a play, and Tom Hanks told her, "There's no crying in baseball." That could have been the mantra for Taylor's youth, except in her world apparently, not only was there no crying in baseball, there was also no crying in kickball, hide-and-seek (even when her brothers forgot about her and left her in the neighbor's shed for two hours), climbing trees, falling two stories out of said trees and breaking her arm, and even fishing when her brothers used her pet caterpillar collection as bait.

Yes, Taylor learned at a very young age that the only way to get boys to shut up and play fairly was to show them that you took crap from *no one*. It was a lesson that served her well working at a large law firm, where women comprised roughly 15 percent of partners despite the fact that they generally constituted, year after year, more than half of every entering first-year associate class. Somewhere along the way, these women were getting lost, ignored, or weeded out, or were choosing a different path.

Taylor, however, was determined not to fall victim to what these law firms accepted as inevitable reality. Even if it meant she had to eat nails for breakfast.

So in response to Sam's directive that she not get "starry-eyed" on this particular assignment, she folded her arms definitively across her chest, having only one thing to say. "Not a chance."

Sam smiled. He nodded, satisfied.

Then something occurred to her. She cautiously asked Sam one last question.

"But I have to wonder, Sam, given the . . . reputation . . . of this particular client, did the fact that I'm a woman have anything to do with choosing me for this project?"

Ever the litigator, Sam paced grandly in front of his desk, ready to show off the interrogation skills he had honed over the past twenty years.

"Taylor, in your sexual harassment practice, who do you tell your clients they should have leading their defense team, a man or a woman?"

"A woman," she replied without hesitation.

"And why is that?"

"Because it makes the client seem more credible if they have a female lawyer saying they treat women fairly."

Sam paused meaningfully before his imaginary jury. "So then you agree, don't you, that there are times when—in addition to being the best litigator—your gender can be an advantage to this firm?"

Taylor got the message. Shut up and play the game.

She smiled at her boss.

"Thursday it is."

TWO

JASON ANDREWS.

He would be at their offices on Thursday. The biggest actor in Hollywood.

Jason Andrews.

The movie star. In every paparazzi-following-your-every-move, crazed-fans-showing-up-naked-in-your-bedroom sense of the term.

Later, when Taylor's secretary did her "research," she would stumble across *Rolling Stone* magazine's June cover interview, which summed up Jason Andrews as: "devilishly good-looking, and a true legend of his day. Like Clark Gable or Cary Grant, he exudes effortless charm and confidence. Thinks he's smarter than most and frankly, probably is. A lethal combination that seemingly has left him with respect for very few."

Devilishly good-looking. Effortless charm and confidence. Jason Andrews.

And she was going to be working with him.